THE LAST RAYS OF THE SUN SHONE HORIZONTALLY
ACROSS THE TERRACE.

—*To Leeward.*

THE COMPLETE WORKS OF
F. MARION CRAWFORD
In Thirty-two Volumes ✒ Authorized Edition

TO LEEWARD

BY
F. MARION CRAWFORD

WITH FRONTISPIECE

P. F. COLLIER & SON
NEW YORK

THE COMPLETE WORKS OF F. MARION CRAWFORD

—3—

TO LEEWARD

TO LEEWARD.

CHAPTER I.

THERE are two Romes. There is the Rome of the intelligent foreigner, consisting of excavations, monuments, tramways, hotels, typhoid fever, incense, and wax candles; and there is the Rome within, a city of antique customs, good and bad, a town full of aristocratic prejudices, of intrigues, of religion, of old-fashioned honour and new-fashioned scandal, of happiness and unhappiness, of just people and unjust. Besides all this, there is a very modern court and a government of the future, which may almost be said to make up together a third city.

Moreover, these several coexistent cities, and their corresponding inhabitants, are subdivided to an infinity of gradations, in order to contain all and make room for all. The foreigner who hunts excavations does not cross the path of the foreigner who sniffs after incense, any more than the primeval aristocrat sits down to dinner with the representative of fashionable scandal; any more than the just man would ever allow the unjust to be introduced to him. They all enjoy so thoroughly the freedom to ignore each other that they would not for worlds endanger the safety of the barrier that separates them. Of course, as they all say, this state of things cannot last. There must ultimately be an amalgamation, a deluge, a unity, fraternity and equality ; a state of things in which we shall say, "Sois mon frère, ou je te tue," — a future glorious, disgusting, or dull, according as you look at it. But, meanwhile, it is all very charming, and there is plenty for every one to enjoy, and an abundance for every one to abuse.

When Marcantonio Carantoni saw his sister married to a Frenchman, he was exceedingly glad that she had not married an Englishman, a Turk, a Jew, or an infidel. The Vicomte de Charleroi was, and is, a gentleman ; rather easy-going, perhaps, and inclined to look upon republics in general, and the French republic in particular, with the lenient eye of the man who owns land and desires peace first — and a monarchy afterwards, whenever convenient. But in these days it is not altogether worthy of blame that a man should look after his worldly interests and goods; for how else can the aristocracy expect to make any headway against the stream of grimy bourgeois, who sell everything at a profit, while the nobles buy everything at a loss? So Marcantonio is satisfied with his brother-in-law, and just now is particularly delighted because Charleroi has got himself appointed to a post in Rome ; and he goes to see his sister every day, for he is very fond of her.

In truth, it is not surprising that Marcantonio

should like his sister, for she is a very charming woman. She is beautiful, too, in a grand way, with her auburn hair, and grey eyes, and fair skin; but no one can help feeling that she might be quite as beautiful, and yet be anything but charming; so many beautiful people are vain, or shy, or utterly idiotic. Madame de Charleroi is something of a paragon, and has as many enemies as most paragons have, but they can find nothing to feed their envy. She was very unhappy years ago, but time has closed the wounds, or has hidden them from sight, and her dearest friends can only say that she was cold and showed very little heart. When the world says that a woman is a piece of ice, you may generally be sure that she is both beautiful and good, so that it can find nothing worse to say. Marcantonio Carantoni's sister is a paragon, and there are only two things to be said against her, — she did not marry Charleroi for love, and she has not done half the things in the world that she might have done.

On the January afternoon which marks the opening of this story, the brother and sister sat together in a small boudoir in the Carantoni palace; there was room for all in the great house, and as Marcantonio was not married, it was natural that his sister and her husband, with their children, governesses, servants, and horses should occupy the untenanted part of the ancestral mansion. Up in the second story there is a room such as you would not expect to find within those grey and ancient walls, where the lower windows are heavily grated, and huge stone coats of arms frown forbiddingly from above. It is a room all sun and flowers and modern furniture, though not of the more hideous type of newness, — modern in the sense of comfortable, well padded and well aired. The afternoon sun was pouring in through the closed windows, and there was a small wood fire in the narrow fireplace. The Vicomtesse de Charleroi sat warming her toes, and her brother was rolling a cigarette as he looked at her. A short silence had succeeded a somewhat animated discussion. She looked at the fire, and he looked at her.

"My dear Diana," said Marcantonio at last, rising to get himself a match, "what in the world can you have against her? We are not Hindoos, you know, to talk about caste in these days; and even if that were the objection, she comes of very proper people, I am sure, though they are foreigners."

Madame moved her feet impatiently.

"Oh, you know it is not that!" she said petulantly. "As if I had not married a foreigner myself! But then, if you had felt about it as I feel about this, I would have thought twice " —

"Have I not thought twice — and three times?"

"Of course, yes — while your head is hot with this fancy. Yes, you have probably thought a hundred times, at least, this very day. Listen to me, my dear boy, and do what I tell you. Go away to Paris, or London, or Vienna, for a fortnight, and then come

back and tell me what you think about it. Will you
not do that — to please me?"

"But why?" objected Marcantonio, looking very
uncomfortable, for he hated to refuse his sister anything. "Seriously, why should I not marry her?
Is there anything against her? If there is, tell
me."

Donna Diana rose rather wearily and went to the
window.

"I wish you would abandon the whole idea," she
said. "I am quite sure you will repent when it is
too late. I do not believe in these young girls who
occupy themselves with philosophy and the good
of the human race. Politics — well, we all have a
finger in politics; but this dreadful progressive
thought — it is turning the world upside down."

"Oh — it is the philosophy that you do not like
about her? Well, my dear sister, that is exactly
what I think so interesting. This young English
Hypatia" —

"Hypatia, indeed!" cried Donna Diana rather
scornfully.

"Yes. Is she not learned?"

"Perhaps."

"And beautiful?"

"No, — certainly not. She is simply a little
pretty."

Marcantonio shrugged his shoulders.

"Of course," he said, "you will not allow it."
His sister looked round quickly.

"That is rude," she said. In a moment her brother was by her side.

"Forgive me, Diana mia; you know I did not mean it. But you see I think she is beautiful, and that is everything, after all."

"Yes," answered she, "I suppose it is everything, now. But philosophy is not everything. Put her out of your head, dear boy, and do not say any more rude things."

Marcantonio had the power to avoid being rude, but he was not able to follow the other piece of advice. He could not put her out of his head. On the contrary, he went out and shut himself up in his own rooms and thought of her for a whole hour.

He was not at all like his sister in appearance, though he resembled her somewhat in character. He was of middle height, sparely built, dark of skin, and aquiline of feature; neither handsome nor ugly, but very decidedly refined,—gentle of speech and kind of face. Without any more vanity than most people, he was yet always a little more carefully dressed than other men, and consequently passed for a dandy. Altogether, he was a pleasant person to look at, but not especially remarkable at first sight.

As regards his position, he bore an ancient name, dignified with the title of marquis; he was an only son, and his parents were dead; he owned the fine old palace in Rome and a good deal of land elsewhere; he never gambled, and was generally considered to be rich, as fortunes go in modern Italy. Of course, he was a good match, and many were the hints he received, from time to time, to the effect that he would be very acceptable as a son-in-law. Nevertheless he was not married, and he did not particularly care for the society of women. In truth, women did not find him very amenable, for he would not marry, and could not play adoration well enough to please them. So they left him alone. Grave old gentlemen nodded approvingly when they spoke of him, and his uncle the cardinal regarded him as one of the mainstays of the clerical party. As a matter of fact, he did not aspire to anything of the kind, and was merely a very honest young nobleman of good education, who had not made for himself any interest in life, but who nevertheless found life very agreeable. Possessing many good qualities, he yet knew very well that he had never been put to the test, nor required to show much strength of character; and he did not wish to be put into any such position. His sister was very fond of him, but she sometimes caught herself wishing he would do something a little out of the everlasting common round of social respectability. He was twenty-nine years old, and she was a year younger.

Of late, however, it had become apparent that Marcantonio, Marchese Carantoni, had not only found an interest in life, but had also discovered in himself the strength of will necessary to its prosecution. The dull regularity of his existence was shaken to its foundations, and out of the vast social sea a figure had risen which was destined to destroy the old order of things with him, and to create a new one. There was no doubt about it; not so much because he himself said so, as because his whole manner and being proclaimed the fact. He was seriously in love. Worse than that, he was in love with a lady of whom his sister did not approve, and he evidently meant to marry, whether she liked it or not.

He was seriously in love; and, indeed, love ought always to be a serious thing, or else it should be called by another name. There is a great deal of very poor nonsense talked and written about love by persons only vicariously acquainted with it; and it is a great pity, because there is absolutely no subject so permanently interesting to humanity as love, whether in life or in fiction. And there is no subject which deserves more tenderness and delicacy, or which requires more strength in the handling.

The relation of brother and sister is unlike any other. It represents the only possible absolutely permanent and platonic affection between young men and young women. Its foundation is in identity of blood instead of in the spontaneous sympathy of the heart, and even when brother and sister quarrel they understand each other. Lovers frequently do not understand each other when they are on the best of terms, and the small difference of opinion grows by that misunderstanding until it makes an impassable gulf. Brothers and sisters may be estranged, separated, divided by family quarrels or by the bloody exigencies of civil war, but if once they are thrown together again the mysterious attraction of consanguinity shows itself, and their life begins again where it had been broken off by untoward fate.

Madame de Charleroi was inclined to be angry with Marcantonio, and when he was gone she sat by the fire, wondering what he would be like when he should be married. Somehow she had never thought of him as married, certainly not as married to a pernicious young English girl, with all sorts of queer ideas in her brain, and a tendency to sympathise with the dynamite party. He might surely have chosen better than that. Donna Diana was not a woman of narrow prejudices, but she really could not be expected to be pleased at seeing her brother, a Catholic gentleman, bent on uniting himself to a foreign girl with no fortune, no beauty — well, not much — and a taste for explosives. He might surely have chosen better.

Donna Diana thought of her father, and fancied what he would have said to such a match, the strict old nobleman. And so, between her thoughts and her memories the afternoon wore on, and she bethought herself that it was time to go out.

The horses spun along the streets through the crisp

golden air, and now and then a ray of the lowering sun caught them as they dashed through some open place on the way, making them look like burnished metal. And the light touched Madame de Charleroi's beautiful face and auburn hair, so that the people stood still to look at her as she passed, — for every Roman knew Donna Diana Carantoni by sight, just as every Roman knows every other Roman, man, woman and child, distinguishing lovingly between the Romans of Rome and the Romans of the north. By and by the carriage rolled through the iron gates of the Pincio, and along the drive to the open terrace where the band plays, till it stood still behind the row of stone posts, within hearing of the music. The place has been absolutely described to death, and everybody knows exactly how it looks. There are flowers, and a band-stand, and babies, and a view of St. Peter's.

The first person Donna Diana saw was her brother, standing disconsolately by one of the short pillars and looking at each carriage as it drove up. He was evidently waiting for some one who did not come. His black moustache drooped sadly, and his face was so melancholy that his sister smiled as she watched him.

Marcantonio was soon aware of her presence, but he had no intention of showing it, and studiously kept his head turned towards the drive, watching the line of carriages. Madame de Charleroi was quickly surrounded by a crowd of men, all dressed precisely alike, and all anxious to say something that might attract the attention of the famous beauty. Presently they bored her, and her carriage moved on; whereupon they pulled their hats off and began to chatter scandal amongst themselves, after the manner of their kind. They nodded to Marcantonio as they passed him in a body, and he was left alone. The sun was setting, and there was a purple light over the flats behind the Vatican, recently flooded by a rise in the Tiber. There was no longer any object in waiting, and the young man sauntered slowly down the steps and the steep drive to the Piazza del Popolo, and entered the Corso.

To tell the truth, he was disappointed, bored, annoyed, and angry, all at once. He had fully expected to see her, and to find consolation in some sweet words for the hard things his sister had said to him. Perhaps also he had enjoyed the prospect of exhibiting himself to his sister in the society of the lady in question, — for Marcantonio was obstinate, and had just discovered the fact, so that he was anxious to show it. Men who are new in fighting are sure to press every advantage, not having yet learned their strength; but in the course of time they become more generous. Marcantonio was therefore grievously chagrined at being cheated of his small demonstration of independence, besides being a little wounded in his pride, and honestly disappointed at not meeting the young lady he meant to marry. In this state of mind he strolled down the

Corso, looked up at her windows, passed and repassed before the house, and ultimately inquired of the confidential porter, who knew him, whether she were at home. The porter said he had not seen the signorina, but that one of the servants had told him she was indisposed. The marchese bit his black moustache and went away in a sad mood.

CHAPTER II.

MISS LEONORA CARNETHY was suffering from an acute attack of philosophical despair, which accounted for her not appearing with her mother on the Pincio.

The immediate cause of the fit was the young lady's inability to comprehend Hegel's statement that " Nothing is the same as Being; " and as it was not only necessary to understand it, but also, in Miss Carnethy's view, to reconcile it with some dozens of other philosophical propositions all diametrically opposed to it and to each other, the consequence of the attempt was the most chaotic and hopeless failure on record in the annals of thought. Under these circumstances, Miss Carnethy shut herself up in a dark room, went to bed, and agreed with Hegel that Nothing was precisely the same as Being. She thus scattered all the other philosophies to the angry airts of heaven at one fell sweep, and she felt sure she was going to be a Hindoo.

This sounds a little vague, but nothing could be vaguer than Miss Carnethy's state of mind. Having agreed with Mr. Herbert Spencer that the grand mainspring of life is the pursuit of happiness, and that no other motive has any real influence in human affairs, it was a little hard to find that there was nothing in anything, after all. But then, since her own being was also nothing, why should she trouble herself? Evidently it was impossible for nothing to trouble itself, and so the only possible peace must lie in realising her own nothingness, which could be best accomplished by going to bed in a dark room. It was very dreary, of course, but she felt it was good logic, and must tell in the long run.

It had happened before. There had been days when she had reached the same point by a different road, and had been satisfactorily roused by a flash of intelligence shedding enough light in her darkened course to give her a new direction. To-day, however, it was quite different. She had certainly now reached the absolute end of all speculation, for she was convinced of the general nothingness of all created strength and life.

"For," said she, "I am quite sure that if I saw a train coming down upon me now, I would not get out of the way, — unless, the train being nothing, and I also nothing, two nothings should make something. But Hegel does not say that, and of course he knew, or he would not have understood that Nothing is the same as Being."

This kind of argument is irreproachable. It is like the old lady who said she was so glad that she did not like spinach, because if she did she would eat it, and, as she detested it, that would be very unpleasant. There is no answer possible to a properly grounded philosophical argument of this kind. On the whole, Miss Carnethy did the right thing when she tried to realise the physical being of nothing.

This Leonora was no ordinary girl. She belonged to a small class of young women who take a certain delight in being different from "the rest" — higher, of course. She had the misfortune to be of a mixed race, so far as blood was concerned, for her father was English and her mother was a Russian. It would probably be hard to find people more utterly unlike than these two, for the beef-eating conqueror is one, and the fire-eating Tartar is quite another, while this unlucky child of an international parentage had something of each. Her history — she was twenty-two years of age, then — might be summed up in a very few words. An English child, an Italian girl, a Russian woman. Her father had many prejudices, and did not believe in much; her mother had no prejudices at all, and believed in everything under the sun, and in a few things besides, so that certain evilly disposed persons had even said of her that she was superstitious.

There is something infinitely pathetic about such a growing to maturity as had made Leonora Carnethy what she was. Imagine such an anomaly as a poor little seed, of which no one can say whether it is a rose or a nightshade, alternately treated as a fair blossom and as a poisonous weed. Imagine a young girl, full of a certain fierce courage and impatience of restraint, chafing under the moral flat iron of a hopelessly proper father, whose mind is of the great levelling type and his prejudices as mountains of stone in the midst, reared to heaven like pyramids to impose a personal moral geography on the human landscape; and imagine the same girl further possessed of certain truly British instincts of continuity and unreasonable perseverance, eternally offending by her persistence a mother whose strong point is a kind of gymnastic superstition, a strange perversity of exuberant belief, forcing itself into the place of principle where there is none, — imagine a young girl in such a situation, in such a childhood, and it will not seem strange that she should grow up to be a very odd woman.

The father and mother understood each other after a fashion, but neither of them ever understood Leonora, and so Leonora tried to understand herself. To this laudable end she devoured books and ideas of all sorts and kinds, not always perceiving whether she took the poison first and the antidote afterwards, or the contrary, or even whether she fed entirely on poisons or entirely on antidotes. Poor child! she found truth very hard to define, and the criticism exercised by pure reason a very insufficient weapon. Moreover, like Job of old, she had friends and comforters to help in making life hideous. She wondered to-day, as she lay in her darkened room, whether any of them would come, and the thought was unpleasant.

She had just made up her mind to ring the bell

and tell her maid that no one should be admitted, when the door opened after the least possible apology for a knock, and she realised that she had thought of the contingency too late.

"Dear Leonora!"

"Dearest Leonora!"

The room was so dark that the young ladies stood still at the door, as they fired off the first shots of their brimming affection. Leonora moved so as to see their dark figures against the light.

"Oh," she said, "is it you?"

She was not glad to see her dear friends, for her fits of philosophical despair were real while they lasted, and she hated to be disturbed in them. But as these two young women were her companions in the study of universal hollowness, she felt that she must bear with them. So, after a little hesitation she allowed them to let some light into the room, and they sat down and held her hands.

"We want to talk to you about Infinite Time!"

"And Infinite Space!"

"I am persuaded," said the first young lady, "that our ideas of Time are quite mistaken. This system of hours and minutes is not adapted to the larger view."

"No," said Leonora, "for Time is evidently a portion of universal pure Being, and is therefore Nothing. I am sure of it."

"No. Time is not Nothing, — it is Colour."

"How do you mean, dear?" asked Leonora in some surprise.

"I do not quite know, dearest, but I am sure it must be. It is quite certain that Colour is a fundamental conception."

"Of course." There was a pause. Apparently the identity of Infinite Time with Colour did not interest Miss Carnethy, who stared at the light through the blinds between her two friends.

"It seems to me that we girls have no field nowadays," said she, rather irrelevantly.

"An infinite field, dear."

"And infinite time, dearest."

"I would give anything I possess to be able to do anything for anybody," began Leonora. "We know so much about life in theory, and we know nothing about it in practice. I wish mamma would even let me order the dinner sometimes; it would be something. But of course it is all an illusion, and nothing, and very infinite."

Poor Miss Carnethy turned on her pillow with a dreary look in her eyes.

"It will be different when you are married, dear," suggested one.

"Of course," acquiesced the other.

"But can you not see," objected Miss Carnethy, "that we shall never marry men whose ideas are so high and beautiful as ours? And then, to be tied forever to some miserable creature! Fancy not being understood! What do these wretched society men care about the really great questions of life?"

"About Time —"

"And Infinite Space —"

"Nothing, nothing, nothing!" cried Miss Carnethy in real distress.

"And yet it would be dreadful to be an old maid"—

"Perfectly dreadful, of course!" exclaimed all three, in a breath. Then there was a short silence, during which Leonora moved uneasily, and finally sat up, her heavy red hair falling all about her.

"By the bye," she said at last, "have you been out to-day, dears? What have you been doing? Tell me all about it."

"We have been to Lady Smyth-Tompkins's tea. It was very empty."

"You mean very hollow, for there were many people there."

"Yes," said the other, "it was very hollow — empty — everything of that sort. Then we went to drive on the Pincio."

"So very void."

"Yes. We saw Carantoni leaning against a post. I am sure he was thinking of nothing. He looks just like a stuffed glove, — such an inane dandy!"

Miss Carnethy's blue eyes suddenly looked as though they were conscious of something more than mere emptiness in the world. Her strong, well-shaped red lips set themselves like a bent bow, and the shaft was not long in flying.

"He is very pleasant to talk to," said she, "and besides — he really dances beautifully." It was probably a standing grievance with her two friends that Marcantonio did not dance with them, or Leonora could scarcely have produced such an impression in so few words.

"What does he talk about?" asked one, with an affectation of indifference.

"Oh, all sorts of things," answered Leonora. "He does not believe at all in the greatest good of the greatest number. He says he has discovered the Spencerian fallacy, as he calls it."

"Alas, then that also is nothing!"

"Absolutely nothing, dear," continued Leonora. "He says that, if there is no morality beyond happiness" —

"Of course!"

— "then every individual has as much right to be happy as the whole human race put together, since he is under no moral obligation to anybody or anything, there being no abstract morality. Do you see? It is very pretty. And then he says it follows that there is no absolute good unless from a divine standard, which of course is pure nonsense, or ought to be, if Hegel is right."

"Dear me! Of course it is!"

"And so, dears," concluded Leonora triumphantly, "we are all going to the Devil do you see?" The association of ideas seemed exhilarating to Miss Carnethy, and in truth the conclusion was probably suggested more by her feelings than by her logic, if she really possessed any. She felt better, and would put off the further consideration of Nothing and Being

to some more convenient season. She therefore gave
her friends some tea in her bedroom, and the conversation became more and more earthly, and the
subjects more and more minute, until they seemed
to be thoroughly within the grasp of the three young
ladies.

At last they went, these two charming damsels,
very much impressed with Leonora's cleverness, and
very much interested in her future, — which she
would only refer to in the vaguest terms possible.
They were both extremely fashionable young persons,
possessed of dowries, good looks, and various other
charms, such as good birth, good manners, and the
like; and it would be futile to deny that they took
a lively interest in the doings of their world, however
hollow and vain the cake appeared to them between
two bites.

"Are you going to-night, Leonora dear?" they
inquired as they left her.

"Of course," answered Miss Carnethy. "I must
hear the rest of the 'Spencerian fallacy' you know!"

When Leonora was alone she had a great many
things to think of.

The atmosphere had cleared during the last hour,
so far as philosophy was concerned, and as she looked
at herself in the glass, she was wondering how she
should look in the evening. Not vainly, — at least,
not so vainly as most girls with her advantages might
have thought, — but reflectively, the English side of
her twofold nature having gained the upper hand.

For as she gazed into her own blue eyes, trying to search and fathom her own soul, she was conscious of something that gave her pleasure and hope, — something which she had treated scornfully enough in her thoughts that very afternoon.

She knew, for her mother had told her, that Marc-antonio Carantoni had written to her parents, had called, had an interview, and had been told that he should be an acceptable son-in-law, provided that he could obtain Leonora's consent. She knew also that in the natural course of things he would this very evening ask her to be his wife; and, lastly, she knew very well that she would accept him.

She wondered vaguely how all those strange unsettled ideas of hers would harmonise in a married life. How far should she and her husband ever agree? She had a photograph of him in her desk, which he had given to her mother, and which she had naturally stolen and hidden away. Now she took it out and brought it to the window, and looked at it minutely, wonderingly, as she had looked at herself in the mirror a moment earlier.

Yes, he was a proper husband enough, with his bright honest eyes and his brave aristocratic nose and black moustache. Not very intelligent, perhaps, by the higher standard, — that everlasting " higher standard " again, — but withal goodly and noble as a lover should be. A lover? What weal and woe of heart-stirring romance that word used to suggest! And so this was her lover, the one man of all others dreamed of as a future divinity throughout her passionate girlhood. A creature of sighs and stolen glances — ay, perhaps of stolen kisses — a lover should be ; breathing soft things and glancing hot glances. Was Marcantonio really her lover?

He was so honest — and so rich! He could hardly want her for her dower's sake, — no, she knew that was impossible. For her beauty's sake, then? No, she was not so beautiful as that, and never could be, though the fashion had changed and red hair was in vogue. A pretty conceit, that mankind should make one half of creation fashionable at the expense of the other! But it is so all the same, and always will be. However, even with red hair, and an immense quantity of it, she was not a great beauty.

Perhaps Marcantonio would have married a great beauty if he could have met one who would accept him. It would not be nice, she thought, to marry a man who could not have the best if he chose. To think that he might ever look back and wish she were as beautiful as some one else! But after much earnest consideration of the matter no image of "some one else" rose to her mind, and she confessed with some triumph that she was not jealous of any one; that he had chosen her for herself, and that she was without rival so far as he was concerned. Not even her friends, the one dark and classic, the other fair and dreamy, could boast of having roused his interest. That was a great advantage.

But did she care for him — did she love him? Of course; how else should it be possible for her, with her high ideas of man's goodness, to think of ever consenting to marry him? Of course she loved him.

It was not exactly the kind of thing she expected, when she used to think of love a year ago; when love was a detached ideal with wings and arrows, and all manner of romantic and mythical attributes. But considering how very hollow and barren she had demonstrated the world to be, this thing had a certain life about it. It was a real sensation, beyond a doubt, and not an unhappy one either.

The room grew dark and she sat a few moments, the photograph lying idly in her hand. Out of the dusk, coming from the fairyland of her girl's fancy, rose a figure, the figure of the ideal lover she used to evoke before she knew Marcantonio Carantoni. He was a different sort of person altogether, much taller and broader and fiercer; a very impossibility of a man, coming towards her, and upsetting everything in his course; trampling rough-shod over the mangled fragments of her former idols, over society, over Marcantonio, over everything till he was close and near her, touching her hand, touching her lips, clasping her to him in fierce triumph, and bearing her away in a whirlwind of strength. A quick sigh, and she let the photograph fall to the ground, sinking back in her chair with a light in her eyes that overcame the darkness.

Dreamland, dreamland, what fools you make of us

all! What strange characters there are among the slides of your theatre, only awaiting the nod of Sleep, the manager, to issue forth, and rant and rave, make love and mischief, do battle and murder, play the scoundrel and the hero, till our poor brains reel and the daylight is turned on again, and all the players vanish into the thinnest of thin air!

Miss Carnethy rang for her maid, who brought lights and closed the shutters and let down the curtains preparatory to dressing her mistress for dinner. Leonora looked down and saw Marcantonio's photograph lying where it had fallen. She picked it up and looked at it once more by the candle light.

"Perhaps I shall refuse him after all," she thought, coldly enough, and she put it back into the drawer of her desk.

Perhaps you are right, Miss Carnethy, and the world is stuffed with sawdust.

CHAPTER III.

THE soft thick air of the ball-room swayed rhyth-
mically to the swell and fall of the violins; the perfume of roses and lilies was whirled into waves of
sweetness, and the beating of many young hearts
seemed to tremble musically through the nameless
harmony of instrument and voice, and rustling silk,
and gliding feet. In the passionately moving sym-
phony of sound and sight and touch, the whole weal
and woe and longing of life throbbed in a threefold
pace.

The dwellers in an older world did well to call the
dance divine, and to make it the gift of a nimble
goddess; truly, without a waltz the world would
have lacked a very divine element. Few people can
really doubt what the step was that David danced
before the ark.

The ball was at a house where members of various parties met by common consent as on neutral
ground. There are few such houses in Rome, or,
indeed, anywhere else, as there are very few people
clever enough, or stupid enough, to manage such an
establishment. Men of entirely inimical convictions
and associations will occasionally go to the house of
a great genius or a great fool, out of sheer curiosity,

and are content to enjoy themselves and even to talk
to each other a little, when no one is looking. It is
neutral ground, and the white flag of the ball-dress
keeps the peace as it sweeps past the black cloth legs
of clericals and the grey cloth legs of the military
contingent, past the legs of all sorts and conditions
of men elbowing each other for a front place with
the ladies.

Conspicuous by her height and rare magnificence
of queenly beauty was Madame de Charleroi, moving
stately along as she rested her fingers on the arm of
a minister less than half her size. But there was a
look of weariness and preoccupation on her features
that did not escape her dear friends.

"Diana is certainly going to be thin and scraggy,"
remarked a black-browed dame of Rome, fat and
solid, a perfect triumph of the flesh. She said it
behind her fan to her neighbour.

"It is sad," said the other, "she is growing old."

"Ah yes," remarked her husband, who chanced to
be standing by and was in a bad humour, "she was
born in 1844, the year you left school, my dear."
The black-browed lady smiled sweetly at her dis-
comfited friend, who looked unutterable scorn at her
consort.

Donna Diana glanced uneasily about the room, expecting every moment to see her brother appear with
Miss Carnethy. She was very unhappy about the
whole affair, though she could not exactly explain to
herself the reason of what she felt. Miss Carnethy

was rich, had a certain kind of distinguished beauty
about her, was young, well-born, — but all that did
not compensate in Madame de Charleroi's mind for
the fact that she was a heretic, a freethinker, a
dabbler in progressist ideas, and — and — what? She
could not tell. It must be prejudice of the most
absurd kind! She would not submit to it a moment
longer, and if the opportunity offered she would go
to Miss Carnethy and say something pleasant to her.
Donna Diana had a very kind and gentle Italian
heart hidden away in her proud bosom, and she had
also a determination to be just and honest in all situations, — most of all when she feared that her personal sympathies were leading her away.

The diplomat at her side chatted pleasantly, perceiving that she was wholly preoccupied; he talked
quite as much to himself as to her, after he had
discovered that she was not listening. And Donna
Diana determined to do a kind action, and the
swinging rhythm of the straining, surging waltz
was in her ears. She was just wondering idly
enough what the little diplomat had been saying to
her during the last ten minutes, when she saw her
brother enter the room with Miss Carnethy on his
arm. They had met in one of the outer drawing-
rooms and had come in to dance. Donna Diana
watched them as they caught the measure and
whirled away.

"She is terribly interesting," remarked the little
man beside her as he noticed where she was looking.

"She is also decidedly a beauty," answered Madame de Charleroi, with the calm authority of a woman whose looks have never been questioned.

People who are in love are proverbially amusing objects to the general public. There is an air of shyness about them, or else a ridiculous incapacity for perceiving the details of life, or at least an absurd infatuation for each other, most refreshing to witness. There is no mistaking the manner of them, if the thing is genuine.

The sadness that had been on Donna Diana's face, and which the resolution to be civil to Miss Carnethy had momentarily dispelled, returned now, as she watched the young couple. She remembered her own courtship, and she fancied she saw similar conditions in the wooing now going on under her eyes. Marcantonio was furiously in love, after his manner, but she thought Leonora's face looked hard. How could she let her brother marry a woman who did not love him? Her resolution to be civil wavered.

But just then, as luck would have it, the waltz brought the pair near to her. Marcantonio was talking pleasantly, with a quick smile that came and went at every minute. Leonora stood looking down and toying with her fan. One instant she looked up at him, and Donna Diana saw the look and the quick-caught heave of the snowy neck.

"I do not know what it is," she said to herself, "but it is certainly love of some kind." She moved towards them, steering her little diplomat through the sea of silk and satin, jewels and lace.

"How do you do, Mademoiselle Carnethy?" she said, in a voice that was meant to be kind, and was at least very civil.

Leonora stood somewhat in awe of the Vicomtesse de Charleroi, who was so stately and beautiful and cold. But she was very much pleased at the mark of attention. It was an approval, and an approval of the most public kind. The few words they exchanged were therefore all that could be desired. The vicomtesse nodded, smiled, nodded again, and sailed away in the easy swinging cadence of the waltz. Marcantonio looked gratefully after her. The air was warm and soft, and the light fluff from the linen carpet hung like a summer haze over the people, and the hundreds of candles, and the masses of flowers.

Marcantonio was silent. Something in the air told him that the time had come for him to speak, — something in Miss Carnethy's look told him plainly enough, he thought, that he was not to speak in vain. The last notes of the waltz chased each other away and died, and the people fell to walking about and talking. Marcantonio gave Leonora his arm, and the pair moved off with the stream, and on through the great rooms till they reached an apartment less crowded than the rest, and sat down near a doorway.

The young man did not lack courage, and he was

honestly in love with Leonora. He felt little hesitation about speaking, and only wished to put the question as frankly and as courteously as might be. As for her, she was obliged to acknowledge that she was agitated, although she had said to herself a hundred times that she would be as calm as though she were talking about the weather. But now that the supreme moment had come, a strange beating rose in her breast, and her face was as white as her throat. She looked obstinately before her, seeing nothing, and striving to appear to the world as though nothing were happening. Marcantonio sat by her side, and glanced quickly at her two or three times, with a very slight feeling of uncertainty as to the result of his wooing, — very slight, but enough to make waiting impossible, where the stake was so high.

" Mademoiselle," he said, in low and earnest tones, " I have the permission of monsieur your father, and of madame your mother, to address you upon a subject which very closely concerns my happiness. Mademoiselle, will you be my wife ? "

He sat leaning a little towards her, his hands folded together, and his face illuminated for a moment with intense love and anxiety. But Miss Carnethy did not see the look, and only heard the formal proposition his words conveyed. She saw a man standing in the door near them; she knew him — a Mr. Batiscombe, an English man of letters — and she wondered a little whether he would have used the same phrases in asking a woman to marry him, — whether all men would speak alike in such a case.

She had looked forward to this scene — more than once. Again the figure of the ideal lover of her dreams came to her, and seemed to pour out strong speech of love. Again she involuntarily drew a comparison in her mind between Marcantonio and some one, something she could not define. On a sudden all the honesty of her conscience sprang up and showed her what she really felt.

A thousand times she had said to herself that she would never marry a man she did not love; and for once that she had said it to herself, she had said it ten times over to her friends, feeling that she was inculcating a good and serviceable lesson. And now her conscience told her that she did not love Marcantonio, — at least not truly, certainly not as much as she would have liked to love. Then she remembered what she had thought that afternoon. How was it possible that she could have thought of him for a moment as her husband, if she did not love him, — especially with her high standard about such things? Oh, that high standard! With a quick transition of thought she made up her mind; but there was a strange little feeling of pain in her, such as the prince might have felt in the fairy tale when the ring pricked him. Nevertheless, her mind was made up.

"Yes," she said very suddenly, turning so that she could almost see his eyes, but not quite, for she instinctively dreaded to look him in the face; "yes, I will be your wife."

"Merci, mademoiselle," he said. The room was nearly empty at the moment, and Marcantonio took her passive hand and touched her fingers with his lips, being quite sure that no one was looking. But the man who stood at the door saw it.

"Such a good match, you know!" said some people, who had no prejudices.

"Such a special grace!" said the resident Anglo-American Catholics; "he is quite sure to convert her!"

"Such a special grace!" exclaimed the resident Anglo-American Protestants; "she is quite sure to lead him back!"

"Il faut toujours se méfier des saints," remarked Marcantonio's uncle, concerning his nephew.

"Never trust red-haired women," said the man who had stood at the door.

The engagement made a sensation in Rome, a consummation very easily attained, and very little to be desired. In places where the intercourse between young marriageable men and young marriageable women is so constrained as it is in modern Europe, a man's inclinations do not escape comment, and a very small seed of truth grows, beneath the magic incantations of society tea parties, to a very large bush of gossip. Nevertheless these good people are always astonished when their prophecies are fulfilled, and the bush bears fruit instead of vanish-

ing into emptiness; which shows that there is some
capacity left in them for distinguishing truth and
untruth. Marcantonio's marriage had long been a
subject in every way to the taste of the chatterers,
and though Madame de Charleroi had accused her
brother of hastiness, for lack of a better reproach, it
was nearly a year since his admiration for Miss Carnethy had been first noticed. During that time
every particular of her parentage and fortune had
been carefully sought after, especially by those who
had the least interest in the matter; and the universal verdict had been that the Marchese Carantoni
might, could, should, and probably would, marry
Miss Leonora Carnethy. And now that the engagement was out, society grunted as a pig may when
among the crab-oaks of Périgord he has discovered
a particularly fat and unctuous truffle.

Probably the happiest person was Marcantonio
himself. He was an honest, whole-souled man, and
in his eyes Leonora was altogether the most beautiful, the most accomplished, and the most charming
woman in the world. That he expressed himself
with so much self-control and propriety when he
asked her to marry him was wholly due to the manner of his education and training in the social propri-
eties. That a man should use any language warmer
or less guarded than that of absolutely respectful and
distant courtesy toward the lady he intended to
make his wife was not conceivable to him. In the
privacy of his own rooms he worshipped and adored

her with all his might and main, but when he addressed her in person it was as a subject addresses
his sovereign; a tone of respectful and submissive
reverence and obedience pervaded his actions and
his words. He would have pleased a woman who
loved sovereignty, better than a woman who dreamed
of a sovereign love.

But she was never out of his thoughts, and if he
wooed her humbly, he anticipated some submission
on her part after marriage. He had no idea of
always allowing her mind to wander in the strange
channels it seemed to prefer. He thought such an
intelligence capable of better things, and he determined, half unconsciously at first, and as a matter of
course, that Miss Carnethy, the philosopher, should
be known before long as the Marchesa Carantoni,
the Catholic. Gradually the idea grew upon him,
until he saw it as the grand object of his life, the
great good deed he was to do. His love consented
to it, and was purified and beautified to him in the
thought that by it he should lead a great soul like
hers to truth and light. He was perfectly in earnest,
as he always was in matters of importance; for of
all nations and peoples Italians have been most accused of frivolity, heartlessness, and inconstancy, and
of all races they perhaps deserve the accusation least.
They are the least imaginative people on earth, apart
from the creative arts, and the most simple and
earnest men in the matter of love. Northern races
hate Italians, and they fasten triumphantly on that

unlucky Latin sinner who falls first in their way as
the prototype of his nation, and as the butt of their
own prejudice.   In the eyes of most northern people
all Italians are liars; just as a typical Frenchman
calls England "perfide Albion," and all Englishmen
traitors and thieves.   Who shall decide when such
doctors disagree?   And is it not a proverb that there
is honour among thieves?

Marcantonio never spoke of these ideas of his to
his friends when they congratulated him on his engagement.   He only looked supremely happy, and
told every one that he was, which was quite true.
But his sister was to him a great difficulty, for she
evidently was disappointed and displeased.   He de-
bated within himself how he should appease her,
and he determined to lay before her his views about
Leonora's future.   To that intent he visited her in
the boudoir, where they had so often talked before
the engagement.

Madame de Charleroi received him as usual, but
there was a look in her eyes that he was not accustomed to see there, — an expression of protest, just
inclining to coldness, which had the effect of rousing his instinct of opposition.   With his other friends
he had found no occasion for being combative, and
his old manner had sufficed; but with his sister he
found himself involuntarily preparing for war, though
his intentions were in reality pacific enough.   Marcantonio was very young, in spite of his nine and
twenty years.   His manner now, as he met his sister,

was a trifle more formal than usual, and he bent his brows and pulled his black moustache as he sat down.

"Carissima Diana," he began, "I must speak with you about my marriage, and many things."

"Yes, — what is it?" asked his sister, calmly, as she turned a piece of tapestry on her knee to finish the end of a needleful of silk. Marcantonio had somehow expected her to say something that he could take hold of and oppose. Her bland question confused him.

"You are not pleased," he began awkwardly.

"What would you have?" she asked, still busy with her work. "I am sure I told you what I thought about it long ago."

"I want you to change your mind," said Marcantonio, delighted at the first show of opposition. Madame de Charleroi raised her eyebrows, gave a little sigh of annoyance, and turned towards him.

"I will always treat your wife with the highest consideration," she said, as though that settled the matter and she wished to drop the subject. But her brother was not satisfied.

"I wish you to love her, Diana; I wish you to treat her as your sister."

Donna Diana was silent, and Marcantonio shifted his position uneasily, for he did not know exactly what to do, and he saw that he was failing in his mission. But in a moment his heart guided

him. He went and sat beside her, and laid his
hand on hers.

"We cannot quarrel, dear," he said. "But will
you love her if I make her like you — if I make
her thoughts as beautiful as yours?"

Donna Diana's face softened as she turned to him
and affectionately pressed his hand.

"I will try to love her for your sake, dear boy,"
she answered gently; and he kissed her fingers in
thanks.

"Dear Diana," he said, "you are so good! But
you know she is really not at all like what you
fancy her. She is full of heart, and so wonderfully
delicate and lovely, — and so marvellously intelligent. There is nothing she does not know. She
has read all the philosophies " —

"Yes, I know she has," interrupted his sister, as
though deprecating the discussion of Miss Carnethy's
wisdom.

"But not as you think," he protested, catching the
meaning of her tone. "She has read them all, but she
will take what is best from each, and I am quite sure
she will be a good Catholic before long."

"I really hope so," said Donna Diana seriously.

"Not that I should love her any the less if she
were not," continued Marcantonio, who was loth to
feel that there could be any condition to his love.
"I should love her just as much if she were a Chi-
nese, — just as much, I am sure. But of course it
would be much better."

"Of course," assented Diana, smiling a little at his enthusiasm.

Somehow the peace was made, — it is so easy to make peace when each can trust the other, and knows it! Just as Madame de Charleroi had determined to say something pleasant on the evening when her brother offered himself to Leonora, so now she made up her mind to stand by Marcantonio, and to help him in his married life by being as sympathetic and as kind as possible.

In due time Marcantonio obtained the permission of the Church to unite himself with his Protestant wife, and after a great many formalities the wedding took place in the late spring, after Easter.

Weddings are tiresome things to talk about, and even the principal persons concerned in them always wish them over as soon as possible. What can be more trying for a young girl than to be set up to be stared at by the hour, be-feathered and be-rigged in a multiplicity of ornaments, made flimsy with tulle and lace, and ghastly with the accumulation of white things, when she is pale enough already with the acute fever of an exceedingly complicated state of mind? Or how can a man possibly enjoy being envied, hated, loved, despised, and considered a fool, by his rivals, his bride, the woman he has not married, and his bachelor friends, — all in a breath? It is absurd to suppose that any one with an intelligence above that of the average peacock can enjoy playing a leading part in a matrimonial parade.

Marcantonio Carantoni and Leonora Carnethy were married, and one of her intimate friends shed a tear as she observed how extremely empty a form it was. But the other looked a little pale, and said she was quite sure she could have chosen some one " better than that."

CHAPTER IV.

"Needles and pins, needles and pins," — the rhyme is obvious, and very old, — "When a man marries his trouble begins." Marcantonio is an Italian, and his native language contains no precise equivalent of this piece of wisdom, with which every English baby is made acquainted as soon as it can know anything.

The real difficulty seems to be that there are as many different ways of looking at marriage as there are people in the world. Marriage is described as being either a holy bond or a social contract. Obviously a holy bond implies at least a certain modicum of holiness on the part of the bound; and it is not likely that a single and very simple form of contract can ever cover the multifarious requirements and exigencies of a thousand million human beings. A contract, in order to be satisfactory, must be thoroughly understood and appreciated by the parties who undertake it, and this seems to be a very unusual case in the world.

When Marcantonio Carantoni married, he was possessed of very noble and exalted ideas, totally unformulated, but, as he supposed, only requiring the seal of experience to define, cement, and consolidate them. He believed that his wife was to be the stately queen of his household, the gentle partner of his deeds and thoughts, a loving listener to his words. He pictured to himself a magnificence of goodness unattainable for a man alone, but within easy reach of a man and a woman together; he imagined a broad perfection of human relations which should be a paradise on earth and an example of beatific possibility to the world. He dreamed of that kind of happiness, which, as it undoubtedly passes the bounds of experience, is aptly termed by poets transcendent, and is regarded by men of the world as a nonsensical fiction. He saw visions in his sleep, and waking believed them real, for he had a great capacity for believing in all that was good; and as he was human he found ceaseless delight in believing in these good things, more especially as in store for himself. He had always been fond of the pleasant side of life, and found no difficulty in conceiving of an infinite series of pleasant situations, culminating in his union with Miss Leonora Carnethy. He never analysed. Only pessimists analyse, and the best they can accomplish thereby is to make other men even as themselves, critical to see the darns in other people's clothes, and learned to spy out infinitesimal mud-specks upon the garments of saints.

Marcantonio was young. There is a faculty which men acquire from mixing with the world, which is not pessimism, nor analysis, nor indifference; it is rather a knowledge of good and evil with a fair appreciation of their proportion in human affairs. Nothing is more necessary to thought than the generalising of laws; nothing is more pernicious than the generalising of humanity into types, the torturing application of the nineteenth century boot to the feet of all, — men, women, and children alike. If men are only interesting for what they are, regardless of what they may be, a day of any one's actual experience must be a thousand times more interesting than all the fictions that ever were written. If art consists in the accurate presentation of detail, then the highest art is the petrifaction of nature, and the wax-works of an anatomical museum are more artistically beautiful than all the marbles of Phidias and Praxiteles. True art depends upon an a priori capacity for distinguishing the beautiful from the ugly, and the grand from the grotesque; and true knowledge of the world lies in the knowledge of good and evil, not confounding the noble with the ignoble under one smearing of mud, nor yet whitewashing the devil into an ill-gotten reputation for cleanliness. The temptation of Saint Anthony may convey a righteous moral lesson, but the temptation of Saint Anthony as described by his namesake's pig would risk being too unsavoury to be wholesome.

But Marcantonio was young, and he troubled himself about none of these things, supposing everything to be good, beautiful, and enduring, excepting such things as were evidently bad, inasmuch as they were ugly and disagreeable.

Now Miss Leonora Carnethy had long been given over to a sort of sleek, cynic philosophy, — the kind of cynicism that uses lavender water in its tub. Her dissatisfaction with the world was genuine, but she found means to alleviate it in the small luxuries and amenities of her daily life. She and her friends had talked the kernel out of life, or thought that they had, but the shell was still fresh and well favoured. Leonora herself was indeed subject to moods and fits of real unhappiness, for she was far too intelligent a person not to long for something beautiful, even when she was most convinced that life was ugly. There were times when she dreamed of an ideal man who should win her, and love her, and give her all the happiness she had missed. And again she would dream of the freedom of the earth-bound soul from ills, and cares, and thorns, and she would enter some silent Roman church and kneel for hours before a dimly lighted altar, praying for rest, and peace, and inspiration of holiness. But there was too much poetic feeling in her religious outpourings. If religion is to be poetic, a very little thing will destroy its harmony; some careless sacristan chatting with a crony in the corner of the church, or a couple of thoughtless children wrangling over a half-penny by the door, or any such little thing, destroyed instantly the fair illusion that lay as balm upon her unrestful soul. Religion must be real to every man if it is to stand the test of reality.

Leonora's views of marriage were therefore more or less subject to her moods. There were days, indeed, few and far between, when her better intelligence got the upper hand of the fictitious fabric of so-called philosophy which she had erected for herself. Then for a brief space she thought of life very much as Marcantonio did, and she contemplated her marriage as a noble and worthy career, — for marriage is a career to most women of the world. But then, again, all her uncertainty returned twofold upon her, and the only real thing was the dream of love, the vision of a lover, and the hope of a realised passion. She was so strong and radiantly human, that from the moment when her mind fell into abeyance the material beauty of life sprang up in her heart, until, being disappointed and cast down through not attaining the end of her passionate dreams, she once more sank into a half-religious, half-poetic melancholy. Nevertheless, the strongest element in her character was the desire to be loved, not by every one, but by some one manly man, and loved with all the strength he had, overwhelmingly. Her studies were a refuge when she saw how improbable such a piece of sweet fortune was, and, as might have been expected, they were far from regular and systematic. She read a great deal, especially of such authors as had a reputation for being profound rather than clear, and, as her mind had received no kind of preliminary training, the result was eminently unsatisfactory to herself. To Marcantonio, who knew more about the opera than about philosophy, she seemed a miracle of learning, and she loved to talk with him about theories, generally finding that, in spite of his ignorance, he made extremely sensible remarks upon them. But he always tried to lead her to different subjects, for, in spite of his immense admiration for what he supposed to be her wisdom, he was aware that it seemed very vague, and that it even occasionally bored him.

Leonora had acquired the unfortunate faculty of deceiving herself, and when the fit was upon her she saw things obliquely. In spite of the little prick of conscience that hurt her when she accepted Marcantonio's offer, she had soon persuaded herself that she loved him, on the principle that, since her "standard" was so very "high," she could not possibly have demeaned herself to accepting a man she did not love. It is a very fine thing to believe that we are so far removed from evil that we cannot do wrong, and therefore that whatever we do is infallibly right, no matter how our instincts may cry out against it. It is a most comforting and comfortable vicious circle which we convert into a crown of glory for ourselves on the smallest provocation. So when Leonora was finally married to Marcantonio, she made herself believe that she loved him, and all her vague theories were temporarily cast aside and trampled upon in her determination to realise in him all the happiness she had dreamed of in her ideal.

She had got a husband who did most truly love her, and whose one and absorbing thought would be her happiness, but he was not exactly what she had longed for. She mistook his courtesy for coldness, and his deference for indifference, and since she had persuaded herself that she loved him she wanted to find him a perfect fiery volcano of love and jealousy. Marcantonio was nothing of the kind; he was calm, courteous, and affectionate; he had not the slightest cause for jealousy, and, not in the least understanding his wife, he was perfectly happy.

Of all tests of true love a honeymoon is the severest, and by every right of sensible sequence ought to come last of all in the history of married couples. It is the great destroyer of illusions, and the more illusions there are the greater the destruction. Two people have seen each other occasionally, perhaps for an hour every day, — and that is a great deal in Europe, — during which meetings they have become more or less deeply enamoured, each of the qualities of the other. People notoriously behave very differently to the people they love and to the world at large; but their behaviour to the world at large is the outcome of their character, whereas their conduct to each other is the result, or the concomitant, of a passion which may or may not be real, profound, and good. But each has a great number of characteristics which practically never appear during those hours of courtship. Suddenly the two are married, and the lid of Pandora's

box is hoisted high with a vicious jerk that scares
the little imps inside to the verge of distraction, and
they fly out incontinent, with an ill savour. If the
lid had been gently raised, the evil spirits would
probably have issued forth stealthily, and one at a
time, without any great fuss, and might not have
been noticed. The two condemned ones travel together, eat together, talk together, until in a single
month they have exhausted a list of bad qualities
that should have lasted at least half a dozen years
under ordinary circumstances.

Marcantonio and Leonora travelled for a time,
and at last agreed to spend the remainder of the
summer in some quiet seaside place in Southern
Italy. They soon discovered the fallacy of wandering about Europe with a maid and a quantity of
luggage, and they both hoped that under the clear
sky of the south they might find exactly what they
wanted. So they gravitated to Sorrento and hired
a villa overhanging the sea, and Marcantonio suggested vaguely that they might have some one to
stay with them if they found it dull. At this
Leonora felt injured. The idea of his finding life
dull in her company!

"How can you possibly suggest such a thing?"
she asked, in a hurt tone.

"Not for myself, my dear," said Marcantonio, with
an affectionate smile. "It struck me that you might
not find it very amusing. I could never find it dull
where you are, ma bien aimée." And indeed he

never did. Leonora was pacified, as she almost always was when he was particularly affectionate.

" But, of course," he continued, "you will enjoy the being able to read and study your favourite books."

" I never want to read them now," said Leonora, who chanced that day to be not very philosophically disposed. She had been perusing the latest French impossibility, — she found it rather amusing to be allowed to have what she liked now that she was married.

" I should be glad if you never read any more philosophy," said Marcantonio, unwisely saying what was uppermost in his thoughts.

" Really, though," answered Leonora, " I know it all so very superficially that I feel I must go back and be much more thorough. I think I shall take a sound course of Voltaire and Hegel, and that sort of thing, this summer."

Her husband was silent. He began to suspect his wife of being capable of an occasional contradiction for the mere love of it. Besides, he saw no particular connection between the two authors she named. But then he knew very little about them. He looked at Leonora. There was not a trace of unpleasant expression in her face, and she seemed to have merely made the remark in the air, without the least intention of being contradictory or captious. He liked to look at her, she was so fresh and fair. Neither heat nor cold seemed to touch her delicate white skin, — her hair was so thick and strong, and her

blue eyes so bright. She was the very incarnation of
life. What if her features were not quite classic in
their proportion?

"I am not so beautiful as Diana," she said
laughingly one day to Marcantonio, "but I am sure
I am much more alive than she is." He laughed
too, well pleased at the distinction drawn. He was
glad that his sister should be thought cold, and he
believed that his wife loved him. He kissed her
hand tenderly.

They had been married two months when they
came to stay in Sorrento. It is a beautiful place.
Perhaps in all the orange-scented south there is
none more perfect, more sweet with gardens and
soft sea-breath, more rich in ancient olive-groves, or
more tenderly nestled in the breast of a bountiful
nature. A little place it is, backed and flanked by
the volcanic hills, but having before it the glory
of the fairest water in the world. Straight down
from the orange gardens the cliffs fall to the sea, and
every villa and village has a descent, winding through
caves and by stairways to its own small sandy cove,
where the boats lie in the sun through the summer's
noontide heat, to shoot out at morning and evening
into the coolness of the breezy bay. Among the
warm, green fruit trees the song-birds have their
nests, and about the eaves of the scattered houses the
swallows wheel and race in quick, smooth circles. Far
along through the groves echoes the ancient song of
the southern peasant, older than the trees, older than

the soil, older than poor old Pompeii lying off there in the eternal ashes of her gorgeous sins. And ever the sapphire sea kisses the feet of the cliffs as though wooing the rocks to come down, and plunge in, and taste how good a thing it is to be cool and wet all over.

To this place Marcantonio and his wife came at the beginning of July, having picked up numerous possessions and a few servants in Rome. They both had a taste for comfort, though they enjoyed the small privations of travelling for a time. To luxurious people it is pleasant to be uncomfortable when the fancy takes them, in order that they may the better enjoy the tint of their purple and the softness of their fine linen by the contrast. For contrast is the magnifying glass of the senses.

At sunset they walked side by side in their terraced garden overlooking the sea. They had travelled all night and had rested all day in consequence, and now they were refreshed and alive to the magic things about them.

"How green it is!" said Leonora, stopping to look at the thick trees.

"Yes," answered Marcantonio, "it is very green."

He was thinking of something else, and Leonora's very natural and simple remark did not divert his thoughts. The cook had arrived with a touch of the fever, and he was debating whether to send for the doctor at once or to wait till the next day. For he was very good to his servants, and took care of them. But Leonora wanted something more enthusiastic.

"But it is so very fresh and green!" she repeated.
"Do you not see how lovely it all is?" She laid her
hand on his arm.

"Oui, chérie," said he, getting rid of the cook by
an effort, "and green is the colour of hope." Then
it struck him that the saying was rather commonplace,
and he began to realise what she wanted. "It is a perfect fairyland," he went on, "and we will enjoy it as
long as we please. Are you fond of sailing, my dear?"

"Oh, of all things!" exclaimed Leonora, enthusiastically. "I love the sea and the beautiful colours, and everything" —

She stopped short and put her arm through his
and made him walk again. She was conscious, perhaps, that she was making an effort, — why, she could
not tell, — and that she had not much to say.

"Marcantoine" — she began. They spoke French
together, though she knew Italian better. She thought
his name long, but had not yet decided how to abbre-
viate it.

"Yes, what would you say, my dear?" he asked
pleasantly.

"I think I could — no — Marcantoine, now that we
are married, are you quite sure that you love me —
quite, quite?" Marcantonio's face turned strangely
earnest and quiet. He looked into her eyes as he
answered.

"Yes, my very dear wife, I am quite sure. And
you, are you sure, Leonora?"

"How serious you are!" she exclaimed, laughingly.

"Well, perhaps I am not so sure as you are, — but I think I could." Somehow he did not smile; he took some things so seriously.

Honeymoon conversations are insignificant enough, but it would be well if they were still more so. They should be limited by an international law to the phrases contained in the works of M. Ollendorff.

"Is it a fine day, sir?"

"Yes, madam, it is a very fine day, but the baker has the green hat of the officer."

"Has the baker also the red cow of the general's wife?"

"No, madam, the baker has not the red cow of the general's wife, but the undertaker has the penknife of the aunt of the good butcher."

It would be hard for the most ill-disposed couple to quarrel if confined to this simple elegance of dialectics, where truths of the broadest kind are clothed in the purest and most energetic words. Young married people are allowed too much latitude when they are turned loose upon a whole language with a sort of standing order to make conversation. When they have exhausted a certain fund of stock poetry and enthusiasm, they have very little to fall back upon, except their personal relation to each other; and unless they are equally serious or equally frivolous, the discussion of such matters is apt to get them into trouble.

Like most Italians Marcantonio had difficulty in understanding English humour. When Leonora said

she was not quite sure she loved him, she had meant
it for a jest, and if the jest had a deeper meaning and
a possibility of truth for herself, that was no reason,
she thought, why Marcantonio should consider it no
jest at all.   She was somewhat annoyed, and she
made up her mind that there must be an element of
Philistinism in his character.   She hated and feared
Philistines, partly because they were bores, and partly
because she had met one or two of them who had
known vastly more than she did, and who had not
scrupled to show it.   But, after all, how could Marcantonio be really like them?   He did not know very
much, nor did he pretend to, and he had very good
taste and was altogether very nice, — no, he was not
a Philistine; he loved her, and that was the reason
he was serious.   All this she thought, springing from
one idea to another, and ending by drawing her arm
closer through his and moving along the terrace by
his side.

The sun had set over there in front of them, and
the air was cool and purple with the afterglow.   They
stood by the wall and looked out silently, without
any further effort at conversation.   Talking had been
a failure, probably because they were tired, and for
a brief space they were content to watch the clouds,
and to listen to the swift rush of the swallows and
the faint, soft fall of the small waves on the sand far
below them.   There they were, linked together, for
better for worse, to meet the joys and the sorrows of
life hand in hand; to stand before the world as repre-

sentatives of their class, to play a part in public, and in their homes to be all in all to each other, man and wife.

Man and wife! Ah me! for the greatness and the littleness of the bonds those names stand for! Is there a man so poor and thin-souled in the world that he has not dreamed of calling some woman " wife "? Is there any wretch so mean and miserable in spirit that he has not looked on some maiden and said, " I would marry her, if I could "? Or has any woman, beautiful or ugly, fair or dark, straight or crooked, not thought once, and more than once, that a man would come, and love her, and take her, and marry her?

But have all the woes and ills of humanity, massed together and piled up in their dismal weight, ever called forth one half the sorrow that has ensued from this wedding and being wedded? Alas and alack for the tears that have fallen thick and fast from women's eyes, — and for the tears that have stood and burned in the eyes of strong men, good and bad! Who shall count them, or who shall measure them? Who shall ever tell the griefs that are beyond words, the sorrows that all earthly language, wielded by all earthly genius, cannot tell? Will any man make bold to say that he can describe what pain his neighbour feels? He may tell us what he does, for he can see it; he may tell us what he thinks, for perhaps he can guess it; but he cannot tell us what he suffers. The most he can do is to strike the sad minor chord that in every man's heart leads to a dirge and a death-song of his own.

A man who tries to tell of great suffering is rebuked. "No human creature," says the critic, "could suffer as this man describes, and live. There can therefore be no such suffering in the world." But does any critic or reader or other intelligent person say, when he reads about great happiness, "This joy is too much for humanity; there is no such joy in the world"?

We shrink from suffering, in others as in ourselves, and we turn to happiness and cannot get enough of it, so that however the tale ends, we would have made it end yet more joyfully; for so would we do with our own lives if we could. The strength of half mankind is spent in trying to remedy mistakes made at the outset, and I suppose that there is not one man in ten millions who is not striving to make himself happier, in his own fashion. A man is only happy when he believes himself to be so, in whatever way the proposition be turned, and no man believes himself so happy but what he might be happier.

Marcantonio Carantoni was in just such a position. He was more than contented, for he looked forward to much in the future that he had not yet attained, and he looked forward to it with certainty. His wife Leonora was trying hard to be as happy as he, but there had been a doubt — a cruel, hot little doubt — in her soul from the first. She had deceived herself — with the best intention — until she could hardly ever be sure that what she felt was genuine. She had asked questions of her heart until it was weary of answering them, and would as soon speak false to her as true.

And here ends the prologue of this story.

CHAPTER V.

A FEW days after the arrival of the Carantoni establishment in Sorrento, Leonora was sitting alone on a terrace of the villa with a book and a great variety of small possessions in the way of needle-work, shawls, cushions, flowers, parasols, fans, and a white cat. Marcantonio was gone to the town alone, intending to buy more possessions; for Sorrento is famous for its silk-weaving and its exquisite carved work of olive wood, and Leonora loved knick-knacks.

"I would give anything in the world for a sensation," she thought, as she looked out over the sea.

It was towards evening, and the water was as smooth as glass and tinged with red.

Marcantonio was right after all. It was very dull in Sorrento, with no one but one's husband to speak to, — and he had made such a fuss about the cook's illness. Of course, it was very beautiful and all that; but life with the beauties of nature is so very tiresome after a time. She longed for some of her friends, — even her mother, she thought, would be a relief. But no one had called, except-ing some very proper people of the Roman set,

who all had gout and rheumatism and a dictionary-
ful of diseases, and were taking sulphur baths at
Castellamare.

She was wishing with all her might that some
amusing person would call, when, as though in answer to her thoughts, a servant brought her a card.
Then she yawned slightly, supposing it to be some
toothless old princess of Rome or some other wearisome bore. But as she looked at the name, —
"Mr. Julius Batiscombe," — she gave a little start
and her light fingers touched her lace and ribbons, and her thick hair, and she said she would
receive.

Mr. Julius Batiscombe was a man of five and
thirty years of age, and a person sure to attract
attention anywhere. He was tall and looked strong,
but he trod as lightly as a woman ; none of his movements were clumsy or awkward. Not that he stepped
daintily or affected any feminine grace of movement;
there was something in his build and proportion
that made it always seem easy for him to move, as
though his strength were perfectly under control.

People were divided in opinion concerning his
appearance. Some said he was handsome and some
said he was coarse. Some said he was refined and
some said he looked ill-tempered. As a matter of
fact he had a rather small head, set upon a strong
neck. His nose was large and broad, and decidedly
aquiline, and he had a remarkably clean-cut and
determined jaw. His mouth was comparatively too

small for his face, but well shaped and well closed,
shaded by a black moustache of very moderate
dimensions. His blue eyes were set deep in his
head and far apart. Of hair he had an unusual
quantity, of a blue black colour, and he brushed it
carefully. A single deep line scored its mark across,
just above his brows. He had an odd way of looking at things, hiding the half of the iris under the
upper lid, showing the white of the eye a little
beneath the coloured portion. His complexion was
of that brilliant kind which sometimes goes with
black hair and blue eyes, and is known as an especial
characteristic of the Irish race. Moreover he was
noticeably well dressed, in a broad, neat fashion of
quiet colour, and he wore no jewelry nor ornament
except an old seal ring.

Opinions varied almost as much about Mr. Julius
Batiscombe's character and reputation as about his
claims to be thought good-looking. He had no intimate friends, or was supposed to have none; and
he never answered many questions, because he asked
none. It was known that he was an Englishman
or an Irishman by birth, but that he had never lived
long in his own country, whereas he seemed to have
lived everywhere else under the sun.

" I am so glad you came to-day, Mr. Batiscombe,"
said Leonora after he was seated, and looking at
him rather curiously.

He was the man who had stood in the doorway
at the ball when Marcantonio offered himself to her.

She knew him as well as she knew most of the stray foreigners who from time to time frequented Roman society. He had been in Rome all that winter, and she had met him two years earlier, when she first went out. He interested her, however, by a certain reserve of manner and by an air of " having a story about him " — as young ladies put it — which was unusual.

" I am very fortunate," he answered, with a slight inclination and a polite smile. " I called entirely at random. Somebody said you were coming here, and so I came to see if you had arrived."

" Yes," said Leonora, " we have been here several days, with all sorts of troubles on our hands. It is such very hard work to settle down, you know."

" What has been the trouble?" inquired Mr. Batiscombe, glancing at the evidences of comfort that were scattered about.

" Oh — it is the cook," said Leonora with a little laugh; she was just beginning to feel the novelty of housekeeping, and she laughed at the mention of the cook, as though the idea amused her. " He has had a little fever, and my husband was dreadfully anxious about him. But he is quite recovered."

" I am very glad," said Mr. Batiscombe. " It must be a terrible bore to have one's cook ill. Did you get anything to eat in the meanwhile?"

And so forth, and so on, through a few dozen

inanities. He would not make an original remark, being quite sure that Leonora would ultimately turn the conversation to some congenial subject.

"Shall you be in Rome next winter, Mr. Batiscombe?" she asked at length rather suddenly.

"It is rather doubtful," he answered slowly. "I am a great wanderer, you know, Marchesa. I can never say with any certainty where I shall be next."

He was looking at her and thinking what a splendid living thing she was, with the evening sun on her red hair. That was all he thought, but it gave him pleasure, and his glance lingered contentedly upon her, as upon a picture or a statue. He supposed from her remark that she wanted him to talk about himself, and he was willing to please her; but he was in no hurry, for he feared she would move and show herself in a less favourable light. She was so good to look at, that it was worth a visit to see her; and yet she was not a great beauty.

"I was thinking a little of going to the East," he added presently.

"But you have been there, have you not?"

"Not for a long time; and it will bear revisiting often, — very often. I mean to go there and study again as I did years ago. You have no idea how interesting those things are." Mr. Batiscombe looked thoughtfully out towards the sea.

"What are those things, as you call them?" asked Leonora.

"What many people call the 'wisdom of the East.'

They make us the compliment of implying that there is a 'wisdom of the West' also, which seems unlikely."

"Dear me, what a sweeping remark!" exclaimed Leonora, rather startled.

"I will prove it," said Mr. Batiscombe. "It seems to me that in the West no two wise men think alike; whereas in the East no two wise men think differently. Is not that a kind of proof?"

"Not a very valuable proof," said the marchesa. "But I do not know much about it."

"You have the reputation of knowing more about it than most people, Marchesa," answered Batiscombe. "I have been told that you know everything." Leonora blushed very slightly.

"What nonsense!" said she; "I might say the same of you."

"I observe that you do not, however," said he, laughing.

"I never flatter any one," she answered calmly.

"Obviously, there is but one thing for me to say," said Batiscombe still smiling.

"What is that?"

"That no one could possibly flatter you, Marchesa, — since the truth is no flattery."

"No, but imitation is," retorted Leonora, well pleased at having got a small advantage of him.

"Very good," said Batiscombe; "but do you know who said so?"

"Shakespeare" — began Leonora, but she stopped. "No — I cannot tell."

"A man called Colton said it. He wrote a book called 'Lacon,' containing innumerable reflections on things in general. He was a wandering sea-parson and wrote books of travels. He died of a complication of nautical and religious disorders — he confused the spirituous with the spiritual — but he was a wise man for all that."

"I suppose you remembered all that for the sake of showing that you really know everything," said Leonora, looking up from behind the fan that shaded her eyes.

The last rays of the sun shone horizontally across the terrace. The book she had been reading slipped from her lap. With a quick movement Batiscombe caught it before it fell and laid it on the little table. Leonora noticed the action and admired the ease of it. She was altogether disposed to admire the man, though she would have confessed that his conversation hitherto had not been at all remarkable. But there was something in his manner that attracted her. He was quick and gentle, and yet he looked so big and strong.

"Thanks," she said. "By the bye, are you going to spend the summer here, or are you only passing?"

"I am only passing — literally passing, for I have come from the north, and am going southward. I believe I am doing rather an original thing."

"You are generally supposed to be always doing original things," said Leonora.

"At all events I am never bored," he answered,

"which cannot be said of most people. At present I am going round Italy in an open boat. It is great fun. I started from Nice six weeks ago."

"How delightful! I should like it immensely!"

"Are you fond of sailing?"

"I enjoy it of all things," she answered. In spite of her remark to the same effect made to Marcantonio on the day of their arrival, she had not yet been on the water. He had been so anxious about the cook.

"There is a man-of-war to be launched at Castellamare the day after to-morrow," said Batiscombe. "May I have the pleasure of taking you over in my boat?"

At this moment Marcantonio appeared at the extremity of the terrace and came towards them.

"Should you like to go?" asked Batiscombe quickly, in a lower voice. "If so I will propose it at once." Leonora nodded, and her husband approached.

"Marcantonio," she said, "you know Monsieur Batiscombe?"

"Mais certainement," cried Marcantonio cordially, and the two men shook hands. Batiscombe was at least as much at home in French as his host, and immediately attacked the subject.

"I came to propose to Madame la Marquise," he said, "that you should come over to Castellamare in my boat the day after to-morrow to see the launch. I trust the plan meets your approval?"

Marcantonio turned to his wife to inquire. She nodded to him; he nodded to her.

"We should be charmed," said he.

And so the matter was arranged; they agreed about the hour, and Leonora said she would bring the luncheon.

"Yes," said Marcantonio, "I am glad to say the cook " —

At this point Mr. Batiscombe rose to go, and the remark about the cook's health was lost in the stir. Batiscombe bowed, smiled, bowed again, and moved smoothly away across the terrace, disappearing with a final inclination, and a sweep of his straw hat.

"He walks like a cat, that gentleman," said Marcantonio as he sat himself down beside his wife.

"He is charming," said Leonora. "He has been so amusing." She looked at her husband furtively to see how he took the remark.

"Perhaps," thought she, "he is one of those men who have to be managed by being made jealous. I have read about them in novels."

But Marcantonio was very glad that she had been amused, and he merely smiled pleasantly and said so. It never entered his head to suppose that Leonora was not satisfied with his show of affection, because he knew in himself that his love was perfectly real. There is a little vanity in such men as Marcantonio, together with a great deal of honesty. Their vanity makes them quite sure that the woman they love is satisfied, and their honesty makes them

think the woman would speak out if she were not,
just as they themselves would do.

Leonora had vanity enough of a certain kind,
but it was not personal. She doubted her own
powers and gifts more than she need have done,
and there was enough uncertainty about her own
affection to make her uncertain of her husband's
love. In the meanwhile she was bored since Mr.
Batiscombe had gone, and she wished Marcantonio
would talk and amuse her. But when he did begin
to say something it was about local Roman politics,
and she understood nothing about that sort of
thing. She longed more and more for "a sensation." It would probably be different to-morrow,
for her moods seldom lasted long. But this evening it was intolerable. She made the most absent-
minded answers to her husband's remarks, and seemed
so impatient that he suggested she must be tired and
had better go to bed.

"But I am not tired at all — on the contrary,"
she objected. "There is nothing to tire me here,
— a little driving, a great deal of sitting on the terrace, a great deal of reading, and very little conversation " —

"Very little conversation!" exclaimed Marcantonio. "Mais, mà chère, here it is two hours we
have been talking, without counting the visit of the
gentleman who walks like a cat — Bat— Botis—
I cannot say his name, but I know him."

"Ah, yes — Mr. Batiscombe. Yes," said Leonora

languidly, " he was very amusing. He talked about all sorts of things."

"Shall we ask him to pass a few days with us? I should be very glad, if you like him."

Marcantonio was really delighted to do anything his wife might wish. Leonora was touched. He was sitting beside her, and she put her arms round his neck and laid her head on his shoulder.

"You are so good," she said in a low voice. " Oh, I do not want anybody else here at all. I only want you — but all of you — and I feel as though I had not all yet."

For the moment she really loved him. He gently smoothed her hair with his delicate, olive-tinted hand.

Meanwhile Mr. Julius Batiscombe had gone to his hotel, and, having eaten his dinner, was sitting on the tiled terrace over the sea, with a cup of coffee at his elbow, and a cigarette in his mouth. There were lamps on the terrace, and there was starlight on the water, and Mr. Batiscombe was alone at his small table.

"I wish I had not gone there. I wish I had not asked them to go to Castellamare. I wish I were at sea in my boat." He said these things over and over to himself, and now and again he smiled a little scornfully, and sipped his coffee.

Julius Batiscombe was generally in trouble. He was a strong man in all respects save one. He had conquered many difficulties in his life, and by sheer determination had turned evil fortune into good, winning himself a name and a position, and such a proportion of wealth as he needed. Of good family, and brought up in luxury and refinement, he had been left at twenty years of age without parents, without much money, and without a profession. He knew some half dozen languages, ancient and modern, and he had a certain premature knowledge of the world. But that was his whole stock-in-trade excepting an indomitable will and perseverance, combined with exceedingly good health, and a great desire for the luxuries of life. He had lived in all sorts of ways and places, getting his pen under control by endless literary hack-work. By and by he tried his hand at journalism, and was successively addicted to three or four papers, published in three or four languages in three or four countries. Last of all he wrote a book which unexpectedly succeeded. Since then the aspect of life had changed for him, and though he still wandered, from force of habit, so to say, he no longer wandered in search of a fortune. A pen and a few sheets of paper can be got anywhere, and Julius Batiscombe set up his itinerary literary forge wherever it best pleased him to work. He had fought with ill-luck, and had conquered it, and now he felt the confidence of a man who has swum through rough water and feels at last the smooth, clean sand beneath his feet. His success had not turned his head in the least; he was too much of an artist for that, striving always in his work to attain something that ever seemed to escape him. But he now felt that he might some day get nearer to what he aimed at, and there were moments, brief moments, of genuine happiness, when he believed that there was wrought by his pen some stroke of worth that should not perish. Ten minutes later he was dissatisfied with it all, and collected his strength for a new effort, still hoping, and striving, and labouring on, with his whole soul in his work.

Strong in body and strong in determination, he was yet very weak in one respect. He was eternally falling in love, everlastingly throwing himself at the feet of some woman and making mischief which he afterwards bitterly regretted. It seemed as though it were impossible for him to live six months without some affair of a more or less serious character. It made no difference whether he wandered off into the recesses of the Italian mountains, or went into hermitage in the Black Forest, or steamed and sweltered under a tropical sun; there was always a feminine element at hand to make trouble for him.

It was not only the universal woman calling to him to follow, it was the universal woman seizing him and carrying him away by main force. For it was no matter of inclination. He struggled hard enough to deserve victory, but without any perceptible result.

What gave him most pain was the dreary consciousness of his own insincerity in his love-making,

the consciousness that came to him after the affair
was over. While it lasted he was carried away
and blinded by a sort of madness that took possession of him and allowed him no time for thought.
But when it was over he remembered, bitterly
enough, how untrue it had all been, to himself and
to the one woman whom he had loved, and whom,
down in the depths of his turbulent heart, he loved
still. His other loves were like horrible creations
of black magic, bodies with no soul, when he looked
back on them. And yet while they lasted they
seemed to him real, and high, and noble.

At first he fought against every new inclination,
and cursed his folly in advance; and sometimes he
conquered, but not always. If once the fatal point
were passed there was no salvation, for then he deceived himself and the deception was complete. It
was no wonder people thought so differently about
him. He had been known to do brave and generous things, and things that showed the utmost delicacy of feeling and courtesy of temper; and he
had been known to act with a sheer, massive, selfish disregard of other people, that made cynics
look grave and mild-eyed society idiots stare with
horror. The fact was that Julius Batiscombe in
love was one person, and Julius Batiscombe out of
love, repentant and trying to make up to the world
for the mischief he had done, was quite another;
and he knew it himself. He was perfectly conscious
of his own duality, and liked the one state, — the

state of no love, — and he loathed and detested the other both before and after.

And now he sat over his coffee, and the prophetic warning of his soul told him that he was in danger, so that he was angry at himself and feared the future. He had known Miss Carnethy, as has been said, for some time, and had danced with her and sat beside her at dinner more than once, without giving her a thought; he therefore had found it perfectly natural to call when he discovered that she was at Sorrento. But his impression after his visit was very different. The Marchesa Carantoni was not Miss Carnethy at all.

She had looked so magnificent as she sat in the evening sunshine, and he had gazed contentedly at her with a sense of artistic satisfaction, thinking no evil. But now he could think of nothing else. The sun seemed to rise again out of the dark sea, turning back on its course till it was just above the horizon, with a warm golden light; by his side sat the figure of a woman with glorious red hair, and he was speaking to her; the whole scene was present to him as he sat there, and he knew very well what it was that he felt. Why had he not known it at first? He would surely have had the sense not to propose such a thing as a day together. "A day together" had so often entailed so much misery.

Nevertheless he would not invent an excuse, nor go away suddenly. It would be quite possible, he knew, and perhaps also he knew in his heart that

it would be altogether right. But it seemed so uncourteous, he was really anxious to see the launch
of the great ship and — and — he would not be
such a fool as to fancy he could not look at a
woman without falling in love with her on the spot.
At his age! Five and thirty — he seemed so old
when he thought of all he had done in that time.
No. He would not only go with them, but he
would be as agreeable as he could, if only to show
himself that he was at last above that kind of
thing.

Some human hearts are like a great ship that
has no anchor, nor any means of making fast to
moorings. The brave vessel sails through the
stormy ocean, straining and struggling fiercely, till
she lies at last within a fair harbour. But she has
no anchor, and by and by the soft, smooth tide
washes her out to sea, so gently and cruelly, out
among the crests and the squalls and the rushing
currents, and she must fain beat to windward again
or perish on the grim lee shore.

Julius Batiscombe went to bed that night knowing that he was adrift, and yet denying it to himself; knowing that in a month, a week perhaps, he
should be in trouble — in love — pah! how he hated
the idea!

CHAPTER VI.

DURING the time that elapsed between Mr. Batiscombe's visit and the expedition to see the launch, Leonora had an access of the religious humour. The little scene with her husband had made a deep impression on her mind, and as was usual when she received impressions, she tried to explain it and understand it and reason about it, until there was little of it left. That is generally the way with those people who make a study of themselves; when they have a good thought or a good impulse, they dissect the life out of it and crow over the empty shell.

It was clear, thought Leonora, that the sudden outburst of affection which made her tell her husband that she wanted "all of him" was the result of some sensation of dissatisfaction, of some unfulfilled necessity for a greater sympathy. But, if at the very beginning she had not the key to his heart, if he did not wholly love her now, it was clear that he never would at all. Why was it clear? Oh! never mind the "why," — it was quite clear. Moreover, if he could never love her wholly as she wished and desired, she was manifestly a misunderstood woman, a most unhappy wife, a condemned existence, — loving and not being loved in return. And he, the heartless wretch, was anxious about the cook! Good heavens! the cook — when his wife's happiness was in danger! In this frame of mind there was evidently nothing more appropriate for her to do than to take a prayer-book and to hide her face in a veil, and slip away to the little church on the road, a hundred yards from the house. For a wrecked existence, thought Leonora, there is no refuge like the Church. She was not a Catholic, but that made no difference; in great distress like this, she could very well be comforted by any kind of religion short of her father's, which latter, to her exalted view, consisted of four walls and a bucket of whitewash, seasoned with pious discourses and an occasional psalm-tune.

What she could not see, what was really at the bottom of the small tempest she rashly whirled up in her over-sensitive soul, was her own disillusionment. She had deceived herself into believing that she loved her husband, and the deception had cost her an effort. She was beginning to realise that the time was at hand when she might strive in vain to believe in her own sincerity, when her heart would not submit to any further equivocation, and when she should know in earnest what hollowness and weariness meant. As yet this was half unconscious, for it seemed so easy to make herself the injured party.

Poor Marcantonio was not to blame. He was the happiest of mortals, and went calmly on his way, doubting nothing and thinking that he was of all mortal men the most supremely fortunate.

Meanwhile Leonora kneeled in the rough little church, solacing herself with the catalogue of those ills she thought she was suffering. The stones were hard; there was a wretched little knot of country people, squalid and ill-savoured, who stared at the great lady for a moment, and then went on with their rosaries. A dirty little boy with a cane twenty feet long was poking a taper about and lighting lamps, and he dropped some of the wax on Leonora's gown. But she never shrank nor looked annoyed.

" All these things are very delightful," she said to herself, "if you only consider them as mortifications of the flesh."

She remembered how often just such little annoyances had sent her out of other churches disgusted and declaring that religion was a vain and hollow thing; and now, because she could bear with them and was not angry, she felt quite sure it was genuine.

" Yes," said she piously, as, an hour later, she picked her way home through the dusty road, " yes, the Church is a great refuge. I will go there every day."

Indeed, she was so resigned and subdued that evening at dinner, that Marcantonio asked whether she had a headache.

" Oh no," she answered, "I am perfectly well, thank you."

" Because if you are indisposed, ma bien-aimée,"

continued her husband with some anxiety, " we will not go to Castellamare to-morrow."

" I will certainly go," she said. " I would go if I had twenty headaches," she might have added, for it would have been true.

" The occasion will be so much the more brilliant, ma très chère," remarked Marcantonio gallantly, as they went out into the garden under the stars.

" It is a hollow sham," said Leonora to herself. " He does not mean it."

But whether it was the effect of the morning, or the magic influence of Mr. Batiscombe's personality, is not certain; at all events when that gentleman appeared at the appointed hour to announce that his boat was in readiness, Leonora looked as though she had never known what care meant. She doubtless still remembered all she had thought on the previous afternoon, and she was still quite sure that her existence was a wreck and a misery, — but then, she argued, why should we poor misunderstood women not take such innocent pleasures as come in our way? It would be very wrong not to accept humbly the little crumbs of happiness, — and so on. So they went to Castellamare.

It is not far, but the wind seldom serves in the morning, and it was an hour and a half before the six stout men in white clothes and straw hats pulled the boat round the breakwater of the arsenal. Everything was ready for the ceremony. Half a dozen Italian ironclads lay in the harbour, decked from stem to stern with flags; the royal personages had arrived, and were boring each other to death in a great temporary balcony, gaudily decorated with red and gold, which had been reared on the shore within reach of the nose of the new ship. The ship herself, a huge, ungainly thing, painted red and bearing three enormous national flags, lay like a stranded monster in the cradle, looking for all the world like a prehistoric boiled lobster with its claws taken off. The small water room opposite the arsenal was crowded with every kind of craft, and little steamers arrived every few minutes from Naples to swell the throng. The July sun beat fiercely down and there was not a breath of air. The boatmen were all wrangling in a dozen southern dialects, and no one seemed to know why the ceremony was delayed any longer. Nevertheless, as is usual in such cases, there was half an hour to wait before the thing could be done.

"I am afraid you will find this a dreadful bore," said Batiscombe to Leonora in English, while Marcantonio was busy trying to make out some of his friends on shore through a field-glass. Batiscombe had sat in the stern-sheets to steer during the trip, and having Leonora on one side of him and her husband on the other, had gone through an endless series of polite platitudes. If it had not been that Leonora attracted him so much he must himself have been bored to extinction. But then in that case he would probably not have put himself in such a position at all.

"Oh, nothing of this kind bores me," said Leonora cheerfully.

"You say that as though there were many kinds of things that did, though," observed Batiscombe, looking at her. It was a natural remark, without any intention.

"Dear me, yes!" exclaimed Leonora. "Life is not all roses, you know." She therewith assumed a thoughtful expression and looked away.

"I should not have supposed there were many thorns in your path, Marchesa. Would it be indiscreet to inquire of what nature they may be?"

Leonora was silent, and put up her glass to examine the proceedings on shore.

Batiscombe, who had come out that day with the sworn determination not to say or do anything to increase the interest he felt in the Marchesa, found himself wondering whether she were unhappy. The first and most natural conclusion was that she had been married to Marcantonio by designing parents, and that she did not care for him. Society said it had been a love-match, but what will society not say? "Poor thing," he thought, "I suppose she is miserable!"

"Forgive me," he said, in a low voice. "I did not know you were in earnest."

Leonora blushed faintly and glanced quickly at him. He had the faculty of saying little things to women that attracted their attention.

"What lots of poetry one might make about a

launch," he said laughing, — for it was necessary to change the subject, — "ship — dip; ocean — motion; keel — feel; the rhymes are perfectly endless."

"Yes," said Leonora; "you might make a sonnet on the spot. Besides, there is a great deal of sentiment about the launching of a great man-of-war. The voyage of life — and that sort of thing — don't you know? How hot it is!"

"I will have another awning up in a minute," and he directed the sailors, helping to do the work himself. He stood upon the gunwale to do it.

"I am sure you will fall," said Leonora, nervously. "Do sit down!"

"If I had a millstone round my neck there would be some object in falling," said Batiscombe. "As it is, I should not even have the satisfaction of drowning."

"What an idea! Should you like to be drowned?" she said, looking up to him.

"Sometimes," he answered, still busy with the awning. Then he sat down again.

"You should not say that sort of thing," said Leonora. "Besides, it is rude to say you should like to be drowned when I am your guest."

"Great truths are not always pretty. But how could any man die better than at your feet?" He laughed a little, and yet his voice had an earnest ring to it. He had judged rightly when he foresaw that he must fall in love with Leonora.

Marcantonio, who did not understand English, was watching the proceedings on shore.

"Ah! it is magnificent!" he cried, with great enthusiasm. The royal personage who was to christen the ship had just broken the bottle of wine, and the little crowd of courtiers, officers, and maids of honour clapped their hands and grinned. They all looked hot and miserable and exhausted, but they grinned right nobly, like so many Cheshire cats. There was a sound of knocking and hammering, a final shout of warning from the dock officers, a slight trembling of the great hull, and then the ship began to move, slowly at first, and ever more quickly, till with a mighty rush and a plunge and a swirl she was out in the water. The people yelled till they were hoarse, the boatmen cursed each other by all the maledictions ever invented to meet the exigencies of a lost humanity, the royal personages stood together on their platform looking like a troupe of marionettes in a toy theatre, and congratulating each other furiously as though they had done it all themselves; everything was noise and sunshine and tepid water; Marcantonio was flourishing his hat, and Leonora waved a little lace handkerchief, while Batiscombe sat looking at her and wondering why he had never thought her beautiful before. Indeed, she was superb in her simple, raw silk gown, with fresh-cut roses at her waist.

"It seems to me, Marchese, that you are very enthusiastic," said Batiscombe to Marcantonio.

"Mon Dieu!" exclaimed the other, shrugging his shoulders, "one cheers these things as one would cheer fireworks, or a race. It signifies nothing."

"Oh, of course," said Leonora; "and besides, it is so pretty."

"I think it is horrible," said Batiscombe, suddenly.

"Why — what?"

"To see a nation squandering money in this way, when the taxes on land are at sixty per cent. and more, and the people emigrating by the shipload because they cannot live in their own homes."

"Oh, for that matter, you are right," said Marcantonio, turning grave in a moment. "I could tell you a story about taxes."

"What is it?" asked Leonora. "Those things are so interesting."

"Last autumn I was in the Sabines; I have a place up there, altogether ancient and dilapidated — a mere ruin. I own some of the land, and the peasants own little vineyards. One day I saw by the roadside a poor old man, a sort of village crétin, whom every one knew quite well. We used to call him Cupido; he was half idiotic and quite old. He was weeping bitterly, poor wretch, and I asked him what was the matter. He pointed to a little plot of land by the road, inclosed by a stone wall, and said the tax-gatherer had taken it from him. And then he cried again, and I could not get anything more out of him."

"Poor creature!" exclaimed Leonora, sympathetically.

"Well," continued Marcantonio, "I made inquiries, and I found that he had owned the little plot, and that the tax-gatherer had first seized the wretched crop of maize — perhaps a bushel basket full — to pay the tax; and then, as that did not cover his demands, he seized the land itself and sold it or offered it for sale."

"Infamous!" cried Leonora, and the tears were in her eyes.

"A cheerful state of things," remarked Batiscombe, "when the whole crop does not suffice to pay the taxes on the soil!"

"N'est-ce pas?" said Marcantonio. "Well, I provided for the poor old man, but he died in the winter. It broke his heart."[1]

"I love the Italians," said Batiscombe; "but their ideas of economy are peculiar. I suppose that without much metaphor or exaggeration one might say that the poor crétin's bushel of corn is gone into that ridiculous ironclad over there."

"But of course it is," said Marcantonio. "The whole thing probably paid for one rivet. You, who write books, Monsieur Batiscombe, put that into a book and render it very pathetic."

"It needs little rendering to make it that," said Batiscombe, and he looked at Leonora's eyes that were not yet dry.

By this time the royal marionettes had been bundled off to their boats, and the crowd of small craft on the water began to disperse. Batiscombe's six men fell to their oars and the boat shot out from the breakwater. Presently they hoisted the bright

[1] The author witnessed the facts here described in 1880.

lateen sails to the breeze. Batiscombe perched himself on the weather rail, and took the tiller, as the brave little craft heeled over and began to cut the water. The wind fanned Leonora's cheek, and she said it was delightful.

Batiscombe suggested that they should run into one of the great green caves that honeycomb the cliffs near Sorrento, and make it their dining-room. So away they went, rejoicing to be out of the heat and the noise. It was twelve o'clock, and far up among the orange groves the little church bells rang out their midday chime, laughing together in the white belfries for joy of the sunshine and the fair summer's day.

"I should like to be always sailing," said Leonora, who had now quite forgotten her woes and enjoyed the change.

"Ma chère," said her husband, "there is nothing simpler."

"You always say that," she answered rather reproachfully; "but this is the very first time I have been on the water since we came."

"My boat and my men are always at your disposal, Marchesa," said Batiscombe, looking down at her, "and myself, too, if you will condescend to employ me as your skipper."

"Thanks, you are very good," said she. "But I thought you were only passing, and were to be off in a few days?" She glanced up at him, as though she meant to be answered.

" Oh, it is very uncertain," said Batiscombe. " It depends," he added in a lower voice and in English, "upon whether you will use the boat." It was rather a bold stroke, but it told, and he was rewarded.

"I should like very much to go out again some day," she said.

Those little words and sentences, what danger signals they ought to be to people about to fall in love! Batiscombe knew it; he knew well that every such speech, in her native language and in a half voice, was one step nearer to the inevitable end. But he was fast getting to the point when, as far as he himself was concerned, the die would be cast. His manner changed perceptibly during the day, as the influence gained strength. His voice grew lower and he laughed less, while his eyes shone curiously, even in the midday sun.

The boat ran into the cave, which was the largest on the shore, and would admit the mast and the long yards without difficulty. Within the light was green, and the water now and again plashed on the rocks. The men steadied the craft with their oars and the party proceeded to lunch. Most of "society" has a most excellent appetite, and when one reflects how very hard society works to amuse itself, it is not surprising that it should need generous nourishment. The unlucky cook had done his best, and the result was satisfactory. There were all manner of things, and some bottles of strong Falerno wine. Batiscombe drank water and very little of it.

"Somebody has said," remarked Marcantonio with a laugh, "that one must distrust the man who drinks water when other people drink wine. We shall have to beware of you, Monsieur Batiscombe." He had learned the name very well by this time.

"Perhaps there is truth in it," said Batiscombe, "but it is not my habit I can assure you. The origin of the saying lies in the good old custom of doctoring other people's draughts. The man who drank water at a feast two hundred years ago was either afraid of being poisoned himself, or was engaged in poisoning his neighbours."

"Oh, the dear, good old time!" exclaimed Leonora, eating her salad daintily.

"Do you wish it were back again?" asked Batiscombe. "Are there many people you would like to poison?"

"Oh, not that exactly," and she laughed. "But life must have been very exciting and interesting then."

"Enfin," remarked Marcantonio, "I am very well pleased with it as it is. There was no opera, no election, no launching of war-ships; and when you went out you had to wear a patent safe on your head, in case anybody wanted to break it for you. And then, there was generally some one who did. Yes, indeed, it must have been charming, altogether ravishing. Allez! give me the nineteenth century."

"I assure you, Marchesa," said Batiscombe, "life can be exceedingly exciting and interesting now."

"I dare say," retorted Leonora, "for people who go round the world in boats in search of adventures, and write books abusing their enemies. But we — what do we ever do that is interesting or exciting? We stay at home and pour tea."

"And in those days," answered Batiscombe, "the ladies stayed at home and knit stockings, or if they were very clever they worked miles and miles of embroidery and acres of tapestry. About once a month they were allowed to look out of the window and see their relations beating each other's brains out with iron clubs, and running each other through the body with pointed sticks. As the Marchese says, it was absolutely delightful, that kind of life."

"You are dreadfully prejudiced," said Leonora.

"But I am sure it was very nice."

And so they talked, and the men smoked a little, till they decided that they had had enough of it, and the oars plashed in the water together, sending the boat out again into the bright sun. In five minutes they were at the landing belonging to the Carantoni villa. There was a deep cleft in the cliffs just there, and the descent wound curiously in and out of the rock, so that in many places you could only trace it from below by the windows hewn in the solid stone to give light and air to the passage. The rocks ran out a little at the base, and there were steps carved for landing. There are few places so strikingly odd as this landing to the Carantoni villa. Leonora said it was "eerie."

When it came to parting, the young couple were profuse in their thanks to Mr. Batiscombe for the enchanting trip.

"I hope," said Marcantonio, "that you will come and dine with us very soon, and change your mind about the water-drinking, and give us another opportunity of thanking you."

"I have enjoyed it very, very much," said Leonora, giving Batiscombe her hand. Their eyes met, and for the first time she noticed the curious light in his glance. But he bowed very low and very elaborately, so to say.

"You will keep your promise," he said, "and use the boat again?"

"Thanks so very much. But of course we will have a boat of our own now, and so I should not think of asking you."

She smiled a little at him. Somehow he understood perfectly that he could nevertheless induce her to accept his offer. He stood hat in hand on the rocks as they disappeared into the dark stairway. Then he sprang into the boat, and the men pulled lustily away.

He leaned back in the stern with his hand on the tiller and his eyes half closed. In the bottom of the boat were the luncheon baskets, and one of Leonora's roses had fallen from the stem and lay withering in the hot July sun. Batiscombe picked it up, looked at it, pulled a leaf or two, and threw it overboard, with a half sneer of dissatisfaction.

"They have forgotten the baskets, though," he thought to himself. "If they had asked me to go up with them, as they should have done, I would have had them carried up. As it is I will — I will wait till they write for them. I could hardly take them myself." And he lighted a cigarette.

As Leonora mounted the stairway, leaning on her husband's arm, she turned to get a glimpse of the boat gliding away in the distance. She could just see it through one of the windows in the rock.

"Why did you not ask him to come up?" she inquired.

"Why did you not ask him, my angel?" returned Marcantonio.

"I thought you might not like it," she answered.

"Comment donc! He is very amiable, I am sure. But I thought you were tired and had had enough of him, — in short, that you did not want him."

"Ah!" ejaculated Leonora. She felt a little curious sense of pleasure, that was quite new to her, at the idea that her husband could have seriously thought she did not want Mr. Batiscombe.

"Naturally," added Marcantonio, "we ought to have asked him."

"I suppose so," said she, indifferently enough.

"I will call on him to-morrow, and we will have him to dinner, if it is agreeable to you, my dear."

"Oh yes — I do not mind at all," said Leonora. She was thinking about something, and did not speak again till they reached the house.

It was very frivolous, but she was really thinking about the curious expression of Mr. Batiscombe's eyes. She did not remember to have ever seen anything exactly like it. Besides, she had known him, more or less, for some time, and had never noticed it before. Perhaps it was the reflection from the water. But she dreamed that night that she saw those eyes very close to her, and the expression of them frightened her a little, but was not altogether disagreeable.

CHAPTER VII.

JULIUS BATISCOMBE was a restless man by day and night, after the trip to Castellamare. Marcantonio called upon him, but he was out, and then he received an invitation to dinner from Leonora, with a postscript about the unlucky baskets. He accepted the invitation. What else could he do?

But when the day came he regretted it. He wished he had refused and had gone away. Then he made a fine resolution.

"I will not go to this dinner," he said to himself, savagely, as he walked quickly up and down his room. "I will not go near her again. It is not right, and I will not do it. I will sail over to Naples at once, and send back a telegram of excuse, saying that a matter of the most urgent importance keeps me there. So it is — I should think so — a matter of very urgent importance. Oh! Julius Batiscombe, what an ass you are, to be sure!" With that he crammed some things into a bag, sent for his man, and descended in hot haste to the shore. There was no time to be lost, for it was already four o'clock in the afternoon and the invitation was for eight. He could just reach Naples and send his telegram in time to prevent the Carantoni from waiting for him.

The lazy breeze was dying away, and he wished
he had had the sense to make up his mind sooner.
But his men rowed lustily, and kept time, so that
the boat spun along fairly enough.

" I shall do it," said Julius Batiscombe to himself.

He was happy enough in the sensation that he
was cheating his fate and was about to escape a
serious affection.   Then he laughed at the comic
side of the case, and lit a cigar and blew great clouds
of smoke over his shoulder.   But fate and Batiscombe were old enemies, and fate generally got the
better of it.

It chanced that on this very day Leonora and
Marcantonio had determined to go out in the new
boat.   For Marcantonio had wanted to give his wife
a surprise, and had got from Naples a beautiful clean-
built launch.   He had said nothing about it, and
had patiently borne her reproaches at his indifference
to sailing, until on the previous evening he had taken
her down the descent to the rocks and had shown
her his purchase, which had just arrived by the
steamer.   Of course she was enchanted, and determined to make the most of it, for she was really
fond of the water.   Accordingly, on this very day,
she and her husband sallied forth with six men, —
for he had not dared to give her a smaller crew than
Mr. Batiscombe's.   She was in such a hurry to go
that she said she did not mind the sun in the least,
— oh dear, no! she rather liked it.   And so it came
to pass that a few minutes after Julius had given

his men the word to fall to their oars at the little beach of the town of Sorrento, a long low craft, painted in dark green and gold, and looking exceedingly trim and "fit" with its long lateen yards and raking masts, shot out from the cleft beneath Leonora's villa.

Batiscombe looked straight before him, steering by the Naples shore, and intent on wasting neither time nor distance. He might have been out half an hour or more when a remark from one of his crew made him look round, and he was aware of a dark green boat two or three hundred yards astern, but rapidly pulling up to him. He started, for though he could not see the faces of the occupants, he recognised a parasol that Leonora had taken to Castellamare.

"It is the new boat of the Marchese Carantoni," said the sailor who had first spoken to Batiscombe. The man had seen it arrive by the steamer on the previous evening, and had helped to put it into the water to be rowed down to the villa. Batiscombe gave one more look and groaned inwardly. He would make a fight for it, though, he thought. He encouraged his men not to allow themselves to be overtaken by a parcel of Neapolitans, as he derisively called the crew of Carantoni's boat. His own men were tough fellows from the north of Italy, bearded, and broad, and bronzed; but his boat, built for rougher weather and rougher work than pleasure-rowing in the bay of Naples, was twice as heavy as the slight green craft astern. His sturdy men set their teeth and tugged hard, but the others gained on them.

Leonora and Marcantonio had recognised the cut of Batiscombe's boat and crew from a distance; and, in profound ignorance of his amiable intentions of flight, they imagined nothing more amusing than to race him.

"If we cannot beat him," said Leonora, breathless with excitement, "I will never come out in your boat again!"

She strained her eyes to make out if they were gaining way. Marcantonio spoke to the men:—

> "Corraggio, Corraggio!
> Maccaroni con formaggio!"

The men repeated the rhyme to each other with a grin, and bent hard to their work. They were not Neapolitans as Batiscombe called them, but strong-backed, slim fishermen from the southern coast, as dark as Arabs and as merry as thieves, enjoying a race of all things best in the world, and well able to row it. Swiftly the dark green boat crept up to her rival, and soon Batiscombe could hear the remarks of the men. His own crew did their best, but it was a hopeless case.

"Monsieur Batiscombe, Monsieur Batiscombe," shouted Marcantonio, almost as much excited as his wife, "we shall conquer you immediately!"

Julius turned and waved his hat, and made a gesture of submission. A few lengths more and they were beside him. He raised his hand, and his men hung on their oars.

"Kismet! it is my portion," he said to himself as he gave up the fight.

"But where are you going in such a hurry, Mr. Batiscombe?" asked Leonora, who was delighted at having won the race. "You see it is no use running away; we can catch you so easily."

"Yes," said Batiscombe, laughing recklessly at the hidden truth of her words, "I see it is of no use, but I tried hard. It was a good race."

He turned in his seat and leaned over, looking at his friends. The boats drifted together, and the men held them side by side, unshipping their oars. Batiscombe admired the whole turnout, and complimented Leonora upon it. Marcantonio was pleased with everything and everybody; he was delighted that his wife should have had the small satisfaction of victory, and he was proud that his boat had fulfilled his expectations. So they floated along side by side, saying the pleasantest manner of things possible to each other. Time flew by, and presently they turned homewards.

"I wonder how long it will be," thought Batiscombe as he held the tiller hard over and his boat swung about, "before I tell her where I was going 'in such a hurry'?" And he smiled in a grim sort of irony at himself, for he knew that he was lost.

"Eight o'clock — don't forget!" cried Leonora.

She had a pleasant voice that carried far over the water. Batiscombe waved his hat, and smiled and bowed. They were soon separated, and their courses became more and more divergent as they neared the land.

Batiscombe swore a little over his dressing, quite quietly and to himself, but he bestowed much care upon his appearance. He knew just how much always depends on appearance at the outset, and how little it is to be relied on at a later stage. So he gave an unusual amount of thought to his tie, and was extremely fastidious about the flower in his coat.

As for Leonora, she was on the point of a change of mood. She had been very gay and happy all day long, and the adventure with the boat had still further raised her spirits. But that was all the more reason why they should sink again before long, for her humours were mostly of short duration, though of strong impulse. This evening she felt as though there were something the matter, or as though something were going to happen, and her gayety seemed to be the least bit fictitious to herself. She and her husband stood on the terrace in the sunset, awaiting their guest.

"My dear," said Marcantonio, "I am in despair. I shall be obliged to go to Rome to-morrow or the next day. My uncle, the cardinal, writes me that it is very important." Leonora's face fell; she had a sharp little sense of pain.

"Oh, Marcantoine," she said, "do not go away now!"

"It is only for a day or two, my angel," he said, drawing her arm through his.

"Must you really go?" she asked, not looking at him.

"Hélas, yes."

"Then I will go with you," said she, in a determined tone.

"Ah, I thank you for the wish, chérie," he answered. "But you will tire yourself, and be so hot and uncomfortable. See, I will only be away a day and a half."

"But I do not want to be alone here without you," she pleaded. She could not for her life have told why she was so distressed at the idea, but it gave her pain, and she insisted.

"As you wish," said Marcantonio, kissing her hand. "I will make every arrangement for your comfort, and do what I can to make the journey pleasant."

He was a little surprised, but, manlike, he was flattered at his wife's show of affection. There are moments in a woman's life when, whether she loves her husband or not, she turns to him and holds to him with an instinctive sense of reliance.

A moment later Julius Batiscombe was announced, and the three went in to dinner. It was a strange position, though it is by no means an uncommon one. A man, his wife, and another man, an outsider; the outsider loving the woman, the husband supremely happy and unconscious, and the woman feeling the evil influence, not altogether opposing it, and yet clinging desperately to her husband's love. Three lives, all trembling in the balance of weal and woe. But no one could have suspected it from their appearance, for they were apparently the gayest and most thoughtless of mortals.

The adventure in the afternoon, the expedition to Castellamare, the baskets and even the cook, — then, the events of the past winter, their many mutual acquaintances, and the whole unfathomable cyclopædia of society facts and fictions, — everything was reviewed in turn, and talked of with witty comments, good-natured or ill-natured as the case might be. Batiscombe was full of strange stories, generally about people they all knew, but he was not a gossip by nature, and he avoided saying disagreeable things. Leonora, on the other hand, would be gay and brilliant for a few moments, and then would let fall some bitter saying that sounded oddly to Batiscombe, though it made her husband laugh.

"You would have us believe you terribly disillusioned, Marchesa," said Batiscombe, after one of these sallies. Leonora laughed, and her eyes flashed again as she looked at him across the table.

"You, who are so fond of Eastern magic," she said, "should give back to this age all the illusions we have lost."

"Were I to do so," answered Batiscombe, looking into her eyes as he spoke, "I fear that you, who are so fond of Western philosophy, would tear them all to pieces."

"My poor philosophy," exclaimed Leonora, "you will not let it alone. You seem to think it is to blame for everything, — as if one could not try, ever so humbly, to learn a little something for one's self, without being always held up for it as an exception to the whole human race. It is as if I were to attribute everything you say and do to the fact of your having written a book — how many — two? three?" She laughed gayly. "I do not know," she continued, "and I will never read anything more that you write, because you laugh at my philosophy."

"It is better to laugh at it than to cry at it," said Marcantonio, without meaning anything.

"Why should I cry at it?" asked Leonora quickly. Her husband did not know how honestly she had shed tears and made herself miserable over it all.

"You laugh now," he answered, "but imagine a little. All philosophers are old and hideous, and wear " —

"For goodness' sake, Marchese," broke in Batiscombe, "do not paint the devil on the wall, as the Germans say."

"The Germans need not paint the devil," retorted Marcantonio, irrelevantly. "They need only look into the glass." He hated the whole race.

"You might as well say that Italians need not go to the theatre," put in Leonora, "because they are all actors." Her husband laughed good-humouredly.

"You might as well say," said Batiscombe, "that Englishmen need not keep horses because they are all donkeys. But please do not say it."

"No," said Leonora, "we will spare you. But you might say anything in the world of that kind. It has no bearing on my philosophy."

"That is true," answered Marcantonio. "I said that philosophers were old and hideous, but not that they were devils, actors, or donkeys. You suggest the idea. I think they are probably all three."

"Provided you do not think so after I have become a philosopher," said Leonora, "you may think what you please at present, mon ami."

"I think that you are altogether the most charming woman in the world," replied her husband, looking at her affectionately.

"Is it permitted to remark that the Marchese is not alone in that opinion?" inquired Batiscombe, politely.

"No," said Leonora, demurely, "it is not permitted. And observe that an English husband would not say that kind of thing in public, mon cher."

"Perhaps because they do not believe it in private," objected Marcantonio.

"More likely for the reason I suggested," observed Batiscombe, "that we are all donkeys."

"All?" asked Leonora. "But some of you are authors " —

"It is the same thing," said Batiscombe.

"Mon Dieu! there are times " — began Marcantonio.

"When you believe it?" inquired Batiscombe, laughing.

"Ah, no! you are unkind; but times when I should like to be an Englishman."

"I have heard of such people," said Batiscombe, gravely, "but I have never met one. You interest me, Marchese."

"You must not be so terribly disloyal," said Leonora. "You know I am English, too, — at least, I was," she added, looking at Marcantonio.

"Precisely," said he. "The wife takes the nationality of the husband."

"I am not disloyal," answered Batiscombe. "I am very glad to be an Englishman, but I cannot fancy any one else wishing to be one. I should think every one would be perfectly contented with his own country. I cannot imagine wanting to change my nationality any more than my person."

"Evidently, you are well satisfied," said Leonora.

"Perfectly, thank you, for the present. When I am tired of myself I will retire gracefully — or perhaps gracelessly; but I will retire. I am sure I should never find another personality half as much in sympathy with my ideas."

As they followed Leonora from the dining-room

out upon the terrace, Batiscombe watched her intently. There was a strength and ease about her carriage that pleased his strong love of life and beauty. He noticed what he had hardly noticed before, that her figure was a marvel of proportion, — no wasp-waisted impossibility of lacing and high shoulders, but strong and lithe, and instinct with elastic motion. He had seen her lately always in some wrap, or lace, or mazy summer garment, whereas this evening she was clad in close silk of a deep-red colour, with the least possible trimming or marring line. The masses of her hair, too, rich in red lights and deep shadows, were coiled close to her noble head, and her dazzling throat just showed at the square cutting of her dress.

" People must be wonderfully mistaken," thought Batiscombe. " She is certainly, undeniably a great beauty, in her very peculiar way. Gad! I should think so indeed! " which was the strongest expression of affirmation in Julius Batiscombe's vocabulary.

It was no wonder she attracted him. For nearly two months he had been wandering, chiefly in his boat on the salt water, and in that time he had not so much as spoken to a woman. His conversation had been with himself during all that time; and if he had enjoyed intensely the freedom of heart and thought in the intellectual point of view, his strong nature, always drawn to women when not plunged deep in work or adventure, could not withstand the sudden magnetism now thrown upon it. He knew and felt the evil of it, and he struggled as best he could, but each fresh meeting made the chances of escape fewer and the danger more desperate.

"Marry," said his best friend to him, when, now and then, in the course of years, they met.

"How can I marry?" he would ask. "How can I ever hope to love one woman again as a woman deserves to be loved?"

"Then go into a monastery and do no more mischief," returned the friend. She was a woman.

"I am no saint," Julius would say, "but I will try to be." And ever he tried and failed again.

They sat upon the terrace in the cool of the early night, with their coffee and their cigarettes. There was a lull in their conversation, the result of having talked so much at table.

"A propos of contentment," said Marcantonio, "we are very discontented people. We are going to Rome to-morrow, or the next day."

Batiscombe was surprised. He paused with his coffee cup in one hand and his cigarette in the other, as though expecting more.

"Of course it is only for a day or two," continued Marcantonio. "We shall return immediately."

"Seriously, Marcantoine," said Leonora, "how long shall we have to stay?"

"Oh—not very long," he said. "I will get the letter. Monsieur Batiscombe will pardon me?" Batiscombe murmured something polite and Marcantonio rose quickly and entered the house.

"Are you really going so soon?" Julius asked in English, when they were alone, and Leonora could see the light in his eyes as he spoke. She looked away, over the starlit sea.

"I am not quite sure," she said. "I think I ought to go."

"I hope you will not," said Batiscombe boldly. She turned and looked at him again, with a little surprise in her face. Marcantonio came back, — it was only a step to his study.

"Here it is," said Marcantonio, sitting down. "He says he thinks that a day should do, if I could be with him all the time. You see, he is old and wishes to put his affairs in order."

"I cannot see" — began Leonora, but stopped.

"Enfin," said Marcantonio, "it might happen to any one, I should think."

"Let us hope it may happen to all of us," remarked Batiscombe, for the sake of saying something.

When it came to parting, Batiscombe made some polite remark about the pleasure he had enjoyed.

"When do you go?" he asked, as he shook hands with Marcantonio.

"I think we will go to-morrow night, — n'est-ce-pas, Léonore?" He turned to his wife, as though inquiring. She looked up from her seat in her deep, cane arm-chair.

"To-morrow night? Oh yes — one day is like another — let us go then to-morrow night."

She spoke indifferently enough, as was natural.

Batiscombe supposed she meant to go. He took his leave with many wishes to his hosts for a pleasant journey.

Marcantonio lighted a cigarette and stood looking out over the water, by his wife's side. She was quite silent, and fanned herself indolently with a little straw fan decked with ribbons.

" Will you really go to-morrow night? " asked Marcantonio at last. He had a way of dwelling on things that wearied Leonora. What possible difference could it make whether they went to-morrow, or the day after? "Because," he continued, " if you will be ready, I will make arrangements."

" What arrangements? " asked Leonora languidly.

" I will write to the cardinal to say I am coming, — one must do that."

" You can telegraph."

" What is the use, when there is time for writing? Why should one waste a franc in a telegram? " He had curious little economies of his own.

" A franc ! " she exclaimed with a little laugh.

" And besides," he continued, not heeding her remark, " old gentlemen do not like to receive telegrams. It gives on their nerves."

" Enfin," said she, weary of the question, " you can write that you will go to-morrow night, if you like."

" And you — will you go then? " he asked.

" It depends," she answered. " I may be too tired."

Marcantonio knew very well that his wife was not

easily fatigued; but he said nothing, and by his silence closed the discussion. She was very change-able, he thought; but then, he loved her very much, and she had a right to be as changeable as she pleased. It was very good of her to have wanted to go at all, and he would not think of pressing her to it. He was a very sensible and unimaginative man, not at all given to thinking about things he could not see, nor troubling himself about them in the least. So he did not press Leonora now, and did not make himself unhappy because she was a little changeable. The one thing he really objected to was her pursuance of what he considered fruitless objects of study; she had not opened a book of phi-losophy since their marriage, and he was perfectly satisfied. Before he went to bed he wrote a line to his uncle, Cardinal Carantoni, to say that he should arrive on the next day but one.

Batiscombe strolled back to the town through the narrow lanes, fenced into right and left by high walls. His thoughts were agreeable enough, and he now and then hummed snatches of tunes with evident satisfac-tion. What a magnificent creature she was! And clever too, — at least she looked intelligent, and said very cutting things, as though she could say many more if she liked; and she knew about most things that were discussed, and was altogether exactly what her husband called her, — the most charming woman in the world. Besides, he thought he could make a friend of her. How foolish of him, he reflected, to suppose that very afternoon that he must needs fall in love with her! Where was the necessity? He had evidently been mistaken, too, about her relations with her husband. It was clear that they adored each other, could not be separated for a moment, since when he went to Rome on business she must needs accompany him, — in July, too! Would she go? Probably. At all events, he would not call for a week, when they would certainly have come back. This he thought as he walked home.

But when he sat in his room at the hotel he remembered what he had thought as he followed her out of the dining-room. He had not thought then as he had an hour later. The magnetism of her glorious vitality had been upon him, and he had envied Marcantonio with all his heart, right sinfully.

" Some people call women changeable," he reflected as he blew out his candles; "they are not half so changeable as we are, and some day I will write a book to prove it."

CHAPTER VIII.

LEONORA would not go to Rome when the moment came to decide. She was so sorry, she said, but the weather had grown suddenly hotter and she really did not feel as though it were possible. She tried to make up for it to Marcantonio by being all that day a very model of devotion and tenderness. She affected a practical mood, and listened with attention while he explained to her the reasons for his going. She insisted on seeing herself that he had a small package of sandwiches, and a bottle of wine, and plenty of cigarettes to last him through the night; and when he finally drove away, she would have driven with him to Castellamare, but that she must have come back over the lonely road alone. To tell the truth, she was a little ashamed of herself; she had been so anxious to accompany him, and now she feared he might be disappointed.

Marcantonio saw it all, and was grateful and affectionate, though he begged her not to take so much trouble.

" En vérité, mon ange," he said more than once, " I might be sailing for Peru, you give yourself so much thought."

But she busied herself none the less, going about

with a queer little air of resignation that sat strangely on her face. He took an affectionate leave of her.

"I will not receive any one, if any one calls," she said, as he was going. He looked at her in some surprise.

"But why in the world?" he asked. "Who should call particularly? Not even Monsieur Batiscombe, — he thinks you will go with me."

Leonora felt the least faint blush mount to her cheeks, but it was dark in the hall of the villa, though it was only just dusk, and Marcantonio could not see.

"Oh, not him," said Leonora. "Only I want to be alone when you are not here." For a moment again she wished she were going.

"Enfin, my dear," he answered; "do as you prefer; it is very amiable — very gentil — of you. Adieu, chérie!" and he got into the carriage and rolled away.

But her words lay in his memory and would not be forgotten. Why should she not want to see any one? Was there any one? Why had she been so very anxious to accompany him, begging so hard that he would not leave her? After all, the only person she could be afraid of was Batiscombe. He wondered for one moment whether there had ever been anything between them; he could remember to have seen them together more than once in the winter, at balls. But then, they always met with such perfect frankness. He had not watched them,

to be sure, but he must have noticed anything out
of the way, — bah! it was ridiculous. Not that he
wanted Batiscombe as an intimate, for the man was
certainly called dangerous. He had known him for
years, and had of course heard some of the stories
about him, — but then, there are stories about every
one, and Batiscombe had evidently become very serious since he had got himself a reputation. Besides,
to see him a little, as they did in Sorrento, it could
do no harm; it meant nothing, and he would think
no more about it. He was not going to begin life
with the ridiculous whims of a jealous husband, when
he had married such an angel as Leonora — not he!
Besides, Batiscombe — of all people! If it had been
his sister Diana, it would have been different. Everybody knew that poor Batiscombe had loved her ten
years ago, when he was as poor as Job, and had nothing
but a fair position in society. But Marcantonio had
been away then on his travels, being just nineteen,
and having been sent out into the world to learn
French and spend a little money on his own account.

Strange that he should almost have forgotten it!
Not that it mattered in the least. The man had loved
his sister to distraction, but had soon recognised the
impossibility of such a match, and had gone away to
make his fortune. He had come to see Madame de
Charleroi now and then of late; Marcantonio knew
that, but it was perfectly natural that they should be
the best of friends after so many years. How they
had first met, or what had passed between them, Marc-

antonio did not know, and never troubled himself to
ask ; perhaps he feared lest it should pain his sister
to speak of it. But the whole story invested Batiscombe with a sort of air of safety as regarded Leonora.
He had certainly behaved well about Diana, and nobody denied it. Nevertheless, it was best that he
should not see Diana too often, especially if he intended to live in Rome, now that he had made his fortune. But Leonora — he might call if he pleased, and
amuse her in the dull summer days. Carantoni would
not begin life by playing the jealous husband. It was
certainly odd, though, that he should have thought
so little about that old story. The fact was, he had
never seen so much of Batiscombe in his life as during
the last week or ten days.

Meanwhile, he rolled along the road to Castellamare, and, after a great deal of shifting, found himself in the night train from Naples for Rome. He ate
his sandwiches and thought affectionately of his wife
as he did so; and then he lay down and slept the
sleep of the just until morning.

When he reached the Palazzo Carantoni, the first
piece of news he received was that Madame de Charleroi was in the house, having arrived the previous
day alone, — that is to say, with her courier and her
maid. The old servant volunteered the information
that the vicomtesse was going to stay a week, or
thereabouts, and had sent a note to the house of
his Eminence, Cardinal Carantoni, the night before.
Marcantonio gave instructions that she should be in-

formed of his arrival, and that he would come and see her later in the morning, and he retired to dress and refresh himself.

He hated family councils, and he saw himself condemned to one, for there was no doubt of the cardinal's intention, since Madame de Charleroi had come, and had communicated with him. The cardinal was old, and felt the need of settling his affairs and of talking them over with his only near relations, — his nephew and his niece. For he was rich, and had money to leave.

Marcantonio and his sister greeted each other affectionately, for they were always glad to be together, and their meeting seemed to have been unexpected. His Eminence had sent for each separately, and they had arrived within twenty-four hours of each other, — Diana from Pegli and Marcantonio from Sorrento. Of course, they talked of trivial matters, for now that Diana had accepted the marriage there was nothing more to be said about it. At twelve o'clock they drove to the cardinal's house, through the hot, glaring streets of Rome, fringed with the red and white awnings of the shops. The carriage rolled under the dark porch of the palace, and the pair mounted the cool stairway and were soon ushered through a succession of dusky halls and swinging red baize doors to their uncle's study, — a curious, old-fashioned room in an inner angle of the building. The blinds were drawn, and the occasional chirp of the lazy little birds came up from the acacia trees in the courtyard.

The room was carpetless, with bright, smooth, red tiles; in the middle was a huge writing table, covered with papers and books; on one end of it stood a large black crucifix with a bronze Christ, and there was an enormous inkstand of glass and brown wood. Around the walls were mahogany bookcases, ornamented with light brass-work in the style of the first empire, and filled with books and pamphlets. The room was cool and dark and high, and as the brother and sister entered, their steps clicked sharply on the clean, hard tiles. His Eminence sat in an arm-chair at the writing table, clad in a loose, purple gown, and wearing a minute scarlet skull cap.

He looked, indeed, as though his life were nearly spent; for, though his dark eyes shone bright and penetrating from under the heavy brows, his cheeks were thin and sunken, of the hue of wax, and his white hands were transparent and discoloured between the knuckles. Marcantonio and Diana touched the great sapphire on his finger with their lips, and then the old man laid his hand on the head of each. They were his brother's children, and he loved them dearly, after his crabbed old fashion; for all the Carantoni are people of heart and kindness.

"My dear children," he began, when they were seated by his side on straight-backed chairs that Marcantonio brought up to the table, — "my dear children, I am growing very old and infirm, and I wanted to see you here together before I leave you all."

A kind smile played fitfully over the waxen features, like the memory of life that haunts a plaster mask. Diana laid her fingers gently on his arm, and Marcantonio broke out into solicitous protestations. His uncle was not yet sixty, — he had many years of life, — this was a passing indisposition, a black humour, a melancholy. One should never expect to live less than seventy years at the very least, he said, and that would not be reached for a long time.

"Ah! no, dear uncle," he concluded, "you will surely live to see my sons growing up to be men, and to marry Diana's little girls!"

The cardinal shook his head. That was not the way of it, he said. He might die any day now, he said, in his meek voice; and it really sounded as though he might, so that Donna Diana felt her eyes growing dim and her heart big. She took one of the old man's thin hands in both of hers, and he with the other pushed back the rich, heavy hair and smoothed it tenderly. A marvellous picture in sooth they made, — the dying prelate in his purple and scarlet, and the great unspeakable freshness and life of the fair woman. Marcantonio passed his hand over his eyes and sighed as he sat watching them.

Then his Eminence explained to the two what his chief plan was in calling them to him now. He had made a deed, he said, which he wished them both to understand. There were certain estates which he had inherited from his mother, — their grandmother, — as being the second son. These he earnestly desired to see incorporated in the property of the Carantoni family. To that end he had made an act of gift, transferring the lands to Marcantonio at once, on the condition that the cardinal should continue to receive a certain income from them during his life. This he insisted upon doing, as he feared lest after his death the lands should be sold by the executors in order to divide the proceeds between the two heirs. In order to make the present arrangement a fair one, however, he at the same time gave to his niece Diana de Charleroi a sum of money from his personal estate which was equal to the value of the lands given to Marcantonio. Whatever they found after his death could then be divided and distributed, — the lands being safe in the male line; they might find something left after all.

Diana protested; she was very glad that the lands should be settled, but she did not wish to accept a large sum of money in that way. In fact, she begged her uncle to reconsider the matter. As for Marcantonio, he looked grave and wished himself well out of it. He was practically to be administrator of his uncle's property during the remainder of the latter's lifetime, and he did not like it. However, as the arrangement was for the ultimate good of his children, and as he had not Diana's excuse for refusing on the ground of not wishing to take a gift,

— since it hardly was one, — there was nothing for him to do but to accept the situation with a good grace.

" You do not deserve anything at all, my boy," said the cardinal, half kindly, half in earnest, " because you married a heretic.   But as I helped you to obtain the permission, I must do something for you."

" But I," said Diana, — " I cannot take all this. It is not fair to Marcantonio, for I ought to pay you the income of it, just as he is to do."

" Nonsense, figlia mia," said the old man.   " You need money more than he does or ever will, with that husband of yours, who is always going from one court to another on his nonsensical diplomatic errands. Ah! my children, diplomacy is not what it used to be!   Altri tempi — altri tempi!"

The end of it was that the two young people agreed to their uncle's provisions, and he insisted on their hearing and understanding all the papers, to which end he sent for his secretary, a wizened little Roman with grey hair and bright eyes and a fondness for snuff; and the secretary read on for two good hours.   The old man from time to time nodded his head to Marcantonio or to Diana, as the one or the other was referred to in the documents, and waved his pale thin hand in appreciation of the completeness and simplicity of his arrangements.   At last the various deeds were signed, and a notary, whom the secretary had provided, was called in from the antechamber where he had waited, and attested the signatures and the general legality of the proceedings. The cardinal was satisfied, and leaned back in his chair. He was one of those old-fashioned noblemen who still believe in the divine right of primogeniture and in the respectability of land as a possession. With the modern laws concerning the division of estates, — the keen Napoleonic knives that cut the strings of succession at every knot, — these conservative aristocrats have infinite trouble; but they generally manage to evade the spirit of the law, and to conform as little to the letter of it as they can.

"Cara mia, one must submit," said Marcantonio to his sister, when they were alone together. "Old men have strange fancies, and he has always been good to us. What he said about my marriage was quite true. If he had not helped me, I should have made a fiasco of it, — or done something rash."

"I suppose so," said Diana, thoughtfully. "By the bye, are you comfortable at Sorrento? How is Leonora?"

She was rather ashamed of not having asked the question before, but Marcantonio was good-natured, and was glad that she had not said anything hard. And, of course, the moment she mentioned his wife, he was delighted at the chance to speak of what was nearest to his heart.

"Leonora is well and more than well," he answered. "Ah, she is an angel! She has not read any philosophy since we married, — imagine! And she was crazy to come with me to Rome — in this heat! — because she did not wish to stay in Sorrento alone without me."

"Why did you not let her come, then?" asked Donna Diana.

"She was tired," he said, "and as I told her how fatiguing it was, she made up her mind to stay. I shall go back to-morrow, I suppose. I wish I could go to-night."

"So soon?" asked Diana. "But I have seen nothing of you, dear boy!"

"Why not come with me to Sorrento? Do come, — there is room for us all, and for all your servants into the bargain, if you like to bring them."

Marcantonio was charmed with his idea; it seemed the most natural thing in the world. Besides, he had longed for an opportunity of bringing Diana and Leonora together. He was quite sure they would become bosom friends. Diana hung back, however, and was less enthusiastic.

"I do not see how I could manage it," she said. "I have so many things to do, and I must go back to Pegli, before long." Marcantonio sat down beside her and took her hand affectionately.

"Cara Diana," he said coaxingly, "will you not come and make friends with Leonora? It would be so kind of you, and she would feel it so much!"

Madame de Charleroi hesitated; not so much on account of her reluctance to stay with Leonora as because she knew that Julius Batiscombe was some-

where in the neighbourhood of Naples. She avoided
him always, though she was his best and most faithful friend; for though she had loved him once, there
was not a trace of that left in her heart, and yet she
knew well enough that he loved her still. Her high
and noble nature could not understand so earthly a
man as he; she could not conceive how it was that
through all his many affairs he still looked on her as
the one woman in the world; but nevertheless she
knew that it was so, and she therefore avoided him,
not wishing to fan a hopeless passion. He came to
see her sometimes, and she was very kind to him,
giving him the best of advice, but she never encouraged him to come. So she was not anxious to meet
him. But the question of her relations with her
brother in the future seemed to make it now desirable
that she should go with him and "make friends"
with his wife, as he expressed it.

"Well," she said at last, "I will go with you, and
do what you wish."

Marcantonio was very grateful. He felt that his
young wife must have friends — young wives have
so few — and he could desire no better friend for her
than his sister, the model of all goodness, gentleness,
and honour.

"Dearest sister," he said, "you are so good! And
if you have much to do here, I can put off going for
a day, you know. You can do your little errands in
a day, can you not?"

"I might, perhaps," said she; "but must you not

take some steps about all this land of yours — or of our uncle's? Do you realise what a position you have assumed, my dear boy? From this day you are absolutely master of the estate, if you like, — but you are also absolutely responsible for the payment of the income. You positively must see the lawyers about it, and you may as well see them at once."

"It is not the whole income of the place that he takes," remarked Marcantonio.

"That makes no difference," said Diana. "If you were to have it all, it would be the same. You are bound to take care of it. Your own lawyer knows nothing about this transaction. You may not be in Rome again for three months. Make some provision for your absence. Who is to collect your rents, in the first place?"

"I suppose somebody would," said Marcantonio laughing. "But you have a much better head for business than I, Diana mia. Perhaps you are right."

"You manage things very well, caro mio, so long as they are under your hand. But you hate to go and look after business when you want to be doing something else."

"After all," he argued, "when a man is just married" —

"He ought to be specially careful of his affairs, for his children's sake," interrupted Donna Diana with remarkable good sense.

She wanted a day or two in Rome, and she thought he was really remiss in his management. She had rather a contempt for a man who cast everything to the winds in order to be one more day with his wife. She did not believe that his wife would have done as much for him.

The end of it was that he agreed to stay a little longer, at least one day more than he had at first proposed; and he wrote an affectionate letter to Leonora, half loving, half playful, explaining his position, and telling her of his sister's coming, that she might be ready to receive her. He added that he hoped to see them very affectionate and intimate, for that Diana was the best friend his wife could have. If Batiscombe had wanted to make a friendship between two women he would not have gone about it in that way. Marcantonio was very young and inexperienced, though he was also very good and honest. His sister saw both sides of his character and understood them. Leonora saw, but only understood the honesty of him. His inexperience she supposed to be a sort of paternal, philistine, prosaic, humdrum capacity for harping on unimportant things, and she already felt the most distinct aversion for that phase of his nature.

Diana and Marcantonio went down by the night train, having stayed the better half of a week in Rome. Marcantonio sent a telegram to Leonora in the afternoon, to say that they would come. They had a compartment to themselves, and as they sat with the windows all open, rushing along through the quiet night, they fell into conversation about

Sorrento. Madame de Charleroi had taken off her hat, and the breeze fanned the smooth masses of her hair into rough gold under the light of the lamp, like the ripple on the sea at sunset. She was a little tired with the many doings that had occupied her in Rome, and her face was pale as she leaned back in the corner. Her brother looked at her as he spoke. 'Of course,' he thought, 'there was never any one so beautiful as Diana.' What he said was different.

"You should see Leonora; she is a perfect miracle, — more beautiful every day. And though she has been on the water several times, she is not the least sunburnt."

"Have you sailed much?" inquired Diana.

"A good deal. I bought Leonora a very good boat in Naples, and had it fitted. It is so pretty. And before it came Monsieur Batiscombe took us to Castellamare."

"Ah!" ejaculated Diana half interrogatively.

"Yes," answered Marcantonio. "He was very amiable, and then we had him to dinner. You know him, Diana?" he asked, as one often asks questions of which one knows the answer.

He did not remember having ever mentioned Batiscombe to her, but his solitary journey to Rome a week earlier had set him thinking, in a lazy fashion, and he wondered whether his sister ever thought of the man after all these years.

"Oh yes," answered Madame de Charleroi. "I

have known Batiscombe a long time, — long before he was famous."

"Yes," said her brother, "I remember to have heard that he was once so bold as to want you to marry him. Imagine to yourself a little! The wife of an author."

There was nothing ill-natured in what Marcantonio said. In the prejudice of his ancient name he was simply unable to imagine such a match. Diana turned her grey eyes full upon him.

"My dear boy, do not say such absurd things. We are not in the age of Colonna and Orsini any more. I came very near to marrying Julius Batiscombe, in spite of your fifty titles, my dear brother."

Diana was a loyal woman, from the outer surface that the world saw, down to the very core and holy of holies of her noble soul. She would not let her brother believe that, if she had chosen it, she would have feared to marry a poor literary hack.

"Do you mean to say, Diana, that you loved him?" asked Marcantonio in great surprise.

"Even you must not ask me questions like that," said Diana, a little coldly. "But this I will tell you, — it was not for any consideration of birth, nor out of any regard of our dear father's anger, that I did not marry Batiscombe. Once I was very near it. We are very good friends now."

She turned a little in her seat and drew the blue woollen curtain across the window to shield her from the draught.

"You do not mind meeting him?" asked Marc-antonio, rather doubtfully.

To tell the truth he feared he had committed a mortal error, and was taking his sister into the jaws of danger and unhappiness. He had never suspected that she had entertained any idea of marrying Bat-iscombe. Julius was a very agreeable man, very amiable, as Marcantonio would have said. What a fearful thing if Diana were to take a fancy to him! Loyal as she was to Charleroi, she did not care a straw for him, — her brother knew it very well. Italian brothers are very watchful and Argus-eyed about their sisters.

"Why should I mind?" asked Diana, looking at him again. "We are very good friends. He comes to see me in Rome, every now and then. I do not object in the least, and he is really very agreeable."

'Worse and worse!' thought Marcantonio. 'She wants to meet him and is glad of the chance. But then, she is so good — what harm can it do?' Be-tween his idea that he ought to keep them apart, and his knowledge of his sister's upright character, Marcantonio was in a sad quandary. It always took him some time to grasp new situations, — and the idea that Diana had ever loved Batiscombe was utterly new to him. True, she had not said it; she had only said that she had been near to marrying him.

CHAPTER IX.

WHEN Leonora was alone, she resolved to have a good fit of thinking. Accordingly, the next morning after Marcantonio's departure she sat by herself in a cool room, surrounded with books and dainty writing materials, — thinking. The little white cat that her husband had procured, because she liked animals, climbed to the back of her chair and made passes at her head with its small, soft paws, seeming to delight in touching her. She put up her hand and pulled the little creature down to her lap.

"Pussy," said she, talking English to it, "were you ever in love?" She kissed it softly and held it up to her fair cheek. "I wonder what it is like," she said to herself. "I wonder whether being in love is always like this! People who love always say they would die for each other. I am not sure whether I would die for Marcantonio. He is very good. Yes — of course — one's husband! Any woman would die for her husband. And yet — if the knife were very sharp and cold, — or the poison very dreadful to take, — I am not sure. Perhaps there might be some other way out of it, and one would not have to die after all."

Poor Leonora, she made herself think she loved

him, and then she applied all kinds of tests to her
love which it would not bear, being but a very thin
and pitiful little ghost of a love.

"I really believe," she said at last, kissing the cat
and half closing her eyes, "that there is not anything
much in anything after all. Things are not much
more real than the shadows in the cave that Plato
talks about. Oh dear me! And then to have people
think that one is clever! They have such an absurd
idea about it, — Marcantonio, I mean. Of course it
is the nicest thing in the world to be loved more than
one deserves, — but, on the other hand, it is just as
terrible a bore to have other people forever thinking
you really worth more than you are. And then, to
have him think that my little bit of knowledge is
dangerous! As if so very little could help or hurt
any one! I must know a great deal more before it
can do me any good. I think I will read something
hard to-day, — how pleasant it is to be alone!"

The last reflection came quite naturally, and she
did not even pause and think about it, the sudden
interest she anticipated in reading having chased
away the dutifully affectionate ideas she made it her
business to build up concerning her husband. With
characteristic quickness of determination she rose,
got herself a volume of Hegel's "Æsthetics," and
buried her whole mind in the question of subjective
and objective art.

To a woman — or a man either — who has not
what is called an interest in life, all manner of things

temporarily take the place which should be occupied
by the leading, absorbing thought. The things that
are but relaxations, amusements, or even unimportant
bits of usefulness to the thoroughly busy woman, to
a woman like Leonora become in turn objects of
intense study and care, only to be cast aside and forgotten when the next day brings in a new era of
speculation, weariness, or excitement. It is good to
read many kinds of books, it is good to do many
pleasant and agreeable things, but it is emphatically
not good to think many kinds of thoughts. If a
woman must change her opinions, it is well that the
change should be gradual and the result of careful
study and examination, instead of taking place
according to the weather, the cut of a gown, or the
conversation of a stray caller. Men change their
minds as completely as women, but not so often, and
above all not so quickly. To be unchangeable is the
quality of the idiot; to change too easily belongs to
children and lunatics; and the happy faculty of a
sensible judgment permitting a change for the better
and forbidding a change for the worse is the high
privilege of the comparatively small class of humanity who are neither fools nor madmen.

With Leonora to live was to change, and to change
often. Brimming over and exulting in strength of
physical life, neither her mind nor her nerves could
keep pace with her vitality, and the result was the
inevitable one. After great excitement there was
morbid reaction, and in the state of rest there was a

restless, insatiable craving for motion. A strong man, ruthlessly ruling her by sheer superiority of massive power, would have brought out all that was best in her, and would have driven her to her very best weapons for defence. But her husband was quite another sort of person. His love for her was by far the best thing about him; save for that, he was not an interesting man. He was young and very tactless, though full of good impulses and gentle courtesy to her and to every one. But he wearied her with useless details, and made her doubt whether his affectionate manner meant love or mere good breeding. He had an entire incapacity for making any one believe that he was capable of great things. His sister knew how real was his goodness of heart and how generous he could be, and she knew also how much he loved his wife. But she had no power to put into him the passionate, burning romance which was precisely what Leonora most longed for; and Diana did not believe that such a woman as Leonora would long be satisfied with such a husband as Marcantonio.

Meanwhile the day wore on, and she read seriously, and had her midday breakfast in solitude and tried to read again. But by and by she nodded over her book and fell asleep in the humming heat of the summer's afternoon. As she slept she dreamed of a strong, black-browed man who kneeled there beside her in her own house, and who presently took her in his arms and bore her fast down the dark stairs and passages through the rocks to the sea, where a boat lay; and as he carried her his eyes gleamed like burning stars, and she felt that her own grew big and bright. And suddenly he would have leapt into the boat with her, but he stumbled and fell, and she heard the deep roar of the waters in her ears as they sank together.

She woke with a start. The white cat had climbed up and lay on her shoulder, purring with all its might. That was evidently where the sound of the sea came from. She laughed, a little startled at the dream and amused at its cause. It had been so strange — so — so wicked. She was shocked. How could her thoughts, of themselves unaided, have gone to such a subject! Besides, it was not the first time. She had dreamed of Julius Batiscombe before, and always of that strange look in his eyes, gleaming wildly with something she could not understand.

"It is dreadful!" she exclaimed, rising and going to the window.

She had slept long, for the sun was low, and when she looked at her watch it was six o'clock. She reflected that she had not been out all day, and that she wanted a walk. She wrapped something thin and dark over her white summer dress and left the house. The white kitten followed her to the door, mewing sorrowfully, and wistfully waving its little tail.

She walked slowly down the road musing on the odd thing she had dreamed, and seeking in her mind for the reason and cause of it, finding fault with herself for being able to dream such things. It is one thing to be able to call up images of ideal men, and to tell the truth she strove even against that; but it is quite another matter to find one particular man so much in your thoughts that you dream of his running away with you.

She looked up, and a little church was before her, the door being open. She hesitated a moment; she had come out to walk, but it would be so pleasant to kneel in the cool, quiet place, in the half lights and deep shadows; to think, and think, and to pray sweet wordless heart-prayers, half mystic, half religious; to pour out the confessions of her soul's suffering, and to find, even for a brief space, that trust in something unseen, which her troubled spirit could not give to earthly wisdom or earthly love. She raised the curtain and entered.

It was a simple little church, with a floor of green and white tiles, whereon stood rows of green benches and a few straw chairs. The light was high, and the sun did not penetrate into the building. Everything was very clean and cool. Over the altar was a great picture, neither bad nor good, of a monk saint, dark in colour and inoffensive in composition; there were two or three small chapels at the sides, and the plain white arch of the roof was supported by two rows of square masonry pillars.

When Leonora entered she saw that she was alone, and the anticipated pleasure of religious exaltation was heightened by the sensation of solitude. She stood one moment, and then, being sure that no one saw her, she touched with her fingers the holy water in the basin by the door and made the sign of the cross, bending her knee slightly towards the altar. Had there been any one in the church she would perhaps not have done so; but being alone she loved to experience the forms of a religion in which she did not seriously believe, but in which she trusted far more than she knew. She went forward, took a straw chair, turned it round and kneeled on the tiles, burying her face in her hands.

At first, as she knelt there, she trembled with a strange emotion that she loved, — a sort of wave of contrition, of faith, of penitence, and of uncertainty, half painful and yet wholly delicious, that seemed to her the sweetest and most salutary sensation in the world. It was just painful enough to make the pleasure of it keener and rarer. She could not have described it, but she loved it and sought it, when she was in the humour. Gradually her troubles, real and fancied, would answer to her command, and array themselves in rank and file for her inspection; the domestic difficulties, small and snappish little knots of mosquito-like annoyance, biting tiny bites to right and left, and with little stings stinging their way to notice in the foreground; then the troubles of the heart, the temptations of a wild, unspoken and ideal love, streaming by her in the sweep of tempest and storm, stretching out sweet faces and fierce hands to take her with them, and to bear her away from hope of salvation or thought of heaven to the strange unknown space beyond; then again the shapeless and awful host of her fancied philosophies, now towering in fearful strength and menace to the sky, and rending and tearing each other to empty nothing and howling hollowness, now falling down to earth in miserable shapes and slinking insignificantly away; but last and worst of all, there was a deep dark shadow, the trouble of her heart, the certainty that she had made the great mistake and done the irretrievable sin against truth, that she had married a man she could never love, but whom — God forbid the thought! — whom she might hate for the very lack he had of anything that could deserve hating. And then all the pleasure of her exultation was gone; and the dull, uncertain pain, that would not take shape because it had no remedy, filled all her soul and mind and body; she had never felt it as she felt it to-day, but she knew that each time she came to the church to let her heart talk to her in the silence, this same pain had come, sooner or later, and that each time it was stronger and more real. She bent low under its weight, and the tears gathered and fell upon her hands and on the rough straw chair.

Julius Batiscombe had passed the day after the dinner in his boat, sailing far out to sea in the early morning, among the crested waves and the dancing sunbeams, smelling the salt smell gladly, and enjoy-

ing the sharp, cool spray that flew up over the bows.
And at noon, when the west wind sprang up, he went
about and ran homewards over the rolling water. All
that day he was thinking of Leonora, but he was per-
suading himself that he could and would make her
his friend, and that the sudden attraction he had felt
for her was nothing but a little natural sympathy of
minds, striving to assert itself.

He found these thoughts so agreeable and edifying
that he determined to repeat the experience on the
following day, and test their reality by their durabil-
ity. But somehow the hours seemed longer, and
before the wind turned, as it does every day in
summer on the southern coast, he put the helm down,
furled sail, and bade his men pull home. He was
discontented, and, having no one but himself to con-
sult, he thought he would try something else. Once
in his room at the hotel he tried to sleep, but he could
not; he tried to read, but everything disgusted him;
he tried to write, and wrote nonsense. At six o'clock
he went out for a walk. It was not unnatural, perhaps, that he should take the road toward Leonora's
villa, between the high walls of the narrow lanes, for
it was still hot, and the dust lay thick in the road.
Besides, he knew that Leonora was away, and that
consequently there would not be the temptation to
call upon her. For in spite of his visions of friendship, he felt an instinctive conviction that he ought
not to see her. Consequently, as he strolled along
the road, smoking a cigarette and studying the ex-

tremely varied types of the Sorrento beggar, he was conscious of a comforting assurance that he was not in mischief.

At the end of half an hour he was passing the gate of the Carantoni villa. He stopped a moment to look at the little vision of flowers and orange-trees that gleamed so pleasantly through the iron rails, in contrast to the dead monotony of stone walls in the lane. A servant was coming toward the gate, and seeing Batiscombe standing there, opened it wide and took off his hat. Batiscombe carelessly asked if the Signora Marchesa were at home, expecting to be told that she was gone to Rome.

"No, Signore," returned the man; "the Signora Marchesa is this minute gone out, it may be a quarter of an hour. Your excellency " — everybody is an excellency in the south — "will probably find her in the little church along the road, where she often goes." The man bowed, and Batiscombe turned on his heel, not wishing to talk with him. But he turned toward the church.

He walked very slowly, as though in hopes that Leonora would meet him as she came home; and when he came to the door he stopped, as she had done, hesitated, and went in. He trod softly, as Marcantonio had more than once observed, and he did not disturb the silence of the place. He stood still, holding his breath, and knowing that he ought not to stay, but unable for his very life to move. His overhanging brow bent as he watched her, and a curious look crossed his bronzed face, as though he were pained, but felt both sympathy and pity for the kneeling woman. The dead silence, the cold light from above, the half-prostrate figure of Leonora clad in white with the dark lace thing just falling from her splendid hair, — it all seemed like a strange scene in a play, and Julius looked for the sake of looking, while his heart felt something deeper than the artistic impression.

Leonora was bending low upon the seat of the straw chair, the bitter tears trickling down through her white fingers, and her whole life within her convulsed in the consciousness of sorrow. It had so long been vague — this sad knowledge of an evil ever present, and yet ever eluding her attempts to see it and understand it. But now it had come upon her suddenly. After two months of wedded life she knew that she had made a mistake beyond all repairing. She had tried hard to love Marcantonio, she had tried hard to believe that she loved him, but the deception could not last in her, and yet it seemed death to lose it. Sometimes she could think almost indifferently of her marriage, talking to herself, and asking questions of which she knew the answer, but to which she hoped to find another. Did she love him? she would ask at such moments; and she would answer that she thought so, well knowing that whatever real love might be, it was not what she felt for him. But to-day it seemed as though the veil were torn and she saw the dreadful truth. He had left her for a day or two, and she had said it was so pleasant to be alone. That was not love — ah, no! And that dreadful dream, too, that haunted her still; it kept returning, with its sinful face, the face of Julius Batiscombe. The whole unfaithfulness of herself to herself rushed upon her overwhelmingly, relentlessly, till she could not bear it, but bowed herself and sobbed aloud before the altar.

There was a slight noise behind her, and with an effort she controlled herself, rose till she kneeled upright and merely bent her head upon her hands, drawing the back of the chair towards her in the act. She had been disturbed, and the sense of annoyance overmastered the expression of her trouble for a moment. Gradually the consciousness of a presence took possession of her, and she knew that some one was watching her; she grew uneasy, tried to repeat a prayer mechanically for the sake of thinking of something definite, failed, touched her hair half surreptitiously with one hand, and finally rose from her knees. As she turned to leave the church she met Julius Batiscombe's eyes, and she started perceptibly. It was so precisely the expression she had seen in her dream, little more than an hour since, that she was fairly frightened, and would have turned and fled had there been any other way out. But when she looked again she saw something that reassured her. There was that which attracted, as well as that which frightened her. She had the length of the church to walk,

and she made up her mind that she would not show
that she was surprised, and would behave as though
nothing had happened. For she was a strong woman
in such ways, and could rely upon herself if not
taken too much off her guard. Meanwhile Batiscombe looked on the ground; for he was often
conscious of the too great boldness of his sight,
and knew that it must be disagreeable to her. So
he moved a step or two, hat in hand, waiting for
Leonora to pass him, and prepared to follow if she
showed any sign of wishing it. He feared, however,
that he had offended her by his inopportune appearance, and he was prepared for a repulse. Nevertheless, after the first start was over, she came boldly
towards him, smiling rather sadly and looking
wonderfully beautiful; for the tears only made her
eyes softer and deeper, leaving a gentle shadow
in them, just as the sea is bluer and pleasanter
in its blueness beneath the shade of an overhanging
cliff. She smiled, and passing out half looked at
him again as he lifted the green curtain for her. He
smiled again, gravely, and followed her. When they
were on the steps, he bowed low again.

"How do you do, Mr. Batiscombe?" she said,
quite naturally, holding out her hand to him. But
in the open air, his hand touching hers, she could
not help blushing a little when she thought of that
dream an hour ago.

"You did not go to Rome, after all?" he said,
as they began to walk along the lane.

"No," she answered, "it was too hot. Do you often go to the little church, Mr. Batiscombe? It is so nice and quiet there, is it not?"

She was determined to put a bold face on the matter. Besides, he perhaps had not heard those sobs, — he had only seen her kneeling, perhaps, and had not understood that she was crying. But Julius had seen all and heard all, and was pondering deep in his heart the causes which could make her unhappy, seeing she was young and, in his opinion, beautiful, — married, as society said, to the man she loved, and not lacking the goods of this world, while praying ardently for those of the next.

"I have sometimes looked in," answered Batiscombe. "It was a chance that took me there to-day."

"Yes?"

"Yes" — he glanced down sidelong at her face — "that is to say — not altogether."

She was silent, walking serenely by his side.

"No, not altogether," he continued, determining suddenly on his course. "The fact is, I was walking by your place, and a servant who was just coming out told me you were in church, and then I went in. I suppose I ought not to have done it," he added with a little laugh; "I am very sorry I disturbed you. Pray forgive me."

"Not at all, — churches are free for every one. But why do you laugh?"

"At my own stupidity," he answered. "I might have known that when you go to church at odd times you go to be alone, and not to have wandering callers sent there after you."

"What makes you think that?" she asked, curious to know how much he had noticed. She argued that if he had heard her crying he would think the question natural, whereas, if he had not, he would not suspect anything from it.

"Because you acted as though you thought you were alone," he said seriously.

"I did think so," she said, blushing faintly. "Do you know? I was quite startled when I saw you there."

"I saw you were," he answered, still very gravely, "and I am very sorry."

"Do you remember what I said to you at Castellamare, Mr. Batiscombe?"

"Yes; you said that life was not all roses, and you said it in earnest."

"Yes," said Leonora. "You see I did. I am not always in earnest."

"Is it rude to ask how one distinguishes between your excellency in earnest and your excellency in fun?" inquired Batiscombe, glad enough to turn the conversation to a jest, for he judged Leonora to be rather imprudent. Indeed, he wondered how she could have said what she had, unless it were from a wish to face out the situation.

"You ought to be able to see," she answered, laughing lightly, "but when you cannot, perhaps I will tell you."

"Pray do," said he. "I am very stupid about such things, — but then, I am always in earnest, even when I want to be funny. Perhaps you might think me most diverting when I am most in earnest."

"No," said Leonora, "I should not think that. I should think you might be very unpleasant when you are in earnest — at least, from the things you write."

"That is a doubtful compliment," remarked Julius, smiling.

"Is it? I cannot imagine anything more delightful than having the power to be as unpleasant as you want to be."

"Is there anything I can do for you, Marchesa? I should be most happy, I am sure, — short of poisoning your enemies, as you suggested the other day."

"You ought not to draw the line," she said with a laugh.

"Oh, very well. I will do the poisoning too, if you wish it."

"Of course. What is the use of having friends if you cannot rely on them to do anything you want?"

"If I could be one of your friends," he said gravely, "I am sure I would not 'draw any line,' as you call it."

"With what seriousness you say that!" she exclaimed, very much amused. She was nervous from the knowledge that he had found her out in the church, and she laughed at anything rather recklessly. But Batiscombe had turned grave again.

"Would you rather that one should ask such a privilege in jest?" he asked.

"No indeed," said she, a little frightened at the point to which she had brought him.

"Then I ask it very much in earnest," he answered.

"To be my friend?" she asked, looking straight before her.

"Yes, to be your friend," said he, watching her closely.

"Really? In earnest?"

"Really — in earnest," he answered. She stopped suddenly in the road.

"I accept," she said, frankly holding out her hand.

"I am very proud," he said quietly. He took off his hat and touched her fingers with his lips. Then they walked on without a word for some minutes.

"What a strange thing life is!" exclaimed Leonora, at last.

"Yes, it is very strange," he answered. "Here are we two, on the smallest provocation, swearing eternal friendship on the high road, as though we were going to storm a citadel, or head an Arctic expedition. But I am really very glad, and very grateful."

Somehow the reflection did not sound light or flippant; and to tell the truth, Leonora was thinking precisely the same thing, wondering inwardly how she could possibly have gone to such a length with a mere acquaintance. But the land of friendship was an untried territory for Leonora, and she seemed to find in the idea a sudden rest from a sense of danger. A friend could never be a lover, — she knew that! This was the meaning of the dream. But she answered quietly enough.

"If things are real at all," she said, "they are as real at one time as at another."

"Yes," answered Batiscombe. "Malakoff or Sorrento, it is all the same."

CHAPTER X.

"You will come in?" said Leonora when they reached the gate.

"Thanks; I should like to very much," answered Batiscombe, and he followed her through the gate into the garden. They passed into the house, and Leonora received from the servant a telegram which had come when she was out. It was the one Marcantonio had dispatched when he had decided to stay a few days in Rome and to bring his sister to Sorrento.

Leonora opened it quickly and glanced over the message. It was very evident from her expression that she was annoyed and somewhat surprised. Batiscombe looked away.

"It is too bad!" she exclaimed; her companion examined the handle of his stick, as though there were something wrong with it. He was not curious, and he had very good manners. Leonora folded the dispatch and put it away.

"Let us go out again," she said, "it is so close indoors."

Batiscombe followed her in silence, obediently. They sat down among the orange-trees on an old stone bench. The air was still and very warm, and the lizards were taking their last peep at the sun wherever they could, climbing up the trunks of the trees and the wall of the house to catch a glimpse of him before he set.

"My husband telegraphs that he will be away some time," said Leonora after a minute. "He has business that keeps him, and his sister is in Rome."

"You must be very lonely here," remarked Batiscombe in answer.

"Do you know Madame de Charleroi?" asked Leonora, taking no notice of the observation.

"Yes," said Batiscombe, "I know her. Somebody told me she was in Pegli."

"So she was. But she had to come to Rome on business, and now my husband is going to bring her here."

"Indeed?" exclaimed Batiscombe. "To pass the summer?"

"Oh no; only for a week, I suppose. Do you know? I am rather glad; I hardly know her at all, and she seems so hard to know."

"Hard to know?" repeated Julius. "Perhaps she is. It is always hard to know very charming women."

"Is it?" asked Leonora, smiling at the frankness of the remark; it seemed to her that he had found it easy enough to swear friendship with her half an hour ago. "Is it? Is she such a very charming woman?"

"Yes, indeed," he answered.

"Yes to which question?"

"Both," said Julius. "Madame de Charleroi is charming, and it is very hard to know women of her sort well. Think how long it is since I first met you, Marchesa, and we are just beginning to know each other."

"Do you think we are?" asked Leonora. She was full of questions.

"I think so — yes. At least, I hope so," he said with a pleasant smile.

"If you were writing a book about us, Mr. Batiscombe, would you say that we were beginning to know each other? no one would believe that we stopped in the road and shook hands and swore to be friends. It would be very amusing, would it not? I do not know why we did it; I wish you would explain." She laughed a little, and stuck the point of her parasol into the earth. Batiscombe laughed too.

"When people have known each other in society for a long time," he said, "and then begin to be friends, there is always some ice to break, and it always seems odd for a little while after it is broken."

"I suppose that is the reason that such things always seem improbable in books, until you know about them yourself."

"Amusing books, and interesting ones, are made up of improbabilities," answered Julius. "And the people who write them are even more improbable. It is always improbable that a man who has lived a

great deal should have the talent, or the patience **if**
you like, to make stories out of his own experience,
— or that a man who has not seen a great deal of
the world should be able to evolve a good novel out
of his inner consciousness. The probabilities for
most men are that they will eat and drink and wear
out their clothes and be buried. All those things
are a great bore to do, a greater bore to describe, and
an intolerable bore to read about. The most amusing books are either true stories of a very exceptional
kind, or else they are rank, glaring, stupendous improbabilities, invented to illustrate a great theory,
or a great play of passions, — like Bulwer's 'Coming
Race,' or Goethe's 'Faust.' I am sure I am boring
you dreadfully."

"Oh no!" cried Leonora, who was interested and
taken out of herself by his talk. "But I think I prefer the 'exceptional true stories,' as you call them,
like Shakespeare, — the historical part, I mean."

"The worst of it is," said Batiscombe, "that the
true stories are generally the ones that no one believes. Critics always say that such things are a
tissue of utter impossibilities."

"Oh, the critics," exclaimed Leonora; "they must
be the most horrid people. I wonder you authors let
them live!"

"Thanks," said Batiscombe, laughing, "I was a
critic myself before I was an author, and I do not
think I was a very horrid person."

"That is different," said Leonora. "Of course a

man may do ever so many things before he finds his real vocation."

"Authors owe a great deal to critics," continued Julius. "More men have come to grief at their hands by over-praise than by too much discouragement. A very little praise is often enough to ruin a man, and a man who has much talent will always survive a great deal of abuse and disappointment. If any one asked my advice about adopting literature as a career, I would certainly tell him to have nothing to do with it; I should be quite sure that if he were born to it nothing would keep him from it for long."

"That is the way with other things," said Leonora, looking rather wistfully away at the setting sun, just below the green leaves of the orange grove. "It is the way with everything, good and bad. Some people are born to be saints, and some people are quite sure to turn out the most dreadful sinners, whatever they do."

"What a depressing theory!" exclaimed Batiscombe, who had much more cause to think so than Leonora.

"Depressing is no name for it," she answered. "One makes such mistakes in life, and then there is no way out of it but to make others."

"And the worst of it is, that one knows one is making them, and cannot help it."

"Yes," said she, "one always knows, — if one only knew." Then she laughed suddenly. "What a ridiculous speech!"

"No," said Batiscombe, "I understand exactly what you mean. Just when one is doing the wrong thing, there is always a little instinct against it. But it is often so very little, that one does not quite know it from ever so many other instincts. And then, before one is quite sure that one knows what is right, — before one's mind has time to think it over logically, — one has done the wrong thing. At least, it seems afterwards as if that were what happened; but I suppose it is because we are weak."

Leonora looked at Julius, who seemed deep in his thoughts. He had exactly put her idea into words, but she could not tell whether he believed what he said, or was merely amusing himself with his faculty for explanation. He interested her extremely. It was just this kind of introspection that most delighted her, — this cutting up and skinning of conscience and soul. Nevertheless she did not think that Batiscombe was the man to analyse his own actions. It was more likely, she thought, that he was very clever, and could talk to please his listener. But he interested her greatly, and she was curious to know how he had got his knowledge of human nature.

"You must have had a wonderful life," she said, presently, saying aloud what she was thinking, rather than hoping to draw him on to talk about himself.

"Oh no — very commonplace, I assure you," said he, with a laugh that sounded natural enough.

"Only, you see, I have had to make capital of what I know. But it spoils one's own enjoyment to analyse anything, and I shall have to give it up, or resign myself to a miserable existence."

"I wonder whether you are right," said Leonora, reflectively.

"Of course I am," he answered gayly. "The man who carves the pheasant does not enjoy it, but the man who eats it does."

"Then let us eat and drink, for to-morrow we die. Is that the end of your experience?" asked Leonora, gloomily.

"Oh — well — if you put it so. Only if you do not eat and drink too much, you may possibly not die until the day after to-morrow."

"Or you may spend your life in cooking the dinner, and die before it is served?" suggested Leonora.

"Or anything — what carnal similes!" laughed Batiscombe. "But they are very apt for any one who cares for eating. If that is really an important enjoyment, it may as well stand as the type."

"Exactly — 'if.' I am sure you do not think it is, nor that any material satisfaction can possibly stand as a type, nor that we should enjoy to-day without thought of to-morrow, nor a great many other things you have said." She watched him as she spoke, and he liked to feel her eyes on him.

"No," he answered, "you are quite right. I do not think those things at all. But I am sure I generally do them," he added, smiling.

"But what do you think — really? Is there any-thing really high and noble in the world? It all seems so little and so hollow, sometimes."

She sighed, thinking how, formerly, she had said such things speculatively, and for the sake of raising an argument with her friends. Batiscombe turned on the stone seat, so that he faced her.

"Of course there are high and noble things in the world," he answered. "It is when you look into the small workings of the mind and soul, as you have been making me do, that you lose sight of the great ones. Material nature is most interesting under a microscope, and generally most beautiful in great masses at a distance. But if you walk close to the grandest cliff in nature, and flatten your face against it, and hold your eye half an inch from the rock, the grandeur and the beauty are all gone, and without a microscope wherewith to examine your particular point, you will find the close inspection tiresome after a time. There is no microscope for the soul, any more than for the heart, or the mind. You gain noth-ing by looking too closely at it. It is ten to one that you hit upon a diseased spot for your examination. It may amuse you for a time to study other people's souls, because you can hardly get so near to them as to lose all impression of the whole, as you can with yourself. What does it matter what you know about your soul, so long as you do what is right?"

"That sounds true," said Leonora, "but I suppose there is something wrong about it."

"All good similes sound true," said Batiscombe, laughing. "That is the reason why popular orators and preachers are so fond of them. The real use of a simile is for an explanation; the moment you make an argument upon it, you are revelling in words without logic, calling illustrations facts and generally making game of your audience."

"What a discouraging person you are," said Leonora. "You make one almost believe a thing, and then you turn round and tell one there is nothing to believe after all."

"Not so bad as that," said Batiscombe, leaning back and clasping his brown hands over his knee. "I have not said there was nothing to believe in. Only take care you do not believe in anything because it bears a tempting resemblance to something you like."

"That is ingenious, but I wish you would be positive about something. I wish you would tell me, for instance, what you yourself believe in." Her eyes turned towards him in the twilight. For the sun had gone down, and the orange-trees brought the shadows early where the two were sitting.

"What I believe in?" he repeated. "I suppose that, apart from religious matters, I believe most in sympathy and antipathy."

"That is not exactly a course of action or a rule of life," remarked Leonora, smiling and looking away.

"No. But in nine cases out of ten they are what

determine both. At all events I believe in them. They always carry the day over logic, philosophy, and all manner of calculation and forethought. You may determine that it is your duty to like a person, you may induce yourself to think that you do, and you may make every one believe you do; but if you really do not — there is an end of it. And the reverse is just as true."

"I should think every one knew that," said Leonora in an indifferent way. But she was wondering why he had said it, whether he had any suspicion of her own state of mind. "It is very safe to say you believe in things of that sort — everybody does. You are a very indefinite person, Mr. Batiscombe."

"What is the use of defining everything? Lots of people have been burned alive, and have had their heads cut off for defining things they knew nothing about. Of course they were quite sure they knew better; but then, is it worth while to die for your personal opinion of an abstract question?"

"It is very fine and noble, though," said Leonora.

"There is a tradition that it is fine and noble to 'die for' anything. It sounds well. Every one admires it. But reflect that the common murderer 'dies for' his individual views of the social state. The woman who maintained that scissors were better than a knife for cutting an apple suffered her husband to drown her rather than give up the point, and as she sank her fingers still opened and closed, to imitate the instrument she preferred. She 'died for' her opinion, just as much as Savonarola or Giordano Bruno, whom my countrymen are so fond of raving about."

"You know that is not what I mean," said Leonora. "I mean it is noble to die for what is right."

"The question is, what is right? There are cases when it is eminently heroic to sacrifice one's life."

"For instance?"

"For instance, to die for the liberty of one's own country, — for the defence and safety of one's king, who represents the embodiment of the social principle, — or for the honour of an innocent woman."

"But about liberty and one's king, and that sort of thing," said Leonora, "where can you draw the line? There is no successful treason, you know, because when it succeeds it is called by other names. There must be a standard of absolute good — or something."

"I should think you must be a very unhappy person, Marchesa, if you are always trying to draw a line and to define absolute good. What is the use? Every one knows that it cannot be done."

Leonora was silent. It had interested her to hear the brilliant, successful man, apparently so happy and contented with his lot, talk seriously about the things she was always puzzling over. But what did it come to? What was the use? Those were his last words.

The warm gloom of the night settled softly round them, laden with the sweetness of the oranges and

the aromatic scent of the late carnations. Batiscombe could just see Leonora by his side, her head
bent forward as she rested her chin upon her hand.
The indescribable atmosphere and faint perfume
that surrounds women of high beauty and degree
intoxicated him. She was so English in her beauty
and so Russian in her delicate exuberance of vitality;
above all, she was so intensely feminine, that Batiscombe felt his senses giving way to the magnetic influence. He leaned forward in the dark till he was
nearer to her, looking at the faint outline of her
face. Leonora sighed, and the gentle sound seemed
like the softened echo of past weeping.

"Marchesa," said Julius in a low voice, "can I
really be your friend? Will you let me help to make
your life happier, if I can?"

Leonora felt the blood rise blushing to her face in
the dark, and her heart trembled in its beating. A
friend! Oh, if she really could find a strong, true
friend to help her!

"How can you?" she asked faintly.

"I do not know," he answered. "Let me try. I
will try very hard. I am sure I can succeed."

She let him take her hand for one moment. It
was a consent, not spoken, but given and understood.
Leonora rose to her feet, and they walked silently
toward the house.

"When may I come?" he asked, as he bade her
good night. He spoke quite naturally, as though it
were already a matter of course that he should see

her every day. She hesitated a moment, standing in the doorway with the warm light of the lamp upon her.

"Come at eleven," she said at last, and with a pleasant smile she left him and went in.

The aspect of life seemed changed for her when he was gone. That afternoon she had suffered intensely. Now there was a strange, calm sense in her heart that soothed all her thoughts, and made the lonely evening sweet and restful. She asked no questions, she made no self-examination, she desired of herself no reasons for her conduct. It was enough that the storm had passed and that the calm was come, she knew not how. A man had spoken to her as no man ever spoke to her before, and the earnestness of his words still rang in her ear. He was loyal, strong, and true. He would be her friend, — he had asked it, she had granted it.

She dined alone and read a little afterwards, closing her eyes now and again to enjoy the peace that had descended upon her. For the first time in many months she was happy, supremely, quietly happy, and she asked no questions.

As for Batiscombe, he wandered homewards through the dark lanes, not heeding or caring where he went. He was wholly absorbed in recalling the events of the afternoon, revelling in the memory of Leonora's face and looks and words. He, too, was wholly disinclined to reflect on the possible consequences of his action; he took it as a matter of course that he should keep his word and be indeed a friend to her; at all events he thought neither of the future nor the past, but only ever and ever of herself, clinging tenderly to the images he called up, and asking nothing better than to call them up again, dreaming and waking. He might be in love, or he might not, — the question no longer entered his head. He was fascinated, charmed, and beside himself with enjoyment of his thoughts.

It was the state he had dreaded a day or two ago. To avoid it he had tried to escape, by a stratagem, beyond the possibility of seeing Leonora again. He had cursed his folly in going to see her. He had promised himself that he would not go again; he had reviewed his past troubles, and had remembered how plausibly they had begun. And at last he had fallen into the ancient trap, the snare of fair friendship set out to catch men and women and to destroy them. But the mouth of the pit was garnished with roses and lilies, sweet and innocent enough.

At eleven o'clock of the next day Julius was again with Leonora, and on the day following and the day after that. They walked together, read together, sailed together, and lunched together. A few stray callers came in now and then, but as they never came twice, not one of them thought it at all worthy of remark that Mr. Batiscombe should happen to be calling at the same time.

Leonora found an extraordinary pleasure in his conversation. He had a fund of varied study and experience from which to draw, that amused her and made her think in new grooves; and when he talked about her ideas and interests he always succeeded in showing them to her in a new light. His comments were by turns light and sarcastic, and then again very serious; and his general readiness to make things seem amusing made his graver sayings doubly strong by contrast. He had a bold way of asserting that accumulated knowledge was of very little importance as compared with action, which would have sounded foolish enough from an ignorant man; but Julius was far from ignorant. He had studied a great many questions, and he possessed the faculty of speaking sensibly in a general way about subjects of which he did not profess to know anything. Most of all she found in him a ready sympathy and a love of human nature and of life for life's sake, that were utterly different from the artificial views she had cultivated. She found in him the strong love of enjoyment and the activity of mind and body, that best harmonised with her own real character; and in their long days together the hollowness and emptiness of life never once recalled themselves to her memory, except as things for her to wonder at and for Batiscombe to turn into jest and laugh to scorn.

The whole situation was utterly new and unexpected to her. After the first few days at Sorrento with her husband she had made up her mind that the beauties of nature were very tedious, and that she would be glad to go back to Rome and begin the

duties of society, — anything, rather than go on from
day to day longing for a sensation, and finding only
a great deal of weariness.   But now, in the discovery
of a new friend, a man of talent and tact, who made
all gloomy musings seem ridiculous by the side of his
sanguine activity, the place was transformed into a
paradise for her.   Not a day but brought some new
thought, some witty saying, some bit of novelty with
it, so that she found herself happy when she was
alone in going over what they had said and done together.

As for Marcantonio, she should be very glad when
he came back.   It seemed to her that he must be
much more amusing now, and that she could say
things to rouse him and make him talk.   She wrote
affectionate notes every day, telling him how beautiful everything was, and how he was to enjoy it, now
that the first difficulties of settling were over.   She
even said she had sent for the cook, and had ascertained that he was very well, having had no return
of the fever; she thought it must please her husband
to know that she was taking care of the household
and looking after the people.

In the meanwhile Batiscombe fell in love, studiously consoling his conscience with the reflection
that he was doing a good deed, and was acting the
part of a friend in making the time pass pleasantly
for Leonora in her solitude.   But his conscience did
not trouble him greatly, though it would be sure to,
by and by.   At present everything was swamped

in a sea of glorious enjoyment, and he was no less really happy than Leonora. Day after day began and ended alike, but yet ever different. They never referred to the singularity of the arrangement by which Julius came every day in the morning and stayed till dark. There seemed no reason why they should not leave well alone, and enjoy each other's society to the very utmost. And they did, most fully, each wholly engrossed in the other.

At the end of a week Marcantonio telegraphed that he and his sister would leave Rome by the night train and arrive in the morning. Leonora in the innocence of her heart was glad, anticipating all manner of new pleasure in her husband's society, the result of her own cure from morbid ennui. But Batiscombe felt his heart sink within him.

CHAPTER XI.

THE sun beat down fiercely as Marcantonio and
Madame de Charleroi drove up to the house at
half-past ten o'clock. They had travelled all night,
but the beautiful Diana was not the less fair for
being a little tired, and as she descended from the
carriage and went up the short steps to the door,
Leonora could not help admiring the perfect smoothness and completeness of her appearance. Donna
Diana did things in a stately fashion, and it would
have been a hard journey indeed that could ruffle
her lace or disturb the smooth coiling of her hair.
Leonora herself was apt to arrive a little dusty from
a night in a train, and not altogether serene, and she
knew it; so that the absolutely finished completeness
of Madame de Charleroi struck her as enviable and
much to be admired.

The two women kissed each other affectionately on
either cheek, and then Marcantonio came running
up and bent over his wife's hand, and, when Donna
Diana was not looking, he just brushed Leonora's
cheek in a rather guilty fashion. Presently Leonora
led Diana away to show her the rooms destined for
her, and to fuss a little over all the arrangements,
as women love to do when another woman is come

to stay with them. Marcantonio was busy for a few minutes, asking questions of the coachman and the men-servants concerning the health of every individual in the establishment, and then he also retired to his room, and the perspiring grooms and servants raged furiously together with the luggage and bundles for a while; and then the front door was closed again, and all was cool and quiet.

Leonora left her husband and her sister-in-law to their toilet, and came down stairs through the darkened halls to the drawing-room. She was wondering whether Batiscombe would appear at his usual hour. Strange to say they had not spoken of it on the previous evening, — probably because they feared lest the mention of the subject should lead to some discussion about the singular intimacy into which they had fallen, and which neither wished to endanger. It would be just like Batiscombe to come, she thought; it would be just like him to show himself at once as her friend, and to establish the custom of coming every day.

She was not mistaken; at eleven o'clock the bell rang, and he was shown in.

"I was quite sure you would come," she said, holding out her hand.

"Of course," said he. "I hope they have arrived safely?"

"Quite, thanks. They are making themselves beautiful at this moment, though I think they must have done it on the way, — they arrived looking as fresh as possible, all smiles and lavender and sunshine. I am so glad they are come, you cannot think!"

"Yes, I should think you must be," assented Julius with less enthusiasm.

At that moment Marcantonio was shaving himself in the cool seclusion of his dressing-room. He was going over in his mind the past and the future, reflecting upon the absurd things he had said to Diana about Batiscombe in the train, and wondering what he could do to make her stay pleasant. Batiscombe must certainly be asked to the house, he thought, if only to show his sister that he, Marcantonio, had no objection to her meeting the man. It had been so thoroughly absurd to take up her speech about the possibility of her having married him, and to build on it the supposition that she had ever loved him. Bah! the fancy of a girl for the romantic! Batiscombe was now a perfectly serious man — decidedly so. Besides, Marcantonio began to dread very much the eternal trio between his wife, his sister, and himself, from morning till night. If only he had thought in time to ask some other man, it would have been such a charming square party. His wife was always more brilliant and good-tempered when there were outsiders present, — probably a peculiarity of all women, he thought, excepting Diana. Supposing that Leonora took it into her head to be dull or bored while Diana was there, how dreadful it would be! It was clearly necessary that Diana should have a favourable

idea of the Carantoni household; that had been the
whole object in bringing her down. And if Leonora
did not seem in good spirits, Diana was sure to think
he was not making his wife happy. The idea grew
in his mind; he was terribly afraid of what his sister
might think, seeing how she had opposed the match
from the first. Really it was absolutely necessary to
ask some one to the house while she stayed. But
whom could he ask at such short notice? There was
nobody but Batiscombe within reach.

Marcantonio had finished shaving one side of his
face, and took a fresh razor for the other. There was
a pause in his thoughts while he tested the edge and
applied more soap to his cheek. As he went to work
again, the original train of ideas continued.

Well! Batiscombe. Why not? He was a very
amiable man, and Leonora liked him. She would
certainly not object. As for Diana, it was probable
that he would keep away from her most of the time.
He would scarcely press his company on her. Monsieur Batiscombe had tact, although he was a crazy
foreigner who went round the world in boats and
wrote books. Bah! it was so convenient! Just the
very person — he knew everything, had seen most
things, and could talk like a mill-wheel. All those
ridiculous prejudices about Diana were absurd, and
were an insult to her. Batiscombe should be asked
to stay a week.

Having successfully finished his shaving operations, Marcantonio sat down to write a note to Julius

while the thing was in his mind. Otherwise, he reflected, he might forget to do it, and Batiscombe could not be obtained until to-morrow. He wrote an invitation and signed it. Then he reflected that it would be as well to speak to Leonora before sending it. She did not know anything about that old story that had happened when she was a little girl, and perhaps not even in Rome. It was a mere formality, but it would be more courteous to ask her, before sending the invitation. He would not ask Diana, however. She had herself said, the night before, that she had no objection to meeting the man. Very well, she should meet him very soon. He hurriedly finished dressing and went down-stairs to find Leonora. Entering the drawing-room he found her talking quietly with the very man he was thinking about.

"Mon Dieu! what a chance!" he exclaimed, cordially shaking Julius by the hand. "Imagine! I was just writing you a note, when you were in the house yourself!"

"Really?" ejaculated Batiscombe, in some astonishment. "How can I serve you — since I am here in the flesh?"

"By remaining!" answered Marcantonio cheerfully. "I was in the act of writing a very pressing invitation to you to stay a week with us, and thus to make up the most agreeable party of four in the world. Madame unites herself with me in the request, I am sure," added Carantoni, turning to his wife, who looked rather pale.

"Mais certainement — we shall be charmed," said Leonora, utterly astonished and confused by the suddenness of the situation.

She had herself thought how delightful such an arrangement would be — more than once. But coming so suddenly, from her husband, without her suggestion, it frightened her and did not seem quite natural. Her voice did not sound very cordial as she spoke, but it was sufficient, and her husband, being full of his idea, noticed nothing.

"You are very kind. It will really give me very great pleasure," said Julius, controlling his voice wonderfully.

For he, too, was taken off his guard. Marcantonio was delighted. It was such a wonderful piece of luck, he said, that Monsieur Batiscombe should have called at that hour.

"But come with me, if madame permits," said he, "and I will show you your room. You can send for your things in the afternoon."

Leonora was only too glad to be left alone for a moment, and the two men went away, Marcantonio rubbing his hands at the success of his arrangements for a pleasant week. With Batiscombe in the house the time could not fail to pass pleasantly, he thought.

There are some men who seem to be pursued by an evil destiny that continually forces them to do the wrong thing out of pure goodness of heart. From an innocent desire to make his household pleasant for his sister, and to amuse the wife of his heart, he

had asked the man of all others whom the one desired
to avoid, and the other ought to have been kept from,
simply because he wanted somebody and the man
happened to be on the spot.   And the whole thing
had originated in a laudable desire to see pleasant
relations established between his wife and his sister,
the two persons in the whole world whom he most
loved.   Poor Marcantonio!   He was under an unlucky star.

Presently Batiscombe returned alone to the drawing-room, his host remaining to give some orders
about the luncheon.   He looked curiously at Leonora as he sat down opposite to her.

" This is very charming," he said, smiling.   " It is
so kind of you."

" I had nothing to do with it," said Leonora,
avoiding his glance.   " But of course I am very
glad.   I was dreadfully afraid of being left alone
with my sister-in-law, and of course you will help me
to make it pleasant for her.   Really, it is just like
my husband, — he is so good."

" It would have been very miserable to have our
good time cut short," said Julius reflectively, " and
I suppose they would have thought it odd if I went
on calling every day at the same hour."   Leonora
blushed very slightly.

" Yes," she said, " I suppose so.   People have such
ideas about the appearances.   You know I should
not mind in the least if it were only my husband;
you might stay from morning till night, and we

should all enjoy it. But I am so afraid of Madame de Charleroi, — she is so tremendously correct, you know."

From which piece of conversation it will be seen that Julius and Leonora had grown intimate of late, and regarded things from a practical point of view.

All this time Madame de Charleroi was in ignorance of the amiable arrangement concluded by her brother, and was looking forward with almost as much dislike as he had done to the family trio in which she was to play a part during the week.

She understood Leonora to a certain extent. She had at least a very strong presentiment that there would be trouble between her brother and his wife; not an open disagreement nor anything dramatic, but the sort of small worry and discord that begins slowly and surely, and finally embitters the whole lives of people who are not suited to each other. She had agreed to come down to Sorrento in order to "make friends" with Leonora, as her brother had expressed it, and in her wisdom and knowledge of the world she knew very well what a difficult task she had undertaken, and how small was her chance of success. She foresaw that she must be continually left alone with Leonora, for she understood her brother well enough to suppose he would adopt that method of fostering the friendship he desired. Poor dear Marcantonio had so very little tact! Consequently Diana wished very much that some other person had been asked to stay at the same time. Mean-

while she lay down for an hour upon a sofa in her
sitting-room, and thought the matter over.

Marcantonio, however, bethought him that in spite
of Diana's expressed willingness to meet Batiscombe,
it might surprise her to find herself suddenly living
under the same roof with him. He therefore determined to inform her of the fact before they all met
at the midday breakfast. He supposed she was busy
with her toilet, and so he would not go himself;
he would send his wife. That was a good idea —
it would be at once a chance of throwing the two
together. To this end he returned to the drawing-
room, where Leonora and Batiscombe were still talking, and with an apology to the latter, he drew his
wife aside for a moment.

"I think, my angel," he whispered, "that it would
be better to tell Diana that monsieur is here for a
week. She is dressing at this moment. Would you
be so amiable as to go to her and say in the course of
the conversation that I have invited Monsieur Batiscombe? It would be very good of you, my dear."

Leonora was not in the humour to refuse her husband anything. Everything was bright and happy
to her, now that she saw a means of defence provided
for her against the stately Diana, whom she feared.
She had recovered from her astonishment at the sudden invitation to Julius, and she saw in it a kind
intention on her husband's part, for which she was
grateful.

"Of course, mon ami," she answered, "I will do

everything you like. Only amuse Monsieur Batiscombe for a moment, and I will run to Diana, and tell
her what you wish."

"A thousand thanks!" exclaimed Marcantonio,
and he turned to the task of amusing Mr. Batiscombe,
more delighted than ever.

Leonora knocked rather timidly at the door of
Diana's sitting-room.

"It is I," she said, through the door; "may I
come in?"

"Oh, I am so glad to see you!" exclaimed Diana,
rising swiftly from her couch, with a bright smile.
She took Leonora's hand and led her to a chair, and
arranged the curtains a little, so as to make more
light, and then sat down by her side.

"You must be dreadfully tired," said Leonora,
"and I ought not to disturb you. I just wanted to
see if you had everything you wanted."

"But everything — everything, I assure you,"
answered Diana. "I am so very comfortable, and
the view over the sea is exquisite, really de toute
beauté."

They made a wonderful contrast, as they sat side
by side. Donna Diana's perfect features were more
mature than Leonora's, her bearing was more noble,
and her look more quiet and self-possessed. She
wore a loose peignoir of white, with lace and white
silk ribbons, such as none but perfect blondes can
wear. But nothing could dim the dazzling whiteness
of her skin, or detract from her marvellous beauty.

She was calm, and statue-like, and it was only now and then that a glance from her deep grey eyes betrayed the warm and sympathising heart within. A grand, regal woman, fit to wear a crown or to have been the priestess of an ancient people. She had it all from her mother, who had been like her, though in a smaller mould, and had died, still young and beautiful, when Diana and her brother were little children. It was impossible to imagine her for a moment deprived of her perfect grace, and ease, and quiet.

Leonora was altogether more earthly. She moved well, but often impetuously. Her extraordinary vitality, when not reduced by reaction to a state of unnatural apathy, was forever seeking an outlet. She loved the light and the stir of society life, while she amused herself with reflecting on its emptiness. She was instinct with strength, and motion, and elasticity. Her skin was always fresh, whether in heat or cold, but from the enthusiasm with which she did things, she sometimes lost the smoothness and correctness — as she would have called it — of her appearance. And yet even at such times she had a strange charm and fascination of her own. As she often said, she was far less beautiful than Diana, but much more alive, — though with a life that might perhaps be less strong and enduring than Diana's. Diana was a queen — Leonora a brilliant and irresponsible princess.

They talked a little together, and Leonora found

it easy to lead the conversation to the plans she was making for the amusement of her sister-in-law.

"By the bye," said she, "I ought to tell you. Mr. Julius Batiscombe is staying here this week. I suppose you know him?"

Leonora had no idea of anything having existed in former times in the way of sentiment between Diana and Julius. She was sent to convey a piece of information, and she did it as well as she could, not even looking at Diana as she spoke. Had she suspected anything she would have watched her, and she could have seen the least possible trembling of the eyelids, and the lightest imaginable shade of annoyance on her guest's fair face.

"Oh yes," she said calmly, "I know him. I have known him a long time. So he is staying with you?"

"Yes. He is so very agreeable, and Marcantonio wished it. He has been in Sorrento some time, and he took us to Castellamare to see that ironclad launched. He is so very clever."

"Because he took you in his boat?" laughed Diana. "Yes, my dear, a man is clever indeed who can get such charming company."

Leonora was pleased with the little speech,—it sounded kindly, and as Diana spoke she laid her hand softly on Leonora's.

"How cold your hands are," said Diana. And indeed they were chilled through, though it was a very hot day in July. "'Cold hands, warm heart,' you know, as the proverb says."

Leonora blushed a little. It seemed so odd to be
talking about Julius Batiscombe to a stranger that it
frightened her a little, and she was conscious that
her heart beat faster. Nevertheless she wondered
vaguely why she felt the blood rise to her cheek.
He was only her friend, and the remark about the
heart could have nothing to do with him.

But Diana supposed she changed colour because she
was thinking of Marcantonio. It was natural for a
young bride to blush at the mention of her heart,
of course, and altogether charming. She patted the
cold little hand sympathetically and talked of something else. It is so easy to misunderstand a blush.
But Leonora felt as though she were being patron-
ised, which is the thing people of her stamp most
bitterly resent of all others; and accordingly there
sprang up in her breast a little breeze of opposition,
which might by and by blow a gale.

When the party met in the drawing-room before
the midday breakfast, everything seemed arranged
for the best, and Marcantonio rubbed his hands with
delight, and made numerous hospitable gestures as he
walked round the three lambs of his fold. Batiscombe rose and bowed low to Madame de Charleroi.
She nodded pleasantly as to an old acquaintance, and
gave him her hand. He turned a little pale under
the sunburnt bronze of his face.

"I am glad to see you," said she. "I thought you
had probably been shipwrecked in that boat of yours.
It was in all the papers, you know."

"The sea would not be so ill-bred as to swallow me up before I had had the honour of making my homage to you, madame," said Batiscombe with a bow and a smile.

It is so easy to say pretty things in French, and as every one does it no one ever knows the genuine from the spurious. Diana was well used to Batiscombe's ways, and she laughed a little. But somehow Leonora did not like the speech. The English part of her revolted against a generality of gallant language, though her Russian blood made it quite possible for her to accept such things as genuine when addressed to herself.

Breakfast was announced.

"Mon Dieu," exclaimed Marcantonio, smiling at everybody, "it is the most charming quartette imaginable. But there arises a terrible question of precedence. I must evidently give my arm to my wife or to my sister. It is very grave. Mesdames, I pray you, select."

"Of course," said Leonora, "Diana is the guest. It is to her that you must give your arm; and Monsieur Batiscombe must console himself as he can."

Everybody smiled politely, as people do over the inanities of a very cheerful and hospitable host.

"Thank you," said Batiscombe in English, as he and Leonora followed the other couple into the breakfast-room at a little distance.

It became the duty of Batiscombe and the two ladies to make Marcantonio believe that they were all enjoying themselves and each other immensely; their duty it was — the sacred and unavoidable duty of society towards its entertainers. Batiscombe found the situation very unpleasant. Diana wished the week well over, and bore her part with the unfaltering serenity and cheerfulness that well-bred sovereigns exhibit when they are obliged to do some of the thousand disagreeable things that make up most of their lives. Leonora was beginning to be quite sure she could never like Diana. How could she like a woman who assumed airs of superiority? Diana was not in the least like the young ladies whom she knew in Rome, and whom, she promised herself, she would rule with a rod of iron now that she was married. And Marcantonio smiled and said all the pleasantest things he could imagine; and they were many, for pleasantness was his strong point. Batiscombe seconded him to the best of his ability, and every now and then reflected for an instant on the extraordinary position in which he found himself.

Indeed, he had cause to wonder at the strangeness of fate. There he sat, eating his breakfast between the woman who had dominated him all his life, and the woman who fascinated him in the present, with ample opportunity to compare them with each other, and a determination not to do it. It seemed as though Diana's coming had roused his instincts of contrariety, as it had in Leonora, though for quite different reasons. Diana knew well enough, he thought, that she ruled him and could bring him to her feet in a moment. Why, then, if she did not want him herself, did she come and disturb his peace and happiness? She need not have prevented him from enjoying the society of a charming woman, but she undoubtedly would. He knew well enough that her presence must be a check on the daily and hourly intercourse with Leonora which he just now most desired. She would not believe in the friendship which had seemed so real to Leonora and so possible to himself. She would watch him with those grey eyes of hers that knew him so well, and when she had an opportunity, she would give him a wholesome lecture on the error of his ways. He knew Diana well, and she knew him better.

He was forced to confess that she was more beautiful, more stately, and more perfect now, at eight and twenty, than she had been ten years ago at eighteen; that, if she lifted her finger to him now, he would be more entirely her servant and slave than ever before; and that in the bottom of his heart he wished she would do so, as he wished no other thing in the world. At the same time he knew perfectly well that she would not, and he thought it was not fair of her to disturb an innocent friendship which had, by force of circumstances, assumed a peculiar aspect. She excited in him all the obstinacy which attends weakness —and Julius was a weak man where women were concerned. And whether he would or not, he made up his mind not to relinquish his daily enjoyment of talking to Leonora for all the Dianas in the world,— if it were only to please his own vanity.

The repast was somehow or other a success so far as Marcantonio was concerned. He felt that everything was proceeding as it should, that all his little plans had turned out well, and that he was a happy husband and a happy brother. He was in complete ignorance of Julius Batiscombe's daily visits to his wife during his absence. She had meant to tell him, honestly, how pleasant it had all been, and how much she had enjoyed it; but, somehow, the invitation to Batiscombe to stay in the house had made her put it off. Marcantonio was so odd about some things, and he was sure to want so many explanations; she could tell him just as well after Diana and Batiscombe were gone; and then, of course, it could not matter so much. She knew that Julius would never refer to all those days unless she herself did. If only that terrible Diana did not see or find out! How dreadful it would be to have her say anything to Marcantonio!

CHAPTER XII.

A COUNTRY-HOUSE is a glass house. The more people there are staying in it, the more fragile and delicate are the walls, and the more probability there is that some one will be inspired by the Evil One to throw stones. Sometimes it happens that two or three of a party fight a pitched battle, and then some lucky lovers who have nothing to do with the hostilities are forgotten and overlooked in the din of war. But if there is one thing in the world more certain to get out than murder it is love, righteous or unrighteous. Lovers who desire secrecy should never go to country-houses together.

It seems to them as though each and every member of the household had especially adopted a set of vile and pernicious habits; a determination to be where they ought not, at all sorts of unexpected hours; to come skulking round corners under the empty pretext of seeking shade, and to be found lurking in wooded dells on pretence of studying natural history. There is the matutinal fiend, who shaves at the window in the grey dawn and sees people who have got up for an early walk; and, verily, they feel like worms when they glance up and see his beak and talons at the casement. There is also the demon that walketh in darkness, smoking a midnight cigar on the lawn before going to bed. There is the midday dragon, green-eyed and loathly to behold, who steals out in old gloves and a parasol immediately after luncheon, because she has left her glasses on the mossy seat under the trees, just out of sight of the house, and must needs find them. There is the vile and sickening bookworm, with his bland smile and unhealthy complexion, who dives into the library in the middle of the summer's afternoon, and ruthlessly opens the blinds to find a quotation, the eighteenth volume of an uncut rarity in vellum; and who wrinkles disagreeably all over when he observes the couple in the corner, staring like blushing owls in the sudden glare.

And, besides all these, there are the low earth-spirits, — a swarm of maids, butlers, grooms, stable-boys, and nurses, — who are supposed to dwell somewhere, underground, and are everlastingly appearing, like phantoms, noiseless and awful, with ears like vast trumpets of endless capacity and eyes of incalculable magnifying power.

A country-house is a terrible test of all the great virtues of mankind and a fearful reflector of all the vices. It is well to begin life in the country with an adequate certainty that, whatever you do, you will be found out, and that you will often be found out when you have done nothing. And a villa hired in the orange gardens of Sorrento, overhanging the murmuring sea and sweet with the breath of the rich south, is not different in this respect from a York-shire manor-house, a château in the south of France, or a "romantic retreat" on the Hudson River.

For two or three days after the events just chron-icled, Leonora and Batiscombe managed successfully to spend several hours out of the twenty-four in each other's society. Marcantonio was busy during a great part of the time with correspondence con-cerning the politics of his party, and once he went over to Naples to see an eminent person on business. The four inmates of the house met at meals, and in the late afternoon, when they generally went out in the boat. Donna Diana occasionally sat with Leo-nora for an hour, and they talked to each other studiously, Leonora trying her best to make the time pleasant for Diana, and Diana doing what she could to cultivate her acquaintance with Leonora. At the end of two days it was perfectly clear that the two women would never be intimate. But they both concealed the fact from Marcantonio; and he rubbed his hands, and wrote his letters, and bought cartloads of things for his wife, in the comforting assurance that she was very happy and inclined to follow his wishes in regard to his sister.

But Diana was not given to looking after Leonora when she was out of her sight, and she spent a great part of the day in writing letters, in reading, and now and then in calling on a few acquaintances who lived along the shore in the villas towards Castella-mare. She was glad that Batiscombe kept out of

her way, but she did not exactly understand why he
did so.   He was generally extremely anxious to see
as much as possible of her when he was in her neighbourhood.   Could it be that he did not love her any
longer?   That after all these years he had at last put
her out of his mind?   Perhaps so.   She was glad if
it were so, most truly.   She had many times prayed
with her whole soul that he might forget her.   It
might be that the prayer was answered.   At all
events, he kept out of her way, and she did not
regret it, nor ever give him a sign to come to her.
She supposed that he spent his hours with Leonora
or Marcantonio or both, and there was no reason why
he should not be intimate in the house, so far as she
herself was concerned.

One day it chanced that the wind was in the southeast, blowing a hot blast and making everything very
hazy and sultry that was out of its reach, and cover-
ing everything it touched with a disagreeable mixture
of dust and hot dampness.   Every one who has lived
in Italy knows what the scirocco is like, and the dismal stickiness it brings.   It seems as though the
universe were under a press and some one were
screwing it down.

It was three o'clock in the afternoon, and Madame
de Charleroi was sitting in her small boudoir, trying
to write a letter to her husband.   Unlike most Italians, she had not the habit of sleeping in the day,
and used the time when other people were taking
a nap during the great heat to keep up an extensive

correspondence. She was a woman who had made this one interest for herself, and thoroughly enjoyed being in constant communication with a dozen intelligent people in all parts of the world.

It was excessively hot. Even she, who was southern born and did not mind it, felt her brain grow dizzy and her fingers tired and clammy. Leonora's white kitten had strayed into the room after lunch, and was walking about near the door, squeaking now and then as though it did not like the quarters and wanted to get out. For the mere sake of changing her position, Diana laid down her pen and rose to open the door. As she did so the cat jumped nimbly through, and a little breath of cooler air blew in from the passage. Diana stood one moment as though enjoying it, and then went out. She took a parasol in the hall, and walked slowly down the garden. The sky was overcast with a dull leaden grey, and the southeast wind blew under the trees, bad enough in itself, but infinitely better than the close heat indoors. There was no one to be seen, and Diana paced slowly along the gravel path. At the end of it were the steps which led through the rocks to the sea.

She had gone down and come up again more than once with the rest of the party in the evening, when they had been out in the boat, and she had thought each time that it would be pleasant to come and sit in some of the cool archways and look out over the sea in the heat of the day. She felt sure, too, of being alone there; it was not a likely place for any one to frequent at three o'clock in the afternoon. Diana closed her parasol, and, just lifting the skirt of her white dress off the ground, began to descend the broad stone steps, hewn out of the solid rock, through a steep vaulted tunnel in the inside of the cliff. Here and there a great arched window looked out, in which were cut wide seats.

She had passed through the darkest part of the descent, carefully picking her way, when she suddenly found herself opposite to one of these windows. She was startled to see two persons there, for she had been certain that she would be alone. They were Leonora and Batiscombe, sitting side by side under the arched opening. Hearing her tread they both looked round, and Julius seemed to pick up from the floor something which had probably fallen while they were talking. Then he remained standing, and Diana, seeing she was discovered, advanced boldly toward the pair. There was nothing so extraordinary in the situation after all, but she had always supposed that Leonora slept in the afternoon while Batiscombe and Marcantonio smoked and talked politics up-stairs. They had certainly been sitting very near together, she thought, but the sudden glare of the light and the distance which separated her from them had prevented her from noticing their faces. As she came near, Leonora rose also and spoke first. She held her back to the light, for she was blushing deeply; but Batiscombe, who never blushed and rarely turned pale, stood calmly pulling his moustache, as though it were all the most natural thing in the world.

"I had always meant to tell you how delightful it is here," said Leonora. "I am so glad you have found it out for yourself."

"En effet," answered Madame de Charleroi calmly smiling, "it is ideal." She came under the arch and looked out, enjoying the sight of the sea after the dark passages.

"And then," said Leonora, "it is strictly true that one is 'not at home' when one is here, — if people call, it is very convenient. Nobody can find one."

"Excepting Madame de Charleroi," said Batiscombe, who was very angry at the interruption.

But he said it so pleasantly and with such an air of paying a compliment, that Diana could not be offended; she only smiled a little bitterly in her lofty way, remembering other times when he would have given his right hand for a meeting of any kind with her.

In that moment a suspicion crossed Diana's mind. She understood the meaning of his remark perfectly, in spite of the bow and the smile, knowing, as she did, every intonation of his voice and every expression of his face. She saw that he was angry, and she argued that Julius preferred being with Leonora to being with herself. That was clearly the reason why he kept out of her way; he spent his time with Leonora. If Leonora attracted him, he was certainly at liberty to talk to her if he pleased, but Diana thought it must be a strong attraction indeed that kept him away from herself. It was long since he had missed an opportunity of spending an hour with his old love.

Diana sat down beside Leonora, and Batiscombe leaned against the rock and looked out over the sea, the fire dancing in his blue eyes, but his face as calm as ever. Diana began to talk to Leonora.

"You are very fortunate in getting such a place," she said. "It is by far the most beautiful on the whole shore."

"I wish it belonged to us," said Leonora. "I am sure I could come here every year and never grow tired of it."

"Ah!" exclaimed Diana, "do you like it so very much then?"

"J'en raffole!" answered Leonora enthusiastically, "I am crazy about it. And then, it is always so charming to have absolutely the best. As you say, there is nothing like this place on the whole bay. I should like always to have the best."

"But, madame," remarked Batiscombe, "it appears to me that you always do. You have the talent of supremacy."

"What an idea! The talent of supremacy!"

"But that is precisely it," continued Julius. "It is a talent. Some people are born with it — generally women."

"That is Monsieur Batiscombe's favourite theory," remarked Madame de Charleroi, just glancing at him, "but he does not believe it the least in the world."

"Is it true?" asked Leonora, innocently, looking up with an expression that did not escape Diana. It was a sort of frightened look, as though it really mattered to her what Batiscombe thought about women in general.

"It pleases madame to be witty," answered Julius, glancing in his turn at Diana. "I have not many theories, but I believe in them as a man who is about to be guillotined believes in death."

"One cannot say more than that," laughed Leonora. "But how about the supremacy of men? There have been more men in the world who have ruled it than there have ever been women."

"Mon Dieu! Men give themselves much more trouble," he replied. "Women, having the divine right given to them straight from Heaven, exercise it without difficulty. A word, a cup of tea, a glance, — and the supremacy of a woman is established. What could a man do with a cup of tea? Or, if he looked at people by the hour together, could he rule them with a glance? When a woman has the gift she finds little difficulty in using it, — whereas the more of it a man has, the more trouble it is to him. Men are so stupid!" And with this sweeping condemnation of his own sex, Julius lit a cigarette, having obtained permission of the two ladies.

"You ought not to have many friends, with such ideas about men," said Leonora.

"En effet," said Diana, "he has none."

"Not among men, at all events," said Julius. "I

do not remember ever having any. I do not sleep
any the worse on that account, I assure you. It is
much more agreeable to have a number of pleasant
acquaintances, who expect nothing from you and
from whom you expect nothing. Friendship implies
mutual obligations; I detest that."

Leonora laughed a little. He had such a vicious
way of saying such things, as though he thoroughly
meant them. But then he was courteous and gentle
to every one, though she suspected he might be different if he were angry. Diana knew very well that
what he said was true, and that he had led an isolated life among other men, fighting his way through
with his own hand and owing no man anything.
She herself had for years been his best friend and his
only confidant, though he saw her rarely enough.
And now she felt as though even that one bond of
his were to be broken, — and whether she would or
not, the thought gave her pain, and she wished it
could be otherwise.

"It is always far more amusing to detest things,"
said Leonora, "unless you happen to want them."
She was forgetting some of her indifferentism.

"It is certainly more blessed to abuse than to be
abused," returned Julius, "and, if one has the choice,
it is as well to be the hammer and not the anvil. I
am an excessively good-natured person, and if I had
friends, they would make an anvil of me and beat
my brains out, — and then I should starve."

"Good-natured people are always made to suffer,"

said Leonora thoughtfully. "I am not in the least good-natured."

"I remember," said Diana, "that Mr. Batiscombe used to say good-nature was a mixture of laziness and vulgarity."

"Yes," answered Julius. "You have a good memory, madame. Good-nature is a compound of the laziness that cannot say 'no,' and of the vulgarity which desires to please every one indiscriminately. I suppose I possess both those faults very finely developed."

"Fortunately," remarked Leonora, "goodness and good-nature are not the same."

"Fortunately for you, Marchesa, — unfortunately for me," said Julius.

"It is too complicated — please explain," she answered.

"As you are so fortunate as to possess goodness without good-nature," said he, "you should be glad that the two are not one and the same, since good-nature is not a desirable quality. I am good-natured, but not good — I wish I were!"

"Ah, I see!" exclaimed Diana. "It was a compliment."

"Of course," said Julius.

"Of course; but your compliments are often complicated, as the Marchesa says."

Diana smiled as she spoke. Batiscombe knew that she was repaying him for the remark he had made when she had unexpectedly appeared twenty minutes earlier.

"I can only repeat," he retorted, "that Madame de Charleroi has a good memory."

Leonora was puzzled. She saw well enough that Diana and Julius were, or had been, much more intimate than she had supposed. They understood each other at a glance, by a word, and they seemed on the verge of quarrelling politely over nothing. She devoutly wished that Diana would go away, instead of spoiling her afternoon. But Diana leaned back against the rock and crossed her feet and prepared to be comfortable. She was evidently not going. Batiscombe stood motionless, with the easy stolidity of a very strong man who does not wish to move, and Leonora could see his bold profile against the grey haze of the sky. There was a short silence after his last remark, during which Leonora felt uneasy: something was in the atmosphere that made her anxious, and she did not like the way Diana looked at Batiscombe, with an air of absolute superiority, as though she could do anything she pleased with him.

"How dreadfully solemn we are," said Leonora, rather awkwardly. Julius turned quickly with a laugh.

"Let us be gay," he said. "I hate solemnity, unless there is enough of it to make me laugh. I remember being at a ball once that produced that effect."

"Allons!" said Diana, "give us some of your reminiscences, Monsieur Batiscombe. They ought to be interesting."

"Not so much as you think. But the ball was very funny. It was in Guatemala, three years ago. I was invited to a huge thing by the president — an entirely new president, too, who had just cut the throats of the old president and of all his relations. I believe there was some sort of revolution at the time, and when it was over the victorious individual gave a ball. The refreshments were simple — brandy for the men and rosolio for the ladies; there was no compromise in the shape of a biscuit or a glass of water."

Leonora laughed, being willing to laugh at anything so as to encourage Julius to talk.

"En vérité, that was very amusing," remarked Diana coldly. Batiscombe took no notice.

"The women sat round the room in a double row," he continued, "like a court ball, excepting that they all smoked large cigars, and industriously passed the liqueur. The men stood behind and gave their undivided attention to the brandy. Not a soul spoke, and they all scowled fiercely at the brandy, the rosolio, and each other. A ghastly and tuneless quartette of instruments doled out a melancholy dirge, slower than anything you ever heard at a funeral; and now and then some enterprising and funereal man led out a less enterprising but equally melancholy female in a strange step, like the tormented ghost of a waltz in chains. It was so hideous that I went out and laughed till I almost had a fit. I have never thought anything seemed very solemn since then — it destroyed the proportion in my brain. A pauper's burial on a rainy day in London is a wildly gay entertainment compared with that ball."

Leonora laughed, and even Diana smiled; whereupon Julius was satisfied, and relapsed into silence. But Leonora wanted conversation.

"What in the world took you to Guatemala, Mr. Batiscombe?" she asked.

"That is a question which I cannot answer, Marchesa," he replied. "I believe I went there for some reason or other — chiefly because I could go for nothing, and wanted to see something new."

"Can you always go to Guatemala for nothing?" asked Leonora. "It must be very amusing."

"A steamer company offered me a free passage to any port in their service," said Batiscombe; "and as the next ship went to Guatemala, I sailed with her. It happened to be first on the list."

"What a queer idea!" exclaimed Leonora.

"You are too modest, Mr. Batiscombe," said Diana. "You ought to tell the whole story — it is very interesting." Her voice was less cold than when she had spoken last.

"Oh, do tell the story!" cried Leonora. "I adore autobiographies!"

"Mon Dieu!" said Julius, "there is very little to tell. I did a service to a ship belonging to the company, and in acknowledgment they presented me with a piece of plate and the free passage in question.

Voilà tout! madame is too good when she says it was interesting."

"If Monsieur Batiscombe will not be so obliging as to relate the experience, I will," said Diana. "He shall correct me if I make a mistake."

Batiscombe looked annoyed. He was not fond of telling his own adventures, and he hated to hear them told by other people. He could not imagine why Diana wanted to hear the story. He was irritated already, and her conduct seemed more and more inexplicable. Leonora looked at him expectantly.

Who can understand a woman? It may be that Diana, who was really fond of him in a strange fashion, was sorry for the position she had taken that afternoon, and was willing to atone by giving him the credit before Leonora of some fine action he had done.

"It was three years ago or more, in the winter," began Diana. "Monsieur Batiscombe was travelling in a ship on the coast of America. There were a hundred passengers on board, or more, and a crew of thirty-five. Is that exact?"

Julius bent his head and turned away.

"Eh bien, there was a great storm — such as there are in the ocean. It is horrible, you may imagine. The ship was driven on the rocks, a long distance from the shore. A reef, you call it, n'est-ce-pas?"

"Yes," said Batiscombe. "Fifty or sixty yards from the shore."

"Good. What do they do? Six brave sailors

volunteer to throw themselves into the sea in a cha-
loupe — a miserable boat " —

"And monsieur was one of the volunteers " —
exclaimed Leonora, enthusiastically.

"Not at all, my dear friend. The boat overturns;
the sailors are immediately drowned; every one is in
consternation. Then Monsieur Batiscombe arrives;
he says he will save everybody; he ties a thin line —
a mere string — to his waist; he throws himself to
the sea. The passengers scream as they cling to the
ropes and the side, while the vessel is beaten horribly
on the reef. He struggles in the waves, swimming;
he is thrown down again and again in the breakers;
he rises and rushes on to the shore. Then he pulls
the string, and after the string a rope. A sailor
ventures down and he also reaches the land. They
fasten the rope, and every one is saved — passengers,
crew, captain, tout le monde. Ah, Batiscombe, why
are you not always doing such things, — you, who
can do them so well?"

Madame de Charleroi's grey eyes were wide and
bright, and a very faint colour rose to her cheeks as
she told the story. The calm, regal woman took a
genuine delight in great actions, and as she turned to
Julius at the end there was a ring of real sympathy
and friendship and regret in her voice that it gave
Leonora a strange sensation to hear.

"It was magnificently brave!" exclaimed Leonora
in English, and she looked at Julius as though she
admired him with all her heart and soul.

She had always had a feeling that he had probably made himself remarkable in such ways, but he always had told her that his life had been uneventful. To think that this calm, smooth, well-dressed, fine gentleman should have saved a whole shipload of lives by sheer strength and courage! Ah, he was a man, indeed!

But Batiscombe never moved. He stood looking seaward, his eyelids half closed, and a thoughtful look on his brown face. Indeed, he was thinking deeply, but not so much of the old story Diana had been telling as of herself. The strange appeal in her last words had touched the good chord in his wayward heart, and he was thinking how fair his life might have been with her, — and how dark it had been without her. And the old true love rose up for one moment, hiding Leonora and the rest, and all the intervening years, and sending hot words to his ready lips. He turned in the act to speak, forgetting where he was, — then checked himself. Both Leonora and Diana had seen that he was going to say something, for they were watching him. He hesitated.

"I ought to thank you, madame," he said to Diana, "for gilding my adventure so richly. But as for the thing itself, and the doing of such things, the opportunity seldom offers, and the faculty for doing them is the result of an excellent digestion and quiet nerves. Meanwhile it is grown cooler, and the boats are below. Shall we go down, and sail a little before dinner?"

The two ladies consented readily enough, and they all descended to the landing and got into one of the boats and pushed away.

"I shall have quite a new sensation in future when I sail with you, Mr. Batiscombe," said Leonora. "It would be impossible to be drowned with you on board."

But Diana was pale again, and settled herself among the cushions in silence.

Far up above, Marcantonio was interviewing the coachman on the terrace. He looked down and saw the boat shoot out with the three members of his household. He rubbed his hands smoothly together.

"Ha," he said to himself, "it is superb! What good friends they are all growing to be! En vérité, Batiscombe is a most amiable man, full of tact."

CHAPTER XIII.

LATE that evening Julius was sitting in a corner of the broad terrace over the sea. The clouds had cleared away before the light easterly breeze that springs up at night, and the stars shone brightly. Down in the west the young moon had set, and the air was fresh and cool after the long, hot day. Julius had drawn an arm-chair away from the house and was smoking solemnly, in enjoyment of the night. He found that he had much to think of. The rest of the household had gone to bed, or at all events had retired to their rooms.

It had been a day of emotions with him, and that was unusual, to begin with. His feeling for Leonora was growing to great proportions. He knew that very well; and in spite of the momentary burst of passion, which, if he had been alone with Madame de Charleroi, would have found expression in words which he would have regretted and she would have resented, he now felt that he was irritated against her and could not forgive her inopportune interruption. All his opposition was roused; and as if in despite of his old love he dwelt on the thoughts of the present, and delighted in recalling the details of the fair Marchesa's conversation, the quickly changing expression of her face, the tones of her voice, the grace of her movements. She was so strong and living that he felt his whole being permeated with the atmosphere and essence of her life.

As he leaned back in his chair, he experienced a sensation by no means new to him, of intense delight in existence, and he breathed in the soft fresh air, and tasted that it was the breath of love.

A small, short step sounded on the tiles of the terrace, coming toward his corner. He looked round quickly, and was aware of the tall and graceful figure of Diana de Charleroi, muffled in something dark, but unmistakable in its outline and stately presence. In a moment she was beside him; he rose and threw away his cigarette, somewhat astonished.

"Get another chair," said she, in a low voice. "It is pleasant here."

He obeyed quickly and noiselessly, as he did everything. She had taken his chair, and he sat down beside her, waiting for her to speak.

"I thought I should find you here, Julius," she said, calling him by his Christian name without the smallest hesitation. "I wanted to speak to you alone."

"You have the faculty of finding me," said Julius with a short, low laugh.

"Since when is it so disagreeable to you?" asked Diana.

Julius was silent, for there was nothing he could say. He wished he had said nothing at first, — it would have been much better. Diana continued.

"You and I know each other well enough to talk freely," she said. "We need not beat about the bush and say pretty things to each other, and I forgive you for being rude, because I know you very well, and am willing to sacrifice something. But I will not forgive you again if you are rude in public. There are certain things one does not permit one's self, when one is a gentleman."

"You are very good, Diana," said Batiscombe, humbly. "I am very sorry. I lost my temper."

"Naturally," she answered coolly. "You always lose your temper, — you always did, — and yet you fancy continually that you hide it. Let that go. I have forgiven you for this time, because I am the best friend you have."

"The only one," said Julius.

"Perhaps. You are well hated, I can tell you. Then treat me as a friend in future, if you please, and not as an inquisitive acquaintance who makes a point of annoying you for her own ends."

She spoke calmly, in a quiet, determined voice, without the slightest hesitation or affectation. Julius bent his head.

"I always mean to," he said.

"Now listen to me," she continued. "I came upon you this afternoon by pure accident. I do not owe you any apology for that, and you know very well that I am the last person in the world to do things in that way, by stealth. That is the reason I come to you here, at night, to tell you my mind frankly."

" Yes," said Batiscombe, in a muffled voice, "I know."

"I came upon you by accident," said she, "and I made a discovery. You pass your afternoons in the society of my sister-in-law, and you lose your temper with me when I find you together, — though you always wish me to understand that you prefer my society to that of any woman in the world."

"Ah — how you express it!" exclaimed Julius.

"I express it as plainly as I can. I cannot help it if you do not like it. It is all true. And the inference is perfectly clear. Do you see?"

"No," said Batiscombe.

"You do not? Very well, I will draw it for you."

She leaned back in the chair and looked at him; her eyes were accustomed by this time to the gloom, and she could see him quite clearly in the starlight. He moved uneasily.

"Pray go on," he said.

"The inference is this. You are making love to Leonora Carantoni."

"You shall not say that," said Batiscombe, between his teeth, still looking fiercely at her.

"You might forbid a man to say it," answered Diana, in low, calm tones. "And for anything I care you may forbid any other woman in the world to say it. But you cannot forbid me. I have the right."

"In that case," said Julius, rising, and struggling

to speak quietly, "there is nothing I can do but to leave you, since I will certainly not listen."

But Diana rose also, and laid her white hand on his arm, as though she could have bowed the strong man to the earth if she chose. She seemed taller than he in the power and determination of her gesture.

"Sit down instantly," she said, under her breath.

Julius obeyed silently and sullenly. Then Diana resumed her seat.

"I have the right, Julius," she continued, "not because you pretend to have loved me for ten years, — nor because I once thought I might accept your love, — nor yet because I am sometimes weak enough to like you still, in a sisterly way. But I have the right because you are making love to my brother's wife, because she is young and innocent, and because there is not another human being in the world to stand by her, or to give her any protection in her danger."

"If you think that, why do you not tell your brother so?"

"Do you call yourself intelligent? Do you call yourself a gentleman?" exclaimed Diana in bitter scorn. "Would you have me destroy the peace of my brother and of his wife, because you are doing a bad action, that has not yet borne fruit? Do you think I am afraid of you? Of you?" She repeated the word almost between her teeth.

"No," said Batiscombe, under his breath, "I **do** not. But I would like to ask you a question."

"I will answer," said Diana.

"Why did you tell that absurd story about me this afternoon? Did you not see it was just the very worst thing you could possibly do, from your own point? That nothing rouses a woman's interest like such tales?"

"I promised to answer your question," said Diana, coldly, "and I will. I told the story thoughtlessly, because I am a woman, and admire such things quite independently of the person who has done them. Do not flatter yourself that a woman like Leonora Carantoni will fall in love with you because you are brave. But I dare say I did wrong, and I am sorry for it. You have qualities which any one may admire, but you have others which I despise."

"I despise them myself, sometimes," said Julius, almost to himself.

"Despise them always,—at least, and be consistent," answered Diana. "But you will not. You like them, those bad qualities, and when you like them, they make a miserable wretch of you, as they do now. You know well enough, however cleverly you may deceive yourself, that you ought not to be here. You stay,—you are a coward, besides being a great many worse things which I leave you to understand."

Batiscombe's eyes flashed angrily in the starlight.

"You are cruel, Diana, and unkind," he said.

Diana was silent a moment, and she drew her dark lace shawl about her, as though she were cold.

When she spoke her voice was infinitely soft and gentle.

"Do not say that, Julius. Do not say I am ever cruel to you, — for to you, of all people in the world, I would be most kind."

Julius bent down and pressed his hands to his temples, and sighed heavily.

"Oh, Diana," he groaned, "I know it, I know it."

"Then I will not say any more. Do this thing because it is right, — not because I ask you to. Have I ever reproached you before, when you have come to me of your own accord and told me your troubles? What right have I to reproach you?"

Julius was silent. He knew in his heart that she had the right, because he still loved her best. He sat immovable, his head buried in his hands. Diana rose and stood beside him; she lightly laid her hand upon his shoulder, allowing it to linger kindly for a moment, and then she turned and moved away.

The spell was broken, and Batiscombe rose swiftly and followed her. There was a light in the drawing-room that opened upon the terrace, which Batiscombe had not noticed before. As they entered they found Marcantonio with a candle, overturning books and papers as if in search of something. He looked up with a curious expression of surprise in his face, holding the candle before him.

"Ah!" he cried, "good-evening, my friends. You have been taking a little air. Eh? I imagined that you were all asleep."

Madame de Charleroi smiled serenely at her brother. She knew it was an accident, and that he had a habit of forgetting things and coming to look for them. She said it had been hot all day, and she and Monsieur Batiscombe had been enjoying the coolness of the terrace. Julius bowed blandly and said good-night. But he suspected Marcantonio of having come to watch his sister. They passed on, and Marc-antonio stood for a moment looking after them as they went out into the hall, where lights were still burning. He shrugged his shoulders.

"Eh!" he exclaimed aloud to himself, in Italian, "I do not understand anything about it — ma proprio niente." And he continued his search for the missing letter, pondering deeply.

Batiscombe spent a sleepless night, which was very unusual with him. The interview with Diana had made a deep impression on him at the time. He knew that whenever she was at hand to exert her influence he should succumb to it. But as the night wore on, the strength of the impression diminished, and the old feeling of obstinate defiance gradually returned. At all events, he thought, he would show her that her suspicions were empty, and that nothing — no harm, at least — could come of his intimacy with Leonora. He would also be sure that if Diana interrupted another interview it could hardly be by accident. Such accidents did not occur every day. In the early dawn he rose and went down in his slippers to the sea, and bathed in the cool salt water, and smoked a cigarette on the rocks, and another in the archway where the scene of the previous afternoon had occurred. Then he went up to the house and walked round it, and surveyed the various angles, and terraces, and balconies, and eccentricities of patchwork architecture that made up the dwelling. Suddenly he stopped as though an idea had struck him.

Houses in the south have often as many as five or six broad terraces, of various sizes and at various elevations, built from time to time to suit the taste and convenience of the owners. The strong brown vines grow up leafless from the ground till they reach the trellis, and then spread out into luxuriant foliage and a multiplicity of rich fruit-bearing branches, making a thick shade, into which even the noonday sun finds it hard to penetrate. Julius had just observed that there was a large terrace of this kind which he had not yet noticed, having been but a very few days at liberty to wander alone about the place. It was as high as the first floor, and on the side toward Castellamare, facing the sea. He had been in Marcantonio's room, and knew that it did not open upon this terrace, and Leonora's apartment was on the other side of the house. Obviously this balcony belonged to Madame de Charleroi's rooms, or was attached to some vacant part of the building. It struck him that if it were vacant, it would be a very agreeable spot in which to pass the afternoon. He thought he might mention it to Leonora that morning, and find out if it were available, since their retreat in the rocks had been invaded. It had the advantage of being large, so that people seated upon it could not be seen from below, and the thick vines would prevent their being seen from above.

He spoke to the Marchesa about it as soon as they were alone for a moment after breakfast. She went quietly and surveyed the place, ascertained that it corresponded with a set of rooms which were not in use, the house being very large and irregular, and agreed that she should spend the afternoon there with Julius, since the sun would then be on the other side. There were long window-doors opening to the ground, of which the blinds were fastened, and only the middle one was left open to give access to the terrace. It was delightful, because it was in the house, so to say, and open to every one, and yet no one knew of it. Why should they not sit there? It was much better than going and hiding in the rocks with an air of secrecy, in order to be annoyed by that terrible Diana! Much better! Though, after all, they need not have troubled themselves, for Diana went out at three o'clock in the carriage to pay a visit.

Accordingly, Leonora and Julius passed a very pleasant afternoon together, and when it was late they found Marcantonio, and made him go out in the boat for an hour or two, and everything was very agreeable. Marcantonio was greatly relieved at finding that his sister was away from Batiscombe, and he talked his best, and really made Leonora take an interest in his conversation. She could always find him better company when she had been with Julius for some time and had said all the things she wanted to say, and which Marcantonio would not have understood.

The next day Marcantonio was obliged to go to Naples on very urgent business. An ex-royalty who sympathised with Carantoni's party, and was now in exile, had come to Naples for a day or two incognito — quite as though he had never been a royalty at all, and Marcantonio felt it his duty to go and salute the august personage according to ancient custom. He therefore left the house at an early hour, to return at dusk. He thought his sister and his wife could chaperone each other for a day without danger. But he said to himself that if he had found Diana alone with Batiscombe again he would not have gone.

The morning passed away as usual. Batiscombe, relying on the afternoon for his hours with Leonora, only stayed down-stairs till she was joined by Diana, and then retired to his room, where he wrote or read in solitude, as the fancy took him. The three break-fasted together at one o'clock; then Madame de Charleroi retired to her rooms, and in the course of a quarter of an hour Leonora and Julius were installed for the afternoon in their newly-found situation on the disused terrace.

Diana's boudoir was a corner room in the front of

the house, facing the sea, and opening, by one window, on a narrow stone balcony running the whole
length of the building; the other window was on the
right side, and if she could have undone the blinds
she would have seen that it opened upon the large
terrace already mentioned. But the aforesaid blinds
had resisted her efforts, and, as she supposed that
they were closed for some purpose, she said nothing
about it, merely opening the glass to admit the air.
Leonora, who did not know the house thoroughly,
and had a habit of leaving everything to the servants,
was not aware of this, and did not realise the exact
position of Diana's sitting-room. Batiscombe, of
course, had taken her assurance that this side of the
house was uninhabited. Accordingly, it came to pass
that when he and Leonora installed themselves, they
took up their position immediately outside Diana's
window, under the shadow of the wall.

Madame de Charleroi, on this particular day, did
not go into her boudoir at once, but spent some time
in her bedroom. When she was ready to begin
writing, she passed through the door and sat at her
desk. She at once heard the sound of voices outside, but she did not listen, nor stop to think who the
talkers might be.

Presently, however, the continued sound annoyed
her, forced its way through the blinds, and prevented
her from writing. They were speaking English.
She understood the language, being a cultivated
woman of the world, and the wife of a diplomatist,
though she avoïded speaking it.

The strong, earnest voice of Julius Batiscombe, — the pleading, protesting, yet yielding tones of Leonora, always dominated by the passionate eloquence of the man, and ever answering more weakly, — all this she heard, and she sat stony and wild-eyed with horror, realising in a moment the whole hideous proportions of the phrases.

Diana de Charleroi was the noblest and most honourable of women. Under other circumstances, if the voices had been those of strangers or indifferent people, she would not have hesitated an instant, but would have given some unmistakable sign of her presence. But this thing was too near her, it was a too horrible realisation of what she had dimly foreseen as possible, when she had spoken such strong words two nights earlier.

It was too utterly and unspeakably awful. Her brother's wife, — not three months married, — and Julius Batiscombe, the man who had for ten years loved herself, — or had made her believe it, — whom she herself had once loved, and had never forgotten!

But Diana was no weak woman, to give way to trouble or danger in the face of it. For a few minutes she bowed her head in her hands, trembling from head to foot, and no longer hearing the quickly spoken words outside. Then she rose to her feet, and made one step toward the closed blinds.

No, she would not put them to open shame. Yet something must be done at once. With one movement of her strong white fingers she overturned the

heavy olive-wood writing table upon the smooth tile
floor with a crash that sounded through the house.
In the silence that followed, she heard a moving of
chairs outside, and the quick tread of departing feet.
Then she went swiftly to her room, heedless of the
streaming ink upon the floor, staining her long white
gown, and trampling the litter of pens and paper
under foot. She threw herself upon her bed and lay
quite still, white as death, and staring at the ceiling.

All the disgrace to her brother's name, — to her
own, — came suddenly upon her, like a nightmare, a
thing that no waking could cast off. All the utter
baseness and unfaithfulness of her old lover was before her, making her scorn and loathe herself for
ever having loved such a man, even in the foolish
haste of a romantic girlhood. Her eyes strained
wildly, striving to shed tears, and could not, and the
whole possible pain of human agony, passing the very
pains of hell, got hold upon her soul.

That night, at dinner, Leonora looked desperately
ill. Her face was white, save for a small red flush
upon each cheek, and her eyes had a strange, furtive
look about them, avoiding all meeting with the look
of the other three persons at table. She said she had
been in the sun, had got a bad headache, and would
go to bed immediately. She had only insisted on
being at dinner in order to greet her husband on his
return from Naples, — but when he touched her she
shrank away, and said she was nervous.

Batiscombe was pale, too, beneath his tan, and

though he looked every one in the face, his eyes were disagreeable to see, having an angry glare in them, like those of a wild beast at bay. He spoke little and drank more wine than usual, after the manner of Englishmen when they are unhappy.

Diana was magnificent. Being often pale in the summer, no one saw any especial change in her appearance, and she threw herself nobly into the breach, asking all manner of questions of her brother concerning his trip, and showing a reasonable amount of sympathy for Leonora. The consequence was that Marcantonio was nearly satisfied, in spite of the strong impression he at first received that something unpleasant had occurred in his absence. But when he had an idea he dwelt upon it, and he promised himself that he would ask many questions of his sister when Leonora had gone to bed.

He accompanied his wife to her apartment when dinner was over, with a solicitude which was perfectly genuine, but which made her tremble at every turn. His careful anxiety lest she should over-tire herself upon the stairs, lest there should be a draught in her room, or, in short, lest anything should be omitted which could conduce to her immediate recovery from the exposure to the sun — so dangerous in the south, he kept repeating — made her almost certain that she was already suspected, and that so much kindness was only preparatory to some dreadful outbreak of reproach.

While Marcantonio was gone, Diana led Batis-

combe out through the drawing-room to the terrace.
Neither spoke till they had reached the end away
from the house, where they had sat together two
nights before.

"Julius Batiscombe," said Diana, her voice trembling with strongly-mastered anger, "you will leave
this house immediately."

"Why, if you please?" he asked, defiantly.

"You know very well why," she answered, turning
full upon him. "Do not ask questions, but go."

"I will do nothing of the kind," said he, folding
his arms and facing her. "You have no earthly
reason to give, save your own caprice."

"I heard your conversation this afternoon outside
my window. It was I who made the noise you heard,
to warn you to be silent." She made the statement
deliberately, choking down her anger, and looking
him in the eyes.

"I heard no noise — I was not outside your window," answered Julius, telling the boldest lie of his
life, and, to say the truth, one of very few, for he
never lied to save himself, with all his faults. "I
was not outside your window," he repeated, "and I
am glad I was not. For, by your own account, you
heard the conversation first, and gave your signal
afterwards."

"Very well," said she. "I will not shame you by
repeating the words I involuntarily heard before I
frightened you away. But you will leave this house
to-morrow all the same. You will also consider that

in future you have no title to cross my threshold, nor to bow to me in the street." She turned swiftly, in utter scorn and disdain. Batiscombe followed her to the door and into the drawing-room, where Marcantonio met them, precisely as he had done before. It was too much for his newly roused suspicions. Something had gone wrong, he was sure, — and why should his sister and Batiscombe be everlastingly alone together on that terrace at night?

"Ah!" he exclaimed, a little sarcastically, "you have again been taking a little air? Well, well, the evenings are very agreeable. If you will, we can sit outside, and monsieur and I will smoke a cigarette."

It was dreary enough, sitting together for an hour and more in the dark. Madame de Charleroi would not speak to Batiscombe, and he confined himself to asking questions of Marcantonio and to general remarks. Marcantonio saw this, and decided that she was playing indifference in public, because she saw enough of Batiscombe in private. The latter did not force the position, but as soon as Donna Diana moved to go in, he bade them both good-night, and went to his room and to his reflections.

There was a long silence after he was gone. Both the brother and sister wanted to be sure that he was out of hearing. Diana spoke first, very gently and kindly.

"Marcantonio," she said, "I have something very important to say to you."

She threw a light paper shade over the bright lamp, and sat herself down beside him on the sofa.

CHAPTER XIV.

DURING the four hours which had elapsed between Madame de Charleroi's involuntary discovery in the afternoon and the dinner hour, she had found time to collect her thoughts and to form a plan of action.

It was absolutely necessary to do something at once, and, if possible, to understand afterwards how Leonora could have allowed herself in so short a time to fall a victim to the eloquence and personal charms of Julius Batiscombe. She wondered vaguely how it were all possible, but in the meantime she knew that the mischief existed, and that she must do her utmost to avert its growth and frightful consequences, since she alone could be of use.

Her first impulse had been to go to the window and disclose herself, whereby she thought she could have put Batiscombe to flight instantly. He could hardly have stayed in the house with her after such a scene as must have followed. But a proud instinct forbade her; she would not have it appear that she could possibly stand to Julius in the position of Leonora's rival. Nor could she have found it in her heart to inflict on her sister-in-law the indelible disgrace of an exposure. All this passed through her mind in a moment, and checked her first step towards the window. She frightened the lovers away by upsetting her table, instead of coming upon them herself, and she knew an hour later that she had thereby lost the power of managing them by anything she could say to Batiscombe. She would not — she could not — go to Leonora and force a confession. Besides, what good would be gained? Leonora was a person to be protected, not attacked. As for Julius, she knew perfectly well, when she led him out to the terrace while Marcantonio was upstairs, that he would deny everything. He could do nothing else, and he did it boldly, though it was of no use. But Diana thought it possible that he would leave the house without a struggle, and abandon the position for a time.

If Julius had been a less passionate man, and a more accomplished villain, if he had loved Leonora less ardently and more designingly, or if he had been less furiously angry against Diana, he would have acted differently. He would have lied just as he had done, but blandly and with a great show of astonishment; he would have made a low bow, answering Diana that he was at all times ready to obey her, and he would have left the house in the morning, with an elaborate excuse to his hosts. But Batiscombe was quite another sort of person. One of the calmest and most diplomatic of men under ordinary circumstances, his passion when roused was wholly uncontrollable. He was madly in love, and madly angry, and he would have cheerfully fought the whole world single-handed for the sake of his love, or of his anger, separately, let alone in the present case, when both were roused to the fiercest pitch.

Diana knew him well, and, after the few words she had exchanged with him on the terrace, she knew what to expect. And she had foreseen the possibility of his refusal to leave the villa, and was prepared for it. The only question of difficulty was to direct Marcantonio's whole anger against Batiscombe, and to shield Leonora as far as possible; but Marcantonio must be told of the danger, since Diana alone was unable to avert it.

She sat beside him on the deep sofa in the drawing-room, and she laid her hand affectionately on his, as though to give him some strength to bear what was in store.

"It is very important," she said, "and you must be very patient. You must give me your word that you will do nothing violent for at least a day, for you will be very angry." She knew that, with all his good nature, she could rely on his courage. He was not easily frightened, after all. He looked earnestly at her, and his face was drawn into a look of determination that sat oddly on his delicate and rather weak features.

"Speak, Diana mia," he said simply. "I will do what I can for you." He supposed, of course, that something had occurred between herself and Batiscombe.

"It is not I," she said, "it is you who are concerned."

"I?" repeated her brother, in some astonishment.

"Yes. You are the person who must act in the matter. You must write a little note to Batiscombe, and tell him that your wife's sudden illness" —

"What? But it is only a little sun — a mere headache," interrupted Marcantonio.

"No matter; — that your wife's sudden illness is so severe that you must beg him to postpone the remainder of his visit to some future time."

Marcantonio looked more and more astonished.

"But I only asked him for a week. He will go of his own accord to-morrow or the day after. I am sorry, Diana, but you said you did not mind meeting him." He spoke seriously, with a puzzled expression on his face.

"It makes no difference," said Diana. "He must go to-morrow morning. He has not behaved honourably to you since he has been in the house."

Her brother looked suddenly very grave, and his voice dropped as he spoke.

"Has he insulted you, Diana?" he asked.

"Yes," said she, in low tones, "he has insulted me. But he has done worse, he has insulted your wife in my hearing."

Marcantonio turned suddenly on the sofa, and grasped his sister's arm as in a vise. His face turned a ghastly colour, and his voice trembled violently.

"Diana — are you telling me the truth?"

Her grey eyes turned honestly and bravely to him.

"You and I never learned to tell lies, Marcantonio. It is true."

She knew well enough that he would never suspect his wife, nor ask a question which could lead to
such a conclusion.   When she said that Batiscombe
had insulted Leonora, she spoke the absolute truth.
What greater insult can man offer an honest woman
than by wittingly forcing upon her an unlawful love?

Marcantonio looked at her one moment, and then
sprang to his feet.   At that instant he could have
killed Julius Batiscombe with his hands, as perhaps
Diana herself would have done.   She seized his hand
as he stood, and drew him toward her.

" No," she said, understanding his thought, "remember your promise.   You must do nothing now —
except write the note."

But Carantoni was in no condition to write notes.
He broke away, and walked wildly up and down the
room, wringing his hands together, and muttering
furious ejaculations.   He was too angry, too much
surprised, too much horrified at his own stupidity
throughout the affair to be able to think clearly.
Diana sat motionless on the sofa, as angry, perhaps,
as he, in her own way, but full of pity and sympathy
for him, and trying to devise some means of helping
him.   She leaned forward, resting her chin on her
hand, and her eyes followed him anxiously in his
quick, irregular walk.   And as she looked he seemed
gradually to fall under her influence, and went and
sat in a deep chair away from her, and buried his
face.

Then Diana rose, and went to the table in the cor-

ner and arranged the light, and wrote, herself, the
note to Batiscombe, leaving a blank at the foot for a
signature. She looked round, and saw her brother
watching her.

"Come, dear boy," she said kindly, "I have written the note for you ; sign it, and I will see that he
gets it in the morning."

Marcantonio rose and came to her with uncertain
steps. He put his hand on her shoulder a moment.
Then he fell on his knees beside her, and pressed her
close to him, silently. Presently he rose, she put
the pen between his fingers, still trembling with his
anger, and he signed the note as best he could.
She put it into an envelope, sealed it, and directed
it to Julius Batiscombe.

"He will be out of the house before we are up,"
she said in a tone of certainty. " Go to bed, dear boy,
and never let him trouble your peace again."

" But I will trouble his peace," answered Marcantonio, bending his smooth brows.

" We will see about that afterwards," said Diana.
" If you think best to fight him, I will not oppose
you ; but we will talk about it. We cannot talk
now. Good-night my dear, dear brother."

She kissed him on the forehead and held both his
hands for a moment, and then led him away. He
obeyed mechanically, and they parted for the night.

Diana often wished her brother were a stronger
man in the ordinary things of life, but she knew that
he was honest, and no coward in danger, and that he

always spoke the truth and kept his word. It was his fault that he always imagined every one to be as honest as himself until the contrary was proved, — after which he never trusted the man again.

Diana went slowly to her room and locked the door behind her. With a candle in her hand she entered the boudoir and looked round upon the scene of the catastrophe. The glass of the long window was still open, and the refractory blinds still closed, the bolts rusted in, beyond her strength to draw them. The servants had raised the desk upright and washed away the ink from the tiles; there was no trace of disorder visible. She could hardly realise that in this neat room, that very day, only a few hours ago, she had passed through one of the most terrible experiences of her life.

She sat down in the chair before the desk and bent her queenly head. She had done her best for the right through that day, but it had all gone by so very quickly that she doubted whether she had done wisely. It seemed as though the burden of it all rested upon her — of the right and of the wrong; and the burden was very heavy. May God in his mercy give strength and courage to all brave women doing the right!

I think that ordinary women have more moral vanity than ordinary men; but that very good men have more of it than very good women. A good man always seems to have a conviction of goodness, to be quite sure when he has done right, and to enjoy the sense of having done it. A woman's sympathies are wider and reach further than a man's. When she has done her best, there always is something more that she would do if she could, and until that is done also she can never feel the comfortable delight in godliness experienced by man, the grosser creature, who hedges his possibilities more closely, and gets rid of his superfluous aspirations by the logical demonstration of the unattainable. But the sphere of ordinary women is narrower, and their sympathies are dispersed in a greater multiplicity and divergence of small channels, so that a little goodness, a little easy charity with a pretty name, is a luscious titbit to the tongue that speaketh vanity.

It was a dreary night to every one of the four, — least of all perhaps to Julius Batiscombe, whose fierce temper was thoroughly roused and would not be calmed again for days, giving him a kind of wicked satisfaction while it lasted. He spent most of the night at his window, smoking and going over the scenes of the day, and the scenes of the future. His mind ran in the direction of fighting, — to fight any one or anything would be a rare satisfaction; and ever as he fancied some struggle possible the hot blood rushed to his temples and longed for action, so that he bit his cigar through and through, and clasped his hands together till the veins stood out like ropes. He slept a little at last, and dreamed savage dreams of hand-to-hand combat, and woke with the roar of cannon in his ears. For he was a man of exaggerated fancies when his brain worked unconsciously, like many men who have ended in celebrity or in insane asylums.

The roar of the guns was only a servant knocking at his door, with hot water and a note. He saw Diana's handwriting, and suspected a new move, so that he was not altogether astonished by the contents. He understood that she had made Marcantonio sign her writing — by what means he could not tell — in order to force the position. There was evidently nothing to be done but to go. He would not have left the villa for anything Diana could have said, in his present humour, but it was impossible to bid defiance to the master of the house. Besides, he supposed that since Carantoni had invited him to leave, Diana had said something which would lead to a challenge from her brother, which could naturally not be delivered under his own roof.

He read the note through twice, and he went about his toilet with his usual care, looking angrily at himself in the glass as he shaved, but gradually composing his features to an appearance of calmness. Then he put his things together, rang the bell, told the servant he was going to Sorrento on business, and gave him a very handsome fee, requesting him to bring the things to the hotel in the course of the day. Julius took his hat and stick, and strolled out of the house toward the town.

Donna Diana and Marcantonio met in the morning. They saluted each other with the quiet, mournful understanding of people who have a common trouble, which they know must be spoken of, though they desire to put off the evil moment. They were both pale, and Diana's eyes were shaded by great dark rings that spoke of a sleepless night.

"Have you seen Leonora? How is she?" was her first question.

"Dio mio! She is very poorly. Poverina! It has made a terrible impression on her. Of course I did not speak of the subject."

"Of course." Diana sighed and looked drearily at the window, as though she wished she were outside, away, and beyond this trouble. She could not know what Leonora would say or do if Marcantonio ever broached the subject. "I do not think," said she, "that it will ever be necessary to say anything about it. She will understand that you sent him out of the house,— she will never see him again."

"Is he gone?" asked Marcantonio.

"Yes — early this morning. I sent to find out."

"Then there need be no time lost," said her brother. "I have just written a note to De Lancray, at Castellamare. It is much better to have a Frenchman in dealing with foreigners. He will be here by one o'clock, and will arrange everything."

Diana had expected that Marcantonio would send for a friend to arrange matters with Batiscombe. She did not look surprised.

"Have you sent the man yet?" she asked.

"He is getting a horse, I suppose. I have not heard him go."

"Tell him to wait five minutes. This is a serious affair, and we had better act deliberately."

Diana intended to prevent the duel if possible. Marcantonio was willing to humour her, and went out to stop the man. When he came back, she made him sit down beside her.

She explained to him the situation very clearly. Batiscombe had insulted Leonora, had done him a mortal offence. But Batiscombe was not the important person in the case. Leonora was the important person. If matters had been different, if, for instance, a man had run away with another man's wife, then, of course, they must necessarily fight, —and the woman made no difference, since her reputation would be already destroyed. But it would be a terrible injury to a young wife to have her husband fighting a duel about her before they had been married three months. People always say there is not much smoke without a little fire; society, being generally averse to standing up to be shot at, says that a man in Marcantonio's position would not go out unless he had very serious cause. Of course it would say in this case that the cause lay with Leonora, that she should never have allowed a man enough intimacy to give him a chance of insulting her, and so forth, and so on.

Diana would not use the argument of the

Church's prohibition of duelling. She knew that Leonora's welfare was the chiefest thing present in her brother's mind, and that if she could show him that, for Leonora's sake, he ought to leave Batiscombe alone, he would assuredly conquer his anger and his pride. He had no sanguine and combative instincts, like Julius; he did not like fighting for the enjoyment of it, and if he could be convinced that his anger was unwise, he would ultimately get the better of it, now that the first sharp moment of wrath was over. To preserve Leonora's spotless fame was a much more important thing than to punish an insolent foreigner for vainly attempting to damage it, and thereby calling the attention of the world to the fact that her reputation was capable of damage.

It was a hard fight, and Diana's patience never wearied through the hours they talked together. More than once she thought it was lost, and that Marcantonio would order the note to be dispatched. Nothing but the real affection and trust that existed between her and her brother made it possible for her to succeed. But at last he was convinced, and silently went out and got the note he had written, and tore it up before his sister. The die was cast, and he did not mention the subject again, but went to see his wife. At her door he was told by her maid that Leonora was asleep, which was not true. But he asked no questions, and retired to his own room to solace himself as he might. He was too

deeply distressed to wonder why Diana did not go
to Leonora and sit with her.

Leonora had hardly spoken to any one since she
and Batiscombe had parted on the previous evening
before dinner. At table, as has been seen, she had
said little, and no one had seen her since except
her husband, who had gone to her in the morning.
After his visit she rang for her maid and told her
to see that no one disturbed her, as she was going
to sleep again and would ring when she wanted
anything.

At the moment when her husband was told she
was not visible, she was sitting in her dressing-
room, just behind the closed blinds of the window,
listening to the monotonous, dry hum of the locusts
in the garden, and wondering whether anything
would ever happen again in the world. She was
utterly dishevelled, her rich hair falling to her
shoulders and halfway to the ground in wildest disorder; the gay coloured ribbons of her peignoir all
untied and ruffled, her bare feet half thrust into
her gold-embroidered slippers, her hands lying idly
in her lap, as though there were nothing more for
them to do. A strange, wild figure, sitting there
surrounded by all the gorgeous little properties
and knickknacks of a great lady's toilet.

Batiscombe was gone! Her husband had told
her that he had been requested to postpone the
remainder of his visit indefinitely. Of course he
had gone, then. Marcantonio had supposed she

would understand and be well satisfied. But she had only turned and hidden her face in the pillow, — as was perhaps natural to a very young woman when her husband mentioned anything that gave her a sense of shame. She must have been very much hurt by the insult, whatever it was, and she could not bear to hear it mentioned. Marcantonio had not told his sister of this, thinking it would be indelicate, and was nobody's business but his own and his wife's.

Batiscombe was gone — when should she see him again? How could he reach her, or she him? What was life to be like without him? And then the dazed, disappointed, terrified look came again to her face, and she stared at nothing, vacantly, and like a woman beside herself.

And oh, that other thought! How much did Marcantonio know? It was Diana, of course, who had made that frightful noise — she could hear the crash still sounding in her ears. She had remembered too late that corner room, cut off from all the others opening on the terrace, and communicating from within with Diana's bedroom — oh, the folly of it! If only Diana were to come to her — she could kill her, she thought! She was not so tall, perhaps, but she was much stronger — she was sure she could kill her! But how much did Marcantonio know? Diana was so truthful, she must have told him all. Those hateful people who always speak the truth! Ah, if only Batiscombe could come back — or see her one moment before he went. But he was gone already. If he could have seen her this morning, she might have arranged — it was impossible yesterday afternoon, he was so wild, so furiously, gloriously angry. It did her good to think of his blazing eyes, and strong, set teeth just showing between his parted lips. He was such a man among men! Never again — never — never, perhaps! She might be shut up — made a prisoner — Heaven only knew what was in store for her! Dreary, hopeless, no light, no life — no anything.

Hollow? She laughed dismally to herself. Yes, life was hollow indeed, now — empty of all joy, or peace, or rest, forever and ever. Pray? How could she pray? Prayer was an innocent amusement for idle young women, with imaginary sins and plenty of time. But now — bah! nothing was further from her thoughts. What could Heaven do for her? Heaven would certainly not give her Batiscombe again. It would be wrong — ha! ha! of course it was wrong; but what was life without him? What had all her life been as compared with the happiness of the last fortnight, culminating in the happiness of yesterday? It might be wrong, but it was life; and all before had been mere existence — a miserable, vegetable, hopeless existence.

The day dragged on; she took no thought of the hours, though she had taken neither food nor drink since the night before. And always the maid outside the door said she was asleep.

At five o'clock she could bear it no longer, but rang the bell and said she would dress, as she felt much better. The maid told her that one of the men had returned from Sorrento and wished to see her excellency, as he had executed a commission for her.

Leonora stared a moment, guessed there was something behind the message, and ordered the man to go into her sitting-room, whither she presently went, wrapped in a voluminous dressing-gown, that completely hid her disarranged peignoir. The man handed her a small parcel and waited. She turned her back, and, opening it, found a little olive-wood box, and inside that there was a small note with neither address nor name on it. She hastily closed the box again, and, turning carelessly, so that the man could see her, she examined it by the window, as though criticising the workmanship. She nodded to the man to go, but he stood looking at her with a queer expression that frightened her. She understood that he had examined the parcel on the way, probably; at all events, that he must be bribed. She quickly opened a drawer of her secretary, found a purse, and gave the fellow a gold piece. He grinned, bowed his thanks, and retired. He was the man who had taken Batiscombe's things to town that afternoon.

Leonora had no experience. In novels, people always bribed the servants; it was most likely the proper thing — the safe thing — to do. The man would not have gone away unless she had given him something, she thought.

The note was brief to terseness. It conveyed in the fewest possible words the information that the writer — name not mentioned — intended to spend the day, in future, in a small boat with green oars — underlined with a very black stroke — in the vicinity of a certain landing known to both the writer and the receiver of the note — name of latter also not mentioned. And the writer added, laconically, "No fee to bearer."

She ought to have read the note through before paying the man. But what could she have done? He had stood staring at her, until he was paid.

Her heart gave a great leap. It was so like him, so daring, to send her word at once. At least she should feel, now, that he was always there, waiting for her — ready to help her at a moment's notice. If only she could be with him on the soft, blue water, out in the sun! She could fight now — she could face them all — for he was out there; at least, he would be there to-morrow. She went back to her bedroom, and gave herself up to her maid, and had strong tea and bread-and-butter brought to her, while she dressed; and an hour later she sallied out, with all her usual elasticity of step and motion, and all the marvellous freshness of face that distinguished her from other women. She found her husband and Diana together on the terrace.

Marcantonio's face softened and flushed with

pleasure as he saw how well and beautiful she looked. She, at least, he thought, had not suffered long by all this trouble. It was so brave of her to forget it, now that the man was gone; he was so glad to think that he could have borne the brunt of it, and had saved her the pain of any discussion. But he said little, just kissing her hand, and affectionately leading her to a comfortable chair.

Diana, who had really carried the heat of the battle alone, and bore the burden of the secret, was very quiet. She saw a little look of hardness in Leonora's face which she had seen long before, but rarely. She said kindly that she was very glad to see her up again, and hoped she was entirely recovered. Marcantonio, said Diana, had been very anxious.

For an instant the two women faced each other, and Leonora thought she was beginning to understand her sister-in-law.

CHAPTER XV.

FROM morning till night, under the broiling sun of August, a wretched-looking boat plied slowly along the rocks in the neighbourhood of the Carantoni landing. It was a miserable old tub, big enough to hold three or four people at the most, and the solitary individual to whom it seemed to belong propelled it slowly about with a pair of old green oars. Now and then he would paddle under the shadow of the cliffs and put down a line, angling for a stray mackerel or mullet, and sometimes catching even one of those sharp-finned red fellows that the Neapolitan fishermen called "cardinals." He did not seem to care much whether he caught anything or not, but he apparently loved that particular part of the coast, for he was never seen anywhere else. A big, shabby man, in rough clothes, with bright blue eyes, and a half-grown, blue-black beard,— Julius Batiscombe as a fisherman,— brown as a berry, and growing rough-fisted from constant handling of oars and lines and nets.

No one took any notice of him as he pottered about in his tub. The watermen, who passed and repassed, knew him as the crazy Englishman who found it amusing to bake himself all day in the sun for the sake of catching some wretched fish that he could buy in the market for half the trouble. What did they care? They never fished there themselves, because there were no fish,—a very good and simple reason,—and if a foolish foreigner chose to register an old boat at the little fishing harbour close by, and pay ten francs for the privilege, it was not their business. Neapolitans and their congeners do not care much for anything foreigners do, unless it happens to bring them money.

And in the evening when it was dark, Julius paddled away to Sorrento, and, meeting his own boat on the way, pulled off his rough clothes, jumped into the water for a swim, and dressed himself like a Christian before going ashore. Save that he was growing a beard, and was almost black with the sun, he was as much Julius Batiscombe as ever when he was on land. He had no acquaintances in the hotel, and no one cared or asked what he did with himself all day long.

It was said amongst the fishermen that he had been seen once or twice rowing a foreign lady about, and they laughed at the idea of a "signore" earning a franc by ferrying a passenger, just like one of themselves—for, of course he was paid for it; it amused him, because he was crazy, poveretto! And sometimes he was heard singing outlandish songs to himself in the heat of the day as he paddled about under the cliffs.

The time had sped quickly since Batiscombe had

left the Carantoni villa, and it was now the first
week in August. Madame de Charleroi had stayed
nearly a week longer than she had intended, but at
last had gone back to Pegli, to Marcantonio's
great regret, and to Leonora's unspeakable relief.
So long as Diana was in the house Leonora had
been obliged to steal occasions, few and far between, when she could safely go down to the rocks
and signal to the shabby man with the green oars
to come and take her off. Many and long and
hot were the days when he pulled his poor crazy
craft about from dawn to dark, without catching
a sight of the strong lithe figure that he loved.
But come when she would, at morning, noon, or
night, he was always there, ready to take her and
to slip off at a quick stroke to one of the many
green caves that line the shore; and there, for an
hour or two, or as long as she might safely stay,
they spent happy moments together, the happier for
being few, forbidden, and somewhat dangerous.

As for the danger, though, there was not much of
it. It would have been hard, indeed, to recognise
in the ill-clad boatman, with his stubbly beard, and
seedy cap of brown knitted wool, the fine gentleman
whom the natives stopped to look at in the street.
Leonora, if any one had met her on the landing,
would have said she had taken the first passing
fisherman to row her about among the caves, and no
one would have suspected anything; and she used
to laugh as she watched the progress of his beard,

knowing that each day made the disguise more complete.

Her own boat had given her some anxiety at first, but she had made Marcantonio lend the whole equipage to a friend further down the bay, telling him it was too hot to be on the water at present. And when Diana was at last gone, she had most of the day to herself; for Marcantonio was perpetually busy with letters, or trying horses, or going to Naples. He always found his wife extremely charming when he had been away all day, or shut up in his rooms, and preternaturally contradictory and capricious when he was with her for long together, and he concluded that she preferred a certain amount of solitude, and humoured her accordingly. Never hearing of Batiscombe, he supposed he had left the neighbourhood for parts unknown, and though he regretted not having had an opportunity of shooting him, he knew in his heart that Diana's advice had been good, and that it was best so. Now and then, when he thought of Julius too long, he grew angry and paced quickly up and down his room; but on the whole life was easy and pleasant enough, and his beloved Leonora was the most charming of women, not half so capricious as some of the wives of his friends.

How long this state of things might have continued it is impossible to say, if a disturbing element had not been introduced. But the disturbing element is seldom far to seek in such cases,

and in due time it came.　There was a man in the
service of the Marchesa Carantoni,— the same whom
Batiscombe had employed to take his things to
Sorrento, and then to convey the note to Leonora,
— and the man's name was Temistocle, as arrant a
knave as ever opened palm for bribe.　Carantoni
had taken him in Rome when he married, because
he needed another man, and the fellow's face was
familiar to him.　He had seen him in good houses,
and had noticed his extraordinary adroitness in
waiting.　The man's character was not altogether
satisfactory.　He had received no recommendation
from his last place, but Marcantonio took him on
trial and brought him to Sorrento.

Temistocle had exceedingly sharp eyes, and Temistocle had an exceedingly smooth tongue; he was
understood among the servants to have made economies, and his tastes were somewhat luxurious.　He
found Sorrento hot and dull, and he cast about for
something refreshing and amusing.

To take sea-baths had always been his chiefest
ambition.　It sounded well to be able to say he had
taken a course of sea-bathing.　But the thing was
by no means easy at Sorrento.　He could not bathe
from his master's landing, and it was a long distance
to go round by the lanes to reach another descent.
At last, however, he discovered that he could climb
over the little point of rocks at the foot of the
Carantoni villa, and reach a small cove, where, in
complete seclusion, he might enjoy himself as he

pleased. Accordingly, when he had finished serv-
ing the midday breakfast he used to make a practice
of going down to bathe. In his little cove he hid
his clothes carefully among the rocks and crept into
the water under the deep shadow of the overhanging
cliff. He could not swim a stroke, but he could sit
just so that the water came up to his chin, and his
round black bullet head lay on the surface like a
floating football, scarcely visible to any one passing
outside in the sun. From this position it amused
Temistocle to watch the boats and the fishermen for
an hour or two, enjoying the idea that they never
dreamed of his presence.

It chanced often, as he sat in the water, that
Julius, in his outlandish costume, paddled his old
boat past Temistocle's retreat; and the sharp eyes
of the Roman servant were not long in discovering
that the fisherman was no fisherman at all. It was
the easier to recognise Batiscombe, as the man saw
him when his beard was only a few days old. From
that day Temistocle watched his opportunity to
descend when the boat with the green oars had just
passed, and would be out of the way for some time.

There was never the smallest doubt in his mind
of Batiscombe's intention in thus disguising himself. The incident of the parcel, which he had
carefully opened and examined, Batiscombe's sudden
departure, and Leonora's simultaneous indisposition,
all combined in his mind into one harmonious whole,
from which he proposed to himself to extract at least
a reasonable amount of money.

One day he was rewarded for his pains. The boat passed very near to the mouth of his water-den, skirting the rocks at a great pace. He just saw that Leonora was seated in the stern, and he incontinently ducked his black head, and kept under water till he thought he must have drowned. When at last he was obliged from sheer suffocation to bring his mouth to the air, they were gone, and Temistocle sprang out of the water like some dark evil genius of a low order, awaiting evolution into the advanced condition of complete devildom. He was not long in dressing, and in a few minutes he had got back to the landing, clambering quickly over the rocks, and hurting himself, in his haste, at every step.

After that, he became more irregular in his habits, lurking in secret places till he saw Leonora going toward the descent at the end of the garden, and presently following her at a safe distance. He ascertained, as he had expected, that Batiscombe spent his whole time within hail of the landing, in the boat with the green oars, and that Leonora went down and signalled to him, whenever she had a chance. Temistocle was so delighted with the skill of the arrangement that for a long time he could not prevail upon himself to interrupt it, even for the sake of the bribe that must inevitably follow. But, one day, he needed money, and he did not want to encroach upon his purse of savings, for he was a miserly wretch as well as a knave. He had seen something pretty in the way of a silk cap, which a stray pedlar had brought with other things, and he thought he should enjoy bargaining for it the next time the pedlar came with his wares. He knew that he should probably bargain for an hour and then not buy it after all,— but nevertheless he might be weak, and then he should like to feel that he had got the thing out of his betters by his own skill, instead of squandering money from his hoard. He seldom indulged in the luxury of buying what he fancied, but when he did he generally made some one else pay for it. There was a certain refinement of miserliness about him.

At first he imagined that it might be best to drop some hint to his mistress, just enough to frighten her into paying for his silence. But his calmer reflection told him that he would be thereby killing the goose that laid the golden eggs. Batiscombe's ingenuity would make some change in the arrangements and he would have to begin all over again. Evidently the best thing was to make his master pay, and let the lovers go quietly on their course, so that he could at any time produce evidence of his veracity. He watched his opportunity. Marc-antonio often inquired whether the signora were in the house, or were gone out. If she was out he supposed she had gone into the garden or to pay visits; he never disturbed her arrangements, knowing how much she enjoyed being perfectly free, and feeling sure she would not get into mischief. She made a point of calling on everybody, telling him

afterwards where she had been, and the two or three
hours she spent with Julius escaped notice in her
clever account of the spending of the day. Now and
then she would say she had been down to the rocks,
in case her husband should ever take it into his
head to go and find her there, and she was quite
sure that by this time Julius was changed beyond
recognition.

Temistocle had not long to wait. One day in
August, Marcantonio chanced to inquire of him
where the marchesa might be. Temistocle was
prepared; with the utmost gravity and respect he
dealt his blow, speaking as though he were saying the most natural thing in the world.

"I suppose," he said, "that her excellency is
gone out in the boat with the Signor Batiscombe."
He pronounced all the letters of the name, as though
it had been Italian; but it was unmistakable. Marcantonio turned upon him in amazement.

"Animal!" he exclaimed, "are you drunk?"

"I, eccellenza?" cried Temistocle in hurt tones.
"I drunk? Heaven forbid."

"Then you are crazy," remarked Marcantonio,
more and more astonished. "The Signor Batiscombe is no longer here."

"Pardon me, eccellenza," retorted the servant
respectfully. "I imagined that your excellency
knew. The Signor Batiscombe comes every day,
and takes the Signora Marchesa out in a boat. He
is become a very strange signore, for he dresses like

a fisherman, and has let his beard grow as long as this — so," the man explained, holding his hand a few inches from his face. "Mi maraviglio, io!" he exclaimed, casting his eyes to the ground.

Marcantonio was speechless with amazement and horror, and turned his back upon the servant. A man less thoroughly a gentleman in every sense would have fallen upon Temistocle and beaten him, then and there. By a great effort, Marcantonio collected himself, and turned again.

"You have not to make any remarks upon the appearance of the Signor Batiscombe," he said briefly. "Basta!"

Temistocle had nothing left but to bow and leave the room. He did not understand his master in the least; he was just like a foreigner, he thought.

But Marcantonio dropped into an arm-chair, the moment he was alone, as though all the strength and life were suddenly gone from him. He could not in the least realise the extent of the revelation contained in Temistocle's words. He did not know what to do, and for the moment it did not even strike him that there was anything to be done. In the course of half an hour he grew calmer and began to review the situation.

He remembered distinctly every word of Diana's concerning the trouble when Batiscombe was in the house. Diana had said **very distinctly** that Julius had insulted Leonora — and Diana always

spoke the truth.   Marcantonio had not asked her
what the insult had been.   He could not bring
himself to do it, and he did not want to know
anything more.   He would have cheerfully fought
with Batiscombe on the strength of his sister's
assertion, but she had dissuaded him, and now he
was sorry for it.

The servant had spoken with an air of conviction,
as though he thought it quite natural, and only wondered at Batiscombe's strange appearance.   There
could not be any doubt about it, at all.

A new sensation took possession of Marcantonio
— an utterly new passion, which he did not recognise as part of himself.   He was jealous.   He did
not, he would not, understand the truth, but he
would prevent his wife from ever seeing Julius
Batiscombe again, and then he would go in search
of him and wreak his vengeance without stint.   At
the same time he hoped he might avoid a scene
with Leonora.   He was brave enough to fight the
man, but he shrank from telling his wife what he
knew.   It seemed so brutal and uncourteous, and
altogether contrary to his principles.

But, after all, he ought to ascertain whether
Temistocle were right — whether Julius really disguised himself.   He would go and see.

No, he could not do that!   He could not play the
spy upon his wife — it was low, ignoble, unworthy.
He would find some other way.   His brain swam
and it seemed too much for him.   He grasped the

arm of the chair and rose to his feet in pure desperation, feeling that he must get out of the way into his own rooms for a while, lest any one should see him in his present state.

In the hall Marcantonio paused a moment, holding his hand to his head, as though it hurt him, and as he waited the door opened, and Leonora faced him, beaming with light, and life, and happiness. Marcantonio looked at her one instant, and tried to speak; he would have said something courteous, from force of habit. But the words choked him, and losing all control of himself he turned and fled up the stairs, leaving his wife staring in blank amazement.

Poor fellow! she thought, he had probably got a touch of the sun. She hastened to her room and sent to inquire if the signore were ill, and if she might come to him. They brought back word that he was dressing, and that nothing was the matter. Then Leonora felt a cold chill descend to her heart, the dreadful presentiment of a real terror, not far distant. But when she met her husband in the evening at dinner, she did not dare to refer to his strange behaviour in the hall.

During dinner he talked much as usual, except that he did not laugh at all, and seemed very grave. There was a preternatural calm about him that increased Leonora's fears. She knew him so little that she could not be sure what he would do, whether anything had really occurred, or whether he were subject to fits of insanity. He had looked like a madman in the afternoon.

When they were alone, he offered her his arm, and led her out into the air, and they sat down side by side in deep chairs. Marcantonio leisurely lighted a cigarette, and puffed a few minutes in silence.

"Leonora," he said at last, "I have heard a curious thing, and I must tell you immediately." His voice was even and cold; his whole manner was different from anything she remembered in her experience of him; he was more imposing, altogether more of a man and stronger. Leonora trembled violently, knowing instinctively that he had discovered something. She did not speak, but let him continue.

"I chanced to inquire if you were at home this afternoon, and the man said he supposed you were gone out in the boat with Mr. Batiscombe, as you did every day. Is it true? The man who told me said it as though it were quite natural, as though every one in the house knew it except myself."

Leonora was dumb for a moment. The accusation came so suddenly that she was taken off her guard, besides being thoroughly frightened at her husband's terrible calmness, so unlike his manner under ordinary circumstances. She lay back in her low chair and tried to collect her thoughts.

"The man had also observed," continued Marcantonio, turning his keen dark eyes upon her, "that Monsieur Batiscombe had a beard, and was dressed like a fisherman. Altogether, it was extremely curious."

Marcantonio and his sister always spoke the truth. Batiscombe never lied in his life to save himself, but could do it boldly when it was absolutely necessary to save some one else. He had no principle about it, except that cowards told lies, and men did not,—that was the way he put it. He was not afraid of anything himself, but for a woman he would perjure himself by all the oaths in Christendom. It was his idea of chivalry to women, and could not altogether be blamed. But Leonora by a long apprenticeship to a very worldly mother, and owing to the singular confusion of her ideas, had acquired a moral obliquity which she defended to herself on the ground that the ultimate results she obtained were intended to be good. The telling of untruths, she argued, was in itself neither good nor bad; the consequences alone deserved to be considered. But as the consequences of lies are not easily cast up into totals of good and bad from the starting point, it sometimes occurred that she got herself into trouble. However, she was not hampered by prejudice, and she was a very clever woman, much cleverer than the great majority, and she was just now in a very hard position. In a few minutes she had made up her mind, and she answered Marcantonio fluently enough.

"Why," said she calmly, "should I not go out with Mr. Batiscombe when I please? If he chooses to dress like a fisherman, I suppose he has the right."

Marcantonio was rather staggered at her sudden confession. He had expected a denial; but there she sat as calmly as possible, telling him to his face that it was all true. However, he was not likely to lose his nerve again now that he was face to face with the difficulty.

"It appears to me, Leonora," he said, "that when I have turned a man out of my house for insulting you, it is sufficient reason " —

"For insulting me?" exclaimed Leonora in well-feigned astonishment. "Mr. Batiscombe never insulted me! You must be dreaming." She laughed a small dry laugh. But Marcantonio was not so easily put off.

"My sister," said he, "told me that Batiscombe insulted you in her hearing. I have always known my sister to speak the truth. Perhaps you will explain."

"What explanation do you want? You sent Mr. Batiscombe out of the house on the pretence that I was ill. Of course Diana made you do it, — I do not know how, nor what she said. You must talk it over with her. She was probably sick of him, and wanted him out of the way."

Leonora spoke scornfully, and almost brutally, and Marcantonio's blood began to grow hot.

"That is absurd," he said instantly. "Perhaps Monsieur Batiscombe would not object to being confronted with me for five minutes?"

"I am sure he would not object," said Leonora, without hesitation. She was quite certain of her lover's courage, at all events. She knew he would face anybody.

"Meanwhile," said Marcantonio, "you will oblige me by giving up your harmless habit of going out with him every day. I should have supposed that you would at least have had the pride to deny it, after what occurred when he was here." Marcantonio was angry, but he reasoned rightly.

"You would have preferred that I should lie to you, my dear," said his wife disdainfully, in the full virtue of having told half the truth — the first half.

"I would not permit myself to apply such a word to anything you say," answered Marcantonio, with cold courtesy. "But I would have you observe that you are mistaken with regard to my sister, and that if she told me she heard the man insult you, he did. Perhaps you did not understand what he said. It is the same. You will not meet him again at the rocks — nor anywhere else."

"Why not? Why shall I not meet him?" she inquired, raising her eyebrows in disdain.

"Because I forbid you." He spoke shortly, as if that ended the matter.

Leonora shrugged her shoulders a little, with an

expression of pity, and shifted her position, so as to face him.

"You forbid me, do you?" she asked, lowering her voice.

"Mais oui! I forbid you to see him anywhere."

"Do you know what you are saying?" she asked, and there was a tone of menace in her words.

"Oh, perfectly," answered her husband calmly; "and I will also take care that you obey me — bien entendu!"

"Then it is war?" asked Leonora, as though she hoped it might be, and to the knife.

"If you disobey, it is war," said Marcantonio, "but you will not."

"Why not?"

"Because I will prevent you. It is useless to prolong this discussion."

"Mon Dieu, I ask nothing better than to finish it as soon as possible," said Leonora.

"In that case, good-night," replied Marcantonio, rising.

"Good-night," answered Leonora, still seated. "I am not sleepy yet. You are not afraid that Monsieur Batiscombe will be announced after you are gone to bed?"

She spoke scornfully, as though trying to drive a wound with every word. She thought she knew her husband, and she felt triumphant.

Marcantonio did not answer, and withdrew in silence. In a few hours his whole character had developed, and he was a very different man from the Marcantonio of that morning. He had passed through a few hours of a desperate crisis, and had come out of it with an immovable determination to clear up the whole affair, and to force his wife to break off her intimacy with Batiscombe. Even now he could believe no evil, — only the foolish infatuation of a young woman for a man who had the romantic faculty strongly developed. It would cost an effort to break it off, — and Leonora would be very much annoyed, of course, — but it must be done. And so Marcantonio had gone about it in the boldest and simplest way, by attacking her directly. He congratulated himself, for at one stroke he had ascertained the truth of the servant's statement, and had gone through the much dreaded scene with his wife. Henceforth she knew what to expect; he had declared himself as a jealous husband, and had said he would be obeyed. He went to bed in the consciousness that he had done the best thing possible under the circumstances, and promising himself an early explanation with Batiscombe.

But for all the success of this first move, he was wretchedly unhappy. He still loved Leonora, as he would always love her, whatever she did, with all his might and main, though he saw well enough that she did not love him. But he was furiously jealous, and he swore by all the saints in the calendar that she should never love any one else. His jealousy had made a man of him.

CHAPTER XVI.

It was clear that after what had passed between Leonora and her husband, the relations must assume the aspect described in diplomatic language as "strained," to say the least of it. The two met many times in the course of the day, and never referred to the subject of their difference; but Leonora was well aware that she was watched. If ever she sallied out into the garden, hoping to escape observation, her husband was at hand, offering to accompany her. She once even went so far as to go down some distance with him towards the rocks, she could not tell why,— perhaps because it would have been a comfort to her to catch a glimpse of Julius in the boat. But he was probably lurking behind the rocks, just out of sight, and she could not see him. She knew that he still kept his watch during half the day, not having yet invented a better plan,— for she was in correspondence with him,— and in the meanwhile, until new arrangements could be made, there was a bare chance that she might escape for a moment in the morning and be able to see him. Her husband never left her side in the afternoon.

Temistocle, the knave, had failed in his attempt to gain Marcantonio's favour, as has been seen, but he now reaped a golden harvest from the lovers, who paid him handsomely for carrying letters, with a reckless feeling that if he betrayed them the deluge might come,— but that without him they were utterly cut off from each other. He had at first carefully opened one or two letters and skilfully closed them again, but had desisted on finding that they were written in English, a language he unfortunately did not understand. It was now his business to encourage the correspondence to the best of his ability, in order that whenever it should be convenient to spring the mine, he might have some letter passing through his hands, which he could show to Marcantonio. He made a bargain with an old man who had a little donkey cart, to hang about the lane leading to the villa in the afternoon hours, when Temistocle, being free from the cares of the pantry, found it convenient to play postman. As the distance was considerable, and as Batiscombe always gave him a gold piece for a letter, and Leonora another, he thought he could afford himself ten sous a day for the hire of his primitive cab, without any reckless extravagance.

The first letter he had carried was to Batiscombe. Leonora informed him briefly of the scene with her husband, and begged that he would wait as usual for a few days, or until something better could be devised. But he waited in vain. Then he wrote and proposed that she should drive somewhere and meet him. But she answered that her husband always drove with her when she went out. He proposed to get into the garden at night, to scale her window,—anything. But Marcantonio had bought a brace of abominable English terriers that howled as though they had swallowed a banshee. Marcantonio also kept pistols, and slept with his windows open.

Meanwhile Marcantonio would have given anything to catch Batiscombe and call upon him for an explanation,—but he was afraid to leave his wife for an hour, lest she should have an opportunity of going down to the sea. He could never be quite certain whether Batiscombe were there or not, for the latter had grown cautious and lay very quietly in his boat just out of sight, knowing that Leonora would call if she wanted him, according to the agreement, and he only came in the morning now and waited till twelve o'clock, in order to be at home to receive her letters in the afternoon. Yet Marcantonio would not employ a spy to watch whether Batiscombe were on the water. He could not do that — it was too utterly mean.

Leonora grew pale and thin. She was as thoroughly in love with Julius as a woman of strong temper and impulse can be with the first man she has ever cared for. She dreamed of him, thought of him, longed for him, during every hour of the day and night. He was to her the realisation of the strongest fancy of her life, the passionate, ruthless, all-daring lover; and the consciousness of utter wrong that underlay her feelings only lent the strength of moral desperation to her passion. Having lost all right to other things, she had that left, and only that, on which to rely for all the happiness the world owed her. She would go to the end of it, and enjoy it all, now that she had found it; and then — then she would die, she said to herself, and no one should suffer by her fault. But she was long past the elementary stage, when love can be put upon a block and modelled and shaped with tools, or pulled to pieces, at will, being as yet but a fragile clay sketch and very yielding. The clay had been done into marble, and the marble set up in the inmost sanctuary of the temple, — and if the idol were broken the pieces could not be joined, and the temple must be empty and bare forever. It had come about very quickly — but what of that? Who shall say that passion born in a moment, ready armed, is not so strong and enduring as that which is evolved like man from a pitiful thing with a tail — a mere flirtation, to the semblance of humanity, to the godlike presence of true love?

Or who shall tell us that love is less a real thing, because it is evil instead of being good? Devils are quite as real as angels, as I have no doubt many of us will find in due time. Do not underrate the strength of a thing because it is bad, nor doubt its reality because you do not like its looks.

Leonora was in love with all her might, and it
makes no difference in the effect upon the individual
whether love is lawful or not, so long as it is
thwarted and opposed at every turn. Her character,
from being vague and indistinct, reaching out after
many things, and never wholly grasping any, had
suddenly become definite and full of a mature
purpose — the purpose to love Julius recklessly,
without consideration or question. The one real
thing which remained possible for her had come,
dominating and crushing down the army of her
most favourite unrealities. The man she loved stood
out from the chaotic darkness of the past and from
the dreary shadows of the present as a glorious
figure of light, magnificent in all that could be
noblest; and she gave to him her soul, her life,
and her strength, without hesitation and without
fear. She had no remorse, no pity for her husband, no present consciousness of sin, for she was
too near the wrong, and too new to it, not to
enjoy it.

The traditional hardened sinner, the very mon-
strosity and arch-deformity of complicated vice,
held up by preachers as a bugbear and a moral
scarecrow to the young, the creature without heart,
conscience, or capacity of good, does not enjoy his
wickedness in the least. It has lost its novelty for
him and its sharp, peppery savour. The people who
really enjoy it are young; they are those who have
tasted little of life, and have yet all the sensibility

and refinement of palate that can distinguish between one sauce and another — between green, red, and black pepper. They have dreamed of the pepper, have never been allowed to have it, and have been fed on a kind of moral pap that disagreed with them from childhood. Suddenly the spice is within their reach, and they make to themselves a glorious feast of hot things, vaguely hoping that they will recover from the indigestion before they are found out. And sometimes they do, though the recovery is very painful — and sometimes they do not.

Leonora had subsisted on what she could get in the way of enjoyment, but her capacity far exceeded the supply that presented itself. She was not one of those people who can live for days in happiness from one sight of something beautiful, from a glimpse at a great picture, or from the memory of one strain of music. She liked all that was artistic, and especially that which was admirable for novelty, fineness of execution, or boldness of conception. She was not impressed with the beauty of small and unpretending things, — the art that amused her was necessarily of the most brilliant kind. The people she liked were the stirring, active, original people who either make history or make public fools of themselves, or both. The philosophies she had dabbled in were such as could produce in her a sensation of odd possibility rather than such as could satisfy a logical intellect, and they resolved themselves into a vast sea of aspirations, emotions, and potential passions, in which she loved to disport herself, diving and splashing and floating, like a magnificent sea-nymph in fullest enjoyment of her wild vitality,— sitting, an hour afterwards, on some lonely rock, and wringing her white hands to heaven in despair, because, being but half divine, she was less goddess-like than the great goddesses of Olympus.

She could not help it if she grew pale and thin, — she was so wretched without him; and, without his letters and the sense that he was not so very far from her after all, she would have gone mad. She would sit for hours in her room staring at nothing; or she would go through elaborate processes of toilet before the glass, looking at herself and wondering if he would find her changed,— perhaps that very day some chance would offer, and she might see him. Everything was possible. That was the colour he liked best, and that bit of jewelry,— put it on, in case he should come. And again, she would change it all, because she would not wear for her husband the things she wore for her sweet lover; and then she would change once more, perhaps, and put back the colours and the ornaments he loved, so that she might the better think of him while she was with Marcantonio; she had a thousand idle thoughts and fancies which she strove hard to train into the semblance of a little happiness, the hollowest image of a little joy.

The days came and went miserably for nearly a

fortnight. In all that time Marcantonio watched her closely, never relaxing in his vigilance. She might have escaped, perhaps, but she would have been missed in half an hour, and she had not the courage to do anything so desperate,— the time must come, she thought, when things should change. But meanwhile she grew haggard and worn.

Marcantonio had abandoned the idea of sending for a friend to deal with Batiscombe. What he had to say could, he thought, best be said directly, and there could then be no difficulty in establishing a pretext for fighting. But first of all he must keep his wife out of danger. Feeling that he held her entirely at his mercy, he was willing to take some time for deliberation. She could not see Julius, and it would be the best possible test to ascertain how she bore the trial. Marcantonio had grown hard and calculating in his jealousy, but he ground his teeth as he watched her and saw that she was falling ill,— and it was not so much for sympathy with her, as for anger that she should so love another. At last he determined upon a new course.

"Leonora," he said briefly, one day, "we will leave this place immediately, since it does not suit you. Will you be so amiable as to give orders to have your things packed?"

Leonora started a little, and looked at him. It was not often that she cared to look at him now.

"Why do you wish to go?" she asked at last.

"Because, as I said, this place does not suit you. You are ill — miserable. Ma foi! do you think I will allow you to stay in a place where you are always pale and eat nothing?"

"I am not ill," said she, "and I have a very good appetite. I do not wish to go away. Besides, you have taken the villa for the whole summer. It would be such a useless waste of money to move again."

"Ah! You become economical. It is very well; but economy does not enter into this case at all. We will go to Cadenabbia, or to any place in the lakes, where it is far cooler."

"I do not mind the heat," said Leonora, "as you know. Why not say at once that you are tired of Sorrento, and wish to go away to please yourself? It would be much simpler and more honest."

"Pardon me, my dear, I am perfectly well here. I could spend the rest of my life at Sorrento. But you are not well — whatever the cause may be — and there is a possibility that you may be better elsewhere. Done "—

"Oh, of course," interrupted Leonora, "if you have made up your mind I must submit. If you think you can make me more miserable anywhere else than you can here, I must let you try. I hardly think you can. You might be satisfied. Nevertheless, let us go."

"I do not wish to make you miserable, you know perfectly. I wish to make you happy and free."

"Free?" repeated Leonora. "Indeed, you have a singular fashion of making me free, to watch me day and night, as though I intended to run away with your silver. Free, indeed! Free from what?"

She laughed, scornfully enough, in his face. It was the first time they had approached any subject of this kind since the memorable night after Marc-antonio's discovery. But since he had made up his mind to take her away he was willing to undergo another scene if it were absolutely necessary.

"To make you free from the society of Monsieur Batiscombe," answered Marcantonio boldly. "You can never be well until you are absolutely out of his reach, and if I must go to the end of the world I will accomplish that."

"You need not insult me in words," said Leonora, disdainfully. "You have done it quite enough already by your deeds."

Marcantonio was silent for a moment. The speech hurt him, for he knew how he believed in her innocence, and how it was his jealousy that now prompted most of his actions. His voice changed a little as he answered, and he was more like his old self than he had been for days.

"Leonora," he said, "I would not insult you for anything. But, would you rather I were not a little jealous, since I really love you?"

Perhaps he spoke foolishly — perhaps he hoped to soften her heart: at all events he spoke seriously enough, and laid his hand on hers. But she did not like his touch and drew her fingers away.

"A little jealous!" she cried. "So little that I am kept like a prisoner and watched like a political suspect! Be jealous — yes — since you say you love me; but behave like a sensible creature. Moreover, you might make sure that you had some cause for jealousy before coupling the name of the first man you chance to dislike with mine. Is not that an insult?"

"Certainly it is — and if I did that you would be quite right," said he; "but things are a little different. You do not understand Batiscombe — I do. You have taken a fancy for him — so did I. But you push your fancy too far. I now understand him, and I do not think him a proper friend for you. You make difficulties, you insist upon seeing him. I forbid you, and prevent you. You turn pale and ill, and I am angry that you should be so foolish. Mon Dieu! I am angry — voilà."

"One must certainly allow," said Leonora, with a sneer, "that you have a singularly delicate way of stating your own case."

It was the best thing she could find to say, though she knew the sarcasm was not merited. He wished once for all to put the matter clearly before her, and he did it honestly and delicately, since he described her passion as a "fancy," her strategy and secret meetings as "insisting upon seeing" Mr. Batiscombe. It would be impossible to state such a case

more delicately if it had to be stated at all. A
cleverer man, or a less jealous man than Marcantonio,
might have gone about it less directly; and that is
all that can be said. But he was a half-formed
character, as yet, with some good possibilities and
hardly any bad ones. He was naturally good, but
good as yet without much experience, and his
teaching in the troubles of life had come upon him
very suddenly. It had never struck him that it
could be difficult to manage a woman, and he did
not like the idea now that it was thrust upon him.
The woman he had made his wife would, he had
supposed, be like his sister, of the kind that manage
themselves, and do it well; and if he had anticipated
exercising any influence over Leonora, it was influence of a very different sort from that which he was
now driven to exert. He had made up his mind,
however, that she must obey him now, or that he
should perish in the struggle, and a certain family
obstinacy of purpose, inherited from his father and
all his race, suddenly made its appearance and
changed him from an easy-going, pleasant-spoken
young fellow into a very determined man, so far as
his wife was concerned.

He had said that she should go at once, and go
she should, without any delay whatsoever. Instead
of answering her sarcastic remark about his indeli-
cacy, he went obstinately back to his proposition.

"Let us not talk any more about it," he said, to
cut the difficulty short. "You will doubtless be so

amiable as to give the necessary orders about your things?"

Leonora shrugged her shoulders very slightly, as much as it is possible for a great lady to do, and as much as would horrify a very strict duenna.

"If you wish it," she said, "I must."

"Then we will start in two days, if it is agreeable to you."

"It is not agreeable to me," said Leonora, wearied to death by his civility, "but we will start when you please,—in two days if you say it."

She was casting about in her mind for some desperate means of seeing Julius and assuring herself that he would follow her. Of course he would do that, but she could not go without seeing him once more in Sorrento; there was so much to be said that she could not write,—so very much!

The conversation with Marcantonio had taken place little more than an hour before dinner. As he left the room Leonora glanced at the clock. There was time yet,—if she could only get some conveyance. She might see Julius and be back before dinner. She could make some excuse for not dressing—if her husband noticed it, which was unlikely. He had gone to his room, contrary to his custom, for he generally did not leave her until she went to dress. His windows were towards the sea, and she could slip out through the garden. It had rained a little, but that was no matter. There would be the less dust.

A garden hat she sometimes wore hung in the
hall, among her husband's hats and whips and
sticks; she snatched it quickly and went out, walking leisurely for a few yards, till she was hidden
by the orange-trees. Then she gathered up her
skirt a little and ran like a deer over the moist path,
through the gate that stood ajar, and down the narrow lane between the high damp walls towards
Sorrento, never looking behind her nor pausing to
take breath, for she feared that if she stopped to
breathe she might stop to think, and not do what
she most wished to.

There are always little open carriages hanging
about the lanes during the height of the season, in
the hope of picking up stray fares, and before she had
gone two hundred yards she overtook one of these,
moving lazily along. The man was all grins and
alacrity at the mere sight of her and pulled up, gesticulating wildly and leaning backward over his box
to arrange the cushions with one hand while he held
the reins with the other. The whole conveyance is so
small that the driver can touch every part of the inside
with his hands from his seat. She sprang in and told
the man the name of Batiscombe's hotel, promising
him anything if he would drive fast. In six or seven
minutes he brought her to the door, and she told him
to wait. She would have dismissed him at once
and taken another to return, but she found herself
without money. She could borrow something from
Batiscombe.

He had chanced to tell her the number of his rooms one day, when she was asking about the hotel, and now she luckily remembered it. Stopping the first servant she met, she bade him show her the way. One of Batiscombe's sailors, resplendent in dark-blue serge and a scarlet silk handkerchief, was seated on a bench outside the door. He was a quick fellow, and Julius employed him as his body servant. Sailors, he said, were always cleaner than servants, and much neater.

The man sprang to his feet, saw the anxious expression in Leonora's face and the general appearance of haste about her, and guessing that he could not do wrong, opened the door and almost pushed her in, closing it behind her and confronting the astonished hotel servant with a perfectly grave face.

Sailors have good memories, especially for people who own boats, and the man remembered Leonora perfectly well, having helped to row her to Castellamare, and having raced her crew on the occasion when Batiscombe had attempted a precipitous flight. In his opinion the Marchesa Carantoni would not wish to be seen waiting outside his master's door, whatever might be the errand which brought her in such hot hurry. The hotel servant grumbled something about the franc he had expected for bringing the lady up, and the stalwart seaman laughed at him so that he cursed the whole race of sea-folk, and went away in anger of the serio-comic, hotel kind.

Leonora found herself in Batiscombe's sitting-room. For Batiscombe was a luxurious man, excepting when he was roughing it in earnest, and he had made up his mind of late years that a human being could not exist in less than two rooms, if he lived in rooms at all.

Leonora had not thought at all, from the moment when she had taken her resolution in her own drawing-room until she found herself standing before Julius Batiscombe in the hotel. At such times, women act first and think afterwards, lest perchance the thinking should interfere with the doing. But now that the thing was done, she realised at once the whole importance of the step, and at the same time she understood with what ease it had been accomplished. She saw how, with one bound, she was out of her prison, and with the man she loved, and though she was frightened at the magnitude of the deed, she knew that with him she should find strength and comfort and happiness. What mattered the past?

She had not seen Julius for a fortnight, and though in that time she knew that her love had increased tenfold, yet the outline of him had lost distinctness, and she found him more than ever the man she had dreamed of, and discovered, and loved. He was one of those men whose magnificent vitality casts a sort of magnetic influence on their surroundings, just as Leonora herself sometimes did. When Batiscombe was away, his faults might be detected and criticised,— his selfishness, his combativeness, his vanities. But when he was talking to people, and chose to be agreeable, it was hard not to fall under the spell. He was so eminently a man of action as well as of thought, that even those who disliked him most were obliged to confess that he had certain large qualities,— comforting themselves by describing them as "dangerous," as perhaps they were, to himself and others.

And now Leonora looked upon him and knew how wholly and truly she loved him, and how ready she was to sacrifice anything and anybody to her love, even to herself and her own reputation and honour. With heroic people that consideration of self might first be thrown to the winds; but Leonora was not heroic. She was very passionate and sometimes very foolish, but with all her "higher standard" she believed in the social regulations and distinctions of life. It was the English part of her nature, fighting for a show of Philistinism amidst so much that was the very reverse. It was a strong passion indeed that could make her throw it all away, or even think such a step possible.

It was not that she had yielded weakly to a first impression of weariness after her marriage, and had at once begun to amuse herself with the first man who crossed her path. Weariness alone, the mere commonplace sensation of being bored, could never have led her to such a length. A great variety of circumstances had combined to bring about her destruction. The wild ideas of her girlhood, investing Marcantonio with just enough romance to make him barely come within the line of her "standard," but nerved and encouraged by the faculty she possessed for deceiving herself, had led her into a rash marriage, in which she had been helped and applauded by all those sensible people who think that when money and position are combined on both sides, marriage must necessarily be a good thing. Then followed the bitter disappointment and collapse of all her theories and hopes, leaving a desperate void and a certainty of misery, which gathered strength even from the command of language she had acquired in the study of the imaginary nothingness of everything. And at the very moment when there seemed nothing before her but a dreary waste of years, an individual had appeared who realised the dream she had lost.

And it is indeed a noble quality so long as it is locked close within the treasury of the soul, and so long as one good woman, and one only, holds the key. But of all the unutterable baseness in this world, there is none more despicable than that of the man who makes one woman after another believe that he loves her to distraction, as he never loved any one else, well knowing, the while, that if the furies spare him to an unhonoured old age, it is out of sheer contempt for the blear-eyed Adonis, shambling weak-kneed to his grave with a flower in his button-hole and a ghastly leer at the last woman he meets before death overtakes him.

Leonora was a woman who was probably incapable of a second passion, and the wholeness of the first might lend it some dignity, some simple loftiness of disregard for lesser things, making it seem nobler for being a single sin, sinned bravely for true love's sake.   There were such loves in the world long before Launcelot loved Guinevere, or Héloise was laid in the grave with Abelard.   But the world has no lack of men like Julius Batiscombe, men in no way worthy of the women who love them, nor ever able to be worthy.

Leonora had chosen, and she would not have given him up for all the joys of paradise, any more than she would have believed a word against his faithfulness and loyalty to herself.   He had sworn—how could he deceive her?

CHAPTER XVII.

When Leonora met her husband at dinner an hour later, her face was set, for her mind was made up, and every moment hardened her determination.

Julius had said to her "come," and she would go to the very end of the world if need be. He had stated the case with a show of fairness. She must fully understand the step, he said, and that there was no return possible from such an exile as they undertook together. She must abandon everything, and not only her husband, but her mother, her father, her position before the world, her whole luxurious, aristocratic existence. She must rely on his arm alone to support her, and on his love to be her only comfort and compensation. They must live an isolated life, whether wandering, or resting in some quiet place where society never came. She must also take the chance of his being killed by Marc-antonio, who would certainly make an effort to destroy him, and the chance was not small, considering the provocation. If it happened that he fell, she would certainly be left alone in the world. This was probably the strongest argument with her against flight, but it had not weight enough to hold her back, for she had the pride of a woman who had

found a man ready to fight for her, in these latter
days when fighting is so terribly out of fashion; and
she felt in her heart that she should always be able
to prevent an encounter.

The resolution she had made had killed any doubt
that might still have remained as to the ultimate
result of her love for Julius. Henceforth it was
her duty to kill doubts in order to be happy; and,
indeed, there were few left, for her love was very
sincere and real. But if any should arise she meant
to smother them instantly. And now she remembered every word her lover had spoken in that brief
stolen interview, and she felt no fear. Her face
was set, and she looked defiantly at her husband.
A few hours more, she thought, and she should be
free from him, from the world, from everything —
forever.

They would have gone at once, that very minute,
but Batiscombe pointed out that the time was ill
chosen. She had been seen to come to the hotel,—
the servant who had shown her up-stairs had noticed
her, perhaps recognised her; in half an hour after
the dinner hour she would be missed at the villa,
and they would surely be overtaken on land, especially as there was no train at that time. Julius said
his boat was moored at the foot of the cliff below
the hotel, but it would be impossible to reach it
without being observed by many people, some of
whom might recognise her. There was also no
wind, the sea was oily with a deadly calm, and the

full moon, just rising, would make pursuit easy, for though his boat could beat anything on the coast under canvas, she was over heavy in the water for his six men to row at any speed.

But at midnight, when the easterly breeze was blowing from the land, he would be down at the landing of her villa, ready. Marcantonio was always asleep at that hour, for he rose betimes in the morning and went to bed early. The dogs? Julius had thought of that, and sending his sailor servant to the kitchen of the hotel, he obtained in a few minutes a couple of solid lumps of meat, which he caused to be wrapped in paper and then tied up in a silk handkerchief for her to carry. She might find it hard, he said, to get anything of the kind in her own house. She was fond of animals, and was sure she could manage to quiet the terriers in a moment if she had something to give them. Besides, they knew her, and would only bark a very little at first. The moon was full, to be sure, but that could not be helped. Once on the water, nothing short of steam could catch them, and that was not available at such short notice. She should not hamper her flight with unnecessary things, he said, for if any one were roused she might have to run for her life as far as the beginning of the descent where he would be in waiting for her. These and a hundred other little directions he had given her, with the quiet forethought for details that was part of his remarkable intellect.

And now she sat opposite her husband at their small dinner-table, looking hard and determined, but listening with more than usual complacency to his talk, and striving to eat something, as Julius had instructed her. She made such a good pretence that Marcantonio noticed it approvingly.

"I am glad to see, my angel," he said, "that you are finding your appetite again. It is most encouraging."

It was just like his want of tact, thought Leonora. It was just like him to suppose that she would eat the more because he wanted her to do so, and watched her! Dieu! What a nuisance to be always watched. It would soon be over now, however, and she could afford to be indifferent.

"Oddly enough," said she, "I am hungry—I do not know why."

"Does any one know why they are hungry?" said Marcantonio, with a little laugh. "It happens to me to take much exercise. I rise with the sun, I walk, I ride, I dispatch my correspondence, I work like a dog—et puis, at breakfast I eat nothing. No appetite. Good! Another day, I lie in bed till ten o'clock, rise with a cigarette, read a novel, and —voyez donc, how droll—I eat, perhaps, for four people. But I have often observed that, if I eat a mayonnaise at dinner, I have no appetite the next day at breakfast. It is extremely singular, for the cook makes the mayonnaise of great delicacy."

What could it possibly matter whether Marc-

antonio were hungry or not, or what he ate for
dinner? But Leonora was glad to have him say
anything, so that she might be spared the effort of
talking.

"It is true," she said, absently, "his mayonnaise
is not bad."

She hoped he would go on; it was an easy, neutral
subject — of many ingredients, concerning each of
which it would be possible to differ and to raise a
fresh discussion.

"Apropos," said Marcantonio, "the gardener's
boy cut his finger very badly this afternoon " —

"Apropos of mayonnaise?" Leonora could not
help asking the question. His conversation was
so absurd.

"Ma foi! mayonnaise — vegetables — gardens —
gardeners and the gardener's boy — all that holds
together. As I was saying, he cut his finger, and
I sent your maid to get something to bind it
with."

"I hope she did not take one of my lace handkerchiefs," remarked Leonora. "It would be just like
her."

"It was not lace, I am sure," said Marcantonio,
with an air of conviction, as he helped himself to
the salad which Temistocle handed him. "But it
looked very new. I hope she made no mistake."

The comic side of the situation suddenly forced
itself on Leonora, as it often will happen with
people on the eve of great danger. A lackey in

Paris once danced a jig on the scaffold before he was broken on the wheel. Leonora laughed aloud.

"Would it amuse you, for instance," inquired Marcantonio with a puzzled look, "to have a good handkerchief destroyed to tie up the boy's finger?"

It seemed so funny to Leonora to think that on the morrow her entire stock of handkerchiefs would be at the disposal of all the gardeners in Sorrento if they chanced to cut their fingers.

"No — not that," she said. "It is so odd that you should take so much trouble about it — or care."

"Poor people," said Marcantonio, "one must do what one can for them."

And so their last conversation tottered to its end in a round of domestic triviality, so that Leonora wondered how she could have borne it so long. But, in truth, Marcantonio was so much afraid of rousing her opposition that evening, after the scene that had taken place, that he purposely avoided every intelligent subject, and did violence to his own preference for the sake of keeping the peace. He liked to talk politics, he liked to talk of Rome, of society, of a hundred things, but of late he had found it very hard to talk peaceably about anything.

After dinner Marcantonio smoked, and Leonora sat beside him, with a little worsted work which she did with a huge ivory needle. Her heart beat fast as the hour approached when she must part from her husband. She glanced at him from time to time, sitting there so unsuspecting of any surprise, with his cigarette and his "Fanfulla," the witty Roman paper that amused him so much. His delicate, dark features, a little weak perhaps, looked handsome enough in the lamplight, and Leonora thought for a moment that she had never seen him look so well. She was already so far from him in her thoughts that she regarded him as from a distance, with a certain abstracted consideration of his merits that was new to her. Poor Marcantonio! A certain curiosity, which would have been pity if she had allowed it, came over her. She wondered how he would look when she was gone. Ten o'clock — two hours to midnight, and he never saw her before nine in the morning now. Nine and two were eleven. In eleven hours he must know — unless something happened. Would he rage and storm, like a wild beast? Or would he break down and shed tears? Neither, she thought. He did not love her — he was only jealous. Heavens! thought she, if Julius had been in his position, and he in Julius's, could things have ever got to this pass without some fearful outbreak? Ah no! Julius was so hot-tempered and strong. Her thoughts went away with her, and she heaved a quick short breath, suddenly interrupted in the recollection of where she was. Marcantonio looked round.

"What is it, my dear?" he asked.

"Nothing — I was going to sneeze," said Leonora with a ready excuse.

"There is too much air," said he, rising and going toward the window.

He looked out for a moment. The first breath of the easterly wind was coming over the mountains and just stirring a ripple on the moonlit bay. It had rained early in the afternoon, and they had sat indoors on account of the dampness. Marcantonio sniffed the breeze, said it was damp, and closed the window.

"It must be late," said he. "En vérité, it is twenty minutes to eleven! I should not have thought it."

Leonora's heart beat fast.

"I suppose it is time to go to bed," she said, with enough indifference to escape notice.

Marcantonio had not enjoyed the evening much, and was sleepy. Leonora moved slowly about the room, touching a book here and a photograph there as though to make the room comfortable for the night. Some women always do it. Her blood was throbbing wildly — the last strong effort of conscience was upon her. A great pity sprang up in her — a terrible regret — a horror of great evil. Her resolutions, her love, her determination to fly, her better self, all struggled and reeled furiously together. She felt an irresistible impulse to throw herself at her husband's feet, to confess everything, to implore his protection, and forgiveness, and help. She turned towards him suddenly. He was in the act of ringing the bell.

The sharp tinkle, sounding from far away through the open doors of the house, checked her when she was on the very point of speaking. Almost instantly, the quick tread of the servant was heard. He came, and the supreme moment was over. The reality of her situation returned, and with it the hardness it needed. The man had the candles ready in his hands, and stood waiting to accompany Leonora to her door.

"Good-night, Marcantoine," said she, holding out her hand.

It was cold and clammy with intense excitement, and her face was pale to the lips.

"Good-night, my angel," said he, touching his lips to her fingers, and she passed from him. Just beyond the door she turned and looked back, with a touch of sadness.

"Good-night," she said once more, faintly — for the last, the very last time.

When Marcantonio was alone, he took his newspapers, and one or two letters which had come by the late post, he looked carefully round the room, to see that he had forgotten nothing, as he had a bad habit of doing, and he marched gloomily off to his room, which was beyond Leonora's, and separated from hers by her sitting-room. Her dressing-room was on the other side of her bedroom, and had a separate door, opening upon the head of the stairs.

As soon as Leonora had dismissed her maid for the night, she began to make her preparations. She had a large silk bag, of many colours, made like an old-fashioned purse, with heavy silver rings. She used it for carrying her work, her books, or anything she needed when she went into the garden to spend the morning. It seemed the best thing to take with her now, for it would hold a good deal and was convenient. She filled it with handkerchiefs, bottles of eau-de-cologne, and hairpins, and she put in a tiny looking-glass in a silver case, which she had used all her life. It was of no use to think of taking anything else, she thought, since she must carry it all in her hand. Then she went over her jewels and took her own, carefully setting aside all that her husband had given her. She tied them up in a handkerchief with two hard knots,—the best she knew how to make,—and she put them into the bag with the rest of the things. Then she found her purse, and put into it all the money she had, for it was her own, and she thought she might as well have it, —and there was her cheque-book in the drawer of the writing-table. Of course she could draw her own money just as well when—she did not finish the sentence to herself.

Presently she went into the sitting-room, and listened at the small side door which opened into Marcantonio's bedroom. She had taken an hour over her preparations; it was half past eleven, and he was asleep,—she heard his regular breathing distinctly. The full moon shone outside upon the gravel walks, and the orange-trees, and the soft wind was blowing steadily through the open windows. She paused one moment before she went back, and she looked out at the scene, so sweet and peaceful in the ivory moonlight. Far off in the town the clocks struck the half hour. Julius must be already on the water, perhaps near the landing. She hastened to her room, treading on tiptoe; her maid had left her in her loose white peignoir; she must dress again, and dress quickly, or she would be late.

It did not take long,—though she put the candle before her glass, and dallied a little with a ribbon and a pin. The dress was soft and dark, fitting closely to her figure. In reality she had selected it because it had a pocket,—that would be such a convenient thing on a journey. A hat—yes, she must have a hat, for of course they must land somewhere, though a veil would be more convenient in the wind.

There was a great vase of carnations, gathered that day, that stood on a little table by the window. At the last minute, Leonora stopped and took one. She went back to the glass with the candle in her hand, and pinned the flower in her dress, eying the effect critically. They were the flowers he loved best,— it was an afterthought, and would please him. She was ready, the bag hung over her arm, the package of meat for the dogs in one hand, and a candle in the other. She blew out the remaining lights as the clocks struck midnight, put the one she carried upon a chair by the door, while she softly turned the latch, looked out cautiously, and left the room. Once out of the passage and on the stairs, she had

no fear of being heard, and she descended rapidly.
One moment more and she was in the open air.
The front door closed behind her. Something
touched her feet, and, looking down, she saw that
the white kitten had followed her out; she had not
noticed it, poor thing, and she could not risk opening the door again to put it back.

She glanced out into the moonlight from beneath
the porch, and she was frightened. It was only a
step — a minute's run, if she ran fast, to the beginning of the passage — but she hesitated and hung
back. Oh, if the last step were not so hard! If
Julius had only met her at the door instead of
being down there — but he was even now at the
head of the steps. She realised his presence, and
the garden was no longer a solitude — she was not
alone any more. The kitten mewed discontentedly.
She bethought herself of the dogs, picked up the
little beast, and moved quickly down the walk,
running faster as she neared the end.

Her running on the path roused the terriers,
prowling about among the shrubbery in the warm
night, and they sprang upon her not ten yards from
the mouth of the descent, barking furiously and
snapping at her dress. She dropped the parcel of
meat instantly, but they did not see it at once,
and pursued her. In one moment more she was
lifted from the ground and held firmly in the mighty
grasp of the strong man who stood ready, and had
run forward to meet her when the dogs sprang out.

But, in the quick act, the kitten fell to the ground almost between the enraged terriers.

It was over in a minute. One frantic, piteous death-scream and the poor little white cat lay dead on the gravel path, and the terriers sniffed her little body disdainfully, as though congratulating each other on their brave deed.

"Oh, Julius, they have killed my kitten!" cried Leonora in real distress. They were already under the archway, and Batiscombe was urging her to descend, but she clung to him, and stared back into the moonlight at the dogs and her dead pet.

Julius himself was enraged at the thing — it was so wantonly cruel.

"Run on," said he, in a whisper; "I will settle them." He had reflected quickly that they had only barked for a moment, and that any one who heard them must have heard the cat also and would have taken no notice of the noise.

At that very moment Marcantonio turned on his pillow, and, half waking, swore to himself, as he had done every night of his life for weeks, that he would send the dogs away in the morning. But all was still, and he fell asleep again instantly.

Julius went back upon the path, and the terriers growled, still scenting their vanquished prey. But he moved quickly and softly, speaking gently to them in a low voice, and holding out his hand to them. He had a sort of influence over animals, and they let him come close, pricking their ears and sniffing about his legs. Suddenly, as they smelled at his boots, he caught them by their necks in an iron grip, one in each hand, and held them up at arm's length, struggling frantically, but utterly incapable of making a sound.

"You killed her cat, did you, you brutes?" he muttered, savagely. "I will kill you."

He broke their necks, one after the other, and threw their quivering bodies far out under the orange-trees.

Leonora had watched him from the archway. She shuddered.

"They will not bark any more," said Julius, as he came to her.

"What strong hands you have!" she said.

A window opened, up in the house, a hundred yards away. Batiscombe's quick ear caught the sound.

"Come, sweetheart," he whispered; "some one is stirring."

His arm was round her as he guided her down the first steps, tenderly and strongly. She stumbled a little.

"Oh, Julius, I am so frightened!" she said piteously.

He stopped and took her off the ground as though she had been a child, and bore her swiftly and surely through the dark way. She could see his fiery blue eyes in the gloom, and in the flashes of white light as they passed the windows and arches where the moon streamed in, and as she looked she could feel her own grow big and dark; and she was frightened and very happy. But she thought of that strange thing she had dreamed — this very flight of hers exactly as it was to happen, so that she hid her face against his coat and clung to him nervously.

"Put me down," she cried earnestly, as they emerged upon the flat rock of the landing, "put me down, Julius, — I dreamed you fell here."

He obeyed her, and set her on her feet, still supporting her with his arm about her waist. One passionate kiss — only one — and then they came out from the shadow of the high cliff, and saw the boat riding lightly in the moonlight, two sailors holding her off the rocks, and the rest busy on board with the sails. The water plashed musically in the little hollows, and from near by there came a deep, mysterious murmur out of the many dark caves that lined the shore.

Leonora stepped lightly in, and Julius arranged the cushions about her carefully. Neither of them spoke. With a few strong strokes of the oars the boat shot out into the breeze from the lee of the gorge. The foresail was already set, and jib and mainsail went up in a moment, wing and wing, the tapering, lateen-yards pointing to right and left, like the horns of a great, soft, white moth; the water rippled at the stern, and curled up and lapped the rudder as the sails filled, and ever swiftly and more swiftly the craft rushed down the bay in the glorious moonlight, before the steady east wind.

Julius held the tiller with one hand, and the other lovingly supported Leonora's head against his breast, as she lay along the cushions in the stern.

"Darling," he said presently, "what was the dream about my falling at the landing? You never told me."

She did not answer, but lay quite still.

"Dear one," he murmured, bending down, "are you so tired? Leonora — sweetheart — speak to me!"

But the strain had been too strong, and Leonora lay in his arms, whiter than death under the white moon, unconscious of Julius or of the sea. Julius saw that she had fainted.

CHAPTER XVIII.

AT half past eight on the following morning Temistocle found Leonora's maid at the door of her mistress's room with an expression of blank astonishment on her face that made him laugh. He often laughed, quietly, without the least noise.

"You look exactly like a lay figure in a milliner's shop," he remarked. "Except, indeed, that you look much more stupid."

The maid glared at him.

"The signora" — she began, and then trembled and looked round timidly.

"What about her?" inquired Temistocle, pricking up his ears.

The maid let her voice drop to a low whisper.

"She is not there," said she.

"Ebbene," said Temistocle with a grin, "what has happened to you? She is probably gone out — gone to church. A good place for heretics, too."

"Macchè," whispered the woman, "she has not slept in her bed, and everything is upside down in the room."

"May the devil carry you off!" said Temistocle, suddenly changing his voice, and whispering hoarsely. "Let me see — let me pass." He put down the can of hot water he was taking to his master, and pushed past the maid, into Leonora's bedroom.

"Bada," said the woman, going after him cautiously, "take care! The signore might come in and find you."

"What harm is there?" asked the servant. And then he made a careful survey of the premises, locking all the doors except the one by which they had entered.

"It is true, what you said," he remarked, pushing the maid out of the room. "An apoplexy on these foreigners who go away without telling one. Fuori! Go along with you, my child. Ci penso io — I will look after all this." And he locked the door behind him, put the key in his pocket, and took up his water-can.

"What are you doing?" asked the maid. Temistocle had seen a chance, and took it.

"Look here," said he, rubbing the thumb and forefinger of his hand together before the girl's eyes, — which means "money" in gesture language — "look here. The signore accompanied the signora to the early train from Castellamare this morning at half past four. They had a hired carriage. She went away and forgot her jewels on the table. She is gone to Rome on business, — they were talking about it last night. Do you understand?"

"No," answered the woman looking puzzled, "you said she had gone out" —

"I said so to you," he answered with a sly grin, "but I will not say so to any one else, nor you either. Remember that she went to Rome this morning. It will be worth your while to remember that."

The woman smiled a cunning smile. She had hated her mistress, and would have liked to make a scandal before all the other servants, but Temistocle's advice would be more profitable. So they arranged the matter between them and parted.

Marcantonio was seated at his writing-table when Temistocle entered. He always got up very early, and did a great many things before he dressed.

Temistocle busied himself a moment about the room, and when he was ready to go he came to the table and laid the key he had taken from Leonora's door at his master's elbow.

"What is that?" asked Marcantonio, looking up.

"It is the key of the Signora Marchesa's bed-room, eccellenza," answered Temistocle, edging away toward the door. "Her excellency must have gone away very early, and she left her room open and all her jewelry strewed about. So I locked the doors and brought you the key."

He was very near the door and could escape in a moment.

But Marcantonio did not move; his jaw dropped, and his colour changed to a yellow waxen hue, which terrified the servant. But he did not move. Temistocle continued.

"I told the servants not to be astonished, as you had accompanied the Signora Marchesa to the early train for Rome before daybreak," he said, putting his hand on the latch.

Marcantonio made as though he would rise. Temistocle slipped nimbly through the door and closed it behind him, running away as though the police were after him. But he knew that when Carantoni had recovered, he would be amply rewarded for his wisdom. It often chances that villains play a good and sensible part in life, which is quite as profitable as villainy, and is always safer.

Marcantonio struggled to rise, and at last got upon his feet, staggering like a man stunned by a physical blow. The door to Leonora's sitting-room was open, but, beyond, the one to her bedroom was locked. He had to go round by the passage, feeling his way as though he were blind. At last he found the lock,— the key turned, and he entered.

It was just as she had left it. The white peignoir she had taken off when she dressed for her flight lay in a heap upon the floor where she had thrown it in her haste. The dismal, half-burned candles stood on the dressing-table. The drawer from which she had taken the handkerchiefs was half open. The windows were thrown back, and the blinds had not been closed, so that the strong glare of the morning poured rudely in on the confusion, and the flies buzzed about the scented soap and the bottle of lavender and the pot of carnations in the corner.

Marcantonio dragged himself from one part of the room to another till he stumbled against the table on which Leonora had left her scattered jewelry,— all the things he had given her. He stood staring down at the glittering gold and precious stones, unconsciously realising that they were all his presents that she had left behind her. There was a strange old Maltese cross of diamonds and sapphires among them, mounted in silver. It had belonged to his mother, and he had given it to Leonora with other things when he married her. His eyes fastened upon it, and his hand crept across the table and took it.

He raised it to his white lips and kissed it once —twice; he would have kissed it again, but the bow of his strength was bent too far and snapped asunder. With a short, fierce cry he threw up his hands, and fell prostrate on the smooth tiled floor, as a dead man might have fallen.

He lay entirely unconscious for hours, so that when he at last came to himself and struggled to move till he could sit up and stare about him, the midday sun was pouring in, and the flies angrily tormented his ghastly face, as though in derision of anything so miserable. For some minutes he sat upon the floor, dazed and stupid with the oppression of returning grief, as well as stunned from the physical pain resulting from his fall. He was not hurt seriously, but he was bruised and weak. At last he got to his feet, steadying himself by the table. He would not see what was about him any more, for he knew it all, and the full consciousness of his misfortune was on him. He regained his own room, carefully locking Leonora's door behind him, and taking with him his mother's diamond cross.

But the mere sense of grief could not long hold the mastery with a man like Marcantonio. He had loved his wife too well not to resent the injury and scorn, as well as weep over it. As he pondered, lying on his bed, there arose in his breast a desperate and concentrated anger against the man who had deprived him of what he best loved in the world, the anger of a mind that has never reasoned much about anything, and will carry unreason to any length when it comes. He must find his enemy; that was the principal thought in his mind. That he would kill him when he found him was a conclusion that seemed a matter of course.

But, in order to find him, it was necessary to move, to search, and turn everything over. He turned on his pillow, feeling the first restless stirrings of the demon that would by and by give him no peace by day or night till the man was found and the blow struck. He turned over and rang a bell by his bedside.

"Give me some coffee, and order the carriage," he said to the servant.

At the end of an hour, he found himself in the town, and inquired for Batiscombe. It seemed as though fate favoured Carantoni at the outset, for he found his name at once on the register of the hotel, and found also the man who had waited on Julius. This servant had been told that a lady had come in great haste soon after seven on the previous evening, and had stayed more than half an hour. As soon as she was gone, Mr. Batiscombe had sent for his bill and had ordered his boat to be ready at eleven,— the servant had heard the order. The man guessed there was something wrong from Marcantonio's face, but Batiscombe's sudden departure had excited no remark. He had arrived late at night in his boat, as many people had done, and as the moon was full it was natural enough that he should sail away as he had come. People arrive continually at Sorrento in yachts, and no one takes any notice of them.

His luggage? Yes, he had taken most of his things with him, except one large box, which he had ordered to be sent to Turin. It had gone to Castellamare at once. Mr. Batiscombe had been in the hotel before. He was a very good signore.

At this hint Marcantonio gave the man a heavy fee. Did he happen to know the address on the box? There was no address, except his name. The box was to be left at Turin until called for. It was to go by fast train, and Mr. Batiscombe had left money to pay for its carriage in advance. Mr. Batiscombe paid his bills by cheques on a banker in Rome. Marcantonio might have the name if he pleased. Before leaving he had paid his bill and given a cheque for five or six hundred francs more.

The proprietor knew him very well, and was always glad to oblige him, so he had procured a little cash. Before going he had sent for a silk merchant — there are hundreds in Sorrento — and had bought a quantity of things of him. He had left the hotel at eleven by the steps to the sea, and the servant had seen him into his boat, — for which parting civility, Batiscombe had given him ten francs. The man had watched the boat for a few minutes. She did not make sail, but pulled away towards Castellamare.

That was all, absolutely all, that the man could tell Marcantonio. But it was sufficient for the present. It was clear that Julius had taken Leonora from the landing of the villa. She must have slipped out soon after midnight. The barking of the dogs suddenly came back to Marcantonio's memory, and the scream of the poor cat. He sprang into his carriage, and drove furiously homeward.

"Where are the dogs?" he asked, as soon as he alighted.

The groom did not like to answer. He thought Marcantonio would be angry and visit their death on him. But, as his master insisted, he went away without saying a word, and brought a large basket. In it lay the two dead terriers and the dead kitten, all three side by side.

"The dogs killed the cat," said the man, apologetically. "There are the marks of their teeth, eccellenza."

"But the dogs? How were they killed?" asked Marcantonio savagely.

"Eccellenza, their necks are broken. I cannot understand how it could have been done. We found them all dead near the descent, the cat on the path, and the dogs under the trees a few paces away."

Carantoni took up one of the terriers in his hands, and looked at it.

"So you killed my dogs, did you, you brute?" he muttered. "I will kill you."

He unconsciously used Batiscombe's own words. His face was yellow, and his eyes bloodshot. He dropped the dead beast into the basket.

"Bury them," he said aloud, and turned on his heel, going into the house.

He had accomplished a great deal in a few hours. He had ascertained that they had fled by sea; that Julius had a bank account in Rome with a banker whose address he had got; that Julius had sent his box to Turin, where he would most likely be ultimately heard of. More than that he could not know for the present. It was four o'clock in the afternoon. He could still catch the train to Rome. He could do nothing more in Sorrento, and he could no more remain inactive for one moment than he could give up the whole pursuit. While his things were being hastily packed he thought of Diana. It was the first time, since the morning, that he had realised that he was not absolutely alone in the world. He sat down and wrote a telegram, intend-

ing to send it from the station.   It was brief and to
the point.

"She has left me.   Can you meet me anywhere?
Answer to Rome."

There are doubtless people in the world who take
a morbid and unwholesome delight in the contemplation of sorrow. They can amuse themselves for
many hours in studying the effect of grief upon
their friends, — and they can even find a curious
diversion in their own troubles, so long as they can
keep them far enough away to secure their bodily
comfort. They have neither the strength to sin,
the honesty to be good, nor the common sense to
be happy. And so they feebly paddle in their
shallow puddles of woe, neither dry nor wet, and
very muddy, when they might just as well sit on
the clean, hard ground and enjoy the cleanliness
and solidity of it, if they can enjoy nothing else.
But they will not. They will lie in the mud, and
kick and scream and swear that they are shipwrecked, when they are a hundred miles from the
sea, and would take to their heels on the first sight
of it.

One of the favourite hobbies of these individuals
is a mysterious thing they call a "sweet sadness."
Their ideas about sorrow are not even artistic.
They might at least understand that even the
intensest grief, apart from its causes, has no grandeur. The contemplation of sorrow is not elevating
unless it breeds a strong desire to alleviate it; nor

is the study of vice and crime in the least edifying unless it exhibits the nobility and power of purity in a highly practical light. No vicious criminal was ever reformed by realistic pictures of wickedness, any more than he can be improved by daily association with other vicious criminals. And a very little realism will throw a great ideal into the shade, as far as most people are concerned.

Marcantonio may therefore be allowed to go to Rome without being watched on the journey. His bitter suffering had settled about him and taken a shape and a complexion of its own, thinking its own thoughts and acting its own acts, without reference to the real Marcantonio, the easy, cheerful, happy man of a few short weeks ago. It was no change of character now, but rather the entire disappearance of the character beneath the flood of strong passions that had come from without, sweeping away the landmarks and beacons of all moral responsibility. One idea had taken possession of him, and destroyed his consciousness of good and evil, and his comprehension of the common things of life; his body and intelligence had become the mere tools of this idea, and would strain their strength to carry it out until one or the other gave way. Man is said to be a free agent, and so long as he remembers the fact, he is; but when he forgets it, the freedom is gone.

That morning, when the blow first struck him, he had still some vague thought that there was a course to follow which should be right as well as brave and honourable; it was the fast vanishing outline of his former self, used always to the ways of honour; it was vague and uncertain, and he had no time nor inclination to think about it, but it was present. The day wore on, bringing a fuller realisation of his desperate çase, and the possibility of good in so much evil disappeared. When he was at last in the express train on his way to Rome he was only conscious of one thing — the determination to find Julius Batiscombe, and to kill him ruthlessly, be the consequences what they might.

Rome looked much as usual when he at last came out of the great ugly station upon the Piazza dei Termini. It was morning, and not yet eight o'clock, but the pitiless August sun drove its fire through everything — through flesh and bone and marrow of living things, through the glaring stones and dusty trees, and even the great jet of water looked like bright melting metal that would burn if it touched one.

But Marcantonio Carantoni was past feeling heat or cold or bodily hurt. He did not even remember that he had a servant with him, and he mechanically hailed a cab and was driven to his own house. They put a telegram into his hand; it was from Diana, in answer to his of the day before. It was briefer than his and breathed authority.

"Have left Pegli. Wait for me in Rome."

That was all. He read it stupidly over two or

three times. He would not have telegraphed to her if he had waited till to-day. Some instinct told him that she would prevent and hinder his vengeance. Yesterday he wanted help; to-day he wanted nothing but freedom from restraint and an opportunity of meeting Julius Batiscombe. She would not aid him in that, he was sure.

But she could not arrive to-day,— it was a long journey from Pegli to Rome; he did not know exactly how long it took,— his memory would not serve him with any details. He should have time in Rome to do the things he meant to do, and he would go to Turin that very night and watch that box of Batiscombe's. He would send for it, of course, wherever he was, and the box would betray him at last, if all other means failed. But meanwhile there were the police — there were detectives to be had, and plenty of them; money could do much, and his high position could do more. He would set a whole pack of sharp-scented human hounds at Batiscombe's heels — they should find him, and bring word, never fear. He laughed at the idea of employing the law to hunt his prey, in order that he might bid the law defiance and destroy his man alone.

He threw down the telegram and went to his room, followed closely by his servant, who had arrived in mad haste in a second cab, believing that his master was going to be insane, unless he had a stroke of apoplexy, which seemed not unlikely.

The man was a skilled valet, and Marcantonio suffered himself to be dressed and combed and smoothed, in perfect silence; and when it was over he ate something that they brought him, without the slightest idea of what he was doing. He knew it was yet early, and that his business could not be done until the officials he needed were in their offices.

No sooner had the clock struck ten, however, than he took his hat and left the house. He found a cab, and had himself driven from one office to another all through the heat of the day, seeing confidential detectives and stating his business with a strange lucidity, never telling any single agent that he was employing another, but giving to each one a sum of money to begin his search and to each the same precise statement of all that he knew. The consequence was that before the sun was low he had dispatched half a dozen of the best men that could be found, and had got rid of about fifty thousand francs. Each one separately might have to go to the end of the world — to America perhaps, but most probably to England — before he could give the required information. It was necessary that his men should be perfectly free to move in any direction. He himself would go to Turin, and there receive their telegrams, himself watching that box of Batiscombe's, which he was sure must some day be claimed by its owner.

He was perfectly calm and self-possessed throughout all these arrangements. Only the strange

ghastly colour that had overspread his face seemed
to settle and become permanent, and his eyes were
bloodshot and yellow, while his hand trembled
violently when he held a pen or lit a match for his
cigarette.   But he felt no bodily ill, nor any
capacity for fatigue.   He had not closed his eyes
for thirty-six hours, and had eaten little enough,
but there was not an ache nor a sensation of pain
in him, and he dreaded to pause or sit down, hating
the idea of rest.

When he had done all that he could think of as
being at all useful in his plan, he went home and
told his servant to prepare for the journey to Turin
that night.   The train left at half past ten — there
were some hours yet to wait.   He moved restlessly
about the house, and ordered all the windows to
be opened.

The great rooms were in their summer dress.
The furniture, the huge pier glasses and the chan-
deliers were all clothed in brown linen.   The
carpets had all been taken up, and the floors —
some of marble, some of red brick, and some of tiles
— were bare and smooth.   There was the coolness
and absence of all colour that seems to belong to
great palaces when the owners are out of town, and
the cold monotony of everything soothed him a little.   After wandering aimlessly for half an hour,
he settled into a regular walk, up and down the
great ball-room, with its clere-story windows and
vaulted ceiling.   Up and down, up and down, with

an even, untiring tread he paced, his eyes bent
always on the floor and his hands behind him. His
walk was like clockwork, absolutely even and un-
changing, with its rhythmic echo and unvarying
accuracy.

The broad daylight softened into shadow, and the
shadow deepened into gloom, but still he kept on
his beat as though counting his steps and measuring
the time. There was a certain relief in it, though
not from his mastering thought, which held him in
a vise and never relaxed for a second, but from his
terrible restlessness. It was an outlet to his over-
wrought activity, and he did it monotonously, without any consideration, because there was nothing
else to do, and it would have driven him mad to
sit still for five minutes.

As the night came on, strange faces seemed to
look upon him from the gathering darkness. The
thick, warm air took shape and substance, and he
could distinguish forms moving quickly before him
that he could not overtake. But there was no
sensation of horror or fear with the sight — he gazed
curiously at the fleeting shadows and looked into
their faces as they came close to him and retreated,
but he could not recognise them, and did not ask
himself whence they came nor whither they were
going, nor why he saw them. It seemed very
natural somehow.

But at last, as he turned, there was one coming
toward him that had more substance than the rest,

so that they all vanished but that one. It was a woman, and she seemed moving towards him; but it was almost quite dark. He came nearer; his waking senses caught the sound of her footstep; she was no shadow — it was his wife coming back to him — it had all been a fearful dream, and she was there again. He sprang forward with a quick cry.

"Leonora! Oh, thank God!" and he fell forward into her arms.

"No, dearest brother — it is not Leonora — would God it were!"

Diana had come already — he could not tell how — and they stood together in the dark, empty ball-room, clasped in each other's arms.

CHAPTER XIX.

DIANA had found ample time to think over the situation during the journey, and she was prepared for difficulties.   Her brother could hardly be in his right mind, she thought, and would certainly be on the verge of doing something desperate, which she must prevent.

As was usual with her in sudden emergencies, she had been wonderfully quiet. She was shocked and horrified at the news, but neither the shock nor the horror were uppermost in her mind.   What she most felt was an unutterable and loving pity for her brother; and as she sat in the express train and looked out of the window at the interminable miles of vineyard and cornland, the kind, womanly tears gathered and fell softly. She could not help it, and she would not. Poor fellow! he deserved all her heart, and her soul's sympathy, and the tears thereof.

Marcantonio was in no state to reason or to be reasoned with. He had a strange illusion for a moment, when he thought his wife had returned to him, but he at once realised his folly and understood that Diana had come to meet him — had come, doubtless, to prevent him from accomplishing his vengeance. He had been so sure that she could not arrive until the next morning that he had anticipated no interruption in his plans, and he was angry with her for being in his way. She would watch him day and night, and hinder all his movements. So long as she was with him it would be impossible to do anything. He answered her very coldly.

"You have come already? I did not expect you so soon."

They moved towards the door, groping in the deep gloom, and presently reached a room where there were lights. Then Diana saw her brother's face and understood that he was mad or desperately ill, or both. The ghastly colour, the bloodshot eyes, the trembling hand, she saw it all. She had not known what change his trouble would make in him, but she knew it would be great. But she was startled now that she was face to face with him. It seemed too terribly real. She could not help it, she bent her beautiful fair head on his shoulder and threw her arms about him and sobbed aloud.

But Marcantonio only understood that she was there to keep him from his ends, from the one thing in the world which he wished to do, and meant to do, and surely would accomplish. As she leaned on him and shed those bitter tears for him, he stood passive and dry-eyed, staring vacantly above her at the wall, and his hands hung by his side, not offering to support her or to comfort her. He only wished she were gone again and had never come to trouble him.

It was only for a moment. Such outbursts of feeling were rare with Diana; people said she was a piece of ice, heartless, and without sympathy for any human being. They judged her by her face and by the dignity of her manner, not knowing of the things she had done in her life that were neither heartless nor cold. But now she recovered herself quickly and dried her eyes, and made Marcantonio sit down. She looked at him intently as though trying to understand him. He had never met her so coldly before in his life; there must be a reason for it,— he was evidently beside himself with suffering, but his temporary madness could hardly take the form of a sudden dislike for herself unless there were some cause.

"You did not expect me so soon," she said, speaking very gently. "It was by a mere chance that I managed it."

"I am very sorry," said Marcantonio in a monotonous voice that had no life in it, and seemed not his own. "If you had waited a little while I could have saved you the journey."

"The journey is nothing," said she. "I am not tired at all, and I would come across the world to be with you."

"Yes," said Marcantonio, "I know you would. It would have been better if we had met further on."

"Further on?" she repeated, hoping he would give her some clue to his intentions.

The old habit of confidence was too strong for him; he wished her away, but he could not help speaking and telling her something. He had never concealed anything from her.

"In Turin," he answered briefly.

"Ah,—is he there?" asked Diana in a low voice.

"He sent his box there,—he will go and get it."

"And then?"

"And then," said Marcantonio, the sullen fire burning in his reddened eyes, "we shall meet."

Diana was silent for a moment, determining what to do. All this she had expected, but she had not thought to find her brother so changed.

"Tell me, Marcantonio," she said earnestly, "did you think I would prevent your meeting with him?" He hesitated. She took his hand and looked into his face as though urging him to answer.

"Yes," he said hoarsely.

Diana understood. This was the reason of his evident annoyance at her coming. He thought she meant to prevent him from fighting Batiscombe.

"You know better than that," she said gravely. Marcantonio turned upon her quickly with an angry look.

"You prevented me before," he said. "If I had shot him then, this trouble would not have come. You know it,—why do you look at me like that?"

"If you had shot him before," said she, "this could not have happened. But if he had shot you, —that was possible, was it not?—you gained nothing. If neither of you had killed the other, there would have been a useless scandal. The case is different."

If she had found her brother overcome with his sorrow and abandoned to the suffering it brought, sensitive and shrinking from all allusion to his shame, she would have acted very differently. But she found him possessed of but one idea, how to kill Julius Batiscombe; he was hard and unyielding; he seemed to have forgotten the wife he had loved so well, in the longing to destroy the man who had stolen her away. She felt no hesitation in speaking plainly of the matter in hand, since his feelings needed no sparing. But her sympathy was so large and honest that she did not feel hurt herself because he was cold to her; she understood that he was scarcely in his right mind, and she could make all allowance for him.

Marcantonio did not answer at once. But her influence on him, as she sat there, was soothing, and he was gradually yielding under it — not in the least abandoning his one idea, but feeling that she might not hinder its execution after all.

"Do you mean to say," he asked suddenly, "that you will not try to prevent my meeting with him?" He turned and looked into her eyes, that met his honestly and fearlessly.

"Assuredly I will not prevent you," said she.

"Really and truly?"

"So truly that if I thought you had meant to leave him alone, I would have tried to make you fight him."

Marcantonio laughed scornfully, in a way that was bad to hear. It had never struck him that he could possibly have not wanted to fight. But in a moment he was grave again.

"What a woman you are, Diana!" he exclaimed. It sounded more like himself than anything he had said yet, and Diana was encouraged. But she said nothing.

In her simple code, fighting was a necessary thing in the world. She had been brought up among people who fought duels under provocation, and it never entered her head that under certain circumstances there was anything else to be done. Women often scream with terror at the mention of such a thing, but very few of them will have anything to do with men who will not fight when they are insulted. In preventing a challenge after the affair at Sorrento she had done violence to her feelings for the sake of Leonora's reputation. In the present instance that was no longer at stake. It was perfectly clear that her brother must have satisfaction from his enemy, as soon as might be.

She had never hesitated, therefore, in her view of Marcantonio's situation, and when he put the question to her she answered it boldly and naturally.

But, somehow, he had not understood his sister before, though he had yielded to her, and he was astonished at her readiness to agree with him. He looked at her with a sort of admiration, and his feeling towards her changed.

"Then you will help me to find him?" he asked.

"I will stay with you until you do," she answered.

"It is the same thing," said he. "Will you come to Turin with me at once?"

"I will not leave you," she said. "We can go to Turin to-morrow, if you like."

"No — to-night," he said, quickly. The idea of wasting twelve hours seemed intolerable.

But Diana had made up her mind that he must rest a while before doing anything more. She shuddered when she looked at his face and saw the change wrought there in six and thirty hours.

"If we start now," she said, "we shall arrive in the evening. You could do nothing at night. Rest until the morning, and then we will go. You will need all the strength you have."

"I cannot rest," he said gloomily.

"You must try," answered Diana. "I will read to you till you are asleep."

He rose and began to pace the room. The doubt that she intended to keep him back sprang up again in his unsettled mind. He stopped before her.

"No," he said, "I will go to-night, and you need not come if you are too tired. You want to prevent me from going at all — I see it in your face."

Diana looked up at him as she sat. No one but a madman could have doubted the faith of those grey eyes of hers, and as Marcantonio gazed on them the old influence of the stronger character began to act. He turned away impatiently.

"You always make me do what you like," he said, and began to walk again.

Diana forced herself to laugh a little.

"Do not be so foolish, dear boy," she said. "I want you to sleep to-night, and to-morrow we will go to the world's end together. You will lose twelve hours somewhere, because there are certain things that cannot be done at night. Better make use of them now, and sleep, before you are altogether exhausted. I promise to go with you to-morrow. Do you mean to have an illness, or to go out of your mind? You will accomplish one or the other in this way, and there will be an end of the whole matter."

"Very well," said Marcantonio, unable to resist her will, "since you promise it to me I will do as you please. But to-morrow morning I will start, whatever happens."

"Very well," said Diana. "And now, dear brother, will you kindly give me some dinner? I have scarcely had anything to-day."

"Dio mio!" cried Marcantonio, "what a brute I am!"

It was like him, she thought, to be angry at himself for having forgotten to be hospitable. The words reassured her, for they sounded natural. There had been moments during the conversation when she had thought he was insane. Perhaps it was more his looks than his words, however. At all events, as he rang the bell and ordered what was necessary, she felt as though he were already better.

One of her reasons for wishing him to stay a night in Rome was that he might immediately have a chance of growing calmer. Nothing distances grief like sleep. Until the first impression had become less vivid in his mind, she could not ask him questions about the circumstances of the flight. She guessed that, although he was willing, and even anxious, to talk of his future meeting with Batiscombe, it would be quite another thing to make him speak of the past fact. And yet she knew nothing of the details — not even exactly the time when it had all happened. She half fancied that they must have got away by the sea, because it would have been so simple; but she had no idea of how much Marcantonio knew, nor whether the matter had yet in any way become public property. It was necessary, she judged, that she should know something, at least, of the circumstances. No one but Marcantonio could tell her, and before he could be brought to speak he must be saved from the danger of a physical illness which seemed to threaten him.

Before long dinner was ready. It was ten o'clock, and the meal had been prepared for Marc-

antonio at eight; but he had behaved so strangely
that no one liked to go near him, and the servants
supposed that if he wanted anything he would ring
the bell.

The two sat down opposite to each other. Diana
was tired and hungry; she had taken off her bonnet
on arriving, and had gone straight to Marcantonio,
and now she would not leave him until she had seen
him safe in his room for the night. But in spite of
the long journey, the fatigue, and the great anxiety,
she was the same, as queenly and unruffled as ever,
as smoothly and perfectly dressed, as quiet and
stately in her ways. No wonder she was the envy
of half the women in Europe. The half who did
not envy her were those who had never seen her.

She watched Marcantonio as she sat opposite to
him. It surprised her to see that he ate well,—
more than usual, in fact, and she attributed it
to a sudden improvement which had perhaps been
brought about by her arrival. She had expected
that he would refuse to eat anything, and would
support his strength on strong coffee and tobacco.
She thought that at all events he would not be ill,
— but, again, as she looked at his face, its death-like
yellowness frightened her, and the injected veins
of his eyeballs made his eyes look absolutely red.

They hardly spoke during the meal, for the servants came and went often, and they could not speak
any language together that would not be understood.

After a time they were left alone, and they pre-

pared to part for the night. Diana laid her hand
affectionately on her brother's forehead, as though
to feel whether it were hot. He looked so ill that
it hurt her to see him.

"You are worn out, dear boy," said she. "Go to
bed and sleep."

"I will try," he said, rather submissively than
otherwise. "But we will go to-morrow, of course,"
he added quickly, turning to her with a half-startled
look.

"Of course," said she, reassuring him.

"Because," he said, "I told the detectives to
telegraph to me there, and I gave them my address
at the hotel."

"Detectives?" repeated Diana, starting a little
and looking surprised. "What do you want them
for?"

"Diavolo!" ejaculated Marcantonio savagely, "to
find him, to be sure."

"Batiscombe is not the man to run away, or to
need much finding," said Diana, gravely, with an
air of conviction. She did not like the idea.

"When men mean to be found they leave an
address," said her brother, between his teeth.

There was truth in what he said. Batiscombe
ought to have let Marcantonio know his whereabouts, it was the least a brave man could do, and
Batiscombe was undeniably brave. Diana felt a
sharp sense of pain; the idea that her brother was
hunting down with detectives, like a common male-

factor, the man who had once **loved her** so well —
the idea that she was helping to find him in order
that Marcantonio might kill him if he could — it
was frightful to her. She was bitterly atoning for
one innocent girlish fancy of long ago.

"Marcantonio," she said, almost entreatingly,
"do not do it. Give up the police. I am sure he
will meet you without that " —

"Ah yes!" he interrupted, "you know him. Of
course you will not help me! I forgot that you
were come to shield him, — you — I know you will
not help me!"

He spoke fiercely and brutally, as he had never
spoken to her before. But mad or not mad, Diana
would not submit to such words from any one. She
turned white, and faced him in the light of the two
great lamps that burned on the table. The whole
power and splendid force of her nature gleamed in
her eyes, and thrilled in the low, distinct tones of
her voice.

"What you say is utterly base, and ignoble, and
untrue," she said slowly.

He hung his head, for he knew he was wrong.
He did not know what he said; indeed he had
hardly known what he was doing all that day.

"I am sorry, Diana," he said, at last, quite
humbly. "I am not myself to-day."

Her anger melted away instantly. Himself! No
indeed, poor fellow, he was not himself, and perhaps
never would be his old self again. He was so

utterly wretched as he stood there before her with his head bent and his hands clasped together, so forlorn and forsaken and pitiful, the moment the sustaining force of his anger left him, that no human creature could have seen him without giving him all sympathy and comfort. Diana went close to him and put her arms about him, and kissed him, and her tears wet his cheek. He suffered her to lead him quietly away to his rooms, and she left him in the care of his faithful old servant.

"The signore is ill," she said. "Some one must watch in the outer room all night, in case he wants anything."

Diana herself was exhausted, in spite of her strength and extraordinary nerve. There were times when she broke down, as she had done at Sorrento when she heard Julius and Leonora outside her window, but it was always after the struggle was over, when she was alone. Moreover she had the advantage of a perfectly serene past life, during which no serious trouble had come near her, and her strength had increased with her maturity. It all stood her in good stead now, and helped her to bear what she had to suffer. She went to bed and slept a dreamless sleep which completely restored her. It is the privilege of very calm and evenly balanced natures to take rest when it can be had, and to bear wakefulness and fatigue better in the long run than extremely active and physically energetic people.

As for Marcantonio, he tossed upon his bed and dreamed broken dreams that woke him again and again with a sudden start; he dreamed he had found his man, and the excitement of the moment waked him. Then he dreamed he was quarrelling with his sister, and was suddenly wide awake at the sound of her reproachful voice. He was talking to Leonora, pleading with her, and using all his eloquence to win her back, and she laughed scornfully at him — and that waked him too.

But at last he slept soundly for an hour or two, just before daybreak, and awoke feeling tired, but more restful. The dawn came stealing through the windows, and he got up and moved about a little, with a sensation of enjoyment in the cool, fresh air.

He looked into the glass, and started at his own face that he saw reflected there. It seemed like a hideous mask of himself, all drawn and distorted and pale. But had he looked at himself on the previous day he might have seen an improvement now. He was deadly pale, but no longer yellow, and his eyes had lost the redness which had frightened his sister. He looked ill, but not crazy, and he felt that he could trust himself to-day not to say the things he had said yesterday.

He would go to Turin of course — that was settled — unless Diana were too tired; but he would not have admitted such a condition when he went to bed the night before.

He rang the bell and ordered his things to be got

ready. The old servant, who had slept on a sofa outside, looked haggard and unshaved, and stared suspiciously as he heard the order. But he did not dare to make any remarks, as he would have done if his master had been well. Marcantonio had been ill once before, when he was a boy of fifteen, and had on that occasion, when he was delirious, shown a remarkable tendency to throw everything within reach at the people about him when he did not instantly get what he wanted. The old man remembered the fact, and was silently obedient, for the Signor Marchese looked as though he were ill again. The mildest people are often the most furious in the delirium of a fever.

CHAPTER XX.

AFTER all, Julius was not quite certain whether Leonora had fainted, or was asleep. She had been comfortably settled in the boat at the first, and a quarter of an hour had passed in hoisting and trimming the sails, and bringing the craft before the wind. She might have fallen asleep from sheer fatigue and weariness, — Julius could not tell. He bent far down over the stern, and fetched up a few drops of water from the sea with one hand, while the other supported Leonora's drooping head, — the tiller could take care of itself for a moment, — and he sprinkled her face softly and watched her; once more — and she opened her eyes as from a pleasant dream, and looking up to his she smiled, and closed them again. He bent down and spoke almost in a whisper.

"Darling, are you quite comfortable?" She moved her head in assent, the quiet smile still playing on her lips. Then she lay quite still for a while, and listened to the rush of the water, and the occasional dull, wooden sound as the rudder moved a little on its hinges. The boat rolled softly from side to side, in a long, easy motion and glided swiftly down the bay.

Presently Leonora moved, sat up, and looked about her, at the sea, and the land, and the fiery-crested mountain.

"Where are we going, Julius?" she asked, with a smile at the question.

"I am sure I don't know," said he, laughing. "There are lots of places we can go to. Ischia, Capri,— Naples if you like. Select, dearest, there is a good boat between us and the water, and we have the world before us."

"But we must go somewhere where we can get some breakfast," said she gravely. "And where I can buy things," she added, laughing again. "Do you know that this is all I have got in the world to wear?"

"That is serious indeed," said Julius. "There are provisions and things to drink in the boat, but there is no millinery. We had better go to Naples."

"I think I could manage for one day," said Leonora, doubtfully. "I have brought heaps of handkerchiefs, and hairpins, and cologne water,— they are all in the bag."

"Handkerchiefs and hairpins!" repeated Julius, and laughed at the idea. A woman leaves her husband, who worships her, scatters trouble and tears and madness broadcast, and she thinks of handkerchiefs and hairpins, and remembers where she has put them.

"Yes," said Leonora, "they will be very useful. We could go to Ischia first, and to Naples to-morrow

night,—or rather to-night, I should say. That is,
— if you think ” —

“ What, dear? ” asked Julius.

“ If you think it is quite — far enough.”

“ We cannot go very far. It is six or seven hours
from here to Ischia, if the wind holds. We should
be there between six and seven o’clock.”

“ I think that would be best,” said Leonora in a
tone of decision. She was silent for a moment.
Presently she looked up into Batiscombe’s face,
and her own was white and beautiful in the moonlight. “ I wonder,” she said, “ whether any one
heard that noise the dogs made? Oh, the poor,
poor kitten,— it makes me quite cry to think of
her! ”

“ Poor thing! ” said Julius sympathetically. “ But
its ghost will not haunt the gardens, for it was
amply avenged.”

“ Yes indeed! ” said Leonora. “ Oh, Julius, you
are so strong,— I like you.”

“ Thanks,” said Julius, “ you are awfully good to
like me.” He laughed, but his hand caressed her
hair tenderly, and Leonora was happy.

“ It was just like us,” said she, “ to stop there
at the top of the steps where we might have been
seen in a moment — but I am glad. I hated those
dogs.”

“ It was just as well,” said he. “ They would
very likely have made more noise, and followed
us.”

"Oh yes — and just fancy the wrath when they are found to-morrow morning. But they might have bitten you dreadfully — I was terribly frightened."

"I fancy there will be more wrath about you, my dear, than about the dogs," said Julius, rather gravely.

"About me? Oh — I hardly know — perhaps. I do not think any one will mind very much."

"What does it matter who minds, as you call it?" asked Julius, pushing her thick hair from her forehead tenderly, and looking at her with loving eyes. "What does it matter to us now? What can anything ever matter again?"

"Nothing, nothing, nothing, dear," she answered softly, and her head drooped happily upon his shoulder.

They were as though alone in the boat, for the broad sail was stretched right across to catch the wind, and hid the men, who sat together forward, chattering in a low voice in the incomprehensible dialect known as the lingua franca, the free tongue in which all Mediterranean sailors understand one another, from Gibraltar to Constantinople, and from Smyrna to Marseilles. They did not care a rush what their master did, nor where he went; they had some confidence in his knowledge of the sea and of the coast, and they had entire confidence in themselves, whatever wind might blow. It was nothing to them, who came from the north coast, whether

their broad-shouldered "signore" took a "bella
signora" from Naples or Sorrento for a midnight
sail in his boat. He paid well, to every man his
wages, and he often gave them a few francs to drink
his health. They had never had so good a "pa-
drone" before, and they asked no questions, wisely
distinguishing the side of the bread upon which a
bountiful providence had spread the most butter
for their benefit. They also said that nothing ever
mattered much so long as they got their pay.

Leonora had found at last the desire of her heart,
— the reckless, stormy passion, careless of everything but itself and its object, of which she had so
often dreamed. She had found the man for her to
love, and she did love him to distraction. As for
the rest of the world, she was more persuaded than
ever that there was nothing very much in anything
after all. What she had was wholly sufficient in
the present, the future was a future full of joy and
love, and divested of everything that could possibly
be wearisome, and the past was cut off, murdered,
dead and buried out of sight.

But though she had killed it and thrown it away,
as Julius had done with the dogs, it had a ghost
and a living memory that would haunt her for many
days and weeks, and months and years. A life is
not a dream to be forgotten, nor an old garment to
be thrown aside at will. Life is an ever present
thing, and all our past is as much a part and parcel
of to-day as the marks we bear in our bodies are

portions of ourselves, no matter how we came by them, nor when.

Out of nothing, nothing can come. Out of confusion and vanity and pure selfishness, out of confused and incoherent fragments of half-expressed wisdom, out of the very vanity of vanities, which is the vanity of wise words wrought into foolish phrases; out of the shell of an imaginary self wrought fine and gilded to please the worst part of the real self,—out of all these things, I say, what can come that is good? Or can anything come of them which is truly evil, seeing that, one with another, they are all but so many empty nothings, melted together and lost in the great void that receives the failures of the soul-world?

If anything results from such a life, it must be the realisation of nothing, which is the extinction and annihilation of that which is,—and woe be to the destroyer. We may destroy all hold and anchorage of mind and soul, we may reason ourselves into a disbelief in reality, in matter, in daily life, in good and evil. But always when we think that everything is done, and that our fabric of philosophy is faultless, there arises the strong tide of human passion and creeps across the sands to our tower. At first we may watch the waves from a long way off, and laugh to see them break and overwhelm the very foolish people who have no tower on the shore and must swim for their lives or perish. But the tide rolls on toward us, and runs cruelly up, crash-

ing and thundering in its rising might, till it rends
and tears our flimsy castle out of the sands beneath
our very feet, and we fall headlong into the rushing
waters. And then we too must struggle like the
rest, if we can; and if we cannot, we must sink
to the bottom, while those who learned when the
tide was low and the water smooth, and have tried
their strength in many a brave buffet with the
waves, swim strongly over our drowned bodies.

It is easy to moralise, it is hard to live. That is
the reason that great moralists are generally either
old men who have done with living and would like
to teach other people, or else young men and young
women who have not enough vitality to animate
the most lymphatic oyster, but who manage to float
about by their own inflation. These latter never
save any one from drowning, and the former save
very few. The people who can help others are the
strong ones who can catch them just below the
shoulder, by the arm, and support them and push
them to land, themselves doing all the work. That
is a watery simile, but most similes are but water,
and can be poured into a tea-cup or into a bucket
— they will take the shape of either.

The night wore on, the full moon sinking slowly
to the west, so that after a time she was hidden
from the lovers by the sails, and there was a broad
shadow behind them. Still the breeze blew fresh
from the land and carried them straight towards
Ischia, and the boat rocked smoothly over the rolling

water. Leonora rested on the thick cushions, and
her head lay nestled in Batiscombe's arm while he
held the tiller carelessly with his other hand, steering by the wind, in the certainty of making the
right course. He did not speak, for he wanted her
to rest, and so it came about that before long she
fell peacefully asleep, and Julius drew a light shawl
tenderly about her, and kissed her ruddy hair, and
looked out over the moonlit water, calmly as though
he were sailing for his pleasure.

He was thinking what strange things happened
in his life, and wondering within himself whether
he could ever grow old and be like other people.
But he could never be like other people now, for
he must live a life apart from the world, and create
an existence of a new kind, utterly free from the
ties and bonds and weariness of society. It would
also be without the amusements, the gayety, the
glitter, and the flattery of society. Batiscombe
liked all that, too; but he thought he could do
without it very well. Just now the fascination of
the hour was upon him. The sweet sea-breeze, the
moonlight on the water, the swirl of the boat's
wake — and, above all, the beautiful woman by his
side sleeping so gently and nestled so lovingly close
to him, — it was all perfect.

But with a curious duality that belonged to him,
he enjoyed the moment and thought intensely of the
future at the same time; not with any fear or regret
or even with the anticipation of remorse for what he

had done, but with a far-seeing love of combination, striving to know exactly what would happen and to provide for it.

He went over in his mind the many places to which he might take Leonora, and tried to select the most beautiful and the most retired — some ideal spot, not yet invaded by society. Society, in the long run, gets the best of everything; artists and poets and adventurous tourists may seek out an inaccessible region and keep it to themselves for a while, revelling in the solitude and driving off intruders by discouraging civilisation and affecting a barbaric display of shirt-sleeves, paint, and beards. But if the place is really beautiful, really healthy or really convenient for flirting in the open air, there will surely come at last a stray princess of eccentric disposition and fond of a little discomfort. She will say it is simply too delightful, and so very natural, you know; and in the course of a summer or two the society battalion will encamp there, the houses will be newly painted, and there will be a band and a casino, and a royal personage.

It is very hard to find the kind of place Julius wanted, and he thought for a long time before he hit upon it. But at last he had a happy idea and was pleased with himself for having it, as he always was. Very cautiously he got a cigarette out of his pocket and lit it with one hand, steadying the helm with his elbow. He did it so smoothly and quietly that Leonora did not wake, and he puffed in silent enjoyment of the tobacco, taking care that the smoke should not blow into her face.

It was very like Julius Batiscombe to risk waking her in order that he might smoke, for he was a selfish man and knew it, and delighted in it. But it came upon him in gusts, and was not always a part of him; only, when it did come, it covered completely the better features of his nature. In carrying away Leonora, he had done one of the most absolutely selfish actions of his life, and for the time being there was nothing he would not do so long as he could keep her with him and make her sure that he loved her. He knew well enough that she loved him. He did not want to know anything about his own motives. He was in love — that was motive enough for anything.

As a matter of fact, deep down in his soul there were other incentives at play; but he would not acknowledge that to himself. It was true that since he had loved Diana he had never loved another woman as he loved Leonora. There was a charm about her which he could not explain, which overcame him and filled his whole life. His lingering feeling for Diana was always real when no other passion was in the way, and it had never happened before that any one of his affairs had crossed her path. But now it had chanced at last, and the strong position she had taken against him from the first had roused a bitter opposition in him. It secretly delighted him to think of her anger, and

sorrow, and humiliation at the success of his enter-
prise. But, nevertheless, he loved Leonora with
all the strength of passion that remained to him,
and that was saying much.

Again, he had the vanity, in some directions, of
half a dozen ordinary men, a common peculiarity
of that unusual physical courage and strength which
he possessed in an eminent degree. But it did
not go into his work, for he was an artist at heart,
besides being a man of the world, and was never
long satisfied with anything he wrote. It was the
sort of vanity that hankers after the admiration of
women, and would not take the admiration of men
as a gift, — an intensely virile characteristic of
immense power. He would like to rule men, to
lead them to do great things or to crush them under
his heel, according to his mood; and he sometimes
ground his teeth because he could do neither. But
he did not want their admiration, much less their
sympathy. They might flatter him, or abuse him
— he was utterly indifferent. But he would sacrifice a great deal for the approbation of a woman, and
he often got it; for women, generally speaking, like
best the men who hang upon their words and will
do anything under heaven for a smile and a word
of praise — as is natural.

Consequently, Leonora's evident interest in himself had pleased Julius from the very first, and he
had often done things for the sake of hearing her
say something flattering, which had meant more

than he had realised. There was no doubt whatever that his vanity had played an important part in bringing him into his present position. Nor was he a very exceptional man in this respect, save in the degree of his qualities. Hundreds of men fall in love every day with women who flatter them, and the passion is not less strong because it is of a low order.

It was over now, however, and the plunge was taken. The falling in love was accomplished, and the being in love had begun. Henceforth the two main considerations in his mind were to make life convenient and easy for Leonora, in order that she might not cease to love him out of discontent, and then to get over his inevitable meeting with Marc-antonio as soon as possible and as well as possible. He easily saw that these two things were insepa-rable. If all question of future complication were not removed at once by a decisive meeting with Carantoni, Leonora might live in a state of fear and trembling for months to come. In order to meet him it was necessary to have some place of abode for the time, where Leonora might be happy — of course she should not know of the encounter until it was over — and at the same time the spot must be so chosen as to be tolerably accessible. He had intended to go to France when it was over, and had therefore sent his box to Turin, meaning to take it as soon as he felt free to move; Turin suggested Piedmont, and Piedmont suggested a place where

he had once spent a month in the summer,—
scenery, trout-fishing, considerable comfort, and not
a soul there excepting some of the local society of
Turin, who found it convenient and cheap. He at
once determined to go thither, and to send Marcantonio information of the fact, in order that he
might find him as soon as he pleased.

He no more expected, or wished, to avoid a duel
than Marcantonio himself. The one virtue which
never deserted him was his courage. He would let
his adversary have a shot at him if he liked, but
he himself would fire in the air, of course. He did
not think much about it, to tell the truth, for he
accepted the fact as the consequence of his action,
and occupied himself in providing for it without
any judgment of himself, for good or evil. He had
once said to Leonora that the enjoyment belonged to
the man who ate, and not to the man who carved,
and she had guessed rightly that however well he
might analyse the lives of others, he never analysed
his own. He had got the forbidden fruit and he
was glad of it, and meant to keep it all for himself,
inwardly rejoicing at the anger of those who would
have prevented him, if they could. And with all
this, the fruit gave him an intense delight, independently of the triumph of having obtained it.
He was not a man who tired of anything he liked
so long as the thing itself did not change and
remained as sweet as ever.

There he sat at the helm all through the hours

from midnight to dawn, and Leonora slept peacefully in the cool sea air, at rest after all her excitement and fatigue. Gradually the moonlight seemed to lose distinctness, while gaining more strength and permeating the shadows of the boat which had before been dark and well defined. The breeze blew cooler and fresher than ever, bearing a faint chill in its breath, and the water, from being like black velvet strewn with diamonds, turned gradually grey and misty, so that the waves could all be seen with their small crests and sharp rough edges. In front the rocky height of Ischia seemed to tower to the sky, and soon it caught the first soft tinge of the dawn. Quickly the rosy light crept downwards, falling gently from tree to tree and from rock to rock, till it reached the water, and the sea rippled and laughed in the sweetness of the summer morning.

Leonora moved in her sleep, and Julius, who was watching her, saw her lips tremble a little as though she were talking in her dreams. Then she started slightly, put out her hand, and opened her eyes. The blood mounted to her cheeks as she met her lover's glance, and he looked from the colour on the water to the colour on her face, and he saw that the blush of the woman was fairer than the blush of the summer sea. She sat up and turned from him a moment, and her hands were busy with her hair.

"Have you slept well, my dear one?" asked Julius. "I am afraid you were terribly uncomfortable."

"Oh, so well," said she, still looking away and deftly putting a hairpin in its place. "But I dreamed just as I woke up."

"What did you dream, sweetheart?" asked Julius, stretching his stiffened limbs. He had scarcely moved for four hours; he could have borne it for four hours longer if he had not wanted anything, — but he had risked waking her in order to get a cigarette.

"I dreamed about you," said she. "You behaved so badly, I am not sure I shall forgive you,— ever." She gave him a hesitating look as she bent her head to arrange her hair.

"Tell me, darling," said he, laughing.

"It is nothing to laugh at," she answered. "And besides,— I don't know whether I ought to tell you." She stopped and watched him with a little shy laugh.

"Please do."

"Well,— of course this is in the strictest confidence,— you will never tell any one. Do give me the bag, dear. I want the cologne water."

"And the hairpins and the handkerchiefs," added Julius, laughing, as he stooped to get the bag out of the stern-sheets. "Please tell me the dream."

Leonora took a handkerchief and wet it from the bottle of cologne water. Then she began to dab it on her face.

"I dreamed that you" — dab — "picked me up in your arms and" — dab, dab — "carried me down the stairs,"—dab, dab, dab,—"and just as you were putting me into the "—dab—"into the boat, you dropped me into the sea." A furious succession of dabs, then more cologne water and another handkerchief.

"But you said something about that last night. You made me put you down on the rocks, because you said you had dreamed I dropped you. Was that another dream?"

Julius was watching her operations with a half-amused interest.

"Yes," said she, drying her face, "I dreamed it all over again, just now."

"But when did you dream it first, dear? Yesterday?"

"Oh no! Ever so long ago,—ages ago." She looked down at the flower she had put in her dress at the last minute. It was still fresh, and she arranged it a little.

"Before you knew me?" asked Julius.

"Oh yes,—that is—before"—she blushed again.

"When was it?" he asked, amused and delighted.

"It was before that evening," she said at last, "when you met me in the church. How long ago is that?"

."About ten years, I should think," said Julius gravely. It seemed an endless time.

"Is it not strange?—and then, that I should dream it all again—it is so funny. Why should you have dropped me? It would have been so easy to carry me into the boat, and yet you seemed to stumble on purpose, and we both fell in and were drowned. Is it not very odd?"

She seemed to have settled herself now, for the remainder of the journey; the sun had risen quickly over the land while they were talking, and she put up a parasol which lay on the opposite seat. She did it unconsciously, not realising that she had not brought one with her, but when she held it up, she looked at the handle and saw that it was not one of her own. Then she remembered.

"Did you get it for me?" she asked, smiling.

"Yes," said Julius; "I knew you would want it, so I sent out for it last night."

"A puggia!" shouted one of the men from behind the sail.

Julius put the helm up accordingly, and, as the boat fell off a little, a big fishing smack ran across her bows.

A dozen rough fellows were lounging about in their woollen caps and dirty shirts. They laughed gayly at the crazy foreigners as they went by, and some of them waved their caps.

"Buon viaggio, eccellenza!" they shouted. Julius waved his hand in answer to the greeting. Leonora was pleased.

"At all events," said she, "some one has wished us a pleasant journey. It was sweet of you to get the parasol, dear."

So they chattered together awhile, and presently

the boat went round the point of the island to the north side, and they took in the sails, and the six men pulled her lustily along under the shore, until they reached the little harbour of Casamicciola.

"We can stay here and rest all day," said Julius, as they entered the hotel on the hill, half an hour later. "We shall not be disturbed, and this afternoon we will sail over to Naples, and you can do your shopping when it is cool."

At half past eight they sat down to a breakfast of figs and bread-and-butter and coffee. At the same moment over there in Sorrento, Temistocle laid the key of Leonora's room on Marcantonio's writing-table, and edged away to make sure of an easy escape through the door.

"How perfectly lovely!" exclaimed Leonora, stopping in the consumption of a very ripe black fig, to look out at the sea and the exquisite islands that lie like jewels between Ischia and the main-land.

A waiter had brought a shabby book of ruled paper, with a pen and some ink. He asked if his excellency would be good enough to write his name. Julius took the pen and wrote something, glancing up with a smile at Leonora, who finished her fig in silence.

"Let me see," said she, when he had done. He handed her the book, while the servant waited respectfully.

Julius had written simply, "MR. AND MRS. BATISCOMBE, ENGLAND."

"Give me the pen," said Leonora. "Oh, dip it in the ink, please — thanks!" She wrote something and gave him back the book. Underneath his writing she had put in another name.

"I wanted to write it," said she with a little laugh. Julius looked, and laughed too.

"Leonora Batiscombe," that was all.

But as she wrote it, Marcantonio, over there in Sorrento, fell upon the hard tiles with his mother's diamond cross in his hand.

CHAPTER XXI.

LEONORA did all her errands — or as many as she
said could be done in so short a time.   There were
a great many things, she explained, which she could
order when they were settled, but which would be
in the way at present.   Julius bought her a box,
and wrote a label for it, and pasted it on the cover.
She began to find out that, besides his other
qualities, he was a very practical man, and understood travelling better than any courier she had
ever had.

They had spent a few hours in Ischia as they had
intended, and had then come over to Naples in a
small steamer which plied daily between the island
and the city.   Julius paid something to have his
boat towed across, and when he was in Naples he
paid the men a month's wages in advance, and told
them to go back to Genoa and wait for him there.
They might steal the boat — or they might not, he
did not care.   The thing had to be sent somewhere,
and if it ever reached Genoa so much the better.

He drove with Leonora up and down the Toledo
for hours, stopping at all manner of shops, and
buying all manner of things.   Now and then he
would succeed in paying for something, but she

generally insisted on using her own money. It was fortunate that she had taken it, she thought, as it would have been so awkward to let him pay for everything. He remonstrated.

"All that I have is yours, darling," he said. "You must not begin with such ideas."

"I do not mean to be a burden to you, Julius," answered Leonora. "I am sure I must be much richer than you. Nobody ever made himself rich by writing books." She laughed, and he laughed with her. It was so very amusing to talk to each other about what they possessed.

"Ideas about being rich are comparative," said Julius. "If I sent Worth two or three hundred pounds for a dress every other week, I should certainly not be very well off. But " —

"Oh, Julius — what an idea! There is no one so cheap as Worth in the long run."

"I was going to say something very pretty," remarked Julius.

"Oh, I would not have interrupted you if I had known. What was it?"

"I was going to say that I must be richer than you — since I have got you, and you have only got me."

"You always say things like that," said Leonora, laughing lightly. "Be sure that you always do — I like them very much."

"Ah," said Julius, gravely, "I will sit up all night and make them for you."

"They ought to be spontaneous," said Leonora.

"Everything that is pretty in the world is spontaneous to you, my dear. But I have to work hard to make pretty things, because I am only a man."

"That is really not bad," said she, laughing again.

She wondered vaguely whether he would always be the same. Her husband used to talk much like that at first. But he grew so dull, and when he said things he never looked as if he quite meant them. Julius said sometimes a few words — just what any one might have said; but there was a tone in his voice, and his eyes were so fiery. She loved the fire; it used to frighten her at first.

"We cannot stay here," said Julius, when they sat over their dinner at the hotel on the Chiaja. "It is altogether too ridiculously hot; it is a perfect caricature of a summer, with all its worst points exaggerated."

"Yes; but where shall we go?" asked Leonora.

"I had thought of a charming place," said Julius. "It is away in the Piedmontese Alps — all mountains and chestnut woods and waterfalls. An old convent built over a torrent. Only the people from Turin go there."

"That sounds cool," said Leonora, fanning herself, though whatever she might suffer from the heat she never looked hot. "Let us go. When were you there?"

"Years and years ago," said Julius. "I used to

catch trout with caddis-worms, and write articles about Italian politics. You may imagine how much I knew of what was going on, shut up in an old convent in the mountains. But it made no difference. Writing about Italian politics is very like fishing with worms."

"Why?"

"You sit on a bank with a red, white, and green float to your line. You have not the least idea what is going on under the water. Now and then the float dips a little, and then you write that the national sentiment of honour is disturbed. That is a bite. By and by the float disappears and your line is pulled tight, and you think you have got a fine fish. Then you write that a revolution is imminent, and you haul up the line cautiously, and find that a wretched little roach or a stickleback has swallowed your hook. The red, white, and green float waves over your head like a flag while you get the hook out and bait it again. You make another cast, and you write home that order has been restored. On the other side of the bank sits another fellow, with a float painted red, white, and blue. He is the French correspondent. Sometimes you get his fish, and sometimes he gets yours. It is very lively."

"You used to say that a simile was an explanation and not an argument," said Leonora, rather amused at his description. She always remembered what he said, and enjoyed quoting him against himself.

"So it is. What I told you was an illustration

of a correspondent's life, not an argument against the existence of very fine fish in the stream."

"You are too quick," said Leonora, laughing.

"One has to be quick in order not to appear too awfully slow in comparison with you, dear," answered Julius at once.

"Again,—there is no stopping you!"

It amused her to talk to him, he was so ready; and always with something well turned, that pleased her. There was something, too, that was refreshing in hearing the small talk of a celebrity, often a little doubtful in grammar, and interspersed now and then with a little generous exaggeration that she liked. She had read his books, and knew what he could do with the language when he pleased. And most of all she liked to speak and to be spoken to in English,— it seemed so much more natural.

It was no trouble to Julius to talk to her. With some people he was as silent as the grave, which produced the impression that he was very profound. With others he was ready for a laugh and a jest at any moment, and they thought him brilliant; but there were very few with whom he talked seriously. Leonora saw all his phases in turn, for she felt that if she did not know his character, she was in sympathy with his mind and understood him.

But Julius was anxious to reach the spot he had chosen, in order to let Carantoni know of his whereabouts. He suggested to Leonora that if it was quite convenient to her they might go the next day, when she had had a good night's rest. She assented readily enough. To tell the truth, with all her gayety and enjoyment of the novel situation, she disliked Naples, and she hated to feel that in the morning she should look out of her window across the bay and see Sorrento, and think of her husband as being there. She did not know that when she laid her head on her pillow that night Marcantonio would be in the station in Naples, on his way to Rome, and not half a mile away from her.

"Are you ever seasick?" asked Julius suddenly.

"Oh, Julius! You know I am not," she said reproachfully. He laughed.

"No? I mean in a steamer. Boats are quite different."

"I don't know," said Leonora. "I have often crossed the Channel, and I was never ill at all."

"Oh, then of course it's all right!" he said. "You would not mind in the least. We had better go to Genoa in the steamer; it is very decent and much cooler than all those miles of rail and dust."

"Oh yes, far pleasanter," said Leonora.

And so they made their arrangements, and the next day — the day when Marcantonio was engaging the detectives in Rome — they went on board the "Florio" steamer and left Naples, and Sorrento, and Ischia, and all the countless reminiscences that attached to the glorious bay, and were carried up the coast.

"The dear place," said Leonora, looking astern as she sat in her arm-chair under the awning on deck, "I shall always love it."

"But you are glad to leave it, darling, are you not?" asked Batiscombe, who stood beside her, and was looking more at her than at the coast, though he held a glass in his hand.

It was a curious question to ask, one might have thought, and yet it was natural enough, and did not jar on Leonora's thoughts. She was not sensitive in that way in the least. She did not mind his referring to the past in any way he chose.

"Glad? Of course I am glad," she answered, looking up into his face. "How could I not be glad?" She seemed almost vexed at the simplicity of the question.

"Then I am happy," said Julius, sitting down beside her.

And he spoke the truth; for the time he was utterly and supremely happy. He felt indeed the grave and serious mood, which the bravest man must feel when he knows that in a very few days his life will be at stake. But his vanity told him he was going to fight for her, and that gave him a happiness apart; so he concealed the serious tendency of his thoughts, talking easily and gayly. It was his vanity that helped him most, telling him it was for her; and, as always in his life, the prospect of a woman's praise was a supreme incentive. He did not reflect that he was not to fight for Leonora's honour, but for the greatest dishonour the world held for her.

The broad sun poured down on the water, but the west wind fanned their faces and the awning kept the heat from them. Leonora lay back with half-closed eyes, now and then carefully opening and shutting a fan she held. She was wonderful to look at, her marvellous skin, and the masses of her red hair — the true red of the Venetian women — contrasting strongly with her soft dark dress, and a Sorrento handkerchief of crimson silk, just knotted about her dazzling throat. She was a marvellous specimen of vital nature, of pure living litheness and elasticity, gloriously human and alive. And the man beside her was almost as singular in a different way: he was so quiet, and moved so easily, and his bright blue eyes were so fiery and clear, his skin so bronzed and even in colour; there was strength about him too; and the passengers as they came and went would steal a glance at the couple, and make remarks, quite audible to Julius and Leonora, about the beauty of those Inglesi.

"Which do you like best, dear," asked Julius presently, "the day or the night?"

"Oh — that night was so beautiful," said Leonora; "I love the moon, and the freshness, and the white sails, and all."

"Does 'all' include anything especial?" asked Julius smiling.

"What do you think?" asked she, instead of

answering. Her red lips remained just parted with a loving smile.

"I don't think," said Julius. "I leave the thinking to you, my dear. You can do it much better. But I like the sunlight, the broad, good sunlight, far more than the moon. It is so hot and splendid."

"Yes; I suppose it is like you to prefer it. All men like the sun — and I suppose all women like the moon. At least I do. But you must always like what I like now, you know."

"Including myself, I suppose?"

"Bah, my dear," laughed Leonora, "you will find that very easy!"

How very unhappy she must have been, thought Julius. She had not a regret in the world, it seemed; and the only fear she had shown had been when she stumbled on the descent, so that he took her up and carried her.

"Tell me," said he, "what did you do in all those dreadful days when we could not meet?"

"I did nothing but write letters to you — very nice letters too. You have never shown yourself properly grateful."

"No," said Julius, "I have not had time."

"What do you mean?" asked Leonora with a little frown.

"Why — it must take a long time to show you how grateful I am. A long time," he added, his voice sinking to a deeper tone, that Leonora loved to hear. "It will take my whole lifetime, darling."

"Thanks, dear one," said she quietly, laying her hand on his. She did not mind the passengers,— why should she? She would never mind the world again, as long as she lived, for the world would never care what she did any more.

Her experience of the world — or of what she understood by the term — had not been very happy, though it had not been the reverse. She remembered chiefly the mere technicalities of society, so to speak. She had enjoyed them after a fashion, inveighing all the while against their emptiness and vanity, and now when she looked back she saw only a confused perspective of brilliantly lighted, noisy parties, of more or less solemn dinners, of endless visits to people who bored her, and of an occasional cotillon with a man she liked, in return for numberless dances with individuals who seemed to be trying to get dancing lessons gratis, or who tore furiously up and down the room till she was out of breath, or who caught their spurs in her skirts, and scratched her arms with their decorations. She did not remember how she had enjoyed motion for motion's sake, and had rarely refused to go out, in spite of the aforesaid annoyances. She did not remember the little thrills of pleasure she had felt, as Marcantonio was gradually attracted to her, till he was always the first to greet her and to put his name on her card for a turn, and was always the last to bid her good-night, devoting himself to her mother when she was engaged with some one else. She did not remember the delight she had often experienced in discussing society with her philosophical friends, bowling over institutions with a phrase and destroying characters with an adjective. There were many things which Leonora did not remember but which had given her great pleasure a few months ago; but most of them reminded her of her husband, and she did not wish to be reminded of him in the least.

There was continually a sort of unconscious comparison going on between him and Julius Batiscombe; she could not help it, and it had been perhaps the earliest phase of her love. Even at the moment when Marcantonio offered himself to her, Julius was standing in the doorway, and she had wondered what he would have said if he had been making the same proposal. She knew, now. She thought she knew the difference between the intonation of the man who loved, and of the man who merely wanted to marry. Ah — if she had only known in time, things would have been different. She would have refused Marcantonio, after all his devotion, and she would have married Julius.

She did not understand that Julius would never have fallen in love with her then; that the mere possibility of being led into marriage reared an impassable barrier between him and the whole of youngladydom. He had made up his mind that he would not marry, and young ladies said he was the most obstinate bore they knew; which was very

unkind, for he kept out of their way, and only
bored them when he was obliged to talk to them,
doing it systematically and successfully in self-
defence. But Leonora innocently supposed that
if Julius had met her more intimately, in time, he
would have fallen in love with her just as he had
done now, and would have proposed after six weeks'
acquaintance, and they would have been happy
forever after. She chanced to think of this now,
and she sighed.

"What is the matter, sweetheart?" asked Julius.

"Nothing," said she, "I was thinking of something,—that is all."

"Tell me, dear," said he, bending towards her.
She hesitated a moment, looking into his eyes.

"I was thinking," she said at last, "of something
that happened once. Do you remember, at that
ball, when you stood in the doorway and looked
so dreadfully bored, and I was sitting not far off
with — with the marchese?"

"Of course," said Julius, calmly, "I imagined he
was just proposing to you."

"Yes," said Leonora, in a low voice, "he was."

"I wish he had been at the bottom of the sea,"
said Julius, fiercely.

Indeed, the idea disgusted him, being as much
in love as he was. Nevertheless, he thought she
was a singular woman to refer to the thing,—so
very soon. He had at first expected that she would
never wish to mention her husband to him; at least,

not for very long; but she seemed rather to seek the subject than to avoid it. He mused for a moment, looking out under his half-closed lids, as was his habit when he was thinking. Suddenly a smile came into his face.

"Do you remember, dear, when you and he raced me in the boat on the bay, one afternoon, ever so long ago?" It was not much more than six weeks.

"Yes — perfectly," said she. "Why?"

"Have you any idea where I was going?" asked Julius, laughing a little.

"Not the least. You were not going anywhere; you were out for a row, I suppose, because you wanted the air." She looked a little puzzled.

"If you had not overtaken me, I should never have seen you again," he said, looking at her affectionately.

"What do you mean?" she asked, rather startled.

"Simply this, I was running away. I was engaged to dine with you that evening, and I was going to Naples to get out of it. I would have sent a telegram about urgent business — or anything."

"What an idea!" she exclaimed, laughing. "Why did you do that?"

"Because I knew what would happen if I stayed," said he, softly.

"But you did not care for me then?" she asked, quickly.

"Oh, yes, I did," he answered; "and I knew

I should care a great deal more." His eyes burned in the bright light of the afternoon.

"But I did not love you in the least then," said Leonora, demurely.

"No, of course not — and I did not flatter myself that you would. But I knew I was going to love you with all my heart."

Again their hands met for a moment, and a couple of sailors, who watched them from a distance, nudged each other and grinned.

"When did you first begin to care, dear?" he said presently.

"Seriously? What a silly question, Julius. How can I tell?"

"It was after I found you in the church, was it not?"

"Yes, indeed. Ever so long after that!"

"About two days?" he suggested gravely.

"How absurd, Julius," she said with a little air of offended dignity that was charming. "You know it was ever so long."

"I wonder what you thought of me, when you turned round and saw me looking at you in the church," said he. He really had not an idea, and was curious to know.

"I thought you were very rude," said she. "And afterwards I thought you were very nice."

"I did not mean to be rude," said Julius, "but I could not help going in. I was in love with you, and I knew you were there."

"In love — already?" asked Leonora.

"Why — yes — it was at least a week after I tried to run away," said Julius innocently.

"It was exactly two days," said Leonora.

They both laughed, for it was quite true. It was very pleasant to recall the beginnings of their love, for it had all been sweet, and easy; it seemed so to them, at least, as the foreshore hid Sorrento from their sight, and with it the scene of all they were discussing.

It was a beautiful voyage, along the coast in the summer sea. There was always enough breeze in the daytime, and there was the moon at night, and they always felt that if they were quite alone, on land, it would be even more charming, if possible. It is a great thing in happiness to know that there is to be more of it, and more and more, till at last the heart has its fill of joy.

They reached Genoa, and rested themselves for a day and a night in the glorious rooms of an old palace, turned into an hotel by the profane requirements of modern travellers. But it is very agreeable for travellers to sleep in palaces, by whatever names they are called, and it is foolish to say that moderns should build new buildings instead of making use of old ones when they have them ready to hand.

There is a set of people in the world who deal in cheap sentiments, and get themselves a reputation for taste by abusing everything modern and kneeling in rows before everything that is old. They grind out little mediæval tunes with an expression of ravished delight, and tell you there is no modern music half so good,— in fact, that there is no modern music at all! Or they garnish themselves in queer white robes and toddle through a vile travesty of some ancient drama; or they build houses of strange appearance and hideous complication of style, having neither beauty without nor comfort within: and last of all, they say to themselves, Verily, we are the most artistic people in the world!

One of these persons could not have passed an hour in the old palace which the Genoese have turned into an hotel. The bare idea of such profanity would have produced artistic convulsions at once, and untold suffering in the future by the mere memory of it. But neither Batiscombe nor Leonora were people of that sort. Julius took a very different view of life, believing to some extent in the simple theory that useful things are good and useless things are bad, and that everything that really fulfils its purpose must have some beauty of its own. Moreover, Julius had very little reverence, but a profound intelligence of the comfortable; he would have slept as well in a king's tomb as in an American hotel, provided the furniture were to his taste in respect of length and breadth and upholstery. As for Leonora, she had been brought up chiefly in Italy, and never troubled herself with the intricacies of the art question in that country, taking everything to be natural so long as she always had the very best of it. And at present, being wholly in love, and having her heart's desire, she would even have been willing to put up with less luxury than usual. Her talent for supremacy, as Julius used to call it, had taken a person for its object, and found the dominion of a heart more interesting than the dominion of fashionable luxury, the finest horses, or even Mr. Worth.

"I used to hate hotels," said she to Julius, late in the evening, "but they seem very pleasant after all. There is never any fuss about anything; and I always seem to get just what I want."

"Oh — hotels are very well, if one understands them," he answered. He did not explain to her that her comfort was chiefly due to his forethought. "You would soon find it a great bore, though," he added.

"I am sure I should not," said she. "You are so clever that you make everything seem easy for me."

Julius laughed, out of sheer satisfaction. These were just the little speeches he loved most from women, and, most of all, from Leonora. It would seem a harmless vanity of itself, but it leads to doing acts of forethought and courtesy for the sake of the praise instead of for the sake of the woman.

"It is very good of you to say so, my dear," he answered, modestly. "But we will change all that, by and by. When the heat is over we will go

away, and live in the Greek islands. There are
places worth going to, there."

"Oh, of all things how delightful!" cried
Leonora, carried away by the new idea. "And
have a house by the sea, and a boat, and Greek
servants,—how lovely!"

"Meanwhile, dear," said Julius, "we will go and
be cool in the old Carthusian monastery. It does
not take long from here."

And so they left Genoa and reached Turin, where
Batiscombe found his box — the one that Marcantonio intended to watch so carefully — and took it
away; thence they went to a place called Cuneo, a
little southwards by the railway, in the Maritime
Alps, which Leonora said were beautiful; and then
they drove in an ancient diligence to the Certosa
di Pesio, an old Carthusian monastery, as Julius
had said, built over a wonderful mountain torrent, and surrounded with ancient chestnut-trees.
Through the valley that opens away to northward
you can catch a glimpse of Monte Rosa, when the
setting sun gilds the snow, and the breeze brings
down with it the freshness of the Alps. Leonora
was enchanted with the place, with Batiscombe's
choice, with him, with everything.

"And to-morrow you will show me where you
used to catch fish, and write your articles on Italian
politics?" said she, as they came in from a short
walk late in the evening.

That night Batiscombe dispatched a letter to
Rome.

Certosa di Pesio, Cuneo,
Maritime Alps, *August* 31.

The Marchese Carantoni will find Mr. Julius Batiscombe at the above address, with a friend.

That was all, but it gave Julius infinite satisfaction to send it. He had grudged the days that had passed before he could send Carantoni the information. As for the "friend," he had seen two or three cavalry officers about the place as soon as he arrived, and he knew that he could rely on the assistance of some of them. Duels are easily arranged in Italy.

CHAPTER XXII.

WHEN Marcantonio met Diana in the morning, she noticed at once the change in his appearance. He was still very pale, and his face was drawn in a peculiar expression; but he did not look so wild, and his eyes had regained their clearness.

Diana greeted him affectionately, but made no remark about his health, thinking it would annoy him. She herself had slept soundly and began the day with a new supply of strength.

"You are still determined to go to Turin?" she said, with half a question in her voice, but as though it were quite certain that he would answer in the affirmative.

"Yes," he said, "I am quite determined. It is the best thing I can do."

"I was wondering this morning," said Diana, "whether we ought not to let our uncle know. It seems to me that he ought not to hear it from strangers."

Marcantonio eyed her suspiciously.

"You cannot expect me to go and tell him now," said he. "The train leaves in an hour — there is not time."

"Of course not," said Diana, seeing how quickly he suspected her of wishing to interfere with his plan. "But, if you like, I will write and tell him."

"We can write from Turin," said he moodily. "No one knows yet."

He hurried her to the station, and got there long before the hour of departure. He was determined not to miss the train, and until he was seated in the carriage and the train rolled out of the city he could not feel sure that Diana would not stop him. He was somewhat relieved when they passed the first station on the way to Florence, and he saw that he was fairly off. Donna Diana sat opposite to him and watched him, thinking sadly of the last journey they had made together, when he had taken her to Sorrento by the night train. He looked quiet, though, and she thanked Heaven things were no worse; he might so easily have done himself a mischief in the first outbreak of his solitary grief.

She still hoped for a chance of learning how it had all happened, for she was very much in the dark, and had no means of learning anything except what he might choose to tell her. Perhaps the intense inquiry in her mind reacted on his, as often happens between brothers and sisters. At all events, he began to speak before half an hour had gone by.

"I have not told you anything about it yet, Diana mia," he said. "I have been so busy, so many

things to do." He passed his hand over his forehead as he spoke, as though trying to collect
himself.

"Of course," said Diana gently. "Do not tire
yourself now, dear boy. Another time will do just
as well. I know all that is absolutely necessary."

Marcantonio laughed very slightly and a little
foolishly, and again put his hand to his head.

"Oh, no," he answered, "I shall not tire myself.
You do not know anything about the — the —
occurrence."

"No," said she, "that is true."

"They went away at night," said Marcantonio
quickly, and then stopped.

"Pray do not tell me about it, dear brother," said
Diana, rising and seating herself near to him on the
opposite side of the carriage. She laid her hand
on his arm, trying to soothe him, for she feared a
return of his old state.

"But I must tell you," he said impatiently, and
she saw it was useless to protest. "They went
away at night," he continued, "in a boat. I heard
the dogs barking, just for a moment, and then they
stopped, and I went to sleep. I went to sleep,
Diana," he cried savagely, "when she was running
away with him, and I could have killed him as
easily as possible. I could have killed them both
— oh, so easily!" He groaned aloud and clenched
his thin hands.

"Hush!" said Diana, softly.

"I could have killed them as easily as he killed the dogs and stopped their barking," he went on; "he killed them both, wrung their necks — poverini — as though they were not right to call me. And I never guessed anything, though I heard them!"

He was working himself into a frenzy, and Diana was afraid he might go mad then and there. She tried to draw his mind to another part of the story. She was a woman of infinite tact and resource.

"Yes," said she, "I am sure you could. But how long was it before you telegraphed to me?"

"How long? I do not know," he said; and he seemed trying to recollect himself.

"Was it in the afternoon?" asked Diana, glad to fix his attention on a detail.

"Let me see — yes. I meant to send it from Castellamare — the dispatch, I mean; and instead I stopped the carriage at a little town on the way — I forget the name, but there was a telegraph office there — and so I sent it sooner."

"Yes," said Diana. "I got it at about seven o'clock. My husband was very quick and got a carriage, and brought me as far as Genoa."

"How good of him!" exclaimed Marcantonio. "How is he? And the children, dear little things; are they all well?"

His face changed again, and a pleasant smile showed that he had forgotten his troubles for a moment. Diana was surprised at the ease with which she could distract his attention, and she determined to make use of her power to the utmost. It would be something gained if she could keep him quiet during the journey. She began immediately to speak of her children, a boy and girl of four and three years old. She told him about their games, their appearance, their nursery maids, and their French governess. She branched off into a dissertation on the beauties of the Riviera, and still he listened and made intelligent answers, and talked as though nothing had happened to him and they were travelling for their amusement. Seeing that she was accomplishing her object, she went on from one subject to another, telling him all manner of details about her life in France, in Austria, and other places where her husband's official duties had called him, during the five years since her marriage. Only about Rome she would not speak, fearing lest the smallest reference to the scenes he had recently passed through might take his mind back to his great grief.

And all the while she marvelled at his calmness, and at the ease with which she could amuse him. For he was really amused, there could be no doubt. He laughed, talked in his natural way, and seemed enjoying himself very well, smoking a cigarette now and then, and commenting on the weather, which was abominably hot.

"Of course," said he, "we shall find it much cooler in Pegli."

Diana started quickly, and then looked away to hide her astonishment.

"Of course," she answered, "it is very much cooler there."

Did he really fancy he was going to Pegli? Had he forgotten Turin and his errand? Was he gone stark mad? She could not tell, and was frightened. It might have been a slip of the tongue,—but he said it very quietly, as though he were anticipating the delights of the climate. Nevertheless, she did not dare to pause, and she talked bravely on in the heat and the dust.

At one of the stations the train stopped ten minutes for refreshments. Marcantonio said he would get out and buy a sandwich and a bottle of wine. He sprang nimbly from the step, and Diana watched him as she sat by the open door of the carriage. He looked more like his old self than she had seen him since the catastrophe, and she watched him with loving eyes, wondering how he would bear what was to come, and for the first time wishing that he might be kept always in this state, without the necessity of a meeting with Batiscombe.

Presently he returned with the provisions,—a brace of rough-looking sandwiches, and a bottle of wine.

"It is the best I could do," he remarked. "It is the last place in the world."

He still looked cheerful and entirely himself. Diana watched him closely, hoping and praying with all her might that he might remain so — forever, even if he were out of his mind. Anything would be better than to see him suffer as he had been suffering that morning. She began to talk again, eating a little of the sandwich, for she was tired, and needed all her strength. He ate, too, and drank some of the wine, but he no longer listened as he had done before, and he did not answer nor make a remark of any kind. Diana had taken up what he said about the station, and was talking about travelling in France.

Suddenly Marcantonio's colour changed; he grew pale again, his eyes stared, and he dropped the bread he was eating. Diana was terrified, brave as she was, for she knew that his mind had gone back to his trouble,—how, she could not tell; but it was clear that for a space he had wholly forgotten it. He seemed to take up the thread of his terrible narration at the point at which he had been led away from it.

"Temistocle brought me the key," he said, and his voice sounded hollow again and far away. "He had told the servants she had gone to Rome before daybreak, and that I had gone with her,—ha! ha! —he is a cunning fellow. I gave him something for himself,—I think I did,—I am not quite certain." Again his ideas seemed to wander, and he tried to remember the detail that had escaped his grasp. Quick as thought Diana seized the opportunity.

"Did you give it to him in the evening?" she asked.

"I am not sure. I am not quite sure that I did give it to him after all. Oh, I cannot remember anything any more."

He clasped his hands to his head as though striving to compress his brain and to compel it to action. The train moved away from the station.

"You can send it to him, in any case," suggested Diana, in an agony of sympathy and suspense. She would have added "from Pegli," if she had dared; but she was not sure he would remember his stray remark, or whether he had meant it. In a moment it was too late.

"Of course," cried Marcantonio, delighted with the idea. "I can send it from Turin. He deserves it well. There will be time,"—he hesitated and spoke slowly,—"there will be time,—yes, there will be time, before I find him." His voice fell almost to a whisper, barely audible to Diana in the noise of the train as it gained speed in starting. He seemed unconscious of her at the moment when he said the last words, and she sat with clasped hands and set lips, not knowing what to expect next. In a little while he began again. She had been too much struck by his quick change of manner to find the thing to say, in time to lead him off.

"I went into her room," he said. He stopped and fumbled in his pockets, producing at last the cross of sapphires and diamonds. "I found this," he added, showing it to Diana. She would have taken it, but he held it nervously in his hand, more than half concealed. "Do you know it?"

"Yes," said she as quietly as she could. "It belonged to our mother."

"It is beautifully made," he said suddenly, looking closely at it. "It is most beautifully made, and the stones are very valuable. Should you not think that they are worth a great deal?"

"They must be — the sapphires are of a very good colour and the brilliants are large," said Diana, humouring him. "I wonder where it was made?"

"I do not care where it was made," said Marcantonio roughly. "I have got it again. I will give it back to her — she must have missed it." He looked at Diana with a strange pathetic inquiry in his weary eyes.

"Leonora?" asked Diana, in surprise. Marcantonio started as though he had been stung. He had thought of his dead mother.

"Leonora? Ah!" he cried with a sort-of muffled scream. "It belonged to Leonora — Ugh!" With a quick movement he flung the jewel at the window. It chanced that the pane was raised to keep out the smoke on that side. The heavy cross cracked the plate glass and knocked a small piece out of the middle, but fell to the floor.

Marcantonio remained in the very act, as he had thrown it, for one instant. Then his head sank on his breast and his hands fell to his sides helplessly.

"Oh, Diana, Diana," he moaned piteously, "I am mad." Then he began to rock himself backward and forward as though in pain.

It was no time to break down in horror or grief, and Diana was not the woman to waste idle tears. The cross had fallen at her feet. She had instantly stooped and picked it up and hid it away, lest he should see it again. Then she heard him say that he was mad, and she made a desperate effort. She took him strongly in her arms, almost lifting him from the ground, and laid his head upon her breast and supported it, and took his hand. He was quite passive; she could do anything with him for the moment — he might have been a child.

Diana bent down as she held him in her arms and kissed him tenderly on the forehead and breathed soft words. It was a prayer.

Poor woman! what could she do? Driven to the last extremity of agony and horror, sitting by and seeing her brother going mad — raving mad — before her very eyes, unable to soothe his grief or to strengthen his soul by any words of her own, not knowing but that at any moment he might turn upon herself — poor woman, what could she do? She breathed into his ear an ancient Latin prayer. What a very foolish thing to do! She was only a woman, poor thing, and knew no better.

O woman, God-given helpmate of man, and noblest of God's gifts and of all created things — is there any man bold enough to say that he can make praises

for you out of ink and paper that shall be worthy
to rank as praise at all by the side of your good
deeds? You, who bow your gentle heads to the
burden, and think it sweet, out of the fulness of
your own sweet sympathy — you, whose soft fingers
have the strength to bind up broken limbs and
rough, torn wounds — you, who feel for each living
thing as you feel for your own bodily flesh, and
more — you, who in love are more tender and faithful and long-suffering than we, and who, even
erring, err for the sake of the over-great heart that
God has given you — is it not enough that I say of
you, "You are only women, and you know no
better"? What greater, or higher, or nobler thing
can I say of you, in all humbleness and truth, than
that you are what you are, and that you know no
better? What better things can any know, than to
bear pain bravely, to heal the wounded, to feel for
all, even for those who cannot feel for themselves,
and to be tender and faithful and kind in love?
And even, being given of Heaven and loved of it,
that you should turn in time of need and trouble
and say a prayer for strength and knowledge, even
that is a part of you, and not the least divine part.
So that when the man who cannot suffer what you
can suffer, nor do the good that you can do, sneers
and scoffs at your prayers and your religion, I could
wring his cowardly neck to death. Even poor
Leonora, praying philosophical prayers to a power
in which she did not in the least believe, was not

ridiculous. She was pathetic, mistaken, miserable, perhaps, but not ridiculous.

Perhaps Diana had done the best thing, out of pure despair. The long familiar words, spoken in her soothing voice, at the very moment when he was conscious that he was on the verge of insanity, chained his faculties and gradually brought him to a calmer state. Perhaps, also, the strong magnetic power of his sister acted more forcibly on him from the moment when he suddenly abandoned himself to her influence. Like many people who possess that strange gift, she was wholly unconscious of it, and she sometimes wondered why it was that those about her yielded so easily to her will. Be that as it may, Marcantonio lay quite still in her arms, and at last his eyelids drooped, his limbs relaxed, and he fell into a deep sleep. The hot hours wore on, and the train rolled by the towns and hamlets and castle-crested hills towards Florence, and still he slept, and Diana tenderly supported him, though her arm ached as though it must break, and her eyes were dimmed from time to time with the sight and consciousness of so much misery.

At length, as they entered the station, she waked him. He was quite calm again, and collected, but very sad, as she had seen him that morning.

"Have I slept like this so long?" he asked.

"Yes, dear boy," said Diana.

"Dear, dear Diana, how good you are," he exclaimed, and he kissed her hand gratefully.

"We have an hour here, to dine, before the train starts."

"Will you go on at once?" she asked. She had vainly hoped that he might be induced to stay in Florence. But he had recovered himself enough to know perfectly well what he was doing.

"Yes — certainly," said he. "We shall arrive in the morning." She dared not object nor make a suggestion, not knowing how soon he might break out again, in some fresh burst of madness.

"Very well," she answered, as a station porter took their handbags and smaller properties, "let us dine at once."

She watched him and saw that he ate with a good appetite. She had heard that lunatics always eat well, and she would almost rather have seen him too sad to care for his food; nevertheless she thought it would do him good.

There is probably nothing more wearing, more racking to the nerves, than the care of an insane person. To be ever on the watch, expecting always an outbreak or a painful incoherence, to attempt to follow the sensible nonsense that madmen talk, always endeavouring to distract the attention from the forbidden subject, are efforts requiring the highest tact and the greatest coolness. Diana could accomplish much by sheer common sense and endurance, and more, perhaps, by the strong affection which had always existed between her brother and herself. But she felt instinctively that she was not equal to the task, even while she hoped that Marcantonio was not really mad.

She was mistaken, however, as any indifferent person would have seen in a moment. He was insane, and on the verge of becoming violent. Nothing but her wonderful courage and strong will had kept him within any bounds, and he might at any moment become wholly uncontrollable.

She would have stopped in Florence if it had been possible, but it seemed dangerous to thwart him at present, and she felt sure that in Turin she could get the help of some first-rate physician. So she submitted once more, and in an hour they were off again, in a reserved carriage, as before, flying north-wards towards the mountains, where the road winds so wonderfully through a hundred tunnels, in its rapid ascent.

It was a very long night for Diana. In all her many journeys she had never felt fatigue such as this. Marcantonio would sleep for an hour, and then start up suddenly and begin to talk, sometimes asking questions and sometimes volunteering re-marks that showed how his mind was wandering. Once or twice he showed signs of returning to the account of his doings after Leonora had left him, but Diana was able to check him in time, for he was growing tired and yielded more easily to her will than in the daytime.

At last they were safe in the hotel, and Marc-antonio was in his room, intending to dress, he said, before going out. Diana was no sooner assured that she was free from the responsibility of watching him for a few minutes than she sent for the proprietor of the hotel, inquired for the address of the best physician in Turin, and dispatched a messenger with a very urgent request for his attendance.

The apartment she had taken with her brother consisted of a large sitting-room, with a bedroom on each side of it. Marcantonio's room had but that one door, which she could watch as she lay on the sofa, awaiting the arrival of the doctor.

When he came at last, breathless in his haste to put himself at the service of the great lady who sent for him, he talked very learnedly for half an hour, after listening to all Diana told him with grave attention. He could not see the patient of course, and the interview took place in a small antechamber, from which he could escape if Marcantonio were heard moving within. He was of opinion that it was not a case of insanity, but of temporary derangement of the faculties from the severe strain they had received. The sudden manifestations of violence were natural enough to an Italian,— if it had been the case of an Englishman, it would have been different, because, as the doctor said, half in earnest and half in jest, Inglesi were generally mad to begin with, and anything beyond that made them furious maniacs. He had a man, he said, long accustomed to dealing with lunatics. He would send him disguised as a servant, and he could be in constant attendance, thus relieving Diana of the care of watching the marchese. He himself would call every day and inquire, and would be ready at a moment's notice to remove him to a place of safety. In his present state, he said, to shut him up, and treat him as though he were insane, might very likely make a permanent madman of him.

The doctor retired, leaving Diana somewhat reassured. All that he had said seemed reasonable, and she would strictly follow his advice. Meanwhile, she went to her own room, feeling sure that she could hear Marcantonio's door open, if he finished dressing and came out. But Marcantonio rang his bell at the end of an hour, and sent word to his sister that he felt tired and had gone to bed, and would not rise till midday.

Poor fellow — she was pleased at the intelligence, but the fact was that his mind had strayed again; he had forgotten the object of his journey, and being worn out had gone to bed like a tired child. The new place, the strange room, and the necessity of unpacking his clothes himself had confused him, and driven everything else out of his head.

Before he awoke, the confidential man had arrived, arrayed in the ordinary dress of an hotel servant. He was a quiet individual, with strong hands and iron-grey hair, neat in his appearance, and a little hesitating in his speech; but his eyes were keen and searching, and he moved quickly. Diana was pleased with him, and understood that the

doctor had given her good advice, and that Marcantonio would be safely watched. The man said he
would serve them in their own sitting-room, and
perform the offices of valet for Marcantonio, and be
altogether in the position of a private servant,
which, however, was not his profession, as he took
care to add.

When at last Diana and Marcantonio met, each
rested and refreshed, he looked the less weary of
the two. Diana had suffered too much to be entirely
herself, and for the first time in her life felt as
though she had taxed her strength too severely.
Moreover, the strain was not removed, but increased
hourly. Her woman's instinct told her that, in
spite of the doctor's opinion, her brother was actu-
ally out of his mind, perhaps past all recovery.
His sudden cheerfulness was horrible to her, and
made her shudder when she thought of the magnitude of what he was forgetting.

"Let us take a carriage and see Turin, Diana,"
he suggested gayly, as they finished their lunch and
he lit a cigarette. "I have never been in Turin with
you. There are some very pretty things to see."

"By all means," said she readily. "Let us go at
once."

The confidential servant was dispatched for a
carriage. The idea of seeing sights with his sister
pleased Marcantonio, and he never relapsed into his
sadder self during the afternoon. Diana did not
know whether to be glad or sorry; his forgetfulness

was terrible, but his memory was worse. She remembered the scene with the cross on the previous day, in the railway-carriage, and she thought that if insanity brought peace it was better to be insane.

They drove about and saw what was to be seen, — the great squares, the memorial statues, the armory, where the mail-clad wooden knights sit silently on their mail-clad wooden horses, and they drove out at last to Moncalieri, in the cool of the evening. The confidential servant sat on the box and directed the driver, pointing out to Diana and Marcantonio the various objects of interest, so that Carantoni suspected nothing. The man acted his part perfectly.

"How charming it is here!" exclaimed Marcantonio, admiring the trees, and the life, and the gay colours at Moncalieri. "Why did we not think of coming here before, my dear?" He spoke in French, which he rarely did with his sister, though he had always done so with his wife. Diana hardly noticed it at the moment, — she was obliged to answer something.

"It was hardly the right season for it before this, I suppose," said she. "But now we can stay as long as we please."

"Oh yes," said he, in his old way, "if it is agreeable to you, I ask nothing better. It is infinitely more pleasant than Sorrento. I never liked Sorrento, I cannot tell why. It never wholly agreed with you, mon ange — n'est-ce-pas?"

"I was always well there,—well enough, at least," answered Diana, puzzled at this new phase of his humour.

"Ah no, you were never well after Diana left us. She is so good, she makes every one well!" He spoke pleasantly and naturally.

It was horrible, and Diana started with a new realisation of his state. He no longer recognised persons,—he took her for Leonora!

But some new object attracted his attention, and he chattered on, almost to himself, almost childishly, but with a sweet smile on his pale, delicate face. Diana could scarcely restrain her tears,—she who had not wept for years until lately!

Poor Diana! Batiscombe and Leonora were sinfully, wholly, happy with each other,—Batiscombe selfishly so, perhaps, but none the less for that, and Leonora with a wild delight in her new life, that swallowed up the past and gilded the present. Even poor, crazy Marcantonio, chattering and making small French jokes about the people's dresses at Moncalieri, was happy for the moment. Only Diana, the brave woman who had fought for the right so well, seemed cut off from it all, bearing the whole burden on her shoulders, and silently bowing her queenly head to the storm of woe and grief and destruction.

CHAPTER XXIII.

DIANA would have taken her brother away from Turin if she could, but there was a danger that the mere suggestion might revive the fixed idea that had driven him mad. His illusions had not the absolutely permanent character which is the most hopeless. For instance, on the evening of the very day when he had called his sister by his wife's name, he had known Diana perfectly well, and had sat for an hour talking about old times with her. Whether, at such moments, he had any recollection of recent occurrences, would be hard to say; and the doctor advised for the present that he should have perfect quiet and should be allowed to amuse himself and to be amused in any way which seemed best. In the course of a day or two the doctor saw him, coming on pretence of seeing Madame de Charleroi. He felt now, he said, from Marcantonio's manner, that he would recover before long, though his memory concerning the circumstances of the time when he was insane would probably be very uncertain.

But Diana felt relieved at this and devoted her time to her brother from morning till night, reading to him, driving with him, or talking to him as the case might be. She could do nothing more for the present. Turin is a pleasant city enough, the weather was not excessively hot, and the hotel was large and comfortable. In the course of time it would be possible to move Carantoni and take him to Paris, but at present any sudden change of place or surroundings was to be deprecated.

A week passed in this way, and Diana grew pale with the constant strain of anxiety, and the great dark rings circled her grey eyes. But she bore bravely up, and rose each day with strength to do what lay before her. She wrote to her husband, and he offered at once to come and help her to take care of Marcantonio, but she would not let him come, fearing the effect of a new face,— even that of an old friend like Charleroi. She received all the letters that came to her brother, and was surprised that there were no communications from the detectives he had employed. The fact was that Marcantonio had given a separate address to them, and as they discovered nothing, after the manner of most detectives, they only systematically telegraphed that they had confidence of being on the track. The telegrams were addressed to another hotel, and were dropped into the box for unclaimed letters and were never heard of again. Diana knew that business communications would be harmless in Marcantonio's present state, and when any came she let him have them. He would read them over and often discuss with her the information they contained, and at last he would let her answer them, saying it was very good of her to save him so much trouble.

All these letters came from Rome, being forwarded by the steward who lived at the Palazzo Carantoni and managed the business of the household. Others came, re-directed over the original address, from friends in different parts of the country, and these Diana carefully put aside unopened, fearing always that some passing reference or message to Leonora might disturb him and bring on a fresh outbreak. She could always distinguish the business letters, because they were either directed in the handwriting of the steward, or they bore the outward and visible printed address of the lawyer, farmer, or merchant, from whom they came.

In the week they had spent in Turin there had been already twenty or thirty communications of various kinds. Poor Marcantonio never knew that his sister sorted the mail for him. It was brought to him by the confidential servant, and he always took it and went to his room with an air of great importance to "get through his business," as he expressed it. He was evidently proud of doing it, showing that unaccountable vanity in small things which characterises so many lunatics. Indeed, he had always been proud of his attention to details, and now it became a sort of passion, though he was never able to carry out his intentions, and always left the unfinished work to Diana.

On the fourth of September Julius Batiscombe's

letter, directed to Marcantonio in Rome, had come
back to Turin. Julius had marked it "very
urgent," and the steward had looked at it, had
thought Batiscombe's handwriting indistinct, and
to secure greater certainty had put it into another
envelope and directed it in his own business-like
way. The consequence was that it was mistaken
for a common business letter, and handed to Marcantonio with the rest.

It seemed to be the last blow that an evil fate
could strike at the unhappy man, and it was a
terrible one in itself and in its consequences.

He sat at his table by the window, opening one
letter after another, and looking over the contents
with a pleased expression, a little vacant perhaps,
but not altogether without intelligence. There was
a lacuna in his mind, and sometimes he was conscious of being confused by faces and things about
him, but he was still capable of understanding the
questions about his estates, and farms, and buildings,
though he always seemed to lack the energy to write
the directions with his own hand.

He turned over the sheets and folded each one
neatly and put it back into its particular envelope.
Then he opened the one from the steward, and
found in it a letter directed to Rome in a strange
hand.

He held it in his fingers with a puzzled look for
a moment; it seemed as though one letter had
suddenly become two. Then he understood and

smiled a little sadly at his own weakness of comprehension, and broke the seal.

The effect was not instantaneous. He read it over again, and a third time, his face still vacant, and he put his hand to his head trying and striving with all his might to remember. The week of insanity had done its work and Diana need not have feared that he could be easily recalled to an understanding of the past. But it was not wholly gone yet; he would try to remember. He rose to his feet, and perhaps the slight physical effort helped to stir his dull mind.

Suddenly he trembled violently from head to foot, and his colour changed from the natural complexion it had taken of late to a deadly pallor. For an instant his whole nature seemed to be convulsed, he reeled to and fro and caught himself by the heavy frame of his bedstead, staring wildly about, and fell backwards across the pillows, clutching the counterpane to right and left of him with his two hands, his face distorted and horrible to see.

It only lasted for a moment, and he regained his feet, stood still for a few seconds, and passed his hands across his eyes and seemed at once to recover his faculties. He took Batiscombe's letter again and read it over, as though fixing the few words and the address in his mind. The vacant expression of ten minutes ago had changed to a look of supernatural intelligence and cunning. He put the letter in his pocket and sat down at the table. He

opened some of the envelopes again and scattered
the papers about, eying the effect rather critically.
He then took his dressing-case, opened it, and
removed one small tray, and then a second. In the
bottom of the box was a revolver, bright and ready,
with all its appurtenances, a few cartridges lying
loose in their little compartment. The weapon was
loaded, but he carefully opened it and examined
each chamber, turning it round slowly by the light.
It was not a large pistol, and when he was sure
that it was in order, he put it carefully into the
inside pocket of his coat, and surveyed the effect
in the glass. No one would have suspected that he
was armed.

He saw that his hat was ready in its place, and
he rang the bell and sat down at his table once
more, holding a letter in his hand, as though reading. The confidential servant appeared.

"Will you please to bring me a lemonade?" said
Marcantonio, with perfectly natural intonation.
The man bowed and retired to execute the order.
His master seemed better than usual, he thought;
the appearance of the papers and Carantoni's bland
smile had completely deceived him.

As soon as he was alone he took his hat, felt that
he had his purse in his pocket, and opened the door
to the sitting-room. Diana was not there, for she
generally wrote her own letters until Marcantonio
appeared with his correspondence, asking her to
answer it for him. The servant was gone to get

the lemonade and Marcantonio slipped quietly out on tiptoe.

Once upon the main staircase of the hotel he ran nimbly down, humming a little tune in a jaunty fashion, to show everybody that he was at his ease. Of course the people in the house had no idea that he was insane. It had been Diana's chiefest care to conceal the fact from every one; and Marcantonio walked calmly past the porter's lodge into the street, and took a cab. It was nearly midday and the thoroughfares were less crowded than in the morning and evening; the cab flew rapidly over the smooth pavement to the station.

There are many trains to Cuneo in the summer season, and before very long Carantoni found himself in a smoking-carriage with three or four men, all reading the papers and smoking long, black cigars with straws in them. He lit a cigarette, bought a paper just as the guard was closing the doors, and he rolled out of the station, looking just like anybody else. He pretended to read, and no one noticed him.

When the servant returned with the lemonade and found that Marcantonio was gone, he did not suspect what was the matter, but put the glass on the table and went back to the antechamber and waited at his post. He waited a few minutes and then knocked at Diana's door, and asked if the signore were with her.

"No," said Diana quickly, and came out into the

sitting-room in her loose morning gown. "Where is he? Is he not in his room? He never comes into mine."

"He is not there," said the man, who by this time was thoroughly frightened. "He sent me for a lemonade. He looked better than usual, and was sitting just there, at his table, reading his letters. When I came back he was gone. He seemed entirely himself, better than I have ever seen him."

Diana was frightened and puzzled. After all it was quite possible that Marcantonio had taken it into his head to go out by himself. He had never suggested such a thing yet, and always seemed unwilling to cross the threshold alone; but since he was so much better that day, he might have gone out. It was possible. She would not have believed that without some immediate cause he could have fallen back into a remembrance of his troubles; for she had studied his moods very carefully, and was convinced that, as the doctor said, there would always be a blank in his mind now, destroying the memory of those three or four days. She glanced hastily over the papers on the table. They were all of the usual sort, for Marcantonio had taken Batiscombe's letter with him.

Nevertheless, she was very much frightened, and was angry with the confidential servant for not having sent some one else to get the lemonade. She lost no time in dispatching him to make inquiries. He was really an active man, and understood his business thoroughly, but Marcantonio's manner had completely deceived him, and he had conscientiously thought his charge perfectly safe. Maniacs have more than once deceived their keepers, and their doctors, and Marcantonio seemed to have fallen into a very different sort of madness — rather foolish and gentle than cunning and dangerous.

The servant soon discovered that Marcantonio had passed the porter's lodge and had taken a cab, not many minutes earlier; but no one had heard the order he gave to the driver. There were no more carriages on the stand. The man lost no time but ran down the street till he found one, and was driven to the station, as he was, bareheaded and clothed in a dress-coat and a white tie, after the manner of hotel servants in the morning. His experience told him that crazy people generally made for the railway when they escaped. But he was too late. A train had just left — he made anxious inquiries of every one, describing Marcantonio's clothes and jewelry, which he knew by heart. No one had noticed him. He might not have come to the station after all.

But a dirty little boy elbowed his way through the crowd of railway porters and guards that soon surrounded the man, and the boy listened.

"Had that signore a great ring on his finger, with a black stone in it, and a red one on each side?" he asked.

"Yes," cried the confidential servant. "You

have seen him?" He seized the small boy by the arm and held him fast.

"Yes," said the little fellow; "but you have no need to pinch me like that. I sold him a paper, and he gave me a silver half-franc, and I noticed his fingers and his ring."

The servant released him.

Some one else had noticed the ring, which was very large and brilliant,— a great sapphire with a ruby on each side of it. The individual remembered hearing the gentleman ask for the train to Cuneo. The confidential servant rushed back to the hotel, after ascertaining that there would not be another train for two hours.

He told Diana what he had learned, and she listened attentively. She was pale and quiet, and she did not reproach the man again. It was of no use now. She had dressed herself, and she sent for a cab; and then she also was driven to the station, the man accompanying her. She did not speak except to give her orders.

She went at once to the station-master, an extremely civil individual with a great deal of silver lace.

"Can you give me a special train to Cuneo at once?" she asked.

The station-master was in despair, he said. There was only a single track, and it would be impossible to arrange the line at such short notice. He bowed, and looked grave, and put everything in the station at the disposal of the magnificent lady who ordered special trains as other people order cabs. But he could do nothing. Diana hesitated. Something must be done at once.

"My brother," she said, "took the last train to Cuneo, and I desire to stop him. He — he is insane."

It was a hard thing to have to tell a stranger, a railway official, and Diana was whiter than death as she said it. She would rather have put a knife into her heart.

The station-master was graver and more polite than ever. He could telegraph to all the stations to have the passengers watched as they descended. Would she give him a description, — the name, perhaps?

It had to be done. She gave the details, and the telegram was sent. Meanwhile she sat in the station-master's private office, to wait for more than an hour until the next train should be ready.

The consequence of all this was that when Marc-antonio finally reached his destination, he was politely asked, in company with the other passengers, whether he had seen or heard of an insane gentleman called the Marchese Carantoni. But his newly-found cunning did not desert him. He shrugged his shoulders, and said he did not know the gentleman. He himself looked so quiet and dignified, that no one could have suspected him of being the person, and the short description telegraphed would have answered to hundreds of Italians all over the country. He had, of course, expected to be pursued, as lunatics often do, and he was prepared to baffle every attempt. His quiet look and frank smile were a perfect passport. He even inquired of a porter at the station how he could best reach the Certosa di Pesio; and the man told him it was an hour's drive or more, and got him a little carriage for the journey, and received a few sous for his pains.

Marcantonio leaned back against the moth-eaten cushions and smoked a cigarette and looked at the scenery. He hummed a little tune occasionally, and, when the dirty driver was not looking, he put his hand into his breast pocket, and felt that his pistol was in its place, and then the cunning smile passed over his features.

He had managed it all so well,— there could be no mistake about it. He chuckled as he thought how Batiscombe would expect to receive the visit of a third party, and would thus be suddenly brought face to face with the principal. He thought he could anticipate just how Batiscombe would look, and he revelled for a while in the contemplation of his hatred. He had forgotten nothing now, except that he had ever forgotten his vengeance for a moment.

On and on he rolled in his rattling little cab. Through a long and gradually-ascending valley, thickly clothed with chestnut-trees of mighty

growth. By the roadside ran a stream, that gradually became a torrent as the inclination of its course
grew steeper, and the road wound up towards the
source. Here and there the water fell over a natural
weir of dark-brown rock, forming a deep pool below,
where the trout lurked in the shadow. Again the
thick woods receded a little on each side, and the
bed of the stream, now shallow from the summer
heat, grew broad and stony; and further on there
was a bit of grassy bank overhung with many trees,
and the small river swept smoothly round.

Suddenly the carriage drew up before an old stone
gateway that seemed to start out of the foliage, and
there was a noise as of a deep fall of water, at once
wild and smooth. Marcantonio had reached the
Carthusian monastery at last. His purpose was
almost accomplished.

It is a strange building in a marvellous situation.
Those old monks knew where to live, as they have
always known in all ages and countries,— from the
priests of Egypt to the monks of Buddha, from the
Benedictines of Subiaco to the holy men of ancient
Mexico, they have all reared spacious dwellings
in chosen sites, where the body might live in peace
and the soul be raised, by contemplating the beauties
of the earth, to the imagination of the beauties of
heaven. They were wise old men; some of them
were good, and some bad, as happens in all com-
munities in the world; but they were men who did
the earth good in their day, and found out the places

that have often become cities in our times, whereby
-hundreds of thousands of souls have profited by
their choice.

The Certosa di Pesio, where Julius and Leonora
had taken up their abode for a time, is turned into
an establishment for cold-water cures. There are
generally some fifty or sixty people there from Turin
and the neighbourhood who take the baths, or not,
as they please, and lead a pleasant life for a few
months in the great cloistered courts, and the bright
gardens, and out in the endless chestnut woods. A
cool breath of the Alps blows down the valley, and
the rush of the water, dammed up by a strong weir of
ancient masonry, and continually pouring down with
a steady, musical roar, pervades all the cool rooms
and the sounding halls and passages. It is an ideal
place for the summer, almost unknown to foreigners.
It is no wonder that Julius had thought it the very
spot for Leonora to rest in until the heat was over.
A little way from the buildings, up the valley, a
dilapidated summer-house overhangs the stream.
Sitting there you can see the whole wonderful
outline of the convent buildings, crowned with
chimneys which the old monk-architects seem to
have delighted in greatly, giving them a variety of
strange and grotesque shapes such as I never saw
anywhere else. Julius and Leonora used often to
come to the old summer-house in the afternoon,
with their books, which were seldom called into
requisition, and they would sit side by side for

hours, till the evening sun warmed the colours of the pine-trees on the heights to a green-gold, and reddened the far-off snows of Monte Rosa with the last, loving touch of his departing light.

An obsequious individual came forward from the archway as Marcantonio drove up to the gate. Marcantonio eyed him, and perceived that he was a functionary of the pension.

"Is there an English gentleman here?" he asked, — "a certain Signor Giulio Batiscombe?" His voice was very calm, and had a certain suavity in its tones; he smiled, too, as he asked the question.

"Si, signore," answered the man, bowing and gesticulating toward the building. "Certainly. A handsome signore, with his wife — both Inglesi. They arrived on the thirty-first of last month — five days. Will the signore do the favour to come in? I will inquire whether the English gentleman is at home."

The slightest shade passed over Marcantonio's face at the mention of the wife in the case. But the man would not have noticed it. Marcantonio felt sure he had not betrayed himself.

"I will wait here," said he, "while you inquire."

The man disappeared, and Marcantonio was alone. He looked up at the windows in the grey walls, and saw no one. Nevertheless, at any moment Batiscombe might appear — from the house or from the woods — he might be taking a walk. It seemed a very long time to wait.

He put his hand into his breast pocket. The stock of the revolver just curved over the edge of the cloth inside his coat; he could get at it without trouble. He longed to take it out and examine it; to see whether it were still in perfect order; and he peeped in when the driver was not looking, just to catch a sight of the lock and the bright barrel. Then he smiled to himself, and hummed a tune, assuming an air of quiet indifference — acting all the time, as only madmen can act, as though he were on the stage before a great audience. It was only for the benefit of the driver of his little carriage, a rough fellow, who had not shaved for a week, and wore a dirty linen jacket, his hands black and his eyes red with the wine of the night before — that was the audience; but Marcantonio acted his part with as much care as though he were in the presence of Batiscombe himself. There must not be the smallest chance of an interruption to his plan.

At last the man returned, bowing with renewed zeal. He came forward with one hand extended, as though to help Marcantonio to alight.

"The English signore is in the garden," he said. Marcantonio smiled more sweetly than ever and got out of his conveyance.

"You can wait," he said to the driver, and the latter touched his battered straw hat.

Marcantonio followed the man through a great court, where there were trees, into a long, tiled passage that seemed to run through the house, and,

on the other side, he emerged into a garden, thick
with laurel-trees and geraniums. The man led the
way. Marcantonio's hand crept stealthily into his
breast pocket underneath his coat, and raised the
lock of the revolver very slowly. The man in front
did not hear the small, sharp click.

"Where is he?" asked Marcantonio, very gently,
still smiling an unnaturally sweet smile. The servant had stopped and was looking about.

"I was told they were here," said he; "but they
must be in the summer-house outside."

Again he led the way to a small door in the
garden wall. It was open.

"There they are, signore," said he, pointing with
his finger and standing aside to let Marcantonio
pass.

He looked, and saw two people sitting in the
dilapidated old bower above the water, not twenty
yards from where he stood.

It was five o'clock in the afternoon. Diana had
taken the train at two, and could not reach Cuneo
till six.

CHAPTER XXIV.

LEONORA's utter recklessness of delight could not last very long. It was a strange mood, as unnatural and uncontrollable at first as her husband's madness. She could not help enjoying to the utmost the new life that had so suddenly begun for her. She knew in her heart that she had bought it at a great price, and she knew that she must make the most of it, or she would have to reproach herself with the bargain.

It was easy enough at first. The quick change had thrown all her thoughts into a new channel. From the midnight departure she had no more time to think, until the long, quiet days at Pesio. There were moments when she was on the verge of thinking, of remembering the past, and wondering how her husband had acted. But she felt that it would be very unpleasant to reflect on these things. It might take her a long time to get out of the train of thought, as it used to do long ago whenever she had one of her fits of philosophical despair; she was able to put it off, and she seemed to be saying to herself, 'I shall have time to think about it, and to satisfy my conscience by feeling the proper amount of regret by and by.'

Of course she did not say as much in so many words, but the unconscious excuse for what she knew an unprejudiced outsider would call her heartlessness went on presenting itself whenever she felt the beginning of a regret. Deeper even than that, and almost hidden in the sea of self-deception, and passion, and riotous love of life, lay the reef on which the ship of her happiness would some day go to pieces — the ultimate knowledge of the wrong she had done, and of her own cruelty to Marcantonio and weakness to herself.

But in Pesio the time came; terribly soon, she thought, though her suffering was only at its beginning. Each morning brought a dull sense of pain, that came in her dreams and became the terror of her waking. She knew before she opened her eyes that it was there, and the first returning consciousness was the certainty of sorrow. It soon wore away, it is true, but she grew to dread it as she had never dreaded anything in her short, luxurious life. It needed all her strength and energy to shake off the impression, and it required all Batiscombe's love and thoughtful care to make it seem possible to live the hours until the evening.

That was in the morning, in the brief moments when Leonora, like most of us, had not yet silenced her soul, and trodden it under for the day; and it spoke bitter truth and scorn to her, so that she could hardly bear it. Then, at last, she was honest. There was no more self-deception then, no more

possibility of believing that she had done well in
leaving all for Julius; she could no longer say that
for so much love's sake it was right and noble to
spurn away the world,—for the world came to mean
her husband, her father and her mother, and she
saw and knew too clearly what each and all of them
must suffer. Their pale faces came to her in her
dreams, and their sad voices spoke to her the
reproach of all reproaches that can be uttered against
a woman. Her husband she had never loved; but
in spite of all her reasoning she knew that he had
loved her, and she understood enough of his pride
and single-hearted nobility to guess what he must
suffer while she dragged his ancient name in the
dust of dishonour. Her father was never to her
mind, for he was a Philistine of the kind that have
hard shells and very little that is soft or warm
within them, but she knew that he had treasured
her as the apple of his eye, and that his old heart
would break for his daughter's shame. Her mother
was a worldly woman, loving Leonora because she
had obtained a success in society, and upbraiding
her with never making the most of it; but Leonora
knew how her mother's vanity must be bowed and
trampled down by the deep disgrace, and that her
vanity was almost all she had of happiness.

And so it came to pass that after a little time
the old tax-gatherer, Remorse, began to put Leonora
in distress for his dues, and she was forced to pay
them or have no peace. He came in the grey of the

morning, when she was not yet prepared, and he sat by her head and oppressed it with heaviness and the leaden cowl of sorrow; and each day she counted the minutes until he was gone, and each day they were more.

Julius saw and pondered, for he guessed what she suffered, and understood now her terrible recklessness at the first. All that a lover could do he did, and more also, employing every resource of his great mind to fight the enemy, and always with success. He could always bring the smile and the brightness of glad life to her face at last, and when once his dominion was established there was no return of sorrow possible for that day; his stupendous vitality and brilliant, overflowing strength fought down the shadows and chased them out.

On the morning of the fourth of September, Leonora and Julius were walking together in the chestnut woods near the monastery. She had been less sad than usual at her first waking, and Julius hoped that the time was coming when she could at last feel accustomed to her new position and would cease to be troubled with the ghosts of the past. He was over-confident, and thought he understood her better than he really did. He was laughing and talking gayly enough, enjoying her happy mood and the freshness and beauty of the bountiful nature around him.

Julius stopped from time to time and picked a few wild flowers that grew amongst the moss and the grass of the wood. Leonora loved flowers, and loved best those that grew wild. It was one of the few simple tastes she possessed.

"It is not much of a nosegay," said Julius, as he put the sweet blossoms together, and tied them with a blade of grass. "It is too late for the best wild flowers here." He gave her the little bouquet with one hand, and the other stole about her waist and drew her to him.

She smelled the flowers, and looked up at him over them, a little sadly.

"The time will come, I suppose," said she, "when there will be no more flowers at all."

"Never for you, darling," he answered lovingly. "There will always be flowers for you — everywhere, till the end of time."

"What is the end of time, Julius?" she asked softly.

"Time has no end for us, dear," he said. "For time is measured by love, and nothing can measure ours."

They were near an old tree whose roots ran out and then struck down into the ground. The moss and the grass had grown closely about the great trunk's foot, and made a broad seat. They sat down, by common accord.

"Can there be no end to our love — ever?" she said.

"Should we be where we are, if either of us thought it possible?" he asked.

"It must be whole — it must be endless — indeed it must," she answered — clinging to the thought which gave her most comfort.

"Do you doubt that it is?" asked Julius, the strong earnestness of his passion vibrating in his deep tones.

"No, darling," she answered; "I do not doubt it — only you must never let me."

"Indeed, indeed, I never will!" said he. He meant what he said. Men are not all intentional deceivers, but they forget. They are less faithful than women, though they are often more earnest.

Is it not the very highest power of love not to allow a doubt? And how many men can say that their lives have been so ordered toward the woman they love best, that no doubting should be reasonably possible in her mind? Few enough, I suppose.

"I have been thinking a great deal lately, Julius," said Leonora presently.

"Tell me your thoughts, dear one," said he, drawing her to him, so that her head rested on his shoulder, and his lips touched her hair.

"You know, dear," said she, "what we have done is not right — at least " — She stopped suddenly.

"Who says it is not right?" asked Julius, with a touch of scorn in his voice.

"Oh, everybody says so, of course; but that makes no difference. Nobody would understand. It is not what people say. It is the thing." She stared out into the woods as she leaned against him.

"How do you mean, sweetheart?" he asked.

"It is not right, you know. I am sure of it." She shook her head gently, without lifting it. "It is all my fault," she added.

"You shall not say that, my own one," said Julius, passionately. He was really grieved and troubled beyond measure.

"Ah — but I know it so well," said she. "You must help me to make it right — quite right."

"It is right — it shall be right! I will make it so," he answered. "Only trust me, darling, and you shall be the happiest woman the world holds, as you are the best. God bless you, dear one." He kissed her tenderly, but she tried to turn away from him.

"Oh, no, Julius — God will not bless me. I have only you left now. You must be everything to me. Will you, dear? Say you will!"

"I do say it, my own darling," he answered fervently. "I will be everything to you, now and forever and ever."

He was astonished and puzzled by the sudden outbreak. She had never spoken like this to him before, though he had expected it at first, and had wondered at her indifference. But now it seemed to have come upon her suddenly with a great force, and she would not be comforted.

"And I say it, too," she said, passionately. "I will be everything to you, now and forever and ever. We will give our lives to each other, and make it

right." She wound her arms about him, and hid
her face against his coat.

"How can true love, like ours, not be right?"
asked Julius, clasping her to him. "God has put
it into the world, dear, and into our hearts."

Oh, the blasphemy and the hollowness and the
cruelty of those words! Even as Leonora lay in
his arms and felt his kisses on her hair, loving her
sinful love for him out to the last breath, she knew
that it was not true, what he said so fervently,—
and she knew that he did not believe it, that no
man can believe a lie so great and wide and deep
and awful.

But the sun does not stand still in the heavens
for a man's lie; he hears too many untrue speeches,
and sees too many false faces in his daily task of
shining alike upon the just and the unjust — he is
used to it and goes on his way; and time follows
him, striving to keep pace and to swell the puny
minutes of its pulse into an eternity.

Such moments — when the rising sorrow and
sense of shame that a woman feels are choked down
and crushed by the overwhelming energy of false-
ness in the man she loves — are passionate, even
terrible; and they may come often, but they never
last long.

Half an hour later, Julius and Leonora were wandering on through the woods, and their talk had
taken again its ordinary course. The morning was
passing, and as Batiscombe talked and amused and

interested Leonora, her doubts and fears disappeared, for the time at least, and her old sense of enjoyment returned again, sweeter to her now than ever before, in proportion as it was more difficult for her to attain it. She was happy again, and the clouds were riven away and rent to shreds by the strong breath of her stirring passion.

They walked for a while, and then returned to their midday breakfast and spent an hour over it in the cool, darkened hall, which had once been the refectory of the monastery, and was now the dining-room of the people who came to the water-cure. Julius had suggested to Leonora that they should have their breakfast and dinner in their own rooms, but she said she liked to see the people. It amused her to watch their faces and to wonder about them and criticise them. They were so unlike the people she had known hitherto, that there was a freshness of amusement to her in learning their ways.

And by and by they had their coffee in a little sitting-room of their own that overlooked the torrent, and Julius smoked a cigarette and read the papers a little, amusing her with his daring comments on the conduct of nations and individuals. He was a man who was never afraid to say what he meant — not only to Leonora, over a cup of coffee in the summer, but to the world at large, in his books and articles. That was one reason why the world at large always said he was an uncommonly fine fellow, with a great deal of pluck and judg-

ment. For the world at large likes rough strength
and keen wit, always understanding that the strong
language is not applied to itself, but to its neighbour
next door.

At four o'clock Julius and Leonora went out
again. Julius carried a pair of shawls and a book
and Leonora's silk bag with the silver rings — the
same she had used to bring her handkerchiefs when
she fled from Sorrento. They went into the garden
and out among the laurels and the geraniums for a
few minutes, but Julius was sure there would be
more breeze outside, in the old summer-house over
the water; for the garden was sheltered by high
walls all around, and the sun was still hot, almost
at its hottest at four o'clock on the fourth of
September.

Accordingly Julius took the things in his hands,
and the two went out of the garden by the door in
the wall and left it open. They walked down the
short open path to the old summer-house, and Julius
made Leonora very comfortable with the shawls for
cushions upon the old, wooden bench, which many
generations of people had hacked with their knives
and adorned with the insignificance of their unknown names.

Side by side they sat in the glory of the summer's afternoon, and the birds perched on the grey
old ribs of the summer-house and hopped upon the
untrimmed creepers that grew thickly about it, making their small comments to each other about the

two people who sat below them, and great green and pink grasshoppers skipped into the open space and out again, a perpetual astonishment in their round, red eyes; all nature was warm and peaceful and happy. The lovers talked together a little, enjoying the sense that speech was not always necessary nor even desirable.

"How do you like the 'Principe'?" Julius asked at last, glancing at the book that lay open on Leonora's knee. He had given it to her to read, because she said she knew so little of Italian thought.

"I hardly know," she said. "It is very wonderful, of course. But I cannot quite believe that Macchiavelli believed in it himself, nor that any one ever acted on the advice he gives. It is too complicated and unhuman."

"It always seems to me," said Julius, taking up the question, "that he wrote like a man who inferred a great deal from his own experience — a great deal more than it is safe to infer. He knew men and women very well. He might have been a despotic lover."

"Why?" asked Leonora.

"Do you notice that he always reckons, everywhere and without exception, on the heart of the people and on their personal affection for their sovereign? But he never takes into consideration the possible affection of the sovereign for his subjects."

"That is true," said Leonora. "He was a very heartless individual."

"Perhaps — though I hardly think it," answered Julius. "But he might have written a guide for despotic lovers much better than a book of instruction for tyrannical princes."

"What an idea!" said Leonora, laughing. "But I think he was heartless all the same. He only believed in the people's hearts as a means for getting power."

"He never says so," said Julius. "I rather think he loved the people, but knew them well — and he loved the ingenuities of his wit much better."

"If the heart does not come first, it never comes at all," said Leonora thoughtfully. "If it does not rule it is ruled, and might as well never exist at all. Are you tyrannical, dear?" She smiled at him, knowing how he loved her.

"Oh, yes, indeed," said Julius, laughing; "but only about love."

"But that is just the question," said Leonora. "You ought not to be. Your heart ought to come first."

"Yes, darling," he answered. "The heart comes first, and the heart is a tyrant. Supposing my heart says to yours, 'You shall love me; I will have it at any cost;' is not that tyranny?"

"Perhaps," said Leonora, smiling and touching his hand. "But then it is quite a mutual tyranny, you know, because I say it to you, too, — and you do it."

"I always do everything you say, darling," he answered lovingly.

"Always?"

"Always; — and I always will, Leonora."

"Do you think, Julius — it is a foolish question — do you think you would die for me, if it were necessary?"

"You know I would, dear," he said quietly.

"Yes; I am sure you would," she answered. "Do you know? I used to think that one ought to be willing to die for those one loves; and I like to think that you would give your life for me. Of course it could never happen — but then — Don't laugh at me, Julius."

"Why should I laugh?" he said. "What you say is serious enough, I am sure."

"No — but I thought you might. You laugh at so many things — I am always afraid you will laugh at my love " —

It was five o'clock.

Marcantonio, issuing from the door in the garden wall, saw Julius and Leonora some twenty yards away, in the summer-house. He gave the servant a franc for showing him the way, and the man retired. He stood alone, watching the pair, for he could see them very distinctly. They were so placed that they would see him if they turned and looked upward, but they did not move, nor hear him. Leonora was nearest to him, and was leaning back a little, so that she could not see him; Batiscombe held her hand, and was looking at it, and gently caressing the fair, white fingers as he talked.

Marcantonio turned away for a moment, and got out his revolver. It was clean and bright, and he had examined it,—but he would look once more, just to be sure there was a cartridge in each chamber, especially in that one beneath the barrels. One could not be too certain of one's weapon. There was no mistake,—everything was in order. The hour was come.

The hideous maniac smile played over his delicate features, and he stepped cautiously forward, holding the pistol behind him. Every step he gained before they observed him was an advantage. And besides, Leonora was between him and Batiscombe. It was not a fair shot, and it was too far.

He did not want to kill her; he would take her home with him, when he had killed Julius Batiscombe. He had ordered the little carriage to wait for them. How happy she would be! Cautiously he moved on, ready for action if they saw him. He trod so softly, so softly, it was like velvet on the grass.

Then, as he came nearer,—not ten paces off,—he brought his pistol before him and held it ready. So softly he had crept to them that they had not yet heard him, as the summer wind blew gently through the long grasses and the vines about the old bower, and made a sweet murmur of its own.

—"I am always afraid you will laugh at my love"

— Leonora was saying, but the words that were to follow were never spoken.

Some slight sound caught her quick woman's ear, and she looked up in the direction whence it came. There stood her husband, not ten paces from her, with an expression in his face which would have frozen the marrow in the bones of a wild beast.

The clean polished barrel of the pistol was pointed full at Batiscombe. Leonora saw that, and saw that Marcantonio's eyes were fixed on her lover and not on herself. Batiscombe saw it all as well as she, one second later. But that one second was enough.

With a spring and a clutching turn, as a tigress will cover her young with herself and turn glaring on her pursuers, Leonora threw her strong, lithe body upon Julius, forcing him back to his seat, and she turned and looked Marcantonio in the face. Their eyes met for one moment. But it was too late: the finger had pulled the trigger and the ball sped true.

Without a sound, without a cry, she fell upon her lover's breast. There she fell, there she died.

From the death wound the heart's blood fell in great drops; it fell down to the ground.

She died for his sake whom she loved; she died, she gave for him her life, the joy and the woe and the love of it for his sake.

Do you ask what is the moral of this? Ask it of yourselves.

Ask it of that quiet man, with delicate features and snow-white hair, who drives in the Villa Borghese. He is well-known in Rome for his honesty, his honour, and his unaffected good sense. He is the Marchese Carantoni, he is Marcantonio, and he is not yet forty years of age.

Ask it of Diana de Charleroi, — Duchesse de Charleroi now, for her husband has succeeded to the elder title. Ask it of her, the mother of brave boys and noble maidens. She has her beauty still, she is as stately as of yore, and grander in the crown of mature womanhood. But there is a streak of grey even in her fair hair, and a line of sorrow on her forehead, the masterly handwriting of a mastering grief; and her grey eyes are softer and sadder than they were ten years ago.

Ask it of Julius Batiscombe, — but of him you will ask in vain. He has the mark of a bullet in his throat, Marcantonio's second shot, that was so nearly fatal to him. He stood aside from the world for a while, and lived a year or two among the monks of Subiaco; he manifested some devotion for her sake who had died for him. And now he is writing novels again, and smoking cigarettes between the phrases, to help his ideas and to stimulate his imagination.

THE END.

www.ingramcontent.com/pod-product-compliance
Lightning Source LLC
Chambersburg PA
CBHW020833030726
47496CB00001B/217